W9-AWB-251

RETURN FIRE

"Now!"

The noise of the guns exploding in unison was more like the roar of a cannon than the crackling of individual small arms, and Jack found himself hugging the floor beneath the window before he even realized that he had moved. Ten slugs of lead from ten rifles dug into the wall of the house, one bullet ripping through the hinge of the shutter on Jack's window, causing the shutter to hang askew from its remaining support. Then came more rifle crackling in a continuous rhythm, mixed with the sound of horses' hooves on the earth as the riders stormed the house.

Jack forced himself up from the floor and back to the window. He shoved the shattered piece of wood aside with the muzzle of his rifle, and came up firing . . .

ST. MARTIN'S PAPERBACKS TITLES
BY CAMERON JUDD

FIREFALL

BRAZOS

DEAD MAN'S GOLD

DEVIL WIRE

THE GLORY RIVER

TEXAS FREEDOM

SNOW SKY

CORRIGAN

TIMBER CREEK

RENEGADE LAWMEN

THE HANGING AT LEADVILLE

CORRIGAN

CAMERON JUDD

St. Martin's Paperbacks

NOTE: If you purchased this book without a cover you should be aware that this book is stolen property. It was reported as "unsold and destroyed" to the publisher, and neither the author nor the publisher has received any payment for this "stripped book."

SNOW SKY / CORRIGAN

Snow Sky copyright © 1990 by Cameron Judd.
Excerpt from *Renegade Lawmen* copyright © 2008 by Cameron Judd.
Excerpt from *Timber Creek* copyright © 1989 by Cameron Judd.
Corrigan copyright © 1980, 1989 by Cameron Judd.
Excerpt from *The Glory River* copyright © 1998 by Cameron Judd.

All rights reserved.

For information address St. Martin's Press, 175 Fifth Avenue, New York, NY 10010.

ISBN: 0-312-94555-8
EAN: 978-0-312-94555-8

Printed in the United States of America

Snow Sky Bantam edition / November 1990
St. Martin's Paperbacks edition / July 1998

Corrigan Bantam edition / August 1989
St. Martin's Paperbacks edition / September 1998

St. Martin's Paperbacks are published by St. Martin's Press, 175 Fifth Avenue, New York, NY 10010.

10 9 8 7 6 5 4 3 2 1

CORRIGAN

Chapter 1

Tucker Corrigan could see that his mother was trying hard not to cry when she came out of the back room where his father lay dying. She called him aside, away from the others.

"Tucker, your pa wants to see Jack one last time. I want you to go get him."

Tucker felt the skin on the back of his neck tighten. "But Ma, you know . . ."

"I know. But your pa needs to see his boy. I want to see him, too. You're the only one who can get him."

"What about Thurston Russell?"

"Don't you think I know the danger, Tucker? I haven't gone without seeing my oldest boy for seven years without good reason. But we can't worry about Russell this time. Your pa needs to see his son before he dies."

"When do you want me to leave?"

"First light. Jack ain't that far off, but there ain't no way to say how long your pa has. You'll have to find him and bring him home just as quick as you can."

"What if he don't want to come? He knows Russell will try to kill him."

"He'll come, no matter what, when he finds out his pa needs him."

She moved away then, leaving Tucker alone with his thoughts. He couldn't blame Pa for wanting to see Jack. It had been with Jack that Pa had come to Wyoming years ago and established a spread near the Crazy Woman Creek. Tucker had been just a little sprout then,

1

doing most of his growing right here on the ranch. Pa
had a good knowledge of the cattle business—he had
worked with cattle all of his days—but knowledge and
skill weren't much if a man didn't have luck.

Luck and wealth had evaded Pa throughout his life.
It didn't seem fair that Pa had to lay dying with his hopes
unfulfilled.

"Don't worry, Bess. This old log home ain't nothing
but temporary," he had said. "In just a couple of years I'll
build you a nice place, one you can be proud of."

Those years had come and gone many times over,
and the new house never came into existence. Bad luck
seemed to rob the Corrigans of any bit of wealth they
might accumulate. When the cattle weren't dying, they
were being stolen by competing ranchers or Indians.
Now Danver Corrigan was on his deathbed. It wasn't
fair. But Tucker had learned long ago that life for a struggling Wyoming ranching family was often a long way
from fair.

If Pa had never achieved wealth, at least he had a
good family. There was Jack, Tucker, Bob, Cindy, Tara,
then little Benjamin Elrod. They were a good family,
hardworking and God-fearing, though a bit lively and
high-spirited, occasionally too much so for their own
good.

Jack had been the wildest of the bunch, often taking
part in games of poker at Scudder's Saloon, an institution
of low repute situated in the middle of nowhere. It was a
log building backed by a slightly larger building where
Mel Scudder, the proprietor of the saloon, lived with his
three cats and nine dogs. Jack became fairly well-known
in the area as a sharp gambler, much to the dismay of his
mother. Many were the times that he stared over a hand
of cards at the cigar-smoke-blurred faces of men who
would not hesitate to kill him if he angered them. Tucker
had sometimes slipped into Scudder's Saloon in the days
when Jack still lived on the ranch, marveling at his
brother's bravery and cool manner while dealing cards

and placing bets. He had been somewhat envious of Jack, for he was a dashing figure there at the table, but Tucker had been blessed with enough good sense to know that Jack's ways would come to no good end.

On an October evening Jack came across a piece of trouble he wasn't able to brush off with a bluff and swagger. Thurston Russell, a brute of a man, one of Danver Corrigan's chief competitors, was angered by Jack's good luck during a high-stakes game of poker. Jack had done his best to avoid bringing things to the fighting stage, but he was unsuccessful. Russell struck him, forcing him to defend himself.

For a time it was just a typical saloon brawl, onlookers told Tucker after it was over. But then the two fighters went at it in earnest, and somewhere along the line a knife was slipped into Jack's hand. No one saw just who gave it to him.

When it was over, Thurston Russell was bloody and screaming, staining the split-log floor red so fast that most who watched feared he would bleed to death. But he didn't die, though it might have been best for Jack if he had.

Thurston Russell went through life thereafter with one ear. Jack had sliced the left one off with the knife. He didn't even know himself if the act had been intentional; he had been slashing blindly, wild with rage. But when Russell recovered from his wounds, he swore that, no matter what, he would avenge himself. He wouldn't be content with merely taking an ear for an ear; he would kill Jack Corrigan, he declared.

Jack knew he meant it. So did Danver Corrigan and his wife, Bess. And rather than face the possibility of a fatal fight and more family shame, Jack moved on, heading north into the Montana Territory, working for ranches all over the eastern Montana plains, and still gambling.

Tucker had been dismayed by his brother's action for a time, for he looked on it as cowardice. Tucker was young in those days, just thirteen years old, and he found it hard to believe that anyone whom he admired as much as Jack would run from a fight. It was only a few years later that he realized the sense in what his brother had done. One moment of insanity did not justify hanging around waiting for another, possibly with worse results than a severed ear.

It was seven years now since Jack had left, and the family's communications with him had been few. They knew only that he was working on a ranch in the southeast section of the Montana Territory, near the Hanging Woman Creek, not far from the Tongue River.

"From the Crazy Woman to the Hanging Woman!" Tucker had laughed when he heard the news. But all of the family were glad Jack was so close. He was scarcely more than fifty miles to the north, and that made him seem closer than when he had been roaming up around Miles City.

But in a way he wasn't a bit closer. Even though he could be home in a two-day ride, he would not return as long as Russell held the grudge against him. It had infuriated Russell when Jack took off. When the family refused to tell him where Jack had gone, he turned a fiery red and got so bitter angry that, in Pa's words, "you could look through his ears and see his brains burnin' just like a coal stove."

But now it seemed Jack would be making the return trip in spite of Russell. That is, if Tucker could find him. When he told him Pa was dying, it would likely not be hard to convince him to come back. If only they could keep Thurston Russell away from him while he was home. . . .

Bob approached Tucker and jarred him out of his thoughts with a question: "Tuck, what did Ma say to you?"

Tucker looked shifty-eyed. "I don't know that I'm supposed to say, Bob. She pulled me to the side and talked low. If she wants you to know, she'll tell you herself."

"She's sending you after Jack, ain't she?"

Tucker said nothing, but the silence said as much as if he had nodded his head. Everyone knew Pa was dying, and it made sense that the family would want to be together one last time.

It crossed Tucker's mind as he crawled into his straw tick that night that Thurston Russell might be expecting the same thing, too. He knew Danver Corrigan was mighty sick, and he was smart enough to put two and two together.

Tucker took the best horse and rode off the next morning. His mother kissed him good-bye and cried a little in spite of herself.

"Don't cry, Ma. I'll do my best to be back with Jack in a week or so. Don't you worry."

He rode away then, for tears were gathering in his own eyes, and try as he would, he couldn't suppress the thought that he might see his pa no more.

The land to the north was beautiful, a paradise of rolling plains of wind-whipped grasses. The streams were lined with birch, and willow.

Their house had been built of straight pines. Tucker could remember how he helped Jack and his father cut the trees and drag them, using a team and chain, to the building site, where they had notched them with crude round notches and set them atop each other. Jack had wanted to take more pains with the work, but Pa said no; it was to be a temporary dwelling, and there was no point in wasting time making it too fancy. It turned out that he had been wrong about the temporary part, and Jack had been right about the notching. The temporary dwelling wound up being their permanent home, and the round notches let the logs slip and settle, making huge cracks in the mud chinking that constantly had to be repaired.

Over the years Pa turned the interior of the house into something more inviting, hewing off the inside part of the logs until the wall was something close to flat. He had installed a heavy, cast-iron stove against the back wall, setting it too close and almost burning the house down. Tucker was given the task of correcting the error by hewing out a section of that wall slightly bigger than the stove, creating a recessed area that kept the threat of fire to a minimum. It was hard work, and all because Pa had so carelessly installed the stove. Tucker loved his father, but there had been many times when the man had irritated him no end. Danver Corrigan often tended to act, then think, rather than the other way around. It was a trait the family had learned and accepted years ago.

Tucker forded the Crazy Woman and headed on toward Clear Creek. He bore to the east, moving away from the mountains and the Bozeman Trail, which cut northwest across the Little Big Horn and eventually on to Virginia City in the Montana Territory. Tucker knew the Hanging Woman cut across the border of the Wyoming and Montana territories in a north-south direction. If he could locate it, it should then only be a matter of following it and stopping at any ranch he could find and inquiring about his brother. He hoped it would be that simple.

He had a good horse and an early start. With steady plodding and few stops, he should be able to cover more than thirty miles with no problem. He would spend the night beneath the stars, then begin the actual search tomorrow.

He had eaten a substantial breakfast before setting out, and in his pack was a good supply of hard biscuit and jerked beef, along with plenty of water in a battered canteen and coffee grounds tied in a cloth sack. The small tin coffeepot dangled from the saddle.

The morning passed quickly, and long before noon his stomach was empty and grumbling about it.

He stopped five miles from Clear Creek and built a fire. Soon the small coffeepot was boiling, and Tucker laid out before him a meal of biscuit and beef, along with a small dab of honey his mother had packed for him.

He allowed himself a few extra moments of rest before continuing. He picked at his teeth with a blade of grass and thought about his father. Would he be alive when he returned with Jack? He had always taken Pa for granted, assuming he would always be around. Now that his father was on the verge of dying, he realized how precious the man was. He wasn't successful, nor perfect, but he was Pa.

Tucker stood, brushing the biscuit crumbs from his denim pants. Now wasn't the time for despairing thoughts —the sun had already crossed the crest of the sky and was heading west. It would be dark in a few hours. He saddled up quickly and started northward again at a steady lope.

He forded a creek and put several miles behind him before he stopped again. He ate a meager supper and made out his bedroll. Only after he had lain down and closed his eyes did he realize that he was lonely.

The following morning he rode until he came in sight of what he felt sure was Hanging Woman Creek. He let the horse drink, then began wandering up the west side of the water.

He came upon a small ranch after a bit more travel. It was a typical spread, consisting of a low, spread-out cabin with a dirt roof and an overhanging roof of boards over the front door. A smaller log house stood to the side of the main ranch house, and behind the whole scene was an expanse of trees partially blocking the view of the barren hills on the edge of the landscape.

Tucker took it all in, at a glance and rode slowly toward the main house. He approached close enough for anyone inside to get a look at him and did not dismount. He wore a revolver, but he kept his hands clear of it. Coming as close as he felt was reasonable, he did what folks called "hollering the house," calling out his name and asking if he might dismount. To dismount before being invited to do so would be considered rude.

A voice came back from inside the house. "Who you say you be?"

"Tucker Corrigan, from the Wyoming Territory. I'm friendly."

The front door opened, and a lanky man stepped out onto the porch. He squinted as he looked the young man over for a moment; then he set the rifle he was holding up against the wall. But he did not move away from it.

"Well, get on down, Tucker Corrigan. I got a feeling I might like to talk to you." He said it in a tone Tucker wasn't sure he liked.

Dismounting, Tucker led his horse toward the house.

Chapter 2

The man's name was Drake.

"So you're a Corrigan, are you? You know anything 'bout a man named Jack Corrigan?"

Tucker's mouth dropped open. He hadn't anticipated having his own question taken right off his tongue.

"Yes, sir—he's my brother, as a matter of fact. I come looking for him."

"Brother, huh? Well, Jack Corrigan's brother, you come a little late. He done took off."

"Took off? Was this the place he was working?"

"Yeah, he worked here. Done pretty good at the first. Then he took up with a couple of drifters named York and Dowell, and pretty soon the three of 'em took off. I knew I never should have hired them two—they had a bad look about 'em. First time I laid eyes on 'em, I says to myself, 'Billy Drake, you just send them two back the way they come,' but I was shorthanded at the time, so I thought again and took 'em on temporary. Worst mistake I could have made. They stayed on no more 'an three weeks afore they took off with your brother right along with 'em. One of the blasted fools left his ol' beat-up saddle here and took one of my best ones with him. Just took out the day after I paid 'em, they did. Took out with the best hand I'd had in years and my best saddle. If'n I see 'em again, I reckon they'll smart for it! I don't figure it was your brother what took the saddle—he didn't seem the type to steal from a man—but if'n he's willing to run with the likes of them two, maybe he ain't the honest man I thought he was."

9

Tucker was dismayed. He hadn't anticipated Jack's taking off for God-knows-where just at the time he needed to see him most.

"Have any idea where they might have headed?"

"Lord, boy, they didn't exactly take off wanting me to know where to find 'em. A friend of mine up about Punkin Creek said he seen three riders up in those parts a little after the time they took off from here. I reckon it was them. Said they was riding northeast, toward the Deadwood Road."

Tucker sighed. It looked as if finding Jack was going to be tougher than he had hoped. He had only a vague hint about where they might have headed, and he was not familiar with the Montana Territory. He had promised Ma he would get back with Jack within a week or so. She would be expecting him, and if he was late, she would likely worry herself sick. But coming back without Jack might put Pa in his grave all the quicker. It was a bad situation.

"Mister, I'm sure sorry about your saddle. I think I know my brother well enough to be sure it wasn't him who took it. If I run across them other two, I'll try to get your saddle back for you."

Drake threw back his head and laughed. "What do you reckon you'll do about it, boy? That saddle's gone. Your brother ain't here, and time's wasting while I sit here talking to you. Now is there anything else I can do for you?"

Tucker bristled. He had done nothing to merit the contempt evident in the rancher's voice, and certainly he could not be held responsible for the actions of his brother or his two companions.

"No, sir, I reckon you've done your best. Now, if you don't care, I'll head on so I don't waste no more of my time. You just have you a real good day."

He wheeled and headed back to his horse. As he mounted, Drake said, "If'n you run across that brother of yours, you tell him he'd best not show his face around here again, you hear? And the same goes for them two friends of his. I ain't a man who treats a thief lightly!"

Tucker rode off at a gallop, not glancing back. The rancher stood glowering until Tucker was almost out of sight, then turned back into his house, shaking his head and muttering under his breath.

Tucker was riding through a flat area of grass and a few trees. After he had put a good distance between himself and the Drake ranch, he stopped, leaning over his saddlehorn and trying to figure out what to do.

Drake had said they were heading in the direction of the Deadwood Road. If that was the case, they were probably heading for Miles City. But he could not know if they would stop there. Perhaps they would hang around town long enough to spend or gamble away their pay, or maybe they would head north or east, looking for work at one of the ranches in eastern Montana or in the Dakotas. There was no way to be sure.

Tucker did have one thing to guide him, though. He knew that Jack had one weakness—the gambling table. If he had money in his pocket, he wouldn't be likely to look for work until it ran out. Miles City would be just the place for him to gamble away his cash.

There was only one thing to do, then—head for Miles City. Tucker worried that his ma would fear for his safety if he didn't return in the time he had stated, but right now it appeared he had no choice. If his pa's last wish was to see the son who had drifted away from him, then Tucker would do his best to see that wish fulfilled.

He started riding again, grateful for the extra food his ma had packed for him.

Miles City lay at the heart of one of the nation's chief cattle-raising areas. Situated in the midst of giant plains, the city was a focal point for the life of eastern Montana.

Tucker had never been to Miles City. Once he arrived, locating Jack might be a problem. He had failed to ask Drake when Jack and his two companions had left, and that could make a big difference in whether or not he could find them in Miles City, assuming they had gone there at all. If Jack had a streak of luck at the gambling table, he might hang around one area for weeks; if not, he might leave. There were a lot of ranches in the territory, and trying to find him amidst all of them would be nigh impossible. He hoped Jack had gone to Miles City and stayed there.

He rode steadily, not pushing his time, for he didn't wish to tire his mount. He thought of Pa, lying there back on the Crazy Woman, drawing nearer the grave with every breath. This was a hard time to be away from him. He whispered a prayer that he could find Jack in time to get back before Pa was dead.

Tucker bore east. He found the crisp air invigorating and traveled for a long time before resting. He gathered enough wood to start a small fire and brewed coffee. It was hot and fragrant, and he made it up strong like his pa had taught him during the many times they had worked the roundups together. "Boil up your coffee till it can get the rust off a nail," he had said. "In about ten minutes after that it'll be ready to drink."

He ate a little meat and two of the biscuits. He wanted more but didn't want to be wasteful. After waiting long enough for his meal to settle, he mounted again and continued riding northeast.

The day passed without incident. He saw two other ranch houses out across the plains but stopped at neither. He knew that Jack and his partners would never stop so close to the same ranch where they had stolen a saddle. The fact that they took property from Drake was evidence that they had no intention of hanging around the area. Besides, Drake had said the three riders had been seen up around the Pumpkin Creek; he had a lot of riding to do before he got that far.

Tucker made camp on the open plains. The wind was cool. It rustled the grass and whistled across the land, unimpeded by any significant obstacles. Tucker marveled at the vastness of the land, surpassed only by the almost ominous emptiness of the dark heavens. It was at times like these that he longed for the feeling of a roof over his head and walls surrounding him. Not because he feared the elements, but because the mysterious void of the sky would seem so deep as he lay looking up into it. There was something awesome in the nothingness of it all, almost frightening, something to make a human feel insignificant.

He shut his eyes to block out the view. Out here on the empty plains he didn't need to get himself all shivery and scared like a child.

Tucker tried to sleep, but the ground was hard and his mind was stirring. Never before had he traveled away from his home for more than a few miles unless someone was with him. Now he was striking off for a region he had never seen, with no one to guide or protect him. It was frightening in a way, yet also strangely appealing. And he knew why—for the first time in his life he felt not like a tagalong boy but like a *man*. And it was a good feeling.

Tucker rolled over and again tried to sleep, but after a few moments he realized it was no use. He stood up and stretched, determined to walk around for a bit in hopes of wearing off his excess energy. The wind struck him and he reached for his jacket, at the same time glancing carelessly toward the south.

There was a light off in the distance, a flickering light of a fire. He picked up the jacket and slipped it on, frowning. Who could it be out there? The fire was too far away from him to estimate its exact location. He had seen no one traveling the area besides himself. Unaccountably, he felt a shiver of concern.

He shrugged the feeling off. Probably the fire was in the camp of some drifter or cowboy who wanted a late-evening cup of coffee.

Tucker felt suddenly weary. He slipped off his jacket and crawled back into his blankets. He closed his eyes and listened to the wind and the sound of his horse grazing nearby, and slowly he drifted off to sleep.

When next he opened his eyes, the sun was rising and the ground was wet with dew. He rose, stretching and yawning, and looked around him. The day promised to be clear, a good one for travel. Forgotten was the awe and vague discomfort the empty land and sky had aroused in the night; now the plains were lovely, almost friendly. Building up his fire, he brewed coffee and fried a few hunks of bacon his mother had stowed deep in his sack of provisions.

He forded the creek and pushed almost due east. The best way to approach Miles City would be to follow the Deadwood Road, and he figured to reach it around Powderville.

Tucker was moving into the midst of one of the busiest cattle ranges, yet he had not yet seen a single cow. So vast was the land that animals and men were easily swallowed up in the distance or were hidden behind the low, rolling hills that spread around him. Only a few years before he would have seen buffalo, but now they were almost entirely gone, hunted to near extinction.

Tucker felt excitement begin to steal through him when he reached the Power River and the Deadwood Road. Soon he would be in Miles City, seeing things he had only heard about before, like the railroad. He was looking forward to seeing the wonder of modern transportation that ate wood and drank water while it chugged all the way from the eastern cities to the western towns, building communities and even new cities along its route. The Northern Pacific had reached Miles City a few years back. Folks were saying that the wonderful new line was changing the cattle industry remarkably. Now ranchers could drive their herds to the Miles City loading pens to be herded into big cars designed to haul stock, and the long drives to the more distant railheads were no longer necessary.

Tucker traveled as far as the light would let him before he made camp beside the road. He lay in his blankets, weary yet happy, and almost dropped off to sleep.

He recalled the fire he had seen the night before, burning toward the south. Giving a sleepy grunt, he rolled over and for a brief moment opened his eyes.

Far to the south—just how far he could not tell—the light was flickering again, just as it had the night before. Whoever had been behind him last night was still there and was apparently moving at about his rate of speed.

Chapter 3

Tucker encountered the track of the Northern Pacific just south of Miles City. Somehow the sight was a vague disappointment.

It was no more than an endless succession of ties binding together the shining rows of steel. It was hardly worth looking at. Slumping down in the saddle, he crossed the tracks and rode into the town.

Miles City was typical of many other towns in that part of the country, with wide streets and wooden buildings, many false-fronted log structures. Tucker rode directly in the middle of the street, looking from side to side at the businesses that lined it. It all looked sleepy and dull, livened only by the people moving up and down the boardwalk or walking the street.

Tucker looked at some of the saloons and wondered about Jack. It wasn't likely that he was gambling right now, for Jack had always said that it didn't seem right to cut a deck of cards until the sun was going down. But if Jack was in fact in Miles City, it seemed probable that he was registered in some boarding house or hotel. That is, unless he had chosen to make his bed on the range outside of town.

Finding Jack was the main problem, but Tucker was more concerned at the moment with buying a good meal. He was sick to his soul of jerky and dried biscuits, and the prospect of a good beefsteak with gravy and a few eggs sounded good. He eyed the stores lining the street, looking for a restaurant.

He found one and tied his horse to the hitching post

outside. Removing his hat, he entered the small log building, sniffing the tantalizing aroma of sizzling steak. He found a table in the corner and sat down.

"What'll it be?"

"Steak, two eggs fried, and about a half dozen biscuits."

The meal was delicious. Tucker topped it off with jelly on the biscuits. Sipping his coffee when the meal was through, he leaned back, feeling content and satisfied.

His leisurely and peaceful thoughts were interrupted by the memory of his father. He hoped that he would find Jack before it was too late. And too late could be very soon.

Tucker rose and paid for his meal, full but no longer happy. It was time to get down to business. Before long the gamblers would converge on the saloons to ply their art, and if Jack was in town, Tucker would find him.

The task of looking through several saloons seemed easy enough until Tucker stepped back out on the street and began counting them. Ten . . . eleven . . . twelve . . . the count continued, until he realized that on this street alone there were fourteen saloons! And there were bound to be others on the side streets. It appeared that Miles City had been founded to provide a place for drinking and carousing for the soldiers stationed at nearby Ft. Keogh.

Night fell swiftly. The last traces of light were fading in the west when Tucker stepped into the Morning Star Saloon. He looked around the interior, surprised at the elegance of the furnishings. There was velvety carpet on the floor, and fine oak and mahogany furniture. A beautifully embellished billiard table sat in prominence in the center of the room, and two men dressed in fancy black suits were engaged in a game of pool, their expensive cigars sending clouds of smoke drifting slowly up to the ceiling. Behind the bar was a large shelf backed by a mirror, and just by looking at the labels on the bottles

Tucker could tell that it was expensive liquor sold here. As the door closed behind him, several of the saloon patrons glanced his way, and something in their expressions made him conscious of his faded denims and dirty checked shirt. He glanced quickly around the room and not spying Jack, moved back outside.

He realized that he had stepped into what was surely an exclusive saloon, probably catering to rich cattlemen. A young rancher's son, still fresh into town and wet behind the ears, had no business even sticking his nose into such a plush establishment. He stepped down the boardwalk, looking for another saloon.

The next one was the antithesis of the one he had just left. The floors were covered with sawdust, and the tables were handmade and simple. Men were everywhere, rough men, most of them cowboys and some nothing in particular. The bartender was a fat, unshaven man wearing a filthy coat and grease-covered trousers on which he continually wiped his meaty hands. He had a black, drooping mustache that completely hid his mouth.

Tucker stepped into the saloon and looked around. There were a couple of card games going on, but nowhere did he see Jack. Tucker sighed but tried not to become discouraged. This was only the second place he had checked.

He was just turning to leave when a sudden disturbance erupted behind him. He wheeled about, startled, and saw immediately that trouble was coming.

Two burly men were standing and facing a third fellow, this one rather thin and hardly older than Tucker. He had been seated at one of the tables with a saloon girl on his lap, and his overturned chair betrayed the haste with which he had risen. And the liquor dripping from his shirt let Tucker know just what had happened.

One of the burly men set an empty glass down on the table and smirked at the young fellow.

"It takes a lot to get your attention, don't it, boy?

Now you just listen to me—you give your pa a message. The Circle X has been losing a lot of calves at just about the time your pa's spread has been getting more than its fair share of 'em. That don't look good to us, and it ain't gonna look good to your pa if it happens anymore. Your pa is a thief and a liar, boy, and if things don't change, he's gonna wind up stretching a rope from some cottonwood. You get your butt outta here and give him that message."

The younger man seemed to grow taller as he spat back, "If you got any messages, you deliver 'em yourself. I ain't your messenger boy, Thrasher!"

One burly man glanced at the other, a faint smile on his face. Tucker recognized in the young man the type of brashness that often got a man in trouble and sometimes got him shot.

"Son, you'd best watch your mouth. I hit you with a drink—I can hit you with a lot more," Thrasher said.

The other burly fellow spoke up. "His name's Thrasher, and he can live up to it. Now get outta here and back to your pa's ranch and deliver that message 'less you want more trouble than you can handle, boy!"

Tucker turned to leave. He didn't know how this was going to wind up, but he had no intention of hanging around to find out. He felt sympathy for the young man; he was obviously in no position to defend himself against two men twice his size, and apparently he was the son of a rancher. That fact made Tucker identify somewhat with the boy, though not enough to take a share of the punishment that was about to come to him.

Tucker was almost to the door when the crowd pressed in front of him, faces grinning, necks craning as men moved around to get a better view of the coming fight. Tucker's way out was blocked, and he stopped.

He began to shift around to the edge of the crowd, hoping to squeeze around them and out the door. Then he stopped again, but not because of the crowd. The young fellow inside didn't stand a chance, and clearly no one in the crowd was breaking his neck to help him. That rubbed Tucker the wrong way. Though he had no desire to tackle someone as big as Thrasher and his partner, he also had no desire to head out into the night knowing he had let a helpless young man get beaten half to death, or maybe even shot, without at least having tried to prevent it. What would Pa say?

Sighing and shaking his head, he turned again and looked at the spectacle on the floor. The crowd had spread itself into a circle around the sides of the room, and clearly the onlookers were prepared to enjoy a slaughter.

Blast it all—what a time to develop a code of honor! Wondering if he were a fool, Tucker began clenching and unclenching his fists, hoping that the young, victimized man would have the sense to walk out without trying to take on his two antagonists.

He didn't. With unbelievable speed the youth's fists flashed forward, crashing into the chins of Thrasher and his partner and knocking them both onto their backs on the floor. A gasp escaped from the onlookers, and whoops and shouts of delight filled the air. On the floor Thrasher gazed in shock at the ceiling, then began to roll to the side to raise himself.

He didn't make it, nor did his partner. The young lightning bolt of a fighter put a firm kick into Thrasher's chin, then wheeled around from the momentum of the kick and placed another into the temple of Thrasher's partner. Both men went down again. The young man leaped into the air, descending to dig his knee into Thrasher's big gut, his full weight smashing into the man's stomach.

Thrasher let out a combination cry and grunt that was punctuated by the sound of the young fighter's fists pounding relentlessly into his face. Thrasher's face grew bloody as the fists took their toll of his meaty features.

Tucker admired the grace and agility of the young man, realizing that the way he was handling Thrasher was gaining the respect of many others in the crowd. The catcalls and hoots were coming almost as much in favor of the young fellow as they were for Thrasher. But still, many were cheering on the burly man, cursing at him for being unable to free himself from the charge of human dynamite atop him.

Thrasher's partner was up now. His hands grasped the young man and pulled him off of the bloody and breathless fat man on the floor. The young fellow twisted loose from his grasp, turned and placed a solid blow into the man's face. Gasping, the man staggered backward, his nose shattered.

Thrasher fell like a mountain onto the young man. Thrasher's supporters sent forth a whoop of delight, urging the man to break the neck of his victim.

The young man struggled, but Thrasher's weight held him pinned to the floor. Though Thrasher held the advantage, he was still not in a good position to do much damage to the young man, for in order to keep him pinned he had to lie deadweight on top of him, making it difficult to land any solid blows.

Just as it looked like he might wriggle free, Thrasher brought his forehead down sharply into the face of the young fellow, knocking the youth's head hard against the floor. Stunned, the boy ceased struggling and Thrasher leaped up, pulling his victim to his feet. He grasped the stunned young man's arms and held him upright.

"Waynewright! Work him over!"

Thrasher's partner came forward, his face a bloody sneer. Grinning into the glazed eyes of the young man, he launched a huge fist into his gut, knocking the breath out of him and making him bend almost double, restrained only by Thrasher's grasp. Waynewright then smashed the young man in the mouth, sent another right to his gut.

His fist came back to land another blow, but absorbed in the pleasure of tormenting his victim, he failed to notice that the crowd had grown strangely silent. He swung his fist forward again.

The blow, which had been aimed for the cheekbone of the young man, never landed. A hand reached from behind Waynewright and grabbed his arm, stopping the swinging fist.

"What in the name of . . ."

Tucker smashed his fist into Waynewright's face as hard as he could, and though it felt as if he had broken his fingers in the process, he felt a strange elation when the bulking man collapsed like a puppet with severed strings. And even more enjoyable was the incredulous look on the face of Thrasher.

A whoop arose from the crowd as Tucker made for the big man, who looked completely at a loss as to how to handle his unexpected adversary while hanging on to the nearly unconscious young man he had been tormenting. Cursing, he shoved his victim forward, sending him reeling right into Tucker.

The crowd exploded. Tucker's movement into the fight was an inspiration to the fight-hungry men all around the room, and before Tucker could even shove the limp form of the young man off him, the entire saloon was rocking with a skull-busting free-for-all.

Tucker made it to his feet and lunged at Thrasher, only to be knocked aside by a flying body that some husky cowpoke had thrown across the room. Thrasher disappeared in the sea of swinging fists and bloodied faces.

Tucker was left standing in the middle of the room, not knowing how to handle what he had started, nor even sure who was fighting for him or against him. From the looks of things, he wasn't sure *anybody* knew—apparently it was a matter of smashing the most convenient face.

The young man who had been the start of it all struggled to his feet, his face bloody from a cut across his cheekbone. He stumbled toward Tucker. His hand grasped Tucker's shoulder.

Tucker jerked at his touch and started to pound his fist into the young man's face before he recognized him. The trembling fellow leaned against him, his voice cracked and low.

"Much . . . obliged to you—I . . ."

A fist struck Tucker's face and knocked him backward. He came up swinging, sending a cowboy reeling into a chair. The cowboy was on the floor nursing a broken jaw before Tucker realized that he wasn't even the fellow who had struck him.

The world became a mass of sweating, fighting muscle and flesh, and Tucker was pounded by fists like hammers. His eyes glazed and he sank into a sea of exploding, brilliant stars.

Chapter 4

Tucker was only vaguely aware of being dragged out of the saloon and helped onto a horse. Then came a ride—just how long a ride he could not tell—and he was led into some sort of dwelling and placed in a bed. His head ached horribly.

He awoke to the touch of a damp towel against his forehead. His gaze first focused on the arm that moved gently back and forth as a towel swabbed his face, then his eyes traveled up that arm to look into one of the most beautiful faces he had ever beheld.

"Hello—I thought maybe a little cold water might bring you around to us," the girl said. Her voice was clear and cheerful, and she smiled in a way that made Tucker's already limp form go limper.

"Frank told us what you did," she said. "He says you might have saved his life."

Tucker stirred and sat slightly upright, propping himself on his elbows until his senses began to return.

"Glad I could help. It wasn't a fair fight, and I thought to even the odds a little. When I jumped in, things really started humming, but after that I really can't seem to remember much . . ."

"You got busted in the head, buddy," said a male voice. Tucker looked to his right. On the other side of the bed stood the young man whom he had defended—whose name, apparently, was Frank.

Frank sat down on a stool beside the bed and extended his hand to Tucker. Still a bit groggy, Tucker reached out and shook the calloused hand, noting its strength.

"The name's Frank Bryan. And this is my sister, Charity."

"Tucker Corrigan, from south of the territory. Where am I right now?"

"I managed to get you out of that saloon without nobody noticing. Once that free-for-all started, I made it out of there all right. Things were still swinging when I got you on your horse and rode you out here to the ranch. This here's where I live, with Pa and Charity. My pa runs this spread."

Tucker looked around him. The room he was in was small, with a low ceiling. The walls were made of hewn log, smooth and almost white, for they had not yet browned with age. Tucker's bed was in the corner of the room, and across from it was a cast-iron cookstove with a flue that ran up through a hole in the roof. The walls had pegs all over them, and from those pegs hung pans and pots, two or three rifles, and some sort of crude, fuzzy painting of a cow's head, apparently hung there to add color to the room.

The ceiling was nothing but the underside of the shingled roof, with huge logs running from one end of the house to the other as support. On the side of the room was a door that opened onto a "dog trot" passageway, and beyond was another door opening into a room that was the twin of this one. Tucker recognized the common technique of making a large home from short logs by joining two small, square cabins with a common roof. Althugh he couldn't be sure from the angle at which he lay, it appeared that the Bryans had boarded up the ends of the dog trot, making the entire structure into three rooms, end on end.

Tucker glanced over at Charity Bryan, who had ceased swabbing his forehead. Her hair was a dusty brown, and her eyes were the deepest green Tucker had ever seen. Her skin was fair and unblemished. He stared at her unabashedly, until her faint smile told him his gaze bordered on rudeness. Embarrassed, he quickly turned away.

Frank Bryan was at the stove, pouring coffee into a tin mug. He walked back to Tucker's bedside and extended the mug to him.

Tucker sat completely up, feeling dizzy. It was difficult to focus his eyes. Muttering thanks, he accepted the coffee. He sipped some of the hot brew, then looked again at Frank.

"Just what was that fight all about, anyway? Why were those big devils giving you a hard time?"

Frank sat back down on the wooden stool. "Those two were Brant Thrasher and Marvin Waynewright, cowpokes for the Circle X ranch a few miles north of here. We're a small ranch, and they're a big one. We've been in operation for about two years, and they've been here for a lot longer. What it comes down to is that they're accusing my pa of rustling cattle. A lot of their pregnant cattle have been losing calves, but our herd is growing. Of course, they take it that we're stealing their newborns before they can get to 'em. Nothing we can do seems to convince 'em any different, and now they're talking about burning us out and lynching me and Pa. It's getting to be a desperate situation. I halfway thought it might not be safe to bring you out here, with folks so worked up. But there was nowhere else I could take you."

Tucker sipped his coffee, gently rubbing his aching head. "Sounds bad. But I can't see that you'll need to worry any about the likes of them two back in the saloon giving you trouble. They must be mighty big cowards to be afraid to take on a young fellow like you 'less there was two of 'em together. You gave 'em what-for for a while, Frank! I rightly admired you."

"They would have busted my head if you hadn't jumped in when you did, Tucker. I can't give you much to show my thanks, but I sure hope you know I appreciate it."

"And so do I," cut in Charity. "It's good to know there's folks like you who'll help even when they're not obliged to."

"Tucker, I'll admit I'm confused about why you did it," Frank said.

"I'm a rancher's son myself, Frank, and I guess I saw a little of me in you. My pa owns a spread down about the Crazy Woman in Wyoming. We have a small operation, too."

"That right? There's some pretty country down that way, good grazing land. What are you doing up about these parts?"

The question brought a pang to Tucker, for momentarily he had forgotten about Pa's illness and the reason he was here. He cast his gaze to the floor.

"My pa's ailing, and I come up here looking for my brother. I thought he was south of here, but folks down there told me he had moved north. Miles City seemed to be the natural place to look. I was in that saloon looking for him today."

Frank pursed his lips and slowly shook his head. "Sorry about your pa. Maybe I can help you find your brother. What's his name?"

"Jack Corrigan. I doubt you know him."

Frank shook his head. "I don't. I'll sure keep my ears open for the name, though. How long will you stay in these parts?"

"Don't know for sure. I'll hunt for Jack about a week, if it takes that, then head back whether I've found him or not. I hope I can find him. Pa was counting on seeing him before he . . . dies."

"Well, Tucker, you'll spend the night with us. It's dark already, and there's no way we're gonna have you ride back to Miles City now. Besides, I owe you for what you did."

Charity cooked up supper, and it was delicious. Thick slabs of bacon with fresh bread, molasses for sweetening. Tucker drank milk—milk that came from a can. It had always struck him as ironic that here in the heart of beef country many folks didn't bother to keep a milk cow.

He ate more than was good for him and sat back happily after the meal. Charity sat across from him, giving him a good excuse to look at her.

Frank lit up a pipe and began blowing smoke rings. The conversation dwindled. The girl became restless after a time, stood up, and walked to the window. Drawing back the curtain, she peered outside.

"It seems Pa would be back by now, Frank. I can't figure what is taking him so long."

"Don't worry, Charity. You know Pa once he gets out on the range. There's always something or other to be done. He'll be back soon enough."

But an hour passed and there was still no sign of the elder Bryan. Tucker could sense that Charity's uneasiness was beginning to be shared by her brother, who was smoking furiously, glancing toward the window every time the breeze made a random noise that might be mistaken for a hoofbeat.

Then came a noise that unmistakably *was* the sound of a hoof striking earth. Charity and Frank rose together and moved to the door. Charity threw it open, there was a moment of silence, and suddenly she said: "Frank—it *isn't* Pa . . . it's Seth Bailey!"

"Seth Bailey? What's he doing out here?"

Tucker heard the horse thunder to a stop outside, and a moment later a breathless, windblown man entered the door of the house and plopped down on a stool.

"Seth?"

"It's bad, Frank, real bad. I figured somebody had to tell you . . ."

Frank glanced at his sister, worry in his eyes. "What is it?"

"It's your pa, Frank. They done got him locked up in the jail—charged him with rustling."

Frank collapsed into a chair. Charity went pale.

"When, Seth?"

"Not long after sundown. Don't know all the details, but I seen the sheriff taking him into the jailhouse myself. And Dan Granger was with him."

Frank bent forward, resting his face in his hands. Charity moved over behind him, biting her lower lip to keep from crying, and placed her hand on her brother's shoulder.

Frank rose up again after a moment and looked seriously at Seth Bailey. "I gotta go into town," he said. "I gotta see my pa."

"I figured you would, Frank. Be careful."

Tucker stood. "Frank, I'm going with you."

The young man turned and looked at Tucker. "Tucker, there's no reason for you . . ." He paused, then grinned in a rather sad way. "Thanks, Tucker. I 'preciate it."

The pair saddled up and headed for Miles City. For quite some time they said nothing to each other, then Tucker pulled up close beside Frank.

"Who is this Dan Granger?"

"Owner of the Circle X, and a real troublemaker. He's been after Pa for months now."

"And who is Seth Bailey? Can you trust him?"

"Sure. Seth has been a family friend for a long time. He's always done his best to stick up for Pa. He lives alone in a shack a couple of miles from our spread. Raises his food, works a few of the roundups when the mood strikes him. He's lazy, but a good man."

"Do you think it was wise to leave him alone with Charity?"

"Sure—better than having her there alone. Don't worry, Tucker. He's trustworthy."

Tucker hoped so. He was surprised at how protective he felt toward a girl he had just met and had hardly spoken to.

They reached Miles City and rode straight for the

jailhouse. It had a foreboding look, and Tucker wondered just what Frank planned to do once he got in there. Tying his horse to the front hitching rail, Tucker followed the young rancher's son onto the board porch of the jailhouse.

Frank didn't hesitate at the door, nor did he knock. He flung the door open and barged inside, walking straight to the desk and the startled lawman behind it. He slapped his palms down onto the desktop and leaned forward until his face was no more than a foot away from the sheriff's.

"My name's Frank Bryan. You got my pa locked up for rustling, and I'm here to tell you he ain't done it. You can turn him loose."

The sheriff rose. Tucker was amazed at how tall he was. As he looked down into Frank's face, he made the young man look puny by comparison. But Frank returned his gaze fearlessly.

"Look, boy, if you're Duke Bryan's son, you'd best know that I got you pa dead to rights. Dan Granger swore, along with two others, that he caught your pa rustling earlier this evening. I had no choice but to lock him up. And until we find out more about this, I got no plans to let him loose."

Frank looked a bit chastened, for obviously there was nothing he could do. He stared into the sheriff's face for a moment, then asked in a slightly less forceful voice: "Could I see him?"

The sheriff sighed. He led the two young men back to the cell area, throwing open the heavy door that separated it from the front office. A scent of unwashed bodies assaulted Tucker's nose.

The jail was full tonight, mostly with drunks and brawlers. Blank faces stared at the three men as they moved back farther into the cellblock. There were two men in each cell; in some there were three.

Frank moved to the cell where a bearded man sat in dejection on a bed chained to the wall. When he saw

Frank, the man brightened, then looked all the more despondent.

"They got me up a creek this time, boy. They surely do."

A slender man sharing the same cell turned to look at the trio. As he laid eyes on Tucker, his mouth fell open in shock. Tucker's did the same.

"Jack? Is it you? Jack!"

Chapter 5

Charity Bryan poured Seth Bailey a cup of coffee, which he accepted with thanks. He watched the young lady walking nervously around the room.

She turned to him and asked pleadingly, "Seth, why is there so much stir over rustling right now? Why is Granger so determined to hurt my pa?"

"I can't answer the second part of that question, Charity, 'cause I don't know what Granger has against your pa in particular. But the reason there's so much trouble over rustling is that so much of it is going on. More and more cattle are disappearing, and when a small rancher like your pa starts doing well at about the time the big ranchers are losing out, it's only natural they would get suspicious. But you ought to not feel real bad about this—it could have been a sight worse."

"Worse? What could be worse than having my pa in jail for rustling?"

"Havin' him strung up, that's what! Granger figures your pa is a rustler, and from his point of view he was doing him a mercy by taking him to the jail instead of hanging him on the spot. That's what a lot of cattlemen are doing to the rustlers lately, whether they have been convicted or not. Some have even took away prisoners from the law and . . ."

He stopped, sorry he had mentioned that lynchings had been occurring under the very nose of the law; with Duke Bryan locked up, such talk was hardly comforting to his daughter.

"Seth, do you think . . ."

"No, Charity. I'd say your pa is safe right now. They ain't gonna bust right in that jail to get him. Don't you worry."

He took a sip from his cup and hoped he was right. He wasn't nearly as confident about it as he pretended. In eastern Montana and western Dakota, ranchers were beginning to talk to each other about the rise in rustling. Many were recommending a range war—a unified effort to wipe out the thieves who took advantage of the ranchers' inability to watch their stock out on the open range. Other ranchers were trying to approach the situation with moderation, favoring moves such as the hiring of range detectives and extra hands to keep watch over their stock, but increasingly their voices were being drowned out with louder, more angry ones. Seth was a good friend of Duke Bryan, but he was realistic enough to know that Granger was a strong enough man to have Bryan strung up to a cottonwood at a moment's notice. So far, he was being merciful.

Charity could tell from the nervous way Seth was sipping his coffee that things were not as bright as he was making them out. He was correct in saying that it was lucky Pa was just locked up instead of dead, but she had lived the life of a rancher's daughter long enough to know that no prison could keep determined men from taking out their wrath on a prisoner. And Dan Granger was a man with a remarkable ability to stir up hatred when he wanted to. Dan Granger got what he wanted, when he wanted it, or others paid the price.

What Granger's motive was for his continued actions against her father baffled her. If only Ma were still living—she could have talked to her about it. Ma had always understood problems like that, it seemed. She had been a woman with a keen insight into the human heart and mind.

Charity walked over to the window and stared out into the darkness. The night was silent but for the wind that whistled around the eaves of the house, the moan of it sad and lonesome. She wondered how Pa was, locked up there in the jailhouse, and if Frank and Tucker had managed to talk to him, maybe even get him freed.

She longed to hear the sound of hoofbeats coming over the rise, yet she also dreaded it. The sound of those hooves could herald either the return of Pa, or perhaps merely more bad news. It was hard to believe that such a short time ago things had been so good, the family all together, the future promising.

"Maybe you should sit down, get a little rest," Seth suggested. "I'll tell you what—I'll go on into the other room if you would like to go to bed. It's getting late, and you might need to catch a little sleep. I'm heading outside for a smoke and some fresh air, but I'll be close by. If you need anything, just holler."

Charity smiled at the ragged man. Seth had proven himself a good friend many times over, and it comforted her to have him near. Seth was a good-hearted soul, as homely as they come, and she felt toward him much as she would toward some sort of ugly, lovable old billy goat. She felt secure with him, too, for she knew he had a reputation as a crack shot. She had seen him only a few times without his Colt strapped to his hips.

"Thank you, Seth. I don't think I'll be able to sleep until Frank gets back, but it might feel good to lie down anyway. If you hear them coming, let me know."

"Sure will, Charity."

Seth stepped outside, leaving Charity alone. She walked over to the stove and placed a few extra pieces of wood inside, making the blaze flare to new brightness. She swung the metal door closed and walked over to her bed.

She didn't undress, for she wanted to be able to rise at a moment's notice when Frank and Tucker returned. She had no intention of going to sleep, but when she laid her head on the feather-stuffed pillow, she became drowsy and soon was dozing.

Outside, Seth drew on his pipe, watching the burning tobacco glow red and bright with every puff. He was deep in thought, and his eyes were continually drawn to the dark slope over which Frank and his young partner would come riding when they returned. He hoped Duke would be with them but knew it was unlikely.

And he knew that he was the only man who understood Granger's true motives. He longed to tell Charity the truth, but that was impossible. Still, it was so hard to continue in a lie, especially at a time like this. But it really wasn't his choice. He had made a promise, one he had to keep.

He leaned up against the wall. He liked the feel of the sturdy logs; it made him a bit sad, though, for it revived an old dream that long ago had perished. He had once dared to hope that one day he would own a ranch of his own, somewhere here on the plains, and maybe he would even have had a fine wife and a daughter like Charity or a son like Frank. That was a dream from years ago, though. At moments like this, it would revive itself for a moment, but something would always happen to pull Seth into the more mundane world of reality.

And in this case that something was a stirring in a grove of trees just a few yards across from the cabin and slightly toward the west. Seth tensed and listened closely; he didn't like what he had heard, for the sound had an element of stealth in it. Slowly his hand crept toward his gun butt.

He stared into the dark growth of trees and spoke in a voice loud enough to carry across the distance while not disturbing Charity inside the house.

"Who is it? I hear you . . . and I'll shoot if you don't show yourself!"

For a moment there was no sound, but then came the faint but easily discernible snapping of a twig beneath a foot, then a clicking noise that could only be one thing.

Seth's pistol whipped from his holster and began spitting red flame into the night, bullets ripping through leafy branches and slapping into tree trunks with a dead, plunking sound.

Then the fire was answered with echoing blasts from the grove, just as Seth was overcome by panic, blindly emptying the chamber of his Colt at a target he could not see.

The sheriff looked at Tucker suspiciously. "You know this fellow?" he asked, gesturing toward Jack Corrigan, who stood staring at Tucker as if he were an apparition.

"Yes, sir. He's my brother."

"Well, you know your brother's a rustler, do you? Maybe you do . . . maybe you know a lot about it!"

Tucker could read the sheriff's thoughts, and it angered him. But it scared him to think that Jack was being held on so serious a charge.

"Tucker—what are you doing here?" Jack asked. "How did you get here?"

"I was about to ask *you* that!" exclaimed Tucker. "What's this about you rustling cattle?"

"It's a stinking lie, that's what it is! A bunch of circumstances that made me look bad. I've never rustled a cow in my life and don't plan to start. But it ain't no use trying to tell that fool sheriff that!"

The sheriff stared coldly at Jack. "You keep up that talk, and I'll cut off your visiting privileges with your brother here. You were caught riding with known rustlers."

Jack's eyes narrowed. He looked squarely into the face of the tall sheriff. "I told you how I met them. I knew absolutely nothing about anything they might have done before, and I sure had nothing to do with it myself. You got no reason to hold me here."

The sheriff simply stared back at him, obviously unmoved. Frank Bryan and his father stood regarding the situation, apparently confused. Duke Bryan had no idea who Tucker was. Frank quietly gave a brief account of how he had met Tucker and how Granger's toughs had tried to beat him senseless in the saloon.

Jack and Tucker fell into a deep conversation, trying in a few moments' time to fill in the events of seven years. Tucker told Jack of their father's illness, and Jack was visibly shaken.

"I knew something like that would happen sooner or later. I never should have left. I should have had it out with Thurston Russell."

Tucker shook his head. "I don't think it matters now. The main thing we gotta do is get you outta here so you can see Pa. It's important to him."

The sheriff was lighting a pipe, slowly drawing on the flame until the tobacco was glowing evenly. He shifted the pipe stem to one side of his mouth and dropped the match to the brick floor.

"Forget it, boy. He ain't going nowhere until we determine the truth about that rustling charge."

Duke Bryan, a lean, tanned man with a stubbly beard and small eyes, laughed contemptuously. "In this country what Granger says will go, and if he so much as hints that somebody is rustling cattle, there ain't nothing to look forward to except a prison rock pile or a noose."

The sheriff looked sharply at Bryan. "Shut up, you. Nobody will hang or go to prison without a trial. Granger has no control over that."

"Granger pulls the strings here, and you know it. You jump when he hollers and dance when he whistles just like everybody else in this territory. And if he came knocking on your door tonight politely asking to lynch every man in this jail, you'd step aside and let him do it," the rancher snapped. "I was locked up here without a trace of evidence against me, just because Granger claimed I was rustling. You're a puppet, Sheriff."

Tucker could feel the sting of contempt in Duke Bryan's voice. He was clearly a man who had been pushed to his limit, harassed until he could stand it no longer.

Duke Bryan turned to Frank. "Where is Charity? Is she alone?"

"Seth Bailey is with her, back at the ranch. She'll be all right."

"I hope so. But I'm worried about Granger. His men took me right on the range. Almost like Granger had decided on the spur of the moment to get me out of the way. I'm worried about what he might do back home."

"I thought about that, too, Pa. But there wasn't much I could do. That's why I came here, hoping that some way I could get you out."

Duke Bryan laughed. "And how did you plan to do that? Bust the sheriff in the head?"

Frank caught the slightly different tone in his father's voice. The young man looked into Duke's eyes and did not miss the covert command in them. He smiled faintly, and his father did the same.

The sheriff was leaning against a brick column, still puffing on his pipe and listening to the talk with a quiet, arrogant air. He did not catch the hidden order Duke Bryan had directed at his son.

So he was not prepared when the young man wheeled suddenly, a hard fist swinging up from his waist to catch him full in the chin. The lawman bit the stem of his pipe in half as the force of the blow lifted him two inches off the floor. He slammed back against the wall, collapsing to his rump with hissing breath escaping his lips.

For a moment there was only silence within the jail, Then the prison became a virtual madhouse, with prisoners roaring out in delight at what Frank had done, demanding immediate freedom. Two men in the adjoining cell began shouting, extending their arms through the bars in supplication to Frank to let them go. Tucker took them to be the pair Jack had taken up with, the same ones who had stolen the saddle from the Drake ranch on the Hanging Woman Creek.

"Frank, do you think you should have done that?" asked Tucker, awed. "When he comes to . . ."

"When he comes to we'll be long gone," responded Frank, now kneeling beside the unconscious lawman and removing the ring of keys from his belt. "We had no choice—I have to get Pa out of here, and there's no way you can get your brother back to your ranch unless you break him loose. Is this the key, Pa?"

"I think so . . . hurry up! There's a deputy here somewhere."

The cell door swung open, and Duke Bryan exited the cell, Jack right after him, looking a bit dazed at his unexpected freedom. Duke bent and took the pistol from the sheriff's gun belt.

"Our stuff is all locked up in the safe outside," he said. "We'll have to make do with what we can find as far as weapons and ammunition."

Tucker caught Frank's arm. "Frank—do you realize what this means? We're putting ourselves on the run from the law. Is it worth it?"

"It's the only choice we have! I won't stand back and see my pa get jailed and maybe lynched. Granger has lynched men before, and I don't doubt he would do it again. He would hang your brother just as quick, too. Now shut up and get moving!"

Tucker obeyed, heading into the jail office. Duke Bryan had already rounded up several rifles and a good supply of ammunition.

"We've got two horses outside—we'll have to steal a couple of others," said Frank. "There should be plenty in front of the saloon."

Tucker stopped short. "Listen, Frank—we're in trouble enough as it is, and I won't be a party to horse stealing! This has gone far enough."

"The only choice you have is to get away fom here any way you can, or march your brother back into that cell! If you leave, you're already in truble with the law, whether you steal a horse or not. We're not playing games, Tucker—are you with us or not?"

Tucker glanced at his brother, and a silent communication passed between them. He said, "We're with you."

Duke Bryan shoved open the door and peered out cautiously into the night before stepping onto the porch. The street wasn't deserted, but no one seemed to be paying attention to them. Tucker's horse was still there, tied to the hitching post beside Frank's.

"Pa, you take my horse. I'll get one in front of the saloon over here. It's more important that you get away than it is that I do."

"I'm waiting on you, Son. We'll all leave together."

"I'll go with you, Frank," Jack said.

Tucker and Duke mounted horses, rifles across their laps. Jack and Frank started walking nonchalantly toward the nearest saloon. There were a half dozen horses tied to the rail in front of it, whose owers, they hoped, were too busy bending their elbows to take notice of what was about to happen outside.

Jack reached the nearest horse. He loosened the ties from the rail and pulled himself into the saddle as Frank did the same with the chestnut tied beside Jack's horse.

Clicking his tongue and moving back from the rail, Jack turned the horse and headed down the street toward the jail. Frank did the same, sending a hurried look toward the saloon door.

A figure appeared there, a staggering man, big and husky and very drunk. Against the bright background of the well-lighted saloon, he was to Frank's eyes a silhouetted form, his features invisible as he pushed the door farther ajar and gazed for a moment at the young man riding his horse toward the edge of town.

"My horse! He's stole my horse!"

All four of the men in front of the jail nudged their heels into the flanks of their horses, urging the animals into a run. The man in the saloon door staggered forward, arms waving, shouting after the rapidly fleeing riders.

Others followed him from the door then, one of

them finding that his horse also was stolen. But the four riders had disappeared into the darkness, and most of the men reentered the saloon.

The big drunken man and the other victim of Frank and Jack's thievery did their best to convince someone, anyone, to go after the vanished riders, but their pleas were unheeded.

It was at that moment that the sheriff appeared on the porch of the jail, rubbing his head with one hand and his jaw with the other. Dazed, straining to focus his eyes, he stared into the darkness, aware that his prisoners would not easily be found.

The two men from the saloon came up to him on the porch, too angry about the theft of their horses to notice the sheriff's condition. The big drunken one leaned right into the lawman's face and demanded that he ride after the thieves.

The sheriff pushed him aside, ignoring him. "Shut up—I gotta go talk to Dan Granger!"

He stepped off the porch and headed for the livery, weaving and staggering. The two men on the jailhouse porch stared after him stupidly, shrugged, and headed back to the saloon.

Chapter 6

The men rode hard for a time, at last stopping for a brief rest about two miles out of town. There had been no sign of pursuit, but still the darkness seemed pregnant with danger and all of the riders were tense.

Frank reined his horse in beside his father's. "Where can we go, Pa? They'll come looking at the ranch."

"I know, Frank. But Charity's there. We gotta go back and see that she's all right. I'm afraid of what might happen if some of Granger's men get there before we do."

"What about Tucker and his brother here? They got no cause to get involved any further."

Tucker turned to gaze at his brother, waiting for a response. He sensed that the logical thing to do was to politely thank Frank and his father for their help in freeing Jack, but something in him was resisting that notion. He found himself hoping that Jack would desire to throw in with the rancher and his son and help them fight their way out of their desperate situation.

Jack looked at Tucker, then at the others. "Men, I don't know just what all of this is about, but I'm obliged to you for my freedom. And if you're in some sort of trouble, I feel inclined to help get you out of it. I don't know a lot about this Granger fellow, but I heard his name thrown around when that lawman locked me up. I think it was him that had me arrested. If Tucker is willing, I'm for seeing this through, as long as we can."

Tucker was willing. Frank broke into a grin, and Duke leaned over to pat Tucker on the shoulder.

"I don't really know you, young fellow, but I'm thankful you're along. And you, too, Jack. I don't know if you're a rustler or not, but right now I don't really care."

"I ain't a rustler, though I do consider myself somewhat of a fool, for I been riding with a couple of them the last few weeks. That's the only reason I didn't ask you to let 'em out when you freed me—they got me into some fine messes already, and I'm happy to take my leave of them."

"Men, I don't want to break up a good conversation, but we'd best be riding," said Frank. "Charity's waiting, and that sheriff might have a posse on our tail before long."

The men set out again, riding steadily, though not as hard as before. Tucker thought over what Frank had said. It seemed likely that the sheriff would get a posse together to pursue them. It seemed equally likely that the posse would catch up with them, probably at the ranch. And then . . . He shuddered to think about it.

Tucker had never been involved in any significant battle in his life, and he had never figured he would be. Most of the time he didn't carry any weapon, except when he was out on the range, and though he was a good shot, he had never enjoyed training his sights on any living thing, whether a jackrabbit or a lame horse. And the idea of lining up a gun on a man and pulling the trigger . . . that was hard to think about.

Tucker didn't have any idea how late it was, though he knew it was well past midnight. Charity would probably be upset by now, worrying all this time about her pa and brother. For a moment he caught himself wondering if she had been worrying about him, too, but he chided himself for such a fool notion.

He felt a great surge of relief to see the ranch house still standing as they rode up within sight of it. From the way Duke had been talking, he had feared that the ranch might have been burned down long before they arrived.

The men rode to the front of the house and dismounted. It wasn't until then that Tucker sensed that something was wrong. Just what it was he couldn't say, but apparently the same sense had gripped Duke and Frank, for both looked at each other, frowning.

Tucker realized then that Charity had not come out to greet them. He gripped his rifle and looked to the others, not sure what to do.

Duke and Frank eased toward the door, holding their rifles. It was a tense situation, for while they did not want to walk into some sort of trap, at the same time they didn't want to startle Charity. Maybe she had dozed off during the long period of waiting. Having four armed men burst through the door would be a shock to her.

Tucker and Jack stood back near the horses while Frank and his father approached the ranch house. Frank crept to the window and peeped over the sill, trying to see through an opening in the curtains. It was no use; they were closed tightly.

Frank crept over to where his father crouched beside the door. "Where's Seth Bailey? If he was still here, I think he would have been on the lookout for us."

"I know. That worries me."

Duke turned to Tucker and Jack, motioning for them to stay where they were. Then he and his son took a deep breath, readied their rifles, and reached for the latchstring.

The door flew open, and a tormented cry escaped from the interior of the house, followed almost immediately by a gunshot. Tucker ducked where he stood near the horses, hearing the lead wing away over his head and into the night.

Duke and Frank leaped into the doorway, aiming their rifles at the crouching figure cowering beside the cookstove on the opposite side of the room.

It was Charity, pale, frightened, and gripping a rifle. She dropped her weapon and ran into the arms of her father. Tucker and Jack, still uncertain about what was happening inside the house, moved carefully to the door and looked in before entering.

Frank and his father were too involved with a rather emotional reunion with Charity to notice what Tucker saw immediately when he entered the room.

Seth Bailey lay stretched out on the bed, his face white and his mouth open, his eyes staring. His shirt was a bloody, bullet-pocked rag. At first glance Tucker could tell he was dead.

Charity was crying, her arms around Frank's neck, when Duke Bryan turned to see Tucker staring at the bed. Following the young man's gaze, he took in the dead form of his old friend, and his face seemed to age ten years.

"Seth . . ."

He walked toward the bed. Frank looked up also and noticed Seth's body. His breath drew in with a hiss. Without realizing it, he gripped Charity's arms with such a force that she had to pull away.

Duke turned toward his daughter. "Charity, what happened?"

The girl wrapped her arms around herself as if she were cold. "I can't tell you exactly what happened, Pa. I was inside, getting ready to lie down and rest until you and Frank got back, and there was shooting all at once. It was over almost as soon as it started. I could hear Seth crying out for help; he sounded like he was hurt bad, and there were men moving around in the trees outside, just up the slope.

"I got the rifle and went to the window. I could see Seth on the ground. There were several wounds in his chest. Then two men started moving toward him up in the darkness, and I fired at them. I didn't really aim, I don't think—I just pointed the gun in their direction and fired.

"They took off running, but I don't think I hit them. And I didn't recognize them—I don't think they were Granger's men."

Duke frowned. "Then why were they there? And why would they shoot at Seth and come toward the house?"

"I don't know, Pa. Maybe they *were* Granger's men. But I've seen most of his riders at one time or another, and I had never seen these. One of them was fat, with a beard. It was dark, but I think the hair was red. The other man was fat, too, with dark hair and a mustache. When I started shooting, they didn't hang around long."

Tucker stepped forward. "You say one had a red beard?"

"Yes."

"Did you notice anything else?"

"No . . . why? Do you think you might know who it is?"

Jack spoke then, for the first time since they had come in. "My name is Jack Corrigan, ma'am. I'm Tucker's brother. I think I might know who it was. It might be a man who is out to get me, a man named Thurston Russell. Tucker came here from the Wyoming Territory because our pa is dying. Russell might have followed him, figuring Tucker would lead him to me."

Jack turned away. Tucker could sense what his brother was thinking. He was wondering if it was because of him that a man was dead, a man he didn't even know. If that *was* Thurston Russell haunting the dark plains outside, then only because of Jack was he in the area.

Frank put his arm around his sister's waist. "Did Seth talk to you?"

Charity pulled away from her brother quickly, looking suddenly evasive. She spoke quickly. "No. He said nothing. Nothing at all." She moved over to the window and looked outside, as if trying to avoid looking at the others. Frank and Duke glanced at each other but said nothing.

Duke walked to the door and opened it, looking at the sky. "It won't be long till morning. I sure as the dickens ain't going to try to sleep. I'm way too tensed up, and it could be that Granger might send some of his men in here after us."

Frank said, "The sheriff will have a posse here before long."

Duke sat down on a bench up against the front wall. "I don't know what to do, Frank. I won't lie to you. If we fight it out, there's a good chance we'll be killed. They won't take us back to the prison. But on the other hand, if we run out, Granger's won. He wants the small ranchers out of here so the range can belong to him. If we give in, it'll make it bad for the others." Duke put his elbows on his knees and dropped his chin into his cupped palms.

Frank turned again to Tucker and Jack. "Pa's right. We can't ask you to risk your lives for us, no matter what we said before. If you want to leave, now's the time. Granger might get here before dawn."

Tucker was scared, and Frank knew it. And Jack hardly knew what was going on, despite the brief explanations. He had been thrown into the middle of the situation through no fault of his own, and Tucker wouldn't blame him if he wanted to move on. Back on the trail he had said he would stay. Turning to his brother, Tucker asked him if he still felt the same way.

Jack's response was firm and clear. "If Thurston Russell did this to this man," he said, gesturing toward Seth Bailey's body, "then I ought to stay around here and do something about it. We said we would stick it out, and I ain't one to change my mind. I got even more reason now that Thurston Russell might be involved."

Duke stood. "All right then. There's something I want you to do for me, Tucker. There might be a gunfight here soon. I don't want Charity around when it happens. I want you to pack up supplies for a good while, then ride with Charity out to an old line-camp cabin ten miles south of here. Stock her up good, get her moved in, then stay there until one of us comes out to tell you it's over.

I'm putting my daughter's safety—and her honor—in your hands. Take good care of her."

Tucker nodded. "Yes, sir."

"Thank you, boy. Jack, if you're willing, stay on here with me and Frank. I might be putting your neck in a noose, but if you really want to stick it out like you said . . ."

"I do. I'll stay as long as need be."

"Thank you. And you, too, Tucker. I hope I can pay you back someday."

Charity cut in. "I'll start gathering supplies, Pa. It won't be long till first light." She began bustling about the room, gathering food and clothing and stuffing them into a burlap bag. She put on a valiant show for a few minutes, then the dread overwhelmed her and she ran to her father, collapsed into his arms, and wept.

Chapter 7

Tucker and Charity rode away from the ranch shortly before dawn, moving swiftly, each carrying a rifle. Tucker had a pistol strapped to his waist as well. Duke Bryan had given it to him.

Tucker tried to concentrate on the trail ahead, but he felt as if eyes were watching him all around, as if the gradually lightening plains were filled with danger. He kept Charity close as they traveled.

In a way it was Charity who led, for Tucker knew nothing of the exact whereabouts of the old line camp. But Charity knew the plains well and guided her horse swiftly and surely toward the south, moving with the assurance of a seasoned rider. Tucker admired her grace and skill in the saddle, knowing that if worse came to worse, she could probably evade any pursuers even without his help.

The dawn broke golden over the eastern horizon, its rays catching the shimmering of sweat on the flanks of the horses and the shining of Charity's hair as it whipped behind her in the morning wind.

Tucker occasionally looked behind to see if they were being pursued, but there was never anything except the eternal rolling of the prairie and an occasional tree or outcrop of rock. That much was good.

Of course, there was still Thurston Russell to think about. Everybody back on the Crazy Woman knew Danver Corrigan was ailing, and it didn't take much to figure out he would want to have his family reunited before the end came. Maybe Russell had anticipated what would happen and had followed Tucker. Tucker thought about the distant fire he had seen as he traveled northward. Could it have been the campfire of Thurston Russell? It made sense.

Tucker and Charity made good time. When the sun was well above the line of the horizon and its rays were hot against their faces, Charity pulled her horse to a stop.

"The line camp is over there," she said, pointing to a slope that was dotted with scrubby trees and brush. "That stream runs within ten feet of it."

"Do you think anybody will be there?"

"It could be. I suppose we should check it out before we ride in."

Charity clicked her tongue, and her horse headed for the slope. The girl had the confidence of any cowpoke in the saddle. She had quiet authority over her mount that came only after years of experience in riding. The girl had worked alongside her father and brother in roundups during the lean years when it was hard to hire help. She knew as much about the ranching business as many of the cattle tycoons who puffed big cigars in the stockgrowers' meetings in Miles City.

When Tucker and Charity reached the brink of the slope, they dismounted and tied their horses inside a clump of low brush. Then they carefully moved forward, crouching to keep out of sight in case there was someone in the line camp.

It was built right into the side of a hill. The rear wall of the little structure was nothing more than the rock and dirt of the hill itself.

"Looks deserted enough," whispered Tucker.

"It probably is," Charity said. "But let's be sure. Toss a stone against that door there."

Tucker did as the girl instructed, lobbing a fairly heavy chunk of sandstone into the rough timber of the door. It made a hollow, clunking sound.

They waited for a full minute. There was no movement or noise. They rose and carefully entered the cabin.

The cabin was a mess, dusty and strewn with old cans, ragged scraps of clothing, and empty bottles. Apparently it hadn't been used as a line camp for quite some time, though drifters had apparently made it a temporary quarters. And from the general smell of the place, it seemed a few animals had used it as a den.

Charity had said little while they were traveling, which Tucker had attributed to worry over her family. He was worried, too, fearing for Jack's welfare. Yet he admired his brother for his willingness to risk his very life to help a family he hardly knew. Jack had his bad habits and a powerful temper, but there was a lot to be said for his bravery and unselfishness.

As the day passed, Charity began to talk more, losing her worries somewhat in the bustle of cleaning up the cabin. Tucker helped her, carrying out trash, sweeping out the old cans and bottles, brushing away cobwebs and dust. He wondered if Charity was uncomfortable in his presence. She didn't seem to be. Everything she said indicated she was glad he was around.

Tucker found her presence enjoyable, but he felt distracted. He wondered what was going on back at the Bryan ranch. If there was to be a battle, he figured it had probably taken place by now. Jack, Frank, Duke . . . they might all be dead already. He wondered if Charity realized that.

She did. And it was primarily because of that realization that she tried to lose herself in her work. It was troubling to be miles away, unable to help.

But what could she do? Pa would never let her take part in the battle. There would be nothing at all she could do.

Unless . . .

One possibility—a slim chance, a daring one, but perhaps one that would help. But could she do it? Failure might only make things worse.

She certainly couldn't do what she was thinking about with Tucker nearby. As long as he was around, she would be tied to this spot. If only there was some way to convince him to return to the ranch, leaving her alone to carry out her scheme. . . .

Tucker brought in a rabbit for their supper about an hour before dusk. Charity had found an old black pot tucked away in the corner of the cabin, and now that it had been cleaned and scoured and a fire had been built in the rough stone fireplace, she was ready to cook up a stew. With some of the potatoes and carrots she had brought along, and topped off with some fresh fire-baked bread, it would be a fine meal.

Tucker sat and watched Charity stirring the stew, feeling a bit out of place. All it took was a glance for her to turn him into a shy, stuttering boy.

The stew was first-rate. Tucker downed two bowls of it. He sat sipping his coffee when the meal was over, eating a slab of the fresh bread, topped by apple jelly they had brought along for sweetening.

Charity grew quiet. Tucker knew what she was thinking about. Conversation dwindled, and for several long minutes they sat in silence, contemplating their own thoughts.

"Tucker?"

"Yes, Charity?"

"What do you think has happened at the ranch?"

"I don't know, Charity. I wish I did."

"Me, too."

"Don't you worry—there wasn't a man there who didn't know how to take care of himself." He winced inwardly when he realized he had inadvertently spoken in the past tense, and he hoped Charity hadn't noticed.

"When do you think we'll find out?"

"Soon. They said they would come and tell us when it's safe to go back."

Charity stood and walked over to the fire. "That was before dawn this morning. If there was a fight, it would have taken place already. But still there's been no word. I'm afraid they might be dead."

Tucker looked down at the dirt floor. He could say nothing to ease her worries, for he was thinking the same thing. If the defenders had successfully held off Granger's men and avoided arrest or lynching, then they would have been able to reach this line camp long ago.

"Tucker . . . I don't think I can stand it any longer. I want you to take me back and see what happened."

Tucker frowned. "You know your pa gave me strict orders to stay here with you until we got word to leave."

"Then go alone and bring word back to me. I'll be all right here alone." Charity held her breath; she had made the first request hoping he would turn it down, a sort of bluff to keep him from realizing that what she truly wanted was the second option she had presented.

"I don't know, Charity . . . I made a firm promise to your pa. He wouldn't be pleased if I didn't keep it. Besides, I can't leave you here by yourself. There ain't no telling who might show up. It's obvious drifters have used this place before."

"I can take care of myself. But Pa and Frank, not to mention your brother, might be in sore shape right now. They might need you. It could be that they're back in that jail again, just waiting for someone to haul them out and lynch them. Maybe they can't come out here— maybe they're hoping you'll come back."

Tucker felt his will breaking. Against his better judgment, he relented. "All right, Charity—I'll go. But promise me one thing—you'll not open this door to anybody except me or one of the others from the ranch."

She agreed readily. Tucker began making his preparations, still believing it was all a mistake. But he had given his promise to her. He tried not to think about the fact that he was already breaking the promise he had made to Duke Bryan.

But even as Tucker threw the saddle on the horse and pulled tight the girth, he knew that his going was not entirely motivated by Charity's request. Deep inside he, too, was worried about the lack of word from the ranch. Something must have happened there to keep them from sending word as they had promised.

Charity watched him leave, moving north in the darkness, and suddenly she felt alone and afraid. The line camp cabin became frightening, dark and ominous, and the empty plains seemed to hold invisible phantoms. But no matter. She would not long remain here. With Tucker gone, there was no one to keep her from fulfilling her mission. It wasn't something she looked forward to, but it was something she had to do. If only she wouldn't be too late . . . if only the battle at the ranch had somehow been put off. . . .

She moved back toward the cabin. There was not a moment to lose. She would give Tucker just enough time to get a good distance ahead of her, then she would follow.

But she would not go to the ranch. She wouldn't have time, as much as she would like to do it. She had to go to the only place where she might be able to stop with words what otherwise might explode into violence, if it hadn't already. She would go armed with information Seth Bailey had gasped out to her the night before, a secret he had kept for years.

She would go to Dan Granger.

Chapter 8

Duke Bryan's heart had been heavy when he watched his daughter ride away beside Tucker Corrigan. Frank stood beside him. "Don't you worry, Pa. They'll be back safe and sound."

Duke nodded. "I know. And what will they find when they get here?"

Inside the log ranch house, Jack was having his own worries. Partly he felt like a fool for being here, risking his neck against heaven knows what danger, and all for folks he hardly knew. But he had been reared with a strong sense of duty, and there was no way he could back out.

Especially if his suspicions about Thurston Russell proved true. Many had been the time when he had thought about Russell over the past years, wondering if the old wound was still festering, pondering the incredible strength of the thing called hate. Russell was a man with a reputation for cruelty, certainly not the kind to forget old grievances.

Outside, the darkness was thick, concealing the surrounding plains. Would Tucker be able to safely guide Charity through the night to the line camp Duke had mentioned? Jack figured he would. Tucker was a lot older now than when Jack had last seen him seven years ago, but even in his more youthful days he had had more than his share of spunk and courage. Tucker would do everything he could to make sure Charity was safe. Duke Bryan had put his daughter's safety into good hands.

Duke and Frank walked back inside the ranch house.

Frank sat down on a stool, propping his rifle across his knees.

"Now what?"

"Now we wait. Granger might come soon, might come later. Maybe not at all."

"You really think so? After us bursting out of jail and all?"

"Could be, Jack. Granger's hard to figure. He'll sometimes do the thing you least expect."

"How well do you know Granger?"

"No better than most, I guess. He ain't friendly to just anybody, 'specially to a small rancher like me. He's got power, and he throws it around a lot. I've only talked to him on one or two occasions. He ain't seen too often. He keeps himself holed up at his ranch, away from folks."

"Do you think he'll show up here if his men come after us?"

"I doubt it. He won't expose himself to danger as long as there's others to do it for him. He has more men hired than a lot of the other ranches put together. Some are cattle hands, but a lot are hired guns. That's the way he operates."

There came a faint rustling noise outside in the trees, and in a moment Frank was up and crouched again beside the window. Carefully he looked out through the gap between the split-board shutters.

"See anything?"

"No . . . I think it was the wind. Sure made me jumpy, though."

"You got cause to be jumpy."

Jack took his place beside the other window, staring into the emptiness of a night that gazed back with threatening silence. It would not be long until sunrise. He couldn't decide whether he looked forward to it or dreaded it.

If the three of them had any sense, they would be running across the plains under the cover of night, Jack thought. But he understood Duke's motive for not doing that. If they ran, it would be like giving in to Granger. And it would not be long before other ranchers started doing the same. A lot was riding on Duke Bryan's shoulders right now.

The dawn began breaking in the east, casting an eerie glow over the world, lending a surreal quality to the rolling plains, splitting the sky with golden beams that caught the shimmer of the cottonwood leaves. Then shadows began to appear, long, westward shadows, every second darkening them, intensifying their contrast to the brightening land around them. The dreamlike quality of the world began to fade, the rising sun pouring in the morning steadily.

Jack, Duke, and Frank all stared in silence at the figures outlined on the hill before them, silent figures, slumping carelessly in their saddles, lined up Indian-style against the brightening horizon, wispy clouds of gold and purple visible behind their silhouetted forms. No noise they made, nor any movement, but all in the ranch house could see the flashes of reflected morning light that glinted from the barrels of the Winchesters that lay across their laps.

There was a quiet kind of arrogance in the way Dan Granger's men sat and viewed the scene before them, a deathly kind of calm assurance that what they came to do would be done quickly and in good order. Not a trace of movement could be seen in the line of riders, save for the occasional bending of an elbow to lift a cigarette to a whiskered lip that then sent forth a cloud of smoke to disperse quietly into the morning breeze. How long the riders had been there no one in the ranch house knew; possibly since shortly after Tucker and Charity left.

Duke Bryan whispered a prayer of gratitude that his daughter had made her escape when she did. It would now have been too late.

A burly figure on a big dun stood out in prominence from the group, and after what seemed a torturously long time, that figure straightened, and a hamlike hand flipped away the butt of a cheap cigar. Frank recognized the figure even though the light behind him made his face invisible. It was Thrasher.

"Bryan! Duke Bryan! We come to get you. You can't just walk out of a jail! The sheriff is offended. It warn't good manners!"

Old fool, Frank thought. Old fool really thinks he's being funny.

There was no answer from the little ranch, only the calling of a morning bird somewhere in the brush bordering the clearing.

"Bryan, you might as well answer. We know you're there, and there ain't no point in playing games."

Still no answer.

"Damn it, man, we come to take you back! You got to stand trial for that rustling charge. You don't want us to have to come down there and get you. That boy and that pretty little girl of yours might get hurt!"

A profound sense of relief swept over Duke Bryan. Thrasher's words told him that Charity and Tucker had made it past Granger's men without being detected. Apparently the big scoundrel thought Charity was still here.

"You and your boys had better move on. If the sheriff wants me, he'll have to come for me himself!" Duke shouted.

Thrasher smiled. "We're doing the sheriff's job for him, Bryan! We're deputized to bring you back."

"You're loco, Thrasher. You've come for Granger, not the sheriff. I ain't giving myself up."

Thrasher was grinning even more now. He was enjoying playing this game with Bryan, like a cat toying with its prey. It would make the taking of him all the more enjoyable.

Thrasher leaned forward, resting a calloused hand on his saddlehorn. "Bryan, I'm a fair fellow and a fair fighter. I'll let you send out your daughter so she don't face no danger when the shooting starts. Otherwise I ain't taking no responsibility for who gets hurt."

Part of Duke Bryan wanted to tell the truth to Thrasher, to flaunt in his face the fact that Charity was already safe, beyond the reach of Granger's treachery, if only for the moment. But he knew it would be best to let the gunmen continue to think she was in the ranch house; if some of them still had a trace of decency left after years of living without regard to conscience, maybe they would be hesitant to attack if they thought their shots might hit a woman.

"I'd sooner send her out into a pack of wolves, Thrasher."

Thrasher shook his head philosophically. "You're a bigger fool than I thought, Bryan. But you've had your chance." The big man looked around him at the stony-faced gunmen. For a tense, long moment there was nerve-eating silence, then Thrasher voiced his command, first softly, then loud and gruff.

"Now . . . NOW!"

The noise of the guns exploding in unison was more like the roar of a cannon than the crackling of individual small arms, and Jack found himself hugging the floor beneath the window before he even realized that he had moved. Ten slugs of lead from ten rifles dug into the wall of the house, one bullet ripping through the hinge of the shutter on Jack's window, causing the shutter to hang askew from its remaining support. Then came more rifle fire, this time not in tandem but instead snapping and cracking in a continuous rhythm, mixed with the sound of horses' hooves on the earth as the riders stormed the house.

Jack forced himself up from the floor and back to the window. The dangling shutter jerked and quivered as another bullet struck it, making a large, splintered hole through it. Jack shoved the shattered piece of wood aside with the muzzle of his rifle and came up firing. A man dropped from the saddle, felled by his bullet. Cold sweat broke out suddenly on Jack's brow, and he felt weak.

Frank and Duke were firing from the other window, both of them bent in concentration, squinting down the barrels of their weapons as they poured a deadly stream of return fire at the riders bearing down on them outside.

Frank followed a hefty man in a wide-brimmed hat with the sight of his Henry, then carefully squeezed the trigger. The man threw his arms to the sky, sending his rifle flying, and tumbled over the rear of his brown stallion to thud into the dirt. Frank didn't watch; he was too busy taking aim on another gunman.

Almost as quickly as they had come, the riders were heading back up the slope, most of them surprised that in one rush they had lost two of their number. The most surprised of all was Thrasher, who sent his horse pounding over the slope of the hill to safety, then stopped long enough to stare numbly at the wound that creased his arm, the skin cut into a long furrow where a bullet had nudged its way past him.

He raged as he watched blood ooze slowly from the wound. With a bearlike roar, he turned his horse around to begin the charge once more.

None of the seven remaining gunmen accompanied their leader. Most had expected to take the house in one rush; none had anticipated such a deadly outpour of fire from the shuttered windows. Thrasher found himself rushing the house alone. With a speed that under other circumstances would have seemed comical, he turned his horse and went speeding up the slope again, three bullets winging past him to inspire increased haste.

Thrasher reined his dun to a stop amid the group of disheartened gunmen, blazing with rage. He spit out a long string of invectives, his face growing redder and his frown more bitter. "Are you going to leave me to take that ranch myself?"

"Thrasher, you saw what happened—the down there is crack shots. We rush again, and two three more of us will be gone."

"You explain that to Granger when he asks you, why ten of the territory's top guns couldn't take four men and a girl! He'll be real interested in hearing you explain that!"

"Thrasher, settle down. Perry's right. Rushing the house ain't the way to do it." The speaker was a tall man in a dusty brown hat and leather vest. He had a rather large, thin nose, deep-set eyes, and craggy features that suggested a distorted handsomeness. He was Mick Brandon, who had carved out a reputation as a fast gun as many a greenhorn had carved out his own epitaph trying to prove he was faster. Brandon was a quiet man, generally, and one Thrasher didn't like, for when he spoke, the others tended to listen. In his slow brain, Thrasher sensed that Brandon was his better both mentally and physically, and it angered him. He wouldn't do anything about it, though—he was far too scared of Brandon's fast gun hand.

"What are you suggesting, Brandon?"

"Burn 'em out! When we're riding down on 'em, they got the advantage, 'cause we can't shoot accurately, and they can aim good and steady. Rushing ain't the thing to do. We gotta burn 'em out."

Thrasher stared icily at the lean gunman, dropping his gaze suddenly when Brandon returned the stare. Speaking low, almost glumly, he said, "I got a little bottle of coal oil in my saddlebag for campfires. We can use it to fuel some torches."

Chapter 9

Th waiting was the worst part, the uncertainty about what Thrasher and his men were up to, the assurance that no matter how complete the silence, the battle was not over. Jack and his two companions sat at their window positions until the waiting became unbearable, then they stood and began walking about the room, trying to ease the tension with movement and conversation.

"Could they have left, Pa? I don't think they were expecting this much resistance."

"No, I don't think they'll leave until they've got us one way or the other. I can't blame 'em. I hear Granger is a hard man to deal with when he don't get what he wants, and what he wants is us."

Jack walked toward the rear of the building. "It's too bad you didn't put windows on this part of the house. We could see if they came up from behind."

Duke slapped his thigh impatiently. "Blast it! I know they're up to something."

"I know what you mean, Mr. Bryan."

"Call me Duke. I never did take to the mister stuff. I'm going to get me some coffee. Anybody want some?"

The idea was appealing, for it injected a bit of the routine into the tense situation. Jack and Frank brightened at the offer. Duke opened the door to the cast-iron oven and tossed in a couple of logs. The fire blazed brighter; he shut the door and adjusted the round eye of the stove with a detachable iron handle. Soon the coffee was boiling in a speckled-blue tin pot, filling the little cabin with a tantalizing aroma. Jack returned to his window, peeking out around the demolished shutter to see if there was sign of any renewed attack. Frank came to him and thrust a tin mug of coffee into his hand, and he began sipping the strong and steaming brew, his eyes studying the horizon.

There was no sign of life, no trace of man or horse to betray the presence of Granger's riders—nothing but brilliant blue of the sky, now lit with the full glory of morning, the billowing heaps of snowy clouds high overhead, the faint movement of the breeze-whipped cottonwoods, the thin, white curl of smoke from over the hill . . .

Smoke?

Jack set the mug of coffee on a stool nearby and gazed with a frown at the curling smoke. It appeared to be coming from just over the crest of the slope, in the general area of where he expected the riders to be.

It could only mean one thing. He called for Duke.

"What is it, Jack?"

Jack gestured toward the thin band of rising smoke. Duke looked at it for a long time, then whistled between his teeth.

"That does it for us. They get this place on fire, and we're goners."

"Fire? What's happening, Pa?"

"They got fire up there, and something tells me it ain't to cook their breakfast. Fire's the one thing I was hoping they wouldn't think of."

Jack looked out the window again, silent. For a moment all his hopes seemed to drift away with the wispy smoke he was watching, but suddenly a strong urge to live flowed through him, no matter what.

"Duke, we can't stay here," he said.

Duke nodded. "Just what I was thinking. Frank, go open up the trap."

"The trap? What do you mean?" asked Jack.

"When we were putting the floorboards in this

place, we came up short on a section, so we just built us a small kind of door to cover it. I figured in cold weather we could just stack up firewood under the house right beneath the door and get it in without having to get our feet cold. Never really used it, though. Got a piece of furniture on top of it right now."

The three men moved into the dog trot, heading for the boarded-up rear wall. A large wardrobe sat there, well-stuffed with old clothing and linens. Frank and his father began hefting the heavy piece to the side. In moments they had exposed a large trapdoor hidden beneath it.

"Well, men, here goes!" exclaimed Duke, reaching for the leather thong that served as a handle for the door. Before he threw it open, he paused, sending Frank scurrying back into the main room to gather all the spare ammunition. The young man came back with hands and pockets stuffed with shells, which he quickly distributed to the others.

Duke threw open the trapdoor then, a rush of fresh air filling the passageway. There was nothing beneath the door but a few scraps of discarded firewood and a rounded hollow in the bare earth where the Bryans' old hound had made a sleeping place in the shady coolness under the cabin.

Jack started to lower himself through the opening, but he was stopped by a low growl from beneath the house as well as the touch of Duke's hand on his shoulder.

"Here—let me or Frank go first. Ol' Rex will raise a ruckus if you go through, you being a stranger to him and all."

Jack climbed back up and made way for Duke, who quickly scrambled down through the trapdoor and onto the ground. Rex came sniffing and wagging his tail around his master, who quickly patted him to keep him from making noise.

"Easy, boy. Just stay quiet."

Frank followed his father out the opening. Jack exited last. Crouching to avoid bumping their heads on the bottom of the cabin floorboards, they moved toward the rear of the building.

Then they stood outside, the house between them and the hill that hid the eight riders. Jack looked to Duke for the next move, having no idea what to do. If even one of the riders caught sight of them outside the protection of the cabin, they would likely be run down and shot, or perhaps captured and hanged.

"We got to have horses," Duke said.

"We'll have to run the clearing between here and the stable," said Frank. "If they see us . . ."

"What choice do we have?"

Jack looked across the clearing, a bare piece of ground beaten flat and hard by the hooves of horses. The area through which they would have to run was small—no more than a hundred feet across at the most—but with eight angry gunmen just across the hill, possibly even now watching the house for sign of movement, the distance seemed vast, formidable.

Jack adjusted his hat and shrugged his shoulders, trying to put on a casual front. "Well, men . . . let's run!"

And run they did. Keeping their heads low, fearing to look to their left up the hill and into the face of possible death, they sprinted across the clearing.

The dark stable loomed up before them. Jack pounded inside, not stopping until his hands touched the opposite wall. He had made it. Not a shot fired.

"I can't believe it!" Frank exclaimed.

From the hill came the sound of rushing hooves. Jack and his companions ducked farther back into the darkness of the stable, then carefully peered out through the open doorway.

A rider was bearing down on the house at full speed, crouched low in the saddle, his hand grasping a flaring torch. Within fifty feet of the house he rode—Jack couldn't help but admire his daring—and the torch became an arching bow of yellow against the blue of the sky as he heaved it to the wood-shingled roof of the house.

"When I think how long it took to build that place, how hard I worked, how many memories . . ."

Jack glanced over at Duke. The man's eyes showed a curious combination of wistfulness and anger. This wasn't going to be just any fire. A life of dreams and labor were going to be destroyed in those flames. Duke was fairly new to the Montana Territory, and the house had only sat there for about two years, but there had been a lifetime of planning and sweating invested in it, all now to be robbed by roaring flames and the inexplicable wrath of the mysterious Dan Granger.

The dry shingles began to smolder; the torch lay flaring on the rooftop, wavy swirls of heat distorting upward. Then came another horseman, and another torch thrown upward. Duke Bryan fingered the butt of his rifle, bit his lip, but did nothing.

Jack realized that their escape attempt had come too late. With the mounted gunmen again in view of the house and stable, they were just as trapped as before. All they could do was watch the flames spread across the roof, steadily growing, crackling and sending a multiplying shower of sparks to the sky.

"In a minute they're going to start wondering why we aren't coming out or at least shooting at 'em," said Frank. "What should we do, Pa?"

"I tell you one thing—we can't sit and wait for them to find us," Duke said. The embittered rancher swung his rifle to his shoulder, his burly hand swinging the lever and pumping a new slug home. He lined up his sights on one of the riders who was bearing down on the ranch house to throw a fresh torch through one of the open windows.

The stable echoed with the roar of the gun. The rider jerked in his saddle and fell sidelong to the earth, his hand still gripping the torch even as he writhed on the dirt. Then Duke's rifle spoke again, and another rider cried out in terror as a high-powered slug ripped through the crown of his hat, missing his head by a fraction of an inch.

Duke's spirit touched off a spark of life within Jack, arousing his fighting instinct, making him desire to sell his life as dearly as possible, if sell it he must. He dropped on one knee, raised his weapon, and joined his fire with that of the rancher. Frank took a position on the other side of the stable door and opened up with a stream of deadly, steady fire as well.

Granger's riders disappeared quickly, stunned to find themselves endangered from a new direction, confused about how the men they thought were trapped in a burning house had managed to miraculously travel to the nearby stable. Thrasher raced his dun over the crest of the slope as a bullet winged by his left ear.

There again was silence, tense and threatening. The three fighters in the stable took the opportunity to reload their hot weapons, then stood listening for any hint of further attack.

The silence continued, eating into their nerves. At last Jack began to suspect that their unexpected blitz from the stable had broken the nerve of the attackers and sent them on their way.

Then came a quiet kind of hissing noise from the opposite side of the stable. Confused, Jack turned to look at the others and found them staring at something in the stable's loft.

The loft was in flames, the straw burning hot and bright and spreading quickly around the torch that had been tossed in through the single ventilation window in the stable. This torch had apparently been tossed not by a rider but by a man on foot, who had stealthily crept over the slope out of view of the stable's occupants.

"They've got us, boys," Duke said in a dull tone. Filled with a sudden courage born of desperation, Jack leaped outside the stable and began pumping a deadly rain of lead up the slope.

Jack was driven back inside as dirt began kicking up

around his heels. Levering his rifle, he sent a futile shot winging up the slope as a final defiant gesture.

Frank had already scrambled into the loft, a saddle blanket in his hands. Bravely he began beating at the flames as his father followed him up the ladder, Jack at his heels.

Duke grabbed another blanket and began working beside his son. The air was a choking mixture of burning straw fragments, smoke, and lung-searing heat. Jack grabbed up his rifle and dug into his pocket for ammunition. Ducking the dangerous exposure of the window, he moved over to the opposite side. He sighted down the length of the muzzle at the faint, fleeing forms he could make out atop the hill and began firing.

Duke and Frank were choking, coughing, occasionally having to stop their seemingly fruitless battling of the flames in order to beat out fire that set into their clothes. The heat grew intense, the air smoke-filled. Though the two firefighters continually beat at the flames, they were losing the battle. In a matter of minutes the stable would be as engulfed in flame as was the flaring, roaring inferno of the ranch house just across the clearing.

Jack wiped sweat from a grimy brow and kept pumping bullets into the distance, the smoke whipping about him, burning into his eyes. Return fire ripped into the log walls about him, close shots occasionally whipping past his head to implant themselves in the opposite wall.

Granger's riders emerged from their refuge in the trees and brush across the hill, riding hard, moving straight toward the stable.

This was it. The final attack, the last rush. In moments the riders would be upon them, and with the finality of a few blasts from their Winchesters, it would be over. Jack emptied the chamber of his rifle and prepared for death.

And then, miraculously, unbelievably, the riders veered to the right, past the barn, running as if the devil himself were on their tails.

Over the crest of the hill appeared a new band of riders, guns blazing, horses running, pursuing the fleeing band of Granger's gunmen.

Chapter 10

Jack joined with Frank and his father in trying to beat out the flames, lashing out at them with a horse blanket, unable to take time even to query Duke about the new riders.

The flames began to lose their hold in the stable. But there was no hope for the house; it was now a smoldering shell, a red-hot skeleton of a building that looked as if a slight wind would bowl it over.

A handful of men entered the open doorway to the stable, and Duke said: "Buck—I'm glad to see you! Quick! Help me save the barn. The house . . ."

"The house is gone, Duke," said a pudgy man in a red-checked shirt and a wide-brimmed slouch hat. He was climbing the ladder to the loft, one burly hand grasping the wooden rungs, the other clinging to a Henry that still was exuding a wispy swirl of thin smoke from the rim of the muzzle.

Duke bit his lip and started whipping at the flames with renewed fervor. The man named Buck took off his leather vest and joined the others, two other men coming up the ladder behind him and adding their efforts to the battle as well.

Little by little the flames died away. Duke treaded out the last remaining fragments of burning straw with his boot. He turned and extended his hand to Buck. His face looked weary, sad, yet tremendously relieved.

"Buck—if you hadn't showed up, I guess we'd either be roasted or shot by now. But how did you know?"

"I didn't. Or I should say, *we* didn't. But we did

know that you had got out of the jail, and it wasn't hard to guess what would happen. I'm just sorry it took so long for us to get here. Some of the ranches are spread out pretty far, you know, and we had to ride hard. We're all plenty worried about what Granger is trying to do to you. If you go, then our ranches go next."

The group descended from the loft and walked into the open air, the smell and taste of hot smoke and sweat clinging to them. Duke looked bitter when he saw what little was left of his log home, even now crumbling away as the flames ate away the last remaining supports that held up the charred roof.

"No matter what, I can't deny that Granger has won part of his battle right here," he said. "There's something gone that can never be replaced. I can rebuild the house, but something will be different. There will be the memory of what was here before, and how I lost it."

The stocky leader of the group approached Jack and thrust out his hand. Jack took it and pumped it firmly. "Buck Treadway."

"Jack Corrigan. Pleased to meet you—more pleased than you might know."

The big man laughed, his eyes disappearing into a sea of wrinkles. "You fellers were in something of a fix!"

"And we still are, if you ask me. And you, too, Buck," Frank cut in. "Dan Granger won't let this pass. He'll be after all of you, too."

"Let him come," said Treadway, his voice now as cold as it was jovial a moment before. "This thing calls for a response from us—we've let it go long enough. We have rights here just as much as Granger, and it's high time we stood up for 'em."

Duke turned away from the flaming remains of his home. "What now, Buck? Where can we go? Granger will have more men on us than we can hope to handle if we stay here. And if we go to any other ranch, it will just wind up like mine—burnt to the ground."

"You got a point, Duke. Maybe we ought to have us

a quick meeting. We'll let the group decide what to do next."

The idea sounded reasonable. Jack was introduced to the group, slapped on the back by about two dozen hands, while congratulations and praise were poured upon him. The ranchers introduced themselves one by one, but hardly had they finished before Jack promptly forgot them all, his mind still spinning from the tumult of the battle.

The meeting took place before the grove of trees that lined the slope facing the ranch. The ranchers sat in a circle on the ground, some crouched on their haunches like Indians, others seated cross-legged with rifles across their laps. Most had cigars or pipes thrust into their mouths, and all looked deadly serious about what they were doing. No one was anxious to submit to a man like Granger, yet none of them would be happy to expose their ranches to danger.

Buck Treadway stood in the midst of the group and looked around him. "Men, you know the situation," he said. "You can see from what Granger did to Duke's ranch how far he will go when he's angry. We got to go somewhere. We've set our course. I don't like risking my home and cattle just to spite Dan Granger. But on the other hand, I ain't willing to turn tail in front of him."

"What are you getting at, Buck?" asked a thin man in a ragged blue shirt.

"That maybe the thing to do ain't to turn tail, but to take on Granger face-to-face."

The words brought stunned silence for a moment, then Duke spoke. "You mean make a raid on Granger's ranch?"

"Not exactly. Better to talk out every angle of a thing before fighting it out. It's never crossed our minds that Granger might be willing to listen to reason. Maybe if we talk to him . . ."

"It won't work, Buck. Granger won't talk to us."

"He's right, Buck," someone else chimed in.

Treadway raised his hand to quiet the voices. "You don't know what he might do. Nobody has tried to reason with the man before and maybe that's been a mistake. I can't guarantee that it won't blow up in our face, but even that seems better to me than waiting for him to come to us when he feels like it."

Duke nodded. "I think I see your point, Buck. If we wait around and do nothing, Granger's men will attack when it's best for them. But if we move in when they don't expect it . . ."

"Then we'll have the advantage. Maybe Granger will be willing to talk it out and settle things."

One man spit a wad of tobacco on the ground and shook his head. "I still ain't convinced, Buck. A man trying to keep from getting snake-bit shouldn't stick his foot into the den."

"We ain't just going to waltz in there and let Granger have his way with us, Bill. We'll be armed and ready to fight if need be."

"I still don't like the idea."

"I understand that . . . but do you have any better ones?"

The man's heavy brows drooped low over deep-set eyes. He shifted the wad of tobacco from one side of his mouth to the other, then shrugged. "I reckon not."

"What do you say then? Are you with me?"

Buck looked at the circle of faces, waiting for a response. And he got one, though not in words. Every man gave a slight nod, a twitch of the finger, or some other faint gesture that let him know his plan was accepted. Buck smiled faintly, then thrust his hands into his pockets and jutted out his prominent belly.

"All right, then. We'll go to Granger's."

Jack's skin was crawling. He saw the sense in what Buck had suggested, but the idea of another possible confrontation with Granger's men was frightening. And he was beginning to think of Tucker again, and his father back in Wyoming.

In the excitement of battle Jack had almost forgotten about his father's illness and the pressing need to finish this business and get back to the ranch on the Crazy Woman. He had no desire to see the defense of the small ranchers crumble under Granger's chastening, and he felt a personal stake in it all due to the likely presence of Thurston Russell in the area. But still there was his own family responsibility to think about. And after all, he had already done more than his part to help out Duke.

As the informal meeting broke up, Duke walked over to Jack's side.

"I appreciate all you've done," he said. "As far as I'm concerned, you're free to go home."

Jack smiled weakly. His mind was full of conflict. Emotion pulled him southward toward home while a sense of duty to finish what he had started made him want to stay here. What to do? He wished he could find the answer easily.

"I don't really know what I ought to do, Duke."

"Of course you do. You've got a responsibility to your father. That's important."

"So is what you're doing. And if our roles were reversed, I'd like to think somebody would care enough to help me fight it out."

Duke patted Jack's shoulder. "You can leave when you want, or stay. It's your choice and I won't push you about it. But there'll be no hard feelings if you go. Think about it."

Jack did think about it, and the more he did the more he was inclined to leave. He had no business getting more deeply involved in this fight, risking his life while his father waited for him back home.

But thinking of his father suddenly made him recall a time when they were together. Jack had been twelve years old, and he and his father had just sold a few head of cattle and were returning from herding them to the pickup point for the buyer. They stopped at a café and ordered a meal. When they were finished with it, they left, and on the way back to the horses passed a saloon.

At that moment the door had burst open and a man had fallen out onto his back. Danver had to sweep Jack aside to keep him from being crushed beneath the fellow.

"Hey now, watch it around my boy!" Danver exclaimed.

The man stood. His lip was bleeding. He turned a crimson scowl on Danver but said nothing; his mind was still fixed on whatever had happened inside the saloon. Jack wasn't even sure the man was really aware of them, distracted as he was.

Another man came to the door. "We'll have no putrid Irish about here," he said. "You drink at your own slop pits and stay away from a decent man's saloon."

The bleeding Irishman snarled and bolted toward the saloon door, but the man inside slammed it shut. The Irishman faltered, hesitated between decisions a few moments, then at last turned away, muttering.

"Hang, draw, and quarter the damnable lot of them," he said in a thick brogue. "I'd sooner drink with a heathen Chinee when it comes down to it. I'll not drink where a good man's treated like a swine."

Only then did he apparently truly notice Danver and Jack. He had looked right through them before. His broad face grew red in obvious embarrassment. He wiped away blood from his lip. "I'm sorry indeed," he said. "I had a bit of a row and did not mean to intrude upon you."

Danver gestured at the saloon. "Irish not welcome, I gather."

"The proprietor seems to have a bit of a problem with such as myself, yes."

Jack was intrigued with the man, who looked and sounded to him like the essence of everything Irish. The fellow looked quizzically at Danver. "And what is your attitude on the subject, sir?" he asked in a slightly challenging tone. Jack wondered if maybe the man was looking for someone to fight to vent his fresh humiliation.

"My name is Danver Corrigan, sprung from the O'Corrigans, so what do you think?"

A broad grin spread across the broader face. The Irishman slapped a hand as big as a steak on Danver's shoulder. "Riley's my name, friend Corrigan. Glad to meet you. Did you come straight from the old land itself?"

"No, but my grandfather did, bringing my father with him," Danver returned.

Riley looked down at Jack. "And this would be your lad?"

Danver introduced Jack, who thrust up his hand and then tried not to wince as Riley crushed it in greeting.

Riley wiped some fresh blood that had risen on his damaged lip and said, "Sorry again to have bothered you, my friends. Yet I'm glad to have met you, for seeing one's own always brightens the sunshine a bit, but I'll be on my way now."

"Not yet, not yet. When two Irishmen meet they ought at least to raise a glass together."

Riley looked interested but uncertain. "You mean in there?" he asked, thumbing toward the saloon.

"There indeed."

Jack looked up at his father with wide eyes. "But Pa . . ."

"No buts, Son." Danver looked at Riley with his eyes twinkling. "Except maybe a few we might have to kick inside that saloon."

Riley's eyes caught the same gleam. "Aye, friend Corrigan. Indeed."

Danver looked down at Jack. "Not a word to your mother, hear? And if anything rowdy begins, it's out the door with you."

Jack nodded. His heart beat more quickly. Excitement stole over him and he smiled.

He was a little disappointed later when they left without having had a fight. Jumping one half-drunken Irishman was one thing for the Irish-hating barkeep and his cronies; jumping two of them, when one was so stout a man as Danver Corrigan, was another. The barroom rowdies had merely skulked in the corner, glaring their hatred at the two Irishmen until they were through. Danver doffed his hat and tipped the bartender five cents as he left.

"Spend it wisely, good friend," he said in his best imitation of his Irish-born father.

Later Danver talked to Jack about what he had done. "It wasn't a matter of needing or wanting a drink, nor of looking for a fight," he said. "It's just that a man can't walk away when he encounters a thing that is wrong, particularly an injustice against another. He has to step in and make it his business to set things right, or do his best to. That's the way of the Corrigans."

Jack looked across at Duke Bryan. Duke's situation was not much different, in a way, than that of Riley the Irishman. He was being trodden upon for no good reason. Being done an injustice.

Jack then knew why he was staying. It was because of what his father had told him so many years back. A man could not walk away from an injustice. Especially when the man was a Corrigan.

Jack heard a rushing of hooves on the earth and turned to see three of the ranchers heading westward toward one of the nearby ranches, probably to pick up more ammunition before the move toward Granger's ranch.

The group decided to wait until dawn to approach Granger's home. Feelings at the Circle X would be hot now in the aftermath of the unsuccessful move on the Bryan ranch, and a cooling-off period might greatly enhance the chances of a peaceful settlement, the men decided.

The three riders returned some hours later with ammunition and food. Eating a hearty meal, the group made camp on the Bryan ranch grounds. Jack made out his bedroll with the conviction that he would get no sleep, then lay down and immediately dropped into an exhausted, dreamless slumber.

Chapter 11

Tucker rode through the darkness, convinced he had done the wrong thing in leaving Charity alone in the line camp. What would Duke think when he came riding in, strictly against orders, leaving Charity alone and virtually defenseless in an abandoned cabin ten miles away?

Tucker felt guilty but kept riding. It had been a full day since he and Charity had set out from the ranch; surely Granger's men had come by now if they were coming at all. Still, Tucker hoped he was not too late to give any help that might be needed.

It was almost pitch-black on the plains, the pale and misty moonlight giving the only illumination of the empty land. The plains seemed to swallow that thin light, drinking it in as if thirsty for it.

He recognized from the lay of the land that he was approaching the area of the ranch. Catching his breath in his throat and feeling a sudden racing of his pulse, he came to the top of the ridge and looked down at what lay beyond.

The barn was there, faintly outlined in the moonlight, standing as it always had at the perimeter of the ranch clearing. But the house . . .

A faint red glow rose from the smoldering coals that lay where the house had been. It was gone, entirely gone, burned right down to the foundation stones. Tucker's heart sank. His pulse pounded at his throat. Immediately there came to mind an image of his father, lying there in his deathbed at the Crazy Woman ranch, waiting for Tucker to return with a young man he had not seen for seven years, a son perhaps now destined to never return.

Tucker feared Jack was dead. He morbidly wondered if his brother had died with a bullet in his head or a noose around his neck.

His head hanging, he moved down the dark and silent slope toward the smoldering corpse of a house that sent forth a faint red glow into the darkness. Tucker didn't know just what he was searching for. Maybe nothing. But he wanted to be close to the place where he felt sure Jack had died.

Tucker brought his horse to a halt and dismounted. Silently he strode toward the remains of the house, then he stopped and knelt down into the dirt.

His fingers traced a line in the dirt, and he noticed the marks of horses' hooves in the soft earth. He looked around. There were hoof marks everywhere, as if maybe as many as two dozen horses had thundered through the area. Granger's men must have been a powerful force.

He stood and walked back to his waiting horse. The animal was tired, covered with a thin lather, but he would work it more this night. He was filled with a bitter desire to look into the eyes of a man who could order the murder of men who had in no way wronged him.

But Tucker had no idea where Granger's ranch lay. Mounting his horse, he sat in the saddle for a moment, thinking.

There were other ranches to the east. He had noticed a handful of them as they rode here to Duke's ranch the night before. Surely someone there would know where Dan Granger's spread was.

Turning his back on the ranch of Duke Bryan, Tucker spurred his horse to a trot and disappeared into the night.

Charity Bryan sat silent in the darkness, watching the first hint of morning light tint the eastern horizon. As the light grew, so did her fears.

She had reached the borders of Granger's ranch some two hours before, coming as close as she dared to the main house, knowing the rancher kept the place closely guarded, like a fortress.

In a sense that was exactly what it was, she thought. Granger was a man with a reputation as an eccentric, one who generally baffled most people. Partly the stories about him were fiction, Charity figured, tales wrought out of people's curiosity about a man who kept himself holed up alone in a large ranch house, separated from contact with his fellow humans, seen publicly only in the company of some of his hired gun hands or the sheriff everyone knew he controlled. The rare occasions when any of the townsfolk caught sight of Dan Granger in public generally became the topics of conversation in the cafés and saloons, the places where the legends multiplied and grew about the unknowable rancher.

Charity had heard the stories—how Granger would never suffer a woman to enter his home, how mere contact with one made him grow angry.

But Charity knew better. If what Seth Bailey had told her in dying gasps was true, then Dan Granger was capable of at least some feeling toward a woman. She shuddered.

Charity had made no move toward the ranch in the darkness, for the guards she felt certain were at the place would have made short work of her. Whether an approach in the daylight would be any safer she did not know, but she was determined to try. Maybe if she could confront Granger and talk to him, he would leave her father alone. She tried not to think about the possibility it might already be too late.

The light broke on a clear morning, streaming across the prairie and revealing the ranch house that had before been shrouded in darkness. The building was a far cry from the usual low, dirt-roofed log sheds that most local ranchers lived in. Charity knew that her father had taken special pains with their house, hewing the logs square and taking the time to build a shingle roof, but his and every other ranch house she had seen paled in comparison to that of Dan Granger.

The house was a two-story log building, three gables breaking through the roof of uniform shingles. The logs were so straight and evenly notched as to require almost no chinking, and two large stone chimneys graced both ends of the house. A rail fence surrounded a spacious yard on all sides of the structure. Flanking the yard on the sides and rear were several buildings, ranging from a large log barn to smaller sod structures. Standing to one side was a huge bunkhouse built of rough, hand-sawed lumber. Between the bunkhouse and the ranch house was a smaller building that Charity guessed to be the kitchen.

There was no sign of movement around the ranch save for the scuffling and shifting of a handful of chickens and the lazy loping of a dog toward the bunkhouse. The sun illuminated the scene through a cool-morning atmosphere touched with just a hint of dew. Such was the serenity of the entire panorama that for a moment Charity almost forgot that within the walls of that massive, impenetrable home lived a man who was doing his best to see her father dead.

She stood gazing upon the ranch from the safety of distance until the sun was well risen over the eastern horizon. Her horse grazed a short distance away in a concealing grove of scrubby trees, rested after the long ride from the deserted line camp. Steeling herself for the ordeal to come, Charity walked toward the horse. Mounting, she moved from the concealment of the trees and down the narrow dirt road that led to the opulent home.

Even now she had been spotted, she guessed. She didn't care; she wanted Granger's guards to see her long before she rode within close range of their rifles. She wanted them to know that she was making no attempt at covert action. Most of all, she wanted them to know that she was a woman. Though Granger was rumored to hate women—the result of a jilting, she had heard—maybe his guard had enough respect for her sex to let her pass safely.

The road to the house seemed extremely long. With every slow, probing step of her horse's hooves Charity counted the seconds. She kept her eyes focused on the house as she rode, unwilling to look to either side for fear of what she might see. She was sure she was being watched now; she had seen the faint movement of one of the pale curtains that hung shroudlike inside the windows.

Charity was within two hundred feet of the house when two men approached, coming from either side of the building, rifles in their hands. She stopped, her breath coming faster. For a long time the men stood regarding her with cold, unreadable expressions, then the taller of the two spoke. He had a rough, grinding voice that grated on her nerves like the scales of a dead fish rubbing flesh.

"Who are you, and what is your business?"

Charity swallowed. "My name's Charity Bryan. I've come to see Mr. Granger."

The tall man glanced at his partner. "Bryan?"

"That's right. My father is Duke Bryan. I'm sure you've heard of him."

The man said nothing, glancing again at his partner, then asked, "Why do you want to see Mr. Granger?"

Charity sat up straight in the saddle, trying to put on an air of confidence and authority. "This is between Mr. Granger and me."

The shorter guard spoke. He had a high, almost effeminate voice that seemed out of harmony with his stocky build. "Don't get sassy, little lady. We got orders to turn away anybody that ain't invited here, no questions asked."

"I think when you tell Mr. Granger who I am, he will want to see me."

"She's right. I do."

The voice came in conjunction with the opening of the heavy front door. The guards moved a couple of steps backward, turning toward the doorway.

A man of medium height and weight, clean-shaven except for a pair of thick, graying sideburns that contrasted with the darkness of his slightly long and wavy hair, stood in the doorway, looking upon the lovely young lady mounted bravely before him. His face was ruggedly handsome, with deep brown eyes beneath expressive eyebrows, a noble-looking nose, and thin, firmly set lips setting off his features with an air of dignity and power. He was dressed in a loose robe of lavender, tied at his waist and hanging almost to his ankles. In his hand was a curved pipe, and he fingered it as he looked at Charity with his dark, expressive eyes.

It was the first time Charity Bryan had ever laid eyes on the famed Dan Granger. Somehow what she saw was not what she had expected. Granger didn't look like the epitome of evil. He looked like a man who could comfortably wear a ministerial collar. Charity had always paid a lot of attention to her first impressions of those she met, and her impression of Dan Granger was so totally at odds with what she had expected that for a time she was speechless.

Granger seemed in no hurry to speak further himself. He regarded Charity for a long time before he again spoke in a voice as smooth as fresh cream.

"So you are Duke Bryan's daughter. I'll admit you're one sight I never expected to see. And I'm surprised that Bryan raised such a lovely child—even if she is a bit immodest."

Charity ignored the obvious reference to her exposed legs, though she suddenly was painfully conscious of the eyes of the two guards upon her. Refusing to break the gaze she held upon Granger, she cleared her throat and tried not to sound nervous.

"I've come to talk to you about my father, Mr. Granger. May I come in?"

Granger looked down then, producing a match from the pocket of his robe. Striking it on the doorpost, he lit his pipe, concentrating on the flame touching the tobacco. His expression was calm, masking his discomfort in the presence of the young woman. For she reminded him of another woman he had known, and the memory stung.

Dan Granger drew in a cloud of smoke and exhaled it into the dewy light of the morning. He stepped back into the doorway.

"By all means, Miss Bryan, do come in. Make yourself comfortable while I go upstairs to dress."

Charity dismounted. One of the guards moved forward to take the reins of the horse. The door shut behind Charity.

Chapter 12

Charity sat in a fancy, engraved mahogany chair atop a plush velvet cushion, looking around her, feeling out of place and scared.

Granger had ascended the stairs to dress, he said, and Charity could do nothing at present but await his return. In a way she dreaded it, for she had no clear idea of just what to say to the man. She hoped it would not be necessary to confront him with what Seth Bailey had told her the night he died.

Granger descended the stairs, trailing a cloud of pipe smoke. He was dressed in a well-cut suit, obviously tailor-made. He was a handsome and dashing figure, even more so than before. Charity's nervousness doubled.

Granger sat down in a cushioned chair across from her and studied her with his expressive eyes. Charity felt like a piece of beef hanging in a butcher's window.

"You are a very pretty young lady, Miss Bryan. Very pretty. Even features, graceful of form . . . a bit sunburned, perhaps, but—"

"Thank you, sir." Charity didn't want to hear more.

"You're very welcome." He took several leisurely puffs from his pipe. "Tell me . . . are you surprised that I let you in here?"

"I . . . I'm not sure what you mean, sir."

"Oh, come now—surely you've heard the stories, about how I never let a female set foot in my house. I hear some view me as quite a strange character. Probably think I make human sacrifices and eat babies for supper."

Charity could think of nothing to say to that, so she simply sat, staring blankly at the pipe-smoking rancher. She had a vague maddening feeling that the man was trying to unnerve her.

Granger stood and moved toward the window, looking out across the plains. Morning light streamed around him and revealed flecks of almost invisible dust floating in the air. At last he turned toward her.

"I assume you had a reason for coming here."

"Yes."

"Well?"

"You had my father jailed on false charges, Mr. Granger. And you've had your men harassing him. I came to ask you to stop." Charity forced out the words as fast as she could, hoping her voice would not falter.

Granger looked at her with the expression of an innocent child accused of stealing candy. "Miss Bryan, I have nothing against your father at all, and I'm sorry you think that I do. I haven't tried to harass him in any way. About his being jailed—well, two of my best men swore they found him rustling my cattle. What else could I do? A man has to protect what is his. I'm sure your father would have done the same."

Charity's courage was bolstered by anger. Granger was playing a game with her, toying with her words. She gritted her teeth, glaring at him in rage.

"Don't try to bluff me, Mr. Granger. Both of us know what you have been doing. You've sought every chance to hurt my father, and both of us know he had nothing to do with any rustling of your cattle. He's never done a thing to interfere with your business—he's never given you any trouble at all. Yet you've continually harassed him in spite of that, again and again. All we want is to be left alone—that's not too much to ask, is it? Why can't you just call off your men and leave my father alone?"

Granger smiled, a faint, teasing smile. "I have to admit I'm mystified by what you say, Miss Bryan. I can't imagine why you would think I have been deliberately harassing your father. So, certainly there's nothing I can do to stop whatever trouble he might be having."

Charity felt exasperation rising. Granger obviously was going to continue this verbal cat-and-mouse until the end. He wasn't interested in reasoning with her.

Granger stood up and walked over to the window, puffing his pipe. "Look out there, Miss Bryan. That's a big land, a vast one. There's room enough for all of us— myself, your father, almost any number of ranchers. I have no hard feelings toward your father or any other rancher. But he was caught rustling, and when a man steals from another, he has to pay the price. It bothers me that you seem to think I'm evil just because I seek to enforce the laws against rustling. I'm not the kind of man to . . ."

Something snapped inside Charity. Rising up like a whirlwind, she lashed out at the arrogant rancher.

"I know what kind of man you are, Dan Granger. You don't have to play games with me. You don't hate my father because you think he's a rustler—you know as well as I that he isn't. You hate my father because he is the man who was married to a lady your sick mind found attractive—so attractive that you broke into her home one night while she was alone and tried to force yourself on her. I know what kind of man you are. You're the kind that hates women and longs for them at the same time. You're the kind that can only relate to a woman the way you relate to all other people—as a thing to be used for your own pleasure. You're an evil man, Granger, and I hate you for what you tried to do to my mother and what you are doing to my father. I hate you!"

Granger turned a dark stare upon the young woman. "Why, you little—"

"Shut up. I won't listen to you. But you're going to hear me out. I know what you tried to do to my mother—I know because I was told by the man that tore you away from her and sent you whimpering back to your ranch. And you so drunk that you never even knew who it was! It was Seth Bailey, Mr. Granger, and it can't hurt him for you to know that now, because he's dead. He told me about it before he died, and now I understand what it is that drives you to torment my father like you do.

"You can't stand it that my father enjoyed a normal, happy life with my mother as long as she lived, can you? It eats away at you, doesn't it? You don't want control of the small ranches around here—that's what everyone says you want, but I know better. All you want is to act out your revenge on my father . . . because he had the privilege of living a happy life with the woman you wanted for yourself."

Granger leaped at Charity, his face livid. He cursed through gritted teeth. Charity nimbly leaped away from the rancher, and he sprawled suddenly on the floor. The young lady backed up against a table that stood against the wall, holding glasses and bottles of expensive liquor.

Granger rose and came at her again. As he lunged forward, Charity's grasp closed on a bottle of whiskey on the table behind her. She leaped aside as the rancher reached her, and he crashed into the table, sending glasses and liquor flying as it overturned.

Charity swung the bottle she was holding by the neck at the back of the chair where Granger had been sitting minutes before. The bottle smashed, leaving her with the broken neck in her hand, the jagged edges as sharp and deadly as any knife.

Cursing, Granger again rose and moved toward her. Charity screamed and blindly lashed out with her makeshift weapon.

Granger cried out and drew back a hand bloody and torn. Charity went pale. Granger stared first at the bleeding hand, then at the young lady. Then, raising his face toward the ceiling, he sent forth a ringing cry.

The door burst open and the two guards appeared, rifles in hand. Confused, they stared at the wounded rancher's bleeding hand, uncertain about what had happened and what they should do.

"Grab her!" screamed Granger. "Hold her!"

Charity darted toward the .door, swinging the broken bottle at the guards. But the men managed to deflect the thrust, and Charity was grasped in strong, muscled hands, the bottle knocked from her grasp.

Granger gripped his bleeding hand and walked to where Charity struggled in the grasp of the burly gunmen. The rancher stood before her and smiled.

"And now, Charity Bryan, you shall pay for what you have said, and for this!" He thrust the wounded hand forward. Blood splattered against her face and she felt faint.

The stocky guard glanced at his partner, then at Granger.

"What's going on here? What are you about to do, Mr. Granger?"

Granger knelt and picked up the broken bottle neck, never taking his gaze off Charity's face. Flipping the neck into his other hand, he said in an icy voice:

"I'm just going to teach our lady friend that it isn't polite to insult a host—much less wound him. Just a little lesson in manners . . . hold her, men."

"No! Please, no . . ."

The taller guard looked troubled. "You're going to *cut* her? You're going to cut a lady?"

"Shut up! I pay you to obey orders, not question them!"

"I ain't going to take part in this, no matter what you pay me. I've done some bad things in my day, but I ain't never hurt no lady!"

The guard relaxed his grip, and Charity pulled free. Hesitating, the other guard let her go as well. Charity bolted through the door and into the morning light.

Granger swore. "I'll have you shot!"

The taller guard struck Granger, knocking him on

his back. The stocky guard still looked hesitant and confused, staring at his partner.

"Why did you . . ."

Granger's good hand came up, gripping a derringer. The stocky gunman scarcely had time to choke out a faint cry before the room was filled with the blast of the weapon, one bullet for each man.

The stocky guard took his in the forehead; the taller man was wounded in the chest. He fell to the floor, moaning. Within five seconds he was dead.

Granger stepped over the bodies and darted toward the open door.

The girl was running hard toward the open plains that stretched out before the house. Cursing, Granger raised his derringer and squeezed down the trigger, forgetting that he had fired both shots at his guards.

He ran to the body of the nearest man and grabbed the rifle that lay beside him. Working the lever and racing back to the open door, he raised the rifle to his shoulder and searched across the sight for the fleeing girl.

Suddenly he dropped the muzzle of the weapon and stared at something materializing on the horizon. Riders were approaching, moving at a steady pace toward the ranch. They were too far away for him to clearly tell who they were, but they could be bringing nothing but trouble.

Charity was forgotten now. Granger stood in silence, watching the approaching riders. As they drew nearer, he moved to a table across the room and picked up a collapsible spyglass. Returning to the door, he adjusted the instrument against his eye.

For a moment he stared through it, then quickly lowered it. He shook his head slowly. Among the riders he had seen Duke Bryan. And with him several of the other area ranchers.

Picking up the rifle once more, he darted out of the house toward the bunkhouse. Out of the corner of his eye he saw the fleeing form of Charity Bryan heading toward the approaching riders.

Still far away from the ranch house, Duke Bryan pulled his horse to a stop.

"Frank . . . is that Charity I see running toward us?"

The young man gazed intently at the feminine figure running hard toward them. Incredible though it was, his father was right. It was Charity.

"How did she get here? And where is Tucker?"

Charity was closer now. Nudging his horse forward, Frank rode out to meet her, followed by Duke.

Duke descended from his saddle and stepped forward, opening his arms to embrace his daughter. Weeping, scared, Charity collapsed into his grasp as the other riders gathered around.

"He tried to cut me, Pa . . . he tried to cut me with a broken bottle." Charity talked in a rush. "I know I shouldn't have come here, but I wanted to try to talk him out of bothering you anymore. I fooled Tucker to get him to leave me so I could come here. It wasn't his fault, so please don't blame him, Pa. I had to try to stop it from coming to a fight. I'm sorry . . ."

Duke embraced his daughter again, angry because of the dangerous move she had made, yet touched that she would so endanger herself for him. He resisted the urge to scold her, instead drawing her close and declaring his love for her. Suddenly he pulled away from her, looking into her face.

"You say he tried to *cut* you?"

Trembling, Charity could only nod.

Duke turned and looked toward the ranch house. Men were coming out of the bunkhouse and mounting horses from the nearby stable. He shook his head.

"Frank, take Charity and head back toward Buck's ranch. It looks like there's going to be a battle here."

Buck was looking at the gunmen mounting up at the

corral. "There's a lot of 'em, Duke. We just might get the worst end of this deal."

Duke wheeled about and looked at the hefty man. "He tried to cut my daughter, Buck. I'm going to find Dan Granger and square things up with him, even if I have to go alone."

"Don't worry, Duke. You ain't going alone. But we'd best get a move on."

Duke gave a cold smile. "I'm ready, Buck."

Chapter 13

Charity and Frank scarcely made it off the scene before the shooting began. Charity's horse was still stabled at the Granger ranch, so she had no choice but to ride behind Frank on his mount.

The extra weight slowed the animal, and Frank worried that they might be overtaken by any of Granger's men that might get past the line of ranchers. Digging his heels into the flanks of the animal, Frank hoped the ranchers would be successful in putting a dent in Granger's forces.

The ranchers moved out of the open just as the shots began, toward the grove of cottonwoods along a narrow stream to their right. Granger's riders bore down on them like an advancing military line, their rifles blazing.

Duke recognized among them Thrasher and some of the others who had raided and burned his ranch the day before. It was likely that Thrasher was plenty mad right now, having his own tactics turned against him. Sliding from his saddle as soon as he had ridden into the relative safety of the trees, Duke levered a slug into his rifle chamber and squeezed off a quick shot at the hefty Thrasher.

The ranchers had lost the element of surprise when they were spotted from the ranch, and the unexpected appearance of Charity had lost them time. Duke was surprised at the number of men Granger had. He had expected that the losses in the previous raid on his ranch would have reduced the size of Granger's force considerably; instead, it appeared that the handful who had attacked the ranch were only a portion of those Granger had at his disposal. Duke wondered if counterattacking Granger on his own ground was wise after all.

No matter now. It was done, and all they could do was keep shooting from the cover of the trees, hoping they could pick off enough of the rapidly moving targets to keep from being overrun. Lifting his rifle to his shoulder, Duke squinted his left eye and bore down upon one of the riders. Squeezing the trigger with as much of a steady grip as the situation would allow, he dropped the man from his saddle. Beside Duke, Buck fired his own weapon—another rider dropped to the dirt.

Shocked by the accuracy of the ranchers' shooting, Granger's men fell back, making a wide circle, heads held low to avoid making a clear target. Duke took advantage of the retreat to place some careful shots at the fleeing men.

Dan Granger viewed the battle across the distance from the safety of the bunkhouse. He had fled there at the first sight of the approaching band of ranchers and had stirred his sleeping men awake, sending them out blurry-eyed to fight while he cowered in the safety of the thick-walled bunkhouse, watching the fight through an open window.

He had sent all of his men out to fight the ranchers—or so he thought. Unknown to him, the slim, dark figure of the gunfighter Mick Brandon was slipping quietly into the rear of the ranch house, intent on solving a mystery that had only minutes before presented itself as he made an early-morning stroll around the ranch.

Brandon had risen earlier than the other men not because it was his usual habit, but because some vague something had kept him from sleeping. Slipping on his boots, he had strapped on his gun belt and walked out into the morning, moving toward the rear of the ranch clearing for a smoke and a breath of morning air.

The mystery he was determined to solve involved two shots he had heard—thin, cracking shots like those a derringer might make. The strange thing was that they had come from the interior of the house.

It seemed likely it was Granger who had fired, for no one but him occupied the huge dwelling. And no one else would be awake except the pair guarding the place—Bill French and Mick Brandon's brother, Lester. But neither of them carried a derringer.

Brandon knew the house was now empty, for he had seen Granger slip toward the bunkhouse when the band of riders appeared on the horizon. Brandon wasn't concerned with the approaching group; he didn't care what happened to Granger, the ranch, the ranchers, or anyone else except himself and his brother. Brandon was a soldier of fortune; the right cause was the one that paid the most money. If Granger died, it wouldn't bother him in the least; there was always work for a man who was indiscriminate with his gun.

And so when Brandon saw the other men pouring out of the bunkhouse toward the stable, he made no effort to join them. He was in no mood for a battle this morning. In the confusion of the fight Granger would never know he had stayed behind, and even if he found out, the worst he could do would be to send Brandon on his way, if he had the guts. And in that case he would just hire out his gun elsewhere. He was about ready to move on anyway.

But those two mysterious derringer shots still interested him. So, slipping quietly to the back door of the log building, Brandon put his hand to the latch and pushed his way in.

He had to blink a couple of times to adjust to the darkness of the back room. He had set foot in Granger's home only once before—the time he was hired. Granger was funny about his house, Brandon knew, letting others in only occasionally, women almost never. Strange how Granger hated women. He had been jilted once when he was young, the story said, and since that time had hardly spent two minutes with any female. That seemed mighty ridiculous to Brandon, who in all his days had never felt anything resembling love, unless it was the attachment he felt to his brother.

Brandon looked around the back room. Nothing there. He moved toward the door and entered the narrow hallway leading to the main room.

The sight of the two bodies on the floor struck him like a hammer blow. It wasn't that the sight of death upset him, for he had looked on it many times after inflicting it himself, and it had never bothered him. In fact, he sort of liked it.

But the dead men on the floor were not just some strangers, like the men he had killed for money.

Bill French lay with his mouth open and his forehead plugged with a neat hole. Brandon didn't care about him—he had never liked the stocky, effeminate-voiced man anyway. But the other man was Lester, his brother.

Brandon's face grew red. Lester . . . the only member of his family whom he had cared two cents' worth about, lay dead in his own blood on Granger's floor.

Frank slowed the horse down as soon as he and Charity were far away from the battle that now sounded like no more than firecrackers popping at a distant July Fourth celebration.

Strangely, he had little to say to his sister. He felt as if he could be angry at her for doing something so foolish as walking right into Granger's ranch, but there seemed little point to anger now.

Charity felt the same way. She was happy to be alive, glad she had escaped Granger, but still things seemed no better than before. Pa was back there, facing a band of killers, shooting it out in spite of her futile attempt to keep things peaceful.

"They burned the ranch, Charity," Frank said in a dull voice.

"What?"

"They burned the ranch. Nearly killed me and Pa

and Jack, and would have if Buck and the others hadn't showed up and run 'em off. The house was burned before sundown."

They rode on farther, still saying little. Sometime later Frank saw a distant figure approaching on horseback; after a moment he recognized him.

"Yonder comes Tucker—see him?"

Charity looked over her brother's shoulder. He was right—it was Tucker. Charity's face grew red. She wondered how Tucker would react to her. Though she still believed she had only done what was her duty, she felt guilty about it at the same time. Likely Tucker had gone back to the line camp, found her gone, and worried over it.

"Howdy, Tucker. Good to see you still in one piece."

"You, too, Frank. I figured when I saw the ranch that you were killed." Tucker was talking to Frank but staring at Charity, who couldn't return his gaze with any steadiness. "Charity . . . what are you doing here? I thought you were supposed to stay at the line camp."

Frank said, "We'll fill you in later, Tucker. Right now I got to get Charity to the Treadway ranch and head on back to Granger's. Pa and Jack are there, along with some of the other ranchers, and they're fighting it out with Granger's men. They're outnumbered, too, and I plan to get back there as quick as I get Charity to Buck's place."

"Fighting . . . well, I ain't surprised. I'm heading for the Granger spread myself. I asked a sodbuster how to get there."

"All right, then. I'll see you soon."

They separated, Tucker riding faster now, his brow beaded with sweat. Riding into battle—it was something he never dreamed he would be doing.

Charity twisted her head to look at Tucker's diminishing form as they rode toward the Treadway ranch. She watched him as long as he was visible, then turned forward again, deep in thought.

Tucker listened to the rushing wind as he rode, trying to pick out the sound of gunfire. He wasn't certain if he was going in the exact direction toward the Granger spread, but he was following the directions given him by the sodbuster, and he had seen Frank and Charity approach from this direction, so he figured he was right.

But according to what he was told, he should be getting close by now. But if he was close, then why didn't he hear gunfire?

Tucker saw it then—the huge, sprawling ranch with its big ranch house and hulking bunkhouse, the grove of cottonwoods several hundred yards in front of it and slightly to the right. And he saw also, as he pulled his horse to a stop, that the battle had been a short one.

Men were congregated around the bunkhouse, standing in a rough circle. Though the distance was great, he saw some men with their hands tied behind their backs.

Tucker was at a loss. There was certainly no way he could hope to free the men single-handed, and there was nowhere to turn for aid. He seemed doomed to watch Granger do what he pleased to the captured men.

Realizing that his position was not good and that he could easily be seen from the ranch if anyone glanced his way, Tucker spurred his mount toward the cottonwoods, hoping to conceal himself there and obtain a clearer view of the ranch. But even then, what good would that do Jack and Duke and the others?

Tucker refused to consider the thought that Jack might not be among the prisoners, that he might be dead somewhere on the ranch grounds.

Tucker slipped quietly into the trees, dismounting as he entered. Tethering his horse to a branch, he slipped quietly toward the stream that ran through the grove.

His eyes fell on something in the leaves, something he couldn't immediately identify. He jumped, conscious of how edgy he was right now. He looked again. It was a brown hat, the brim ripped by what apparently had been a bullet. A brown hat . . .

Just like the one Jack wore.

"Jack?"

No answer, only the whisper of the breeze in the cottonwoods.

"Jack, are you here?"

Tucker stepped forward, treading on something soft, something other than the moist earth that lined the stream.

It was a hand.

"Jack!" Tucker cried out loudly, forgetting the danger of it.

He pushed aside the bushes that covered the face of the figure. Staring into the face of a dead man, he felt a mixture of revulsion and relief.

The man had been struck by a rifle bullet, messing up his features considerably. But it wasn't Jack. Probably one of the ranchers.

He moved on past the body, crouching in the leaves. Parting the branches just enough to let him see, he looked across the distance at the ranch house.

The men gathered there seemed to be arguing among themselves. Occasionally someone would shove one of the men standing with his hands bound, as if somehow punctuating a point by the action.

Tucker tried to make out the faces of the men. As he squinted and forced his eyes to accommodate to the distance, he made out the face of Duke Bryan among the bound men. Others he didn't recognize. But Jack . . . where was Jack?

There. He saw him, there not far from Duke, occasionally blocked from view as Duke moved about. Jack's hands were bound just like the others, but at least he was alive.

"Don't move a muscle, boy. Don't even twitch."

For a moment Tucker thought the voice had only been his imagination. But then he felt the cold touch of a .44 against the back of his neck and knew it was real.

Chapter 14

As he was led up the road toward the house with a gun pressed to his back, Tucker could tell from the somber expressions of the prisoners that they anticipated no mercy. Dan Granger stood gloating over the scene. Tucker identified him by his imperial bearing.

"I found this one down in the grove," said Tucker's captor. "I figured you'd want him, Mr. Granger."

"That I do. Who are you, boy?"

Tucker looked at Granger with contempt.

The rancher laughed. "Tough one, are you? It doesn't matter. It'll all be over soon enough anyway."

"Sorry they got you, Tucker. I reckon we won't make it back to the Crazy Woman after all," Jack said. It was evident both from his words and bearing that he had abandoned hope.

Granger walked over to Duke Bryan, a smug smile on his face. "You wouldn't yield, would you? You just wouldn't give up. And now I've got you."

He swept his glance over the others. "You didn't even have to be involved in this. But you made your choice and you'll take the consequences. All I really wanted was to deal with my dear friend, Duke Bryan. That's all."

"Why, Granger? Why do you hate me so?"

Granger said nothing, but his gloating smile faded. For a moment hatred gleamed in his eyes, then he turned away.

"Hang 'em."

Some of the gunmen guarding the prisoners looked

at each other, slightly unsure if they had heard rightly. Thrasher voiced the question.

"What did you say, Mr. Granger?"

"Are you deaf? I said hang 'em. The stable rafters will do just fine."

Tucker sensed a mounting tension among the gunmen. It hung in the air like static, a kind of vague dissatisfaction that could be perceived in the faces and eyes of the men.

Granger's eyes snapped as he looked around the group. "What are you waiting for? I told you to hang them, and I want it done now!"

Nervous glances, the sound of someone clearing his throat, uncomfortable fidgeting.

"No."

Tucker wasn't sure who the speaker was, but the quiet monosyllable caused Granger to jerk around, glaring at the group of men. Faces dropped; eyes focused on boot tops.

"Who said that?"

No answer came back, and Granger repeated the question in a tone like a patient father chiding a stubborn child.

"I asked who said that."

"I did, Mr. Granger. I ain't gonna take part in no hanging," said a blond man. "I don't know about anybody else, but ever since we tried to take this here fellow"—he gestured toward Duke—"all I've seen is trouble and folks getting shot. It seems to me that hanging these folks will get us all hanged ourselves sooner or later. It ain't worth it for what you're paying us."

The man spoke quickly, in a trembling voice. Granger stared at him as if he were an oddity.

"Are you refusing to obey an order?"

The man appeared somewhat intimidated by Granger's domineering manner, but also defiant. "Yes, sir. I am."

Granger looked at the rest of the group, studying

faces. "Is anyone else inclined to go along with Hank here?"

There was a pause. Granger slowly began to smile. His men were still under his control; his will still ruled.

That illusion was shattered by a quiet voice that spoke up, followed by others, the courage of the defiant ones growing as their numbers increased.

"Yes, sir, I'll go along with him."

"And me."

"And me. I don't want to hang."

"That's right. It's one thing to shoot a man from cover, where nobody knows who done it, but it's another to hang a man right on your own place where everybody will know it's you."

Granger sputtered, tried to speak, and failed. And in the defiance of the men Tucker found a new trace of hope.

"I don't know about these yaller devils, but I'm with you, Mr. Granger. I'm with you all the way."

The speaker was Thrasher. Granger turned to smile briefly at him, and the burly man grinned like a child who had pleased his father.

Thrasher's words drew similar responses from some of the other men. In a matter of moments the men were divided among themselves, one side ready to leave, the other ready to do whatever Granger ordered.

The rancher walked up to the man who had first defied him and thrust his face inches from the man's nose. Steely-eyed, he raised his arm and pointed to the distant horizon.

"Get out of here, the lot of you. And if I ever see you again, you'll die. Get out of here—out of the territory if you know what's good for you."

"That suits me, Granger. I been ready to cut out for weeks now anyway."

The men turned and strode to their horses, a few of them heading for the bunkhouse. Granger stopped them.

"Forget the bunkhouse. I said for you to get out of here."

"But I got—"

"*Move!*"

The men glared in anger but made no further move toward the bunkhouse. They joined those already in the saddle, and the lot of them moved off at a run, putting as much distance as they could between themselves and the ranch in as short a time as possible.

Thrasher watched them depart. "I would have been glad to have shot 'em for you, Mr. Granger."

"Shut up. Don't you see that there's only a handful of us left?"

It was true. There were only six men left guarding the ranchers—fewer guards than prisoners. But with the prisoners' hands bound and all the weapons in the possession of Granger's loyal remnant, the advantage of greater numbers was of little consequence.

"Well, men, we got a hanging to take care of," said Granger, slapping his palms together. "Take them to the stable."

Tucker felt the cold nudge of a Winchester muzzle against his back, shoving him forward. Reluctantly he moved, the gunmen steering him and his partners toward the stable on the other side of the clearing.

Granger was gleeful as he walked toward the stable. Duke Bryan would not look at him, concentrating his gaze straight ahead, refusing to hurry in spite of the nudging and goading of the men leading him.

The stable was dark and smelled of hay and horse manure. Granger stared up toward the massive rafters that arched across the top of the building. Finding the one he thought best located for the hanging, he ordered a rope thrown across it.

Granger tied the knot himself, pulling it tight and leaving it to dangle. Granger's men pulled a wagon up beneath the rope, adjusted the noose, and tied off the other end. Hitching a mule to the wagon tongue, they looked to Granger for further directions.

"We'll take 'em one at a time," the rancher said. "And though I'm tempted to save the best for last, I think we'll start with my friend Bryan."

Duke was hustled up onto the wagon. Granger stood to the side, grinning broadly at Duke, who stood almost proudly at the end of the wagon, ready to take his fate without a whimper.

"Put the rope around his neck. Bryan, I guess this is good-bye."

Duke cleared his throat and spit directly toward the arrogant rancher, the matter striking him squarely in the face. Then Duke threw back his head and laughed uproariously.

Granger swore and wiped his face on his sleeve.

"Do it! Hang him! *Hang him now!*"

"Hold it right there . . . drop the guns."

Granger whirled, along with the others, to see who had just entered the stable door, guns drawn. Though the sunlight outside silhouetted the two figures, Jack blinked and looked closely, then his mouth dropped open.

"Thurston Russell!"

The burly, red-bearded man moved around into the shadow and out of the glare of the light. He was a large man, red-faced, balding, but with a thick beard. Over his left ear was a leather patch held in place by a strap that ran across his brow and around his head.

"Well, Jack—I figured I would find you in here. I've been keeping a close watch on you the last few days. You ain't been nowhere but I knew about it. And I figured from the looks of what was going on around here that if I didn't come and get you now, I would never get my chance."

Granger stepped forward. "Who is this—"

"Shut up. And the rest of you drop them guns like I told you. That means you, too, fat boy." He waved his pistol at Thrasher. Thrasher reluctantly dropped the weapon he was fingering.

"What do you want?" Granger asked, more polite this time.

"The question is 'who,' feller. I want my old friend Jack, here. We got some old problems to settle, don't we, boy?"

"I don't figure it that way," Jack said.

Russell glanced at the noose around Duke's neck. "It don't look like you have a good choice of options right now."

Jack nodded. "You got a point."

"Then come on. I'll leave the rest of you to continue what you started."

Russell and his partner, a fellow Tucker recognized as one of the Crazy Woman's resident no-goods, hustled Jack outside at gunpoint. Russell waved his pistol in the direction of the stable occupants, making it clear that sudden moves would not be wise.

For a moment there was only silence in the stable, then everyone became suddenly conscious that the guns were on the floor, available to whoever could get their hands on them. Of course, that was a problem for the prisoners, with their hands bound behind them, but Tucker decided to try to free himself, for his bonds felt loose. With a sudden wrenching motion he yanked his hands free of their restraints.

The stable became a sudden flurry of movement, with the prisoners suddenly butting into their captors, knocking them aside. Only Duke, with the rope tight around his neck, was unable to move.

Buck Treadway sent his bulky form flying into Granger, sending him sprawling in the straw and manure. Then the rancher was a whirlwind, moving in all directions, sending bodies flying as he barreled into them.

Tucker's hand found a pistol. Not even having time

to see if it was loaded, he stood and brandished the weapon.

"Hold it!"

The fighting continued. Tucker raised the weapon above his head and fired. The reverberation echoed through the stable, deafening in the enclosed building. The fighting ceased suddenly.

"Granger—back off. The rest of you, too."

The guards moved back, inching toward the rear wall. Out of the corner of his eye Tucker saw a hand inching toward a pitchfork; as the fork was suddenly thrown full-force at him, he ducked, firing at the same time.

The man gripped his chest and fell backward, just as another of the guards leaped for a fallen weapon. He never made it. Tucker's shot struck him full in the side, knocking him off his feet before he fell dead to the stable floor.

There were no further moves. Tucker noticed a knife in the belt of Thrasher.

"Toss that knife over in this corner—hilt first."

Thrasher complied. Tucker edged over and picked the knife up, motioning for Buck Treadway to come to him. The man obeyed, and Tucker cut his bonds. Immediately Treadway picked up a rifle, then headed for the wagon where Duke stood, his neck in the noose.

Whether it was a deliberate action of one of the guards or whether the mule just spooked, Tucker never knew. But for some reason the animal decided to move forward.

Duke tried unsuccessfully to keep his footing on the moving wagon, but he became unbalanced and fell forward. Buck Treadway yelled, dropping his weapons and moving toward Duke with a speed that was incongruous for such a big man.

He caught Duke around the legs, saving him by a fraction of an inch from having his neck snapped by the jerk of the rope. But after he had hold of him, there was nothing he could do but stand there, supporting Duke's weight to keep the rope slack.

Tucker moved forward, scooping up the knife and leaping into the wagon. Keeping his pistol trained on Granger and his remaining men, he slashed the rope above Duke's head, and Treadway let his friend ease to the ground. Another slash of the knife and Duke's hands were free.

Duke and Treadway picked up weapons and took over the duty of guarding Granger and his men while Tucker freed the hands of the other ranchers.

Duke looked squarely at Granger. "It looks like your party was spoiled. Where's your army now?"

Chapter 15

Jack couldn't decide if the arrival of Thurston Russell was good or bad for him. It had saved him from the hangman's noose, but it didn't seem likely that what Russell had in store for him would be better. The big, red-bearded man was riding along directly behind him, and Jack could feel the rifle aimed at his back.

They rode eastward, putting distance between themselves and the ranch at a furious rate. And though he was concerned for his own welfare, Jack was also anxious about Tucker. By now his younger brother might be dead, swinging from a stable rafter.

The three men rode until they reached an area where a low hill dipped into a shallow valley filled with occasional rough boulders and scrubby brush.

"That's far enough. We can take care of our business right here. Are you surprised to see me, Jack?"

"No. Tucker said he thought he was followed. I figured it was you."

"That's right. I knew ol' Danver was dying, and would want to see his boy before he kicked over. He won't get that chance. And from the looks of things back there at that ranch, I don't believe Tucker will make it back home either."

Jack had nothing to say to that. He watched Russell dismount, the grin still on his face.

"Let me ask you something," Jack said. "Was it you that shot the old fellow a couple of nights back at the little ranch that got burned down?"

Russell shrugged. "I reckon it won't hurt to tell you,

since you won't be spreading any stories after I get through with you. Yeah . . . it was me. But the man shot at me first. He had it coming. You can't condemn a man for defending himself."

Jack said, "What do you plan to do with me?"

"Just a little evening up of the score," Russell said. "I've carried around the memory of you for seven years—and it comes back every time I look in the mirror and see this." He gestured toward his damaged ear and the leather patch that covered it.

"I'm sorry about that. I didn't want to hurt you, but you jumped me that night. And like you say, a man has a right to defend himself."

"And he has a right to revenge if he wants it," Russell snapped. "Down off that horse."

Jack complied, forcing himself to move slowly. He didn't want to lost his calm; a quick move might be fatal. His mind worked furiously. He knew Russell was a dull-witted and proud fellow. If there was only some way to turn that against him . . .

"Jack, you know Tater Blevins, here," Russell said, indicating the silent partner that rode with him. "Tater's agreed to help me out. We figure that the old eye for an eye principle holds true right now. Tater, you hold him, and we'll see if he likes losing an ear any better than I did."

Jack's expression didn't change. He spoke in the same calm voice as before. "Tater, you come near me and I'll thrash you. I'm warning you."

Tater glanced nervously at Russell, a bit unnerved. Russell appeared irritated at the hesitation.

"Don't worry about him, Tater—I got a gun on him."

"But what if . . ."

"I said don't worry about him. He won't hurt you. He's too scared."

Jack laughed. "It don't look like I'm the one that's

scared, Thurston. You're the one holding the gun on an unarmed man, afraid to come within ten feet of him."

"You shut up—"

"No. I might as well speak my mind, since I got nothing to lose. You've always been as big a coward as they come, Thurston. You were scared the night I cut your ear, and you're scared now. Big, brave Thurston Russell! Afraid to take me on man to man—got to have some fool to hold me so you can slice on me without worrying about it."

"I ain't afraid of nobody."

"Then fight me—no knives, no guns—just man to man. And if you can whip me, why, I'll cut my own ear off! Sound fair enough?"

Russell looked scared. Jack could read his thoughts. Russell didn't want to have to take a personal risk to get his revenge, but he also didn't want to look like a coward.

Jack smiled deliberately. "I figured as much—too scared. Tell me, Thurston—will you feel like you've had your revenge, knowing that you were scared to face me one on one? You'll kill me, sure, but will that give you satisfaction when down inside you know you're a sniveling coward?"

Russell jerked up straight. "That does it, boy! Tater, back off. Hold the gun on him if you have to, but don't fire unless you get the order from me. Understand?"

Tater nodded, slipping his .44 from its holster. Russell moved forward, slapping his fist into his palm, trying to hide his trembling. Jack dusted his hands on his thighs and smiled, unnervingly calm.

"Come on, Thurston, come and get me! I've tried for seven years to avoid trouble with you, but it hasn't done any good. Come and get me!"

Thurston roared like a bull and lunged forward, grappling for Jack's neck. The agile younger man skipped to the side, laughing as Russell stumbled past him. As he passed, Jack sent forth a wide-swinging kick that landed on the seat of Russell's pants.

"Missed me, jackass! Try again!"

Russell came back quicker than Jack had expected, managing to get a grip on Jack's shirt. He pulled the slim, younger man to him, wrapping bearlike arms around him and beginning to squeeze. Jack felt his ribs bending beneath the force, threatening to snap.

With his arms pinned to his sides, he did the only thing possible—he snapped his head forward and clamped his teeth down on Russell's nose.

The balding man cried out and released Jack. Jack stumbled backward, inhaling refreshing air into his strained lungs, but also managing to gasp out a taunt at the man who was rubbing his nose vigorously.

"You'd . . . best not try that again," he said. "You look ugly enough with just one ear. You'd look worse without a nose."

"You want me to shoot him, Thurston?" called out Tater.

"No! Leave him to me!"

Russell moved forward, arms flailing wildly. He managed to connect a solid right to Jack's jaw, knocking him to his side on the earth. Bellowing like an enraged buffalo, he threw himself in the air and fell straight toward the downed younger man.

Jack's knee came up and caught Russell in the stomach as he fell, sending his breath rushing out in a great foul-smelling burst. Before the man could recover, Jack shoved him aside and rolled over, rising to his feet.

Russell stood up, but Jack planted a hard kick against his thigh, making his leg collapse beneath him. Then he moved forward, raining punches into the fleshy face, blackening the heavily browed eyes.

Russell struck Jack hard in the belly. Jack stumbled, falling back.

Russell was on top of him, pounding him about the kidneys. Jack felt consciousness begin to slip away.

"How . . . does it . . . feel, boy?" gasped Russell. "How do you . . . like it?"

Jack wasn't sure just what he did next; he simply let his body explode into movement. But whatever he did, it worked, for Russell gasped and rolled back off him.

Jack managed to rise, still dazed and throbbing with pain. But now wasn't the time to quit; he stumbled forward, punching Russell hard in the left kidney.

Tater stood to the side, watching it all with great concentration, not paying attention to anything around him except the battle on the grass. And so he was taken completely by surprise when he felt the cold barrel of a Winchester nudge his left ear.

"Drop the gun."

The speaker was Tucker. He had approached unnoticed, along with Duke and a handful of the other ranchers. Taking Tater's weapon, he looked down at the combatants.

"Should we break 'em up?" asked Duke.

Tucker frowned, then shook his head. "No. This is something that has been festering for seven years. It's time they had it out and ended this once and for all."

Duke shrugged. "Whatever you say. He's your brother."

Russell had Jack around the neck right now, doing his best to choke him. But Jack was pouring a steady series of blows to Russell's stomach and kidneys, every one weakening the big man a little further. Gradually the grip on Jack's neck lessened, then let go.

Jack moved in then, still pounding Russell's gut, giving an occasional uppercut to the chin. There was no sound in the little valley other than the grunts and moans of the two men and the sound of fists slapping flesh.

Russell did his best to rally, trying to return the blows he was receiving, but the agile Jack managed to deflect most, still relentlessly letting the big man have it on the gut. Russell's face was fiery red, and his cheeks puffed out with each blow to his stomach. When Jack saw the man's eyes roll up in his head and his mouth drop open, he knew it was over. He sent a final punch into the man's face, and Russell dropped straight back, moaning and drifting in and out of consciousness.

Jack knelt beside him and lifted his head up by the shirt collar. "Listen, Thurston, from now on this war is over—understand? You won't ever bother me or any of my kin again, no matter what. If you do, you'll get worse than what you got today. And don't ever think you can take me on with a gun, 'cause I can whip you that way just as good as I can with my fists. Now I'm going to let you get up from here and ride away, because I don't want to hurt you—I never did, even when I cut your ear. The trouble is over—I'll never run from you again, and you'll never chase me. Understand?"

Bleary-eyed, breathless, filled with pain, Russell could only manage to grunt out an assent. Jack let Russell's head drop back to the dirt, then he stood and noticed for the first time the band of men watching him on the hill. When he saw Tucker among them, his hard-pounding heart leaped within him.

"Tucker! Lord, boy, I thought you would be dead!"

Tucker headed down the slope toward his brother. "Not quite, Jack. I was worried the same for you."

Jack snorted. Glancing down the slope to where Russell was picking himself up from the dirt, he said, "I don't think I'll have anything to worry about from Thurston anymore. I think he'll leave all of us alone from now on. I'm going back home, Tucker. Ma will be needing us both if Pa dies. I ain't running no more."

"I'm glad to hear it, Jack."

"But how did you get away from Granger? And where is he now?"

Tucker walked back up the slope toward the waiting men, his hand on his brother's shoulder. "Granger's our prisoner now, Jack. We managed to overpower them in the stable. Duke and me and the others came after you, worrying about what Russell might do. It looks like we didn't have anything to worry about."

"What have you done with Granger?"

"Buck is taking him back to his ranch, along with the men left with him."

Jack shook hands with Duke. "Well, I figure the worst of it is probably over."

Duke smiled weakly. "I hope so. But we got a problem, still. And that's what we're going to do with Granger."

"We could turn him over to the law . . . well, I guess not the law around here. Granger runs that."

"He sure does. And what kind of proof do we have against him that would stand up in court? We're stuck with a prisoner and nothing to do with him."

"I see the problem. Maybe if we head on to Treadway's ranch we can figure out something once we all get there."

The men mounted up, first seeing off Thurston Russell and his partner. The one-eared man looked like an injured child, his pride completely shattered, cowardice replacing what spirit he had possessed before. He headed due south, probably going back to the Crazy Woman, Jack figured. And although fighting it out with his adversary had lifted a burden from Jack's mind, still he wondered what would happen when their paths inevitably crossed again.

The men started westward toward the ranch.

Spirits were low in spite of the victories of the last hours. Several ranchers had been killed in the battle at the Granger ranch, and breaking the news to the waiting families would not be easy. There would be several bodies to gather and burial services to be held.

The day was almost gone when the men arrived at the ranch. Frank was with them now; he had met them along the way. He had already encountered Buck Treadway returning with Granger in tow, and he had received a complete report on the battle. But he was fascinated to hear about Jack's fight with Russell and made Jack repeat the story more than once, laughing at what he consid-

ered funny details. Jack couldn't figure it out; it wasn't
funny to him.

Buck Treadway lived alone in the small cabin that
constituted his ranch house. And it was obvious that a
woman's touch was lacking in the place; empty tin cans
were strewn about everywhere, the bed looked as if it
were covered with the same linens it had worn five years
before, and the floor had almost a half inch of dirt on it at
some places. But after the traumas of the day, it was an
inviting place, and Tucker entered it joyfully.

Seeing Charity was the best part. She sat in a handmade chair beside the fireplace, staring with obvious discomfort at Dan Granger, who lay bound on the bed
across the single room. When the men entered, she
brightened. And Tucker couldn't help but notice that she
brightened all the more when he brought up the rear of
the party.

Buck Treadway greeted them all cordially, slapping
Jack on the back and declaring he was glad to see him.
Once more Jack had to tell the story of his bout with
Thurston Russell.

Night fell, and Tucker grew restless. He walked over
to Charity and quietly asked if she would be willing to
take a walk with him about the ranch grounds. He was
honestly surprised when she said she would.

Dan Granger watched Tucker and Charity walking
out together, and he both hated and envied them. The
girl was the image of her mother, and that stirred uncomfortable feelings in the man. Like Duke and his wife before them, Tucker and Charity appeared destined for the
kind of human relationship Granger could never know.
Granger had learned many things in his life, but giving
and receiving love was not one of them.

His childhood life had been spent on gray New York
streets, back alleys, and in dimly lit tenements. Strange
thing, memory; though in his youth he never really saw
his surroundings sharply, never found anything amid the

unfocused drabness to stand out from the rest, yet all these years later he saw it all vividly.

In particular, the often-uplifted hand of the man he had called his father. But he was a father only in a manner of speaking and gave nothing to his secondhand son except the last name of Granger and scars on his mind and body that had never faded.

Granger remembered his father's grimacing face glaring down as he beat his stepson. He remembered the throb of every blow through him and the unending ache that remained like the wake left by a ship. He heard the curses, the abusive talk, and remembered pleading for help from his mother and that she never gave it.

Granger's mother had been a prostitute, practicing her profession openly before her son, for she had lost shame early on. Granger had received a blatant and gritty understanding of human relations at base level by simple observation. He gained two things from that: hatred of his mother and a simultaneous longing for and loathing of women in general. Throughout his life he had never overcome that. His relationships with females were from his earliest days mere encounters that lasted as long as it took to force himself physically upon them. He had narrowly escaped prosecution on rape charges three times, once only by bribing his way out. That itself would have been impossible except for Granger's closest thing to a redeeming characteristic: he was an excellent businessman.

Granger's first business venture, financed by stolen money, was a partnership in a slaughterhouse. From there he followed a basically backward route into the cattle business, first buying into cattle farms in New England, then finally heading west as his wealth and acumen grew. His combination of streetwise ruthlessness and natural dealing skills worked well for him, eventually making him into a major Montana Territory rancher who wielded much political power and had as many gunmen as cowboys in his hire.

He had come from enclosing streets of poverty to the land of open sky and wealth. Granger thought over his pilgrimage often, and it brought him the closest thing to happiness he had ever known. If that was not a great thing, it was at least something.

He cursed beneath his breath and tried to loosen the bonds around his wrists.

Chapter 16

The prairie was a wide ocean of grass covered by a dark blanket of sky pinpointed by stars. Tucker recalled how he had felt a vague loneliness beneath the stars on the journey up from the Wyoming Territory. He felt something akin to it tonight, though not quite the same, for Charity was beside him.

They walked around the back of the house, toward the corral. So peaceful were the plains that the horrors of the day seemed unreal. Tucker stopped by the corral fence and leaned one foot upon it. Charity stood beside him, so close he could feel the warmth of her on his shoulder, tingling through him like electricity.

"It's beautiful," she whispered.

"What? The corral?"

Charity laughed. "No, silly—the sky."

Tucker blushed, feeling like a fool. He realized suddenly that Charity's opinion of him was very important. He began to wonder what she did think of him.

"Tucker . . . I'm sorry I fooled you out there at the line camp. I didn't want to get rid of you . . . I just knew you wouldn't let me go to Granger's ranch, and I felt like I had to go. It was a mistake, I can see now."

"It was," he said. "But everything turned out all right, so it don't matter. I admire you for it, really. It was a brave thing to do."

"Tucker?"

"Yeah?"

"I want to thank you for what you've done for us. You risked your life when you didn't have any real call to, you and Jack both. If not for you, my Pa would be dead right now, maybe Frank, too."

"Oh, I don't see that anything I did was that important."

"It was . . . and I admire you for it. I hope you know I'm grateful."

They didn't talk much after that but instead walked about the ranch, admiring the beauty of the wild, night-shrouded prairie and the distant hills that stood out mysterious and beckoning in the moonlight. Tucker found himself wishing that the night would go on forever with Charity beside him.

They walked farther. Tucker knew it would not be wise to range far, so he and Charity stayed within quick running distance of the ranch house, enjoying the night breeze.

An hour passed. Tucker began to consider going back to the ranch house. He knew that a continued absence from the others might worry them. Reluctantly he turned to her to suggest a return.

He looked into eyes wide with horror. Something struck his head, lightning flashed across his vision, then he was down, his mind reeling into the oblivion of senselessness.

Hands picked him up; he was dragged somewhere. He was conscious of the opening and closing of a door; vague, shadowy faces hovered above him; he lay on something soft.

When he came to at last, he was in the ranch house, on the same bed on which Granger had been tied. The rancher had been evicted from it and was sitting glumly in the opposite corner. Tucker stared up at the circle of faces hovering above him.

"Charity?"

"Gone," said Duke. His voice was cold and heavy, like lead.

"Who . . ."

"It must be Thurston Russell," said Jack. "I don't know who else it could be."

"But why would Thurston Russell want Charity? What good would she do him?"

"I don't know."

Tucker sat up in the bed, his head throbbing. Duke touched his shoulder. "Do you think you should be up?"

"I want to help look for Charity."

"You up to it?"

"I am. Nothing could keep me from it."

"Then let's go. There's some already out looking. I waited around for you to wake up."

Tucker stood, rubbing his head, shaking his pounding skull to clear the cobwebs. Blinking, staggering a little, he moved toward the door, hoping his strength would return.

Duke, Jack, and Tucker headed out into the night.

"We found you over there. You had been gone a long time; we had started worrying," Jack said, pointing to the east.

"We don't know how long you had been lying there, and we couldn't find any decent sign of anyone else to follow. But Charity was gone—there was no doubt about that," Duke said.

"Look yonder—here comes Buck and the others," said Jack.

"Do they have Charity?"

"I don't believe so."

Buck Treadway approached at the head of a group of men. His face reflected disappointment. "We couldn't find her, Duke. And whoever it was that took her covered his trail real well."

"No sign at all?" Duke's voice sounded cracked and weak, as if his nerves were near snapping.

"None, Duke. I'm sorry."

"Well, I'll just have a look for myself . . . there's got to be some sign."

"If you want, Duke. But you won't find anything tonight."

Duke closed his eyes and shook his head. Tucker noticed that he was trembling. The strain of losing his ranch house and nearly his life, then having his daughter snatched from under his nose, was too much for him.

Unexpectedly, he turned on Tucker. "Why couldn't you have protected her? Too busy thinking about something else, maybe? Just what did you have in mind to do with her?"

Tucker's mouth dropped open; he was too taken aback to speak.

Duke struck him, hard. Then he leaped upon him, pounding Tucker about the face.

Buck and Jack moved simultaneously, taking Duke by the shoulders and pulling him off his dazed victim. Duke yelled, flailing his arms and trying to break free. Then, just as suddenly, he collapsed into Buck's arms, weeping.

"Get him inside," Buck said.

They moved Duke back into the house. He was still weeping loudly, apologizing for what he had done. Granger, seated in the corner, smiled for the first time since his capture. Tucker gave him a look that caused the smile to fade immediately.

Tucker sat at the table across from Duke. Duke raised his head and looked at the young man through bleary eyes. "I'm sorry, Tucker. I didn't mean what I said, and I didn't mean to jump you. It's just that when I think about Charity out there . . ."

"I understand, Duke."

A voice called from the plains, a distant voice, faint.

"I've got the girl, and I'll kill her unless you listen to me and do what I tell you."

Duke leaped up. Rushing to the door, he flung it open and stared out into the darkness. He could see no one.

"Who are you?"

"Never mind that. Yell out, sweet thing, and let them know I got you."

Charity's voice, trembling and thin, carried through from somewhere in the darkness. Duke called out to her, profoundly relieved to hear her voice, yet also frightened.

"Are you all right, Charity? Are you hurt?"

"I'm fine, Pa. But please do as he says—he means it when he says he'll kill me."

"You hear that, Bryan? She's telling the truth."

Tucker glanced over at Jack, who had a somber expression on his face. "That ain't Russell, Tucker."

"I know. But who, then?"

"I don't know. I never heard that voice before."

"We're listening," Duke called. "What is it you want?"

"I want Dan Granger."

The rancher leaped up from his chair in the corner, straining at his bonds. "No! Don't let him near me! You can't."

"Shut up, Granger," muttered Duke. Then he called out again. "What do you mean, you want Granger? Why should we turn him over to you? Who are you?"

"Never mind who I am—just do what I tell you, or the next shot you hear will be the one killing your daughter. I know you got Granger. Show him at the door."

Duke withdrew into the house. He looked at Buck Treadway and asked, "What do you think?"

"That's what I was going to ask you. I don't want to see Charity put to no harm, but I don't like giving in to a demand like that, either."

"That's Charity out there, Buck. That's my daughter."

Buck nodded. "You're right." He turned to the trembling Granger. "C'mon, mister. Show yourself at the door like he said."

The rancher pulled back, violently shaking his head. "No—you can't make me do that!"

The unidentified voice came ringing again across the distance. "I'm waiting! My patience is running out!"

Duke grabbed Granger and jerked him forward. "C'mon! C'mon or I'll shoot you dead right here!"

The cattleman struggled and fought all the way, but soon Duke held him in place in the doorway.

"Is that Granger?" the voice called.

"It's him!"

"Much obliged."

Three shots came in such rapid succession that the noise of them was like a blur of sound. Two slugs pounded into the wall, but a third clipped away some of the flesh of Granger's right leg. He collapsed. Duke pulled back inside out of instinct.

That Granger could move quickly enough to escape did not seem possible, but he did. He rose on his bleeding leg, his hands tied behind him, and bolted out the door as a fourth shot coughed out in the night and slapped another slug into the wall. The unknown man out on the range cursed loudly.

A loud feminine scream followed. Duke ran outside. Granger was nowhere to be seen. "Charity!" Duke shouted. He looked about; nothing could be seen of her.

Another scream, this one closer. Duke saw her then, running out of the night toward him.

"Pulled free," she said, coming into his arms. "Pulled free from him."

"Who is it?"

Charity was breathless. Duke could tell she had been badly scared. "Don't know. I don't know."

"Get back inside," Duke said. His arm still around her, he drew her toward the lighted open doorway. "You're all right, dear girl. You're all right now."

Out in the darkness, Dan Granger ran on a bleeding leg, struggling to free his wrists, bound behind his back. He was pursued and he knew it.

Two or three of the men in the cabin took out after

Granger but quickly gave up the chase. The fact was that they had no good plan about what to do with him anyway, so they let him go.

Not even Duke felt that Granger would be a threat again.

The gunmen who had been captured with Granger sat against the wall, looking imploringly at Duke. He walked over to them and looked them over. He drew a knife from his pocket, opened it, and cut their ropes.

"You may as well go, too," he said.

Glances flew among the ranchers. "Duke, you think we should do this?" Treadway asked.

"Why not? You think they'll give trouble now?"

Treadway gave the prisoners an up-and-down perusal, then shook his head.

"Thank you, thank you so much," Thrasher said. "We won't forget this, I promise."

"All I want you to promise is to get out of the country," Duke said.

"Yes, sir. Yes, sir," Thrasher said. He and the others left at top speed.

"Who do you think shot at Granger?" Treadway asked.

Duke shrugged. "Don't know, but whoever he is, I wish him luck."

It was clear, Duke Bryan saw, that Charity was deeply in love. She sat beside Tucker right now, and the two of them were lost in quiet conversation. It gave Duke a rather peculiar feeling. Always before he had been the one to whom his daughter turned when there were important things to say.

Treadway joined Duke. "They grow up too fast," he said.

"So they do." Duke gestured subtly toward Tucker. "But when they do, you hope they find one with the right kind of spirit and the right way of looking at things."

"What do you figure will come of this, Duke?" Treadway asked.

Duke smiled. "Before it's through, I'd say a houseful of grandchildren."

Chapter 17

Dan Granger lay in a draw, covered in sweat and trying not to breathe too loudly despite his exhaustion and the pain of his wounded leg. He had run hard from the ranch cabin with his hands still tied behind him, and it had seemed like the hot-breathed devil himself was nipping at the back of his neck. Yet when at last he had collapsed into the draw, he had found no one behind him. There he lay, panting, working at his bonds as he had secretly been doing for several hours back in the ranch house.

Almost loose now, and it was a good thing, like the fact his leg had stopped bleeding. A relatively superficial wound it apparently was; it didn't hurt nearly so bad now.

But that was only small comfort. Whoever was after him obviously was not one for scruples: he had tried to blast Granger away right in the doorway. Who could it be? The ranchers already had Granger at the time and would have no need of murder.

Granger gave a painful pull and his left wrist came free, leaving skin and blood on the rope. He rubbed the abraded skin, face twisted in pain. Then he untied the other wrist and tossed away the rope.

If not a rancher after him, then who? Granger strained to figure it out. Then a suspicion came.

Probably it was a rancher after all. Probably the whole incident had been a charade set up by the more unscrupulous of his captors to let Granger be murdered but still provide them an alibi for the law and their weaker-kneed friends. Who shot Granger? they would be asked. We don't know. Some killer out in the dark. Surely wasn't us.

Clever and heartless, those damnable ranchers. Granger glowered, still rubbing his wrists. He wouldn't stand for such. He wasn't a man to be toyed with. He had power, gunmen at his command . . .

Then he remembered. His gunmen had been routed, his power stripped, at least for the moment. Suddenly he felt even more helpless than before, and utterly alone there on the dark prairie.

Noise . . . he dropped on his face, his breath almost choking off. He nearly panicked.

How close the man passed, Granger did not know, for he never lifted his face from the dirt. But somehow, despite Granger's uncontrollably loud breathing and pounding heart, the man did pass by. After a few moments Granger knew he was alone again.

He had to get back to his ranch, figure out where he stood. He saw no real logic to it—likely there would be nothing gained by going home again—but away from his familiar refuge he couldn't even think. It was an ironic situation to feel more trapped out in the open than in enclosing walls, but that was how it stood.

He stood and immediately went down again. His leg was completely numb; the wound must be worse than he thought. But then Granger laughed to himself. He had realized it wasn't his wounded leg that had no feeling, but his good one. He had lain upon it in such a way as to cut off the circulation of blood. Now it began to tingle electrically, a million needle jabs of pain bolting through it from the inside out.

He danced clumsily about until the tingling left and feeling returned. He began walking across the prairie toward his ranch.

Like many of Granger's worst memories, it was a recollection old yet fresh: fingers wrapped too tightly around his throat, squeezing until stars exploded in his brain. "You've got the neck of a chicken, you have. I can wrap my fingers around it like it was a sapling, and snap it like a twig. Prestilent little thief! If I did kill you, who would complain? Your father? Your sow of a mother?"

The fruit seller laughed foul breath into the boy's face. His features were big and distorted by proximity, his skin gray in the shadows of the towering New York buildings on either side of the alley where the pear-stealing boy had been caught. "Light as a feather you are, Danny Granger. Toss you into the harbor and you'd float to France, eh? How light are you, anyway?"

The fruit seller lifted his young victim by the neck and held him aloft. "Hang you will someday, my little thief. Maybe by then you will have put enough meat on your bones to let you choke it out proper." He threw Dan Granger to the pitted alley floor.

The boy rubbed his neck and gasped for air. The fruit seller pointed at him and said, "You come about my stand again and you'll have my boot bruising your backside, or maybe a knift betwixt the shoulder blades."

Dan Granger's voice squeaked out, weakened because of the choking: "Someday I'll be big and strong enough that men like you will be afraid of me. Someday I'll wipe out men like you with a word."

The fruit seller laughed and turned away. Dan Granger rubbed his neck again and marked it in his mind that one day he would get his revenge.

Seven years later he raped the fruit seller's daughter.

Now, as he stumbled on his wounded leg through a grove of cottonwoods, Granger smiled at the thought. Taught that old man to treat him so, he surely had!

Granger had lost track of time as he crossed the prairie, but he felt the coming of dawn not far ahead. His house lay far before him, and he pushed on.

"You were wrong, old man—I won't hang," he said

aloud. "You were wrong and I was right: I won't hang, and I can wipe out men like you with a word."

He pushed on until he reached his ranch.

Many hours later he sat huddled in the corner of his bedroom, hands around his knees. Around him stretched his ranch, empty but for corpses and dust. Granger stared into the opposite corner as a fly buzzed in his ear. He did not swat it away.

Only now was the possibility that it was all over really beginning to strike him. His power was gone. The small ranchers had defeated him with grit and determination. The dollars Granger paid his gunmen simply hadn't been sufficient to give them purpose enough to overcome the men whose comrade Granger had terrorized.

Duke Bryan. He silently mouthed the name as if it had a bad taste. A pitiful, penny-ante rancher who had nothing—except the one lady Granger had wanted more than anything else.

She had been a fine woman, worthy of better treatment than Granger had given her, and even he knew that. But from his earliest days Granger had never known any other way with women.

Another memory from childhood arose.

Granger, kneeling, hands uplifted. Mama, I'm sorry. I saw him hurting you and grabbed the knife. I didn't know, mama. I'm sorry.

Then came brutal blows from his father, beating down upon him. Bad for business to knife a customer, boy. Ought to throw you into the street.

He remembered his mother's wiping blood from the floor when the beating was done, and he didn't know if it was that of the man he had knifed or that of himself. She was crying. He put his arms out to her but she did not respond.

The rancher snapped his head up; the memory disappeared like smoke in wind. He had heard something outside the house. Granger stood, amazed to see ruddy evening light coming in through the west-facing window, casting brown shadows from the tall cottonwood that stood outside it. He must have been half asleep.

He crept to the window and carefully looked out. Nobody there that he could see. Something banged and he started, but it was just a shutter on the loft door of the barn. Yet that wasn't what he had heard before.

He went to a gun cabinet against the wall and threw it open. Empty! Someone had cleaned it out in the midst of the day's confusion. Maybe even one of his own men. He cursed and slammed the cabinet shut; the noise echoed through the house.

He walked out of the room and onto the stair landing. He peered down but saw no one below. He walked down the stairs. Every thump of his feet on the steps sounded unnaturally loud. Granger grew winded merely descending the staircase. He realized what a toll anxiety was taking on him, and also that he had not eaten a real meal for many hours now.

He went to the dining room and found half a loaf of bread on the table. Gnawing at the dry bread, he walked uneasily through his house as if he were looking for something but not remembering what. He didn't look to see if the bodies of the men he had shot down remained where he had left them; he didn't want to see any more of death tonight.

What could he do? Was there any place for him to go? He still had money, still could buy his own justice if he wanted. So he told himself, but it didn't seem true anymore. His spirit was broken by what had happened today, and he no longer felt like the man he had been. And even Granger knew that a man who did not believe in himself any longer could gain loyalty from no other.

The noise again. It sounded like someone moving in the back of the house.

"Granger."

The rancher stumbled back against the wall. The voice had surprised him. "Who's there?" he demanded.

The speaker must have moved, for the voice now came from a slightly different location. "I've come for you, Granger."

The voice was more familiar now but still unplaced. "Who are you? What do you want?"

"I wasn't sure you would come back here, Granger. Thought you'd be smarter than that. Guess I was wrong and you're more a fool than I thought."

Granger paused. "Brandon—Mick Brandon, is that you?"

"Who do you think it is?"

"Why are you here?"

"I come to pay you the price for a dead brother. Death for death."

Granger's heart hammered. His blood raced through his veins like whitewater. "I didn't want to do it, Mick. They forced me."

"But you did do it. You . . . and so it's you who pays."

"I don't want trouble with you, Mick."

"Too late. Too late when you pulled the trigger on my brother."

Granger was backing away. He still could not see Mick Brandon even though he sensed he was drawing nearer. The house seemed very dark now.

"What do you want from me?"

"Nothing but what I was denied out there on the prairie: a good clean shot. This time I'll do a lot more than nick you."

Granger turned to his left and ran. A gunshot roared, echoing in the house. Panicked, the rancher lunged up the stairs.

He realized when he reached the landing that he had made a mistake. From here there was nowhere to go. He ran back into his bedroom for the lack of any alternative. He slammed the door and lowered the latch as if somehow that could do some good.

On the stairs the boots of Mick Brandon beat out a slow, ascending funeral-march rhythm.

"No!" Granger yelled. "Go away! Leave me alone!"

Still the boots against the stairs, then the landing.

"No!" Granger screamed again. He lurched to the window and threw it open. Out on the porch roof he climbed. The cottonwood reached up its branches toward him like the arms of a mother finally responding to a child who has reached out to her.

Granger did not miss the irony of that even as he leaped.

One kick gained Brandon entry into the bedroom. He thrust out his pistol, swept the room with it. Granger was gone. The window stood open with the curtains trailing out of it into the thickening dark.

Brandon went to the window, bent, and stuck out his head and his pistol. "Granger!" No answer. He cursed and called the name again as he pulled himself out the window and onto the roof.

He walked to the edge and looked down into the cottonwood. He lifted his pistol, then slowly lowered and leathered it. No need for a bullet now; the job was already done.

He turned his back and reentered the window, descended the stairs, left the house, and rode away. Behind him the corpse of Dan Granger bounced slightly up and down, as if hung from a spring, each time the wind moved the branches of the cottonwood. Granger's snapped neck was tightly wedged in the crotch of the largest branch, his limp body dangling below. He had, at least, died quickly.

Chapter 18

Jack and Tucker set out in the morning for the Crazy Woman. After all that had happened, it didn't seem possible, somehow, that they were at last doing what they had planned to do in the first place.

But Tucker couldn't regret having stayed and helped out the Bryans. Especially when he thought about Charity Bryan. He was sad to leave her. Jack sensed his brother's feelings as he rode beside him.

At last he ventured a question. "Missing her, Tucker?"

Tucker glanced over at Jack rather sharply, surprised by the query. For a moment he felt defensive, as if he should deny the truth. But instead, he shrugged and quietly nodded.

Jack looked ahead and grinned. "Well, if the looks of things are any indication, I'd say she's missing you, too. I could tell from the way she watched you from the beginning that she thought you were really something."

Jack and Tucker came to Pumpkin Creek and began following it down its course, heading almost due south. They rode steadily, with few breaks, and by nightfall they had come almost to the southern extremity of the creek. There they made camp.

They talked of their father, and of the difference the past seven years had made in their lives. In the bustle and danger of the recent days, Tucker had had little time to think of his father, but now that he was alone with Jack beneath the stars, with no one around to distract him, the sadness returned, and he prayed that he would find his father alive.

Jack was talkative the next day, for they were approaching familiar territory. They reached the Powder River and followed along the bank, steering east of the Hanging Woman Creek.

"I don't want to get around ol' Drake anymore. He'd probably have my tail for that stolen saddle, even though it wasn't me that took it. He's as sour as week-old buttermilk," Jack said.

They camped that night on the banks of the Powder and the following day rode until they were in the Wyoming Territory. The next day would bring them to the Crazy Woman and Danver Corrigan.

They rose early the next morning, before dawn. After eating a quick breakfast, they rode southwest along the river.

They rode all day without stopping, for the excitement of being home kept them from growing tired or hungry.

The ranch looked deserted when they approached, but a thin white trail of smoke from the chimney told them that the family was there. Tucker's heart jumped to his throat as he drew near, and Jack felt such a turmoil of emotions that he didn't know if he was happy or sad.

The door opened when they were within two hundred yards of the house. Ma stepped out into the yard, crossing her arms as she always did, watching the approaching pair. They rode up close, and only then did they see the tears in her eyes as she looked at Jack.

"Welcome home, Son," she said.

"Hello, Ma," answered Jack. "It's good to be back."

He dismounted and walked slowly toward the mother he hadn't seen in seven years. Then he took her in his arms.

"Is Pa . . ."

"He's still living," she said. "But he isn't good. It's only been the hope of seeing you come back that has kept him going."

Tucker dismounted and led the horses to the stable.

It didn't bother him that his mother had not even greeted him; he knew that the return of Jack was of such profound significance for her that all other considerations faded from her mind. After seeing to the horses, he entered the cabin and slipped quietly past the silent children to the back room.

Ma stood with her arm over Jack's shoulder, and both of them were at the bedside, looking down into Pa's face. And the best thing of all was that in spite of the tears that filled his eyes, Pa was smiling, his face radiant. Pa had aged so fast, it seemed, getting old before his time over these past seven years. But now that Jack was home, again back within these walls where he belonged, it was as if everything was right again, as it had been in the days before Jack left.

Tucker turned away. Somehow it was too much to watch. He returned to the main room of the house, where the children sat in silence, not sure just what to think about the sudden materialization of a man who for seven years had been almost mythlike in their minds. Little Tara and Benjamin Elrod were more taken aback than the others, for when Jack had left home Tara had been only a year old and Benjamin hadn't even been born.

"Is that Jack, Tucker?" Tara asked.

"Yes, honey, that's him."

"Is he here to stay?"

"I believe so, Tara."

"That's good. Pa's been hoping he would."

Jack stayed in the room with his father a long time, even after Ma came back out and joined the rest of the family. Only then did she come over to Tucker and hug him, thanking him for what he had done.

"We were worried about you, though. What slowed you down?"

"That's a long, long story, Ma. I'll wait till Jack's with me to tell it."

Jack came out of the back room at long last, a look of

contentment on his face. He came to each of the family members and greeted them, shaking the boys' hands and hugging the girls. When he met Benjamin Elrod, he didn't know what to say; he hadn't been aware he had a new little brother before Tucker told him about it.

Tucker heard Pa calling his name. He entered the rear room. Pa lay on his back, his head propped up on a feather pillow. He motioned for Tucker to come over and sit on his bedside.

"You did good, Son. I'm proud of you. Jack told me what happened. You proved yourself a man."

"Thank you, Pa."

"Of course, we don't want to tell your mother all about it."

"I understand that, Pa."

Pa let his head settle back into the softness of the pillow. He stared upward at the ceiling, looking very tired, but with a peaceful expression on his face, something calm about him that hadn't been there before.

"Seeing your brother was a dream fulfilled for me. I figure I'm still on the road to my grave, but I can go with a lot more peace now. But that's going to leave you with a lot of responsibility—Jack, too.

"Jack is going to stay, he says, and he wants to run the ranch. But you're going to have to keep an eye on him to see that he don't go to the gambling table any too often. A man can lose everything he has a lot faster than he might think."

"I know, Pa."

"Your biggest responsibility will be to look out for your ma after I'm gone, and keep an eye on Jack, at least until you leave."

"Leave, Pa?"

Danver Corrigan looked into his son's eyes. "You know you can't stay, not if you love her like I love your ma."

Tucker was surprised. Jack must have told Pa about Charity.

"I did figure on leaving to court her a little, nothing permanent, at least not yet."

"Do you love her?"

Tucker looked away from his father's intent face. "I do."

"Then it'll be permanent. That's how it's supposed to be. I'm happy for you, Son. Me and your mother—we never had nothing to amount to much as far as money was concerned, but we've had a lot of love. I wish the same for you. I wish it for all of my children and their children, too."

Tucker walked over to the window. To leave . . . to put aside his home and roam away . . . it was a peculiar thing to think about.

In the past few days he had lived not like a boy but like a man. Even Pa had said that just now.

And a man needed a mate, someone to share his life with and to love more than he loved himself.

"You're right, Pa. I will be leaving. Funny . . . I didn't know it myself."

"When do you figure you'll leave, Son?"

Tucker shook his head. "I don't know. I know I'll stay until . . ."

Danver Corrigan smiled. "Go ahead and say it . . . until I'm dead. There's no point in mincing words."

"I figure that after that I'll stay around and see that the ranch is in good order, give Jack a hand and all. Then I'll head north again."

Danver Corrigan's eyes closed, and he breathed deeply. It was obvious he was growing weary. The new burst of life Jack's return had brought him was beginning to wear off, and his face was growing gaunt and pale once more.

Tucker stood and watched him until he thought he was asleep. Then quietly he turned and started to leave the room.

"Tucker?"

"Pa?"

"There's something else I want you to do for me. Jack told me about his fight with Thurston Russell, and how he thinks the trouble is over. Maybe he's right—I hope so. But look out for Thurston Russell. He don't forget fast."

"I will, Pa. I promise."

"Good. Go on, Son. I think I'll rest a bit."

It was early the next morning that Tucker was awakened by his mother's hand, jostling him gently. He sat up in bed and looked at her weary face.

"He's gone, Tucker. He died peaceful and easy, and he died happy."

Tucker looked out through the window toward the brilliant light of the stars. The wind moaned around the eaves of the house, infinitely mournful. To Tucker it seemed a fitting farewell to the soul of Danver Corrigan.

Tucker and Jack watched the approach of the wagon bearing the simple pine coffin made of planks. The elderly man driving it pulled the mules to a halt and climbed down. He came to the young men and bobbed his head in hello.

Jack walked over and touched the coffin. "We appreciate you, Pete. You did a fine job."

"When you're old as me, you've had plenty of practice," the man said. "I've built coffins for more than I could count. Good men, bad men, men somewhere in between like most of us." He paused. "Your pa, he wasn't like most. A good man, no finer to be found." Pete slipped off his hat. "If your ma's inside, I'll pay my respects to her."

"Thanks again, Pete."

It seemed a strange and alien thing for Jack and Tucker to unload the coffin from the wagon and know it would hold their father's body. They carried it to the porch and set it there, then stood looking at it.

"I lost a lot of years with him," Jack said reflectively. "I never should have left just because of Thurston."

"You had no choice," Tucker said. His voice sounded tired.

"Yes, I did. I just didn't know it." Jack chuckled thoughtfully. "You know, Tucker, many's the time I wondered if I left to avoid trouble, or just because I was afraid. I've thought myself a coward often enough."

Tucker looked at his brother in mild surprise. "You? No. Anything but a coward."

Jack nodded. "I know that now. The trouble we had up there"—he pointed northward—"showed me that much at least."

"It showed me something else, too," Tucker said. "There's more than one way to look at success. Pa never thought he had much of it, but as far as I'm concerned, he had a heck of a lot more than Dan Granger ever did. Money, power, none of that did Granger much good that I can see."

"That's a fact. One minute a rich man with gunmen and land, the next nothing."

"You know," Tucker said, "I don't think I'll ever completely understand men like Dan Granger. I know I don't want to be like that myself."

"Amen to that, brother."

Pete the coffin maker came to the door. "Bring it in, boys," he said. "We're ready."

Tucker and Jack picked up the coffin and carried it into the house.

Danver's body lay on his bed. His eyes were closed. His whiskers had been shaved and his hair was neatly combed. He looked peaceful. The lines and gauntness left by his sickness didn't seem so evident now.

Carefully they lifted the body from the bed and placed it in the coffin. They folded Danver's arms across his chest.

Tucker looked at Jack. In his older brother's eyes tears brimmed. Jack looked down at his father's face.

"I could have been a better son," he said. "I could have stayed close by him. But somehow I never thought about the years I was losing. I never thought about him being gone."

"No regrets, Jack," Tucker said. "You can't let there be regrets."

"There's always regrets, Tucker. More for some of us than for others."

Chapter 19

Danver Corrigan was buried in a small plot beside the ranch clearing. His tomb was marked with a single wooden cross with no inscription other than his name and date of birth and death. Tucker and Jack dug the grave and stood beside it as a preacher who lived over toward the Bighorn Mountains conducted the brief and simple graveside ceremony.

Ma put up a good front, not letting herself cry except just a little, but all of the children knew that in her heart she grieved deeply for her mate. The family stood with her beside the grave for a time, then left her alone with her thoughts.

Tucker and Jack walked off together to the far end of the ranch at Tucker's request, for he needed to talk to his brother.

"Jack, I can't stay long. Me and Pa talked about it, and I know now that I'll have to be leaving soon."

"I can understand that, Tucker. But Ma needs you right now. Charity's important, but so's Ma."

"I know that. I ain't about to run off at first light or anything. It's just that . . . I don't know. I can't explain it. It's like it's eating at me or something. Ever since I talked to Pa. I know my life ain't centered here no more."

Jack shook his head. "Tucker, I've been roaming for seven years, and I'm sick of it. This ranch is home for me now, and I don't plan to leave it. I hope you can learn from my experience without trotting all over the country yourself. Stay around, Tucker. You'll be happier for it."

Tucker walked around the ranch grounds that evening and thought over what Jack had said. He found himself with conflicting impulses, pulling him in all directions.

What Jack said made sense, in a way. He knew that with Pa gone, Ma needed all of her kin close around her, especially Jack and him, who were more mature and understood her needs and feelings better than the others. He didn't want to desert Ma . . . but . . .

His father's words kept playing through his mind. Jack understood some things, but not how Tucker felt about Charity. Jack had been forced from his home and had wandered without real motive or purpose, but for Tucker it was different. He had good reason to want to head north.

But for now, he would stay here. At least until the ranch was going well and Jack had things under control.

The days passed, and Tucker did just what he knew his Pa would have wanted—he worked hard and steady, from dawn until the last light faded. Jack was with him always, working as if he was hungry for the home labor he had missed for seven years.

About dusk exactly five days after the burial of Danver Corrigan, Tucker noticed Jack slipping on his hat and heading for the door. "Where are you going, Jack?"

"Scudder's. I thought a beer would go good."

Tucker sighed. His father's warning about Jack's gambling came back to him. But he knew better than to argue with his brother.

"Hold on a minute," he said, "and I'll come with you."

The pair mounted outside and rode toward Scudder's, the night falling fast. Jack was whistling beneath his breath but saying little. Tucker recognized the symptoms of the old gambling fever.

Scudder's was a bright spot on the side of the road, an isolated structure. There were several horses hitched to the rail out in front of the building, and music from the battered old piano spilled out through the open door and was swallowed up in the night.

They pushed their way into the saloon, getting casual glances at first from the men at the bar and around the tables, then open stares as Jack was recognized. Word of his return had not spread yet, and those who knew him were surprised to see him.

Jack walked up to the bar, ignoring them. He ordered beer for himself and Tucker. Mel Scudder filled two heavy mugs until the foam spilled over the top, then shoved them toward the brothers.

"Good to see you back, Jack," he said. "Didn't expect it after all this time."

"Had to come back when I heard Pa was ailing," Jack said, draining a swallow of beer. "I figure I'll stay awhile."

A man approached the bar, a shot of whiskey in his hand. "Howdy, Jack," he said.

"Hello, Denny. How you been?"

"Fine, mighty fine. How about you? Where you been keeping yourself the past few years?"

"I been doing some punching up about Montana, different spreads," Jack said. "I figured it was time to come home."

Denny raised his shot glass to his lips and drained a small sip of the fiery liquor. "Run into Thurston Russell lately?"

Jack looked at him blankly. "No . . . I ain't seen him since I left."

Tucker looked quickly at Jack, surprised and a bit confused. But suddenly he understood what Jack was trying to do. As far as Jack was concerned, the trouble with Russell was over. Russell had been humiliated in the fight with Jack already, and Jack wasn't about to spread that humiliation any further.

Denny gave a little grunt. "Ain't seen him, huh? I heard a different tale. I hear you and Thurston had quite a ruckus a few days back, up in Montana. Ol' Tater told me about it. Said you worked Thurston over real good."

"It ain't true, Denny. I ain't seen Thurston Russell in seven years." Jack spoke in a dull monotone, casually sipping his beer.

Denny smiled, then shrugged. "Whatever you say, Jack. I guess you'll get a chance to talk about it with Thurston himself before long. He's coming here tonight."

Only Tucker caught the almost imperceptible tensing of Jack's fingers on the handle of his beer mug. His expression and voice remained unchanged.

"That right? It'll be good to see him again."

Denny frowned at that. He hadn't expected such a calm reaction from Jack, and it confused him. He mumbled something and headed back to his table.

"Jack . . . do you think we should hang around here and wait for Russell?" Tucker whispered.

"I can't run. I'm going to be living here now, maybe for the rest of my days. I'll run into Thurston somewhere or other, sooner or later, anyway. Part of the reason I came here tonight was that I figured he would show up. I got to see if this thing is really over, or if he figures on giving me more trouble."

Tucker shook his head. "Well, I don't like to think about what might happen. Russell is a crack shot."

A voice called from the opposite corner of the room. "Got a space for one more in this poker game, Jack. Interested?"

Jack turned around and looked across the room at the speaker. Tucker watched his brother's face, seeing the sudden fever, knowing the temptation that was calling to him.

Tucker could have dropped in his tracks when Jack answered after a lengthy pause, "No . . . I better skip it, Tom. I don't play no more."

Admiration shone in Tucker's eyes as he looked into

his brother's face. Jack looked back at him with a peculiar expression.

"What are you staring at?"

Tucker grinned. "Nothing." He didn't fail to catch the vague smile on Jack's face as he turned back around.

The pair were on their second set of beers when the noise of boots on the floor at the threshold caught their attention. Jack turned slowly to find himself looking straight into the cold, expressionless face of Thurston Russell.

The noise in the saloon stopped. Mel Scudder stepped back a little. A picture of a bloody fight some seven years before was running through the saloon-keeper's mind.

"Howdy, Thurston."

No answer but a cold stare.

"Buy you a beer?"

Russell turned away, walking toward a far table. Every eye in the place was upon him, and he felt it. He cast a violent glance across the men, and heads suddenly dropped back to hands of cards, and liquor glasses were quickly raised to lips.

"Mel, bring me a beer. And I'll pay for it myself," said Russell.

The barkeep hustled quickly, pouring off a beer. He carried it across the room, foam dripping off to splash on wood already stained from years of tobacco juice, muddy boots, spilled drinks, and a little blood.

Russell took the drink and began sipping it slowly, his eyes burning into the back of Jack Corrigan, who had turned his back on the big fellow and returned to sipping his beer.

Denny stood and walked over toward Russell. Speaking in a voice that all could hear, he said, "Thurston, is that a bruise I see on your jaw?"

The burly red-haired man glared up sharply at the smiling Denny. "So it is. What is it to you?"

Denny put forth a hand, palm outward, in a gesture

of mock conciliation. "Hey now, take it easy there, Thurston. No point in being snappy. I was just asking. How did you get that bruise there anyway?"

Russell's features were stony. "Ain't none of your business, Denny."

"Why, Thurston, you got no manners at all tonight! You didn't even say hello to your old friend Jack over there, and him being gone for seven years! But maybe you got good reason to not say hello."

"What's that supposed to mean?"

"Well, I heard that you two run into each other not long ago and said your hellos then. Thurston, how did you say you got that bruise?"

Russell stood, eyeball to eyeball with Denny, who stepped back a couple of feet to keep safe distance.

"Denny, you'd best shut up or I'll have to do something about it. You understand me?"

Denny spread his arms out in a gesture of innocence. "Why, Thurston, I was only trying to be nice . . ."

Russell's arm flashed out. Jack turned around in time to see Denny hit the floor, rubbing an injured jaw. Russell towered over the fallen man, looking as if he could easily squash him out with his boot like an insect.

Denny looked scared now, but also angry. He stood, backing away from Thurston Russell. Glaring, he pointed a finger at the big man's face.

"Are you afraid I'll say what everybody knows already—about how you took off after Tucker here so you could find Jack, and how when you did find him, he whipped you so good that you came crawling home? Is that what you're afraid of?"

Jack grabbed Denny's shoulder and wheeled him around. "Listen, Denny, I told you that I ain't seen Thurston Russell in seven years. Me and Thurston, we got no trouble. We're friends now. Ain't that right, Thurston?"

Russell looked confused. He stammered, unable to

gather his thoughts, then said, "Yeah . . . that's right. Friends."

Denny frowned. "But I thought . . ."

"You ought to quit thinking then, Denny," said Jack. "It puts a strain on your mind."

Abashed, Denny returned to his seat, where he glanced up occasionally at Jack, muttering something to the men around him. Jack noticed but was unconcerned. Denny wasn't worth getting upset over.

Tucker felt an admiration for his brother that he had never felt before. Jack had become almost a new person, a matured, seasoned version of the boy he used to be, with the rough edges worn off. Pa would have been proud of his eldest son.

When the brothers left Scudder's a few hours later, they found Thurston Russell outside, waiting for them. Jack walked up to the man, unafraid, making no move to threaten him.

"I . . . I 'preciate what you done in there," Russell said, his head lowered and his voice hesitant. "You're a good man, Jack Corrigan."

He turned, mounted his horse, and rode away without looking back.

Chapter 20

Jack and Tucker never again saw Thurston Russell after that. Rumors abounded about where the man had gone, but no one knew for sure.

The days passed, and the business of everyday life on the ranch began to overshadow the sorrow the family felt at the loss of Danver Corrigan. Increasingly, Tucker felt the call of the northern plains.

Summer came on full and strong, and the cattle grew fat on the plains, eating the rich green grass. Tucker and Jack spent much time there keeping an eye on their cattle, especially the expectant ones.

Tucker knew he would not be around long. Though Jack still encouraged him to stay, the ache to move on was becoming increasingly stronger, and at night he would toss restlessly and dream of travel.

Ma did well, getting on without Pa, though he knew she could daily feel the pain of his absence. It was Ma more than anything else who made him hesitate about leaving, for he didn't want to add to her loneliness. She had the rest of the family around her, and having Jack home was a delight to her, but still . . .

Tucker knew he could never replace his father, and it was pointless to try. No matter how close he stuck to Ma, he could never be what Danver Corrigan was to her. And she didn't expect him to be.

And still the words his father had said to him on the night he died went running through his mind, urging him northward.

Charity grasped one end of the log and heaved it

upward, biting her lip as she strained beneath the weight. But Buck Treadway was beside her, pushing along with her, and together they managed to hoist the log upward to where Frank and Duke could roll it into place on the rapidly growing wall. After the burden was taken from her, she whistled in relief and wiped the beads of sweat from her brow.

"Heavy, ain't it, Charity?" puffed Treadway, also sweating profusely. "Keep this up and you'll be muscled like a man."

"I hope not," she said. "I'd sure hate to look like you."

Treadway laughed and walked away.

Since they had started rebuilding the ranch house, Charity had had little time to think of anything other than hard work. But nothing was able to squeeze out of her mind the thoughts of Tucker Corrigan or the desire that he would return as he had promised.

It was funny, in a way. Just as she had realized that Tucker was much more than just another stranger whose path had crossed hers, he was taken from her. And now it seemed that she spent half of her time glancing toward the southern horizon, hoping to see him approaching.

Frank and Duke were aware of Charity's feelings. Duke approved of his daughter's interest, for Tucker had proven himself a worthy and brave man.

Duke spent many long hours mulling over the departed Dan Granger, asking aloud on many occasions if anyone had any idea why he had chosen to antagonize him so. Charity never spoke up, and she never would.

When Seth Bailey in his dying breath told her about the night he found Granger molesting her ma, it shook her to her soul, and she understood why Ma had never said anything about it. It must have been a heavy burden on the victimized lady.

Charity knew she had been right about Dan Granger. It was inconceivable to her how Granger could have lived in the way he did, locked away from humanity, his only dealings with women apparently being the violent type in which he had sought to involve her mother.

Granger was buried on the grounds of his ranch. His estate was in confusion, for he had no heirs and no living relatives anyone knew about. Many ranchers were helping themselves to any Granger cattle they ran across on the plains.

The house the Bryans were building was on the same site as the old one, but it was larger and better. Duke was in no danger because of the phony accusation of rustling or the jailbreak; the sheriff was alone now, not backed up by Granger, and he wouldn't make a move against him.

Duke had seemed ten years younger ever since he started work on the new house, and in spite of the backbreaking labor he had retained enough energy at the end of most days to make an evening trip into town for some relaxation with his friends at one of the local saloons.

The house was completed before the coming of summer. Charity was given the task of helping restock the house. Duke had included an honest-to-goodness kitchen in the new house, which excited Charity. Before, it had been only a cast-iron stove and a shelf; now she had several cabinets with swinging doors, a heavy wooden table . . . but the same old stove, which Duke had managed to salvage from the burned-out remnant of the old house.

Duke found his daughter sitting alone about dusk in early August, her skirt spread around her, her hands fingering a soft blade of grass. He approached her and sat down beside her.

"You kind of like that boy, don't you, Charity?"

She smiled, rather sadly.

Duke eased himself down into the grass, slipping his arm over his daughter's shoulder. "He's a good boy, Charity. He'll be back."

Charity looked at her father. "Will he, Pa? It's been months, and I haven't seen him. He's forgotten me, Pa."

Duke hugged his daughter close, looking westward to where the sun sent out final dying rays. In that fading light Duke took in all the land at a glance, sweeping his gaze all across the remote distance of the horizon. The face of his wife came to mind, generating the strange mixture of love, joy, and torment that her memory always brought.

Duke watched night fall like mist on the land. As the sun winked out in the west, he smiled vaguely.

"Charity."

"Yes, Pa?"

Duke stood, the mysterious smile on his face breaking into a full grin. He was gazing southward.

"Pa?"

"Hush, child—go back to the house and fix yourself up. And throw on a pot of beans. Tucker's been riding a long way, I expect, and likely he'll be hungry!"

HERE'S A LOOK AT
THE GLORY RIVER—
BOOK ONE IN CAMERON
JUDD'S
EXCITING NEW *UNDERHILL*
***SERIES*!**

Just outside Coldwater, near the Muscle Shoals of the Tennessee River, Spring 1787

"Move carefully and slowly, Skiuga," the gray-haired Cherokee, speaking in his native tongue, said to the boy at his side. "Many a man has been laughed at for falling into a stream like a clumsy bear, simply because he didn't take the time to be careful on rocks that are slick and wet."

"I've never fallen into the water, Tuckaseh," the young one bragged. "And see those rocks across the water? I've run over them many times, from one bank to the other, and never even wet my feet."

The man looked in the direction the boy pointed, and nodded, but the boy was unsure whether Tuckaseh really saw the rocks he had indicated. The aging man's eyes were growing glassy with the years, clouding over, and vision that had once been keen was now fast dimming into a kind of perpetual twilight. Yet Tuckaseh was so confident in his movements, so adept at the skills of life in the forest and on the river, that the boy often forgot the man's creeping blindness until such moments as this.

"If you've run those rocks, then you are certainly fortunate, just as you are certainly headed for a broken bone or two, and laughter from your friends. Now, go down to the bank, Skiuga, and see how we have done for fish."

The boy's light, thin frame danced lithely down to the riverside. He knelt and reached into the water, pulling up a kind of loosely woven reed basket held beneath the surface by the weight of rocks. The cleverly designed contraption, made by Tuckaseh, was enclosed and rounded at one end, open at the other. But the reeds at the opening were not cut off and bound down as on a normal basket; instead they were left long, sharpened, and curved back into the interior of the basket, which was in fact a fish trap. Fish could easily swim into the basket through the mouth, but once inside, could not easily find their way out again past the sharp reeds they found pointing at them and trapping them inside.

"Eight fish!" the boy called up to the man. "Eight fat ones!"

Tuckaseh smiled and nodded. "Very good. A good trap we've made there."

The boy, bearing the trap with the fish flopping inside it, returned to his companion. "We didn't make it. *You* made it."

"That is true. So you'll make the next one. And why not do it now? You should be well prepared for it. You watched me closely as I put this one together?"

"I did." Just now the boy was wishing he'd watched a little more closely than he had. Tuckaseh's deft fingers moved fast when he made his baskets and traps, skills that he'd practiced increasingly since his vision began to fade some years ago. It was hard even to trace, much less recall, the movements of those swift fingers when Tuckaseh was working at full speed.

Tuckaseh, it was said by some, had never been a great warrior. He'd been a peace chief in earlier days, never a war chief. He'd fought many battles, nonetheless, and had done many a brave act and earned war titles, but he'd never seemed to glory much in them. It was in more peaceful and gentle pursuits that Tuckaseh revealed his true and deeper self, the version of the man that young Bushrod Underhill—whom Tuckaseh and most of the Indians of Coldwater called Skiuga, or "ground squirrel"—had come to cherish and admire.

"I don't see why I should make another fish trap when this one is still in good condition," Bushrod said. "Besides," he added, bluffing, "making fish traps is easy. I can do it when need be without taking time out for it now."

"When I was your age," Tuckaseh said, "my mother's brother told me it was time I learned to chip arrow flints. I watched him do it many times, thought it looked easy. But when I sat down to try, I could do nothing right. So he made me do it again and again and again until at last I could do more than break worthless pieces of flint into smaller worthless pieces of flint.''

Bushrod nodded, knowing that an afternoon of fish trap manufacturing lay in his immediate future.

But a shout from the edge of the nearby village changed that. ''Bushrod! Bush!''

It was Freneau, yelling for him. Bush glanced at the sun and realized he was late again for Freneau's daily schooling, which he usually called, rather formally, *L'Instruction.* Bush learned much from Freneau's tutoring, but the time was always much more like work and less like pleasure than the time he spent with Tuckaseh.

One good thing, though: Freneau never scolded him for his lateness when Tuckaseh was responsible for it. Freneau admired Tuckaseh, spoke often of the man's insight, his *sagesse,* and considered the time Bush spent with him almost as much a part of Bush's *instruction* as his own daily contribution.

''I must go,'' Bush said to Tuckaseh, glad for once to be called away. He was in no humor to make fish traps this afternoon.

''Go,'' Tuckaseh said. ''I'll see to these fish, and when you are done with your white-man's learning, you may replace the trap.''

Bush darted away toward the town. It was a beautiful day, one best spent out of doors, and for a moment he considered asking his adoptive father and tutor if they might take their lessons outside. But he wouldn't. He'd asked before, and Freneau's answer was always the same: A young man learns best when there are no distractions about him. And they would stay indoors.

Bush liked Tuckaseh's way of teaching better. Instead of hiding from ''distractions,'' Tuckaseh used them as the tools and even the objects of his teaching. The woods, the streams, the rivers, the barren mountaintop knobs—these were Tuckaseh's classroom. And what he taught seemed to Bush to have far more value than the English and French and mathematics and history that Freneau forced upon him. Certainly it was much more fun.

But Freneau's schooling, useless as it seemed to Bush, was not optional. The Frenchman had immersed Bush in his academics virtually from the moment he'd found Bush and his sister six years before. There was no sign yet that *L'Instruction* was anywhere close to ending.

Except for the tiny, dark-haired, white-skinned girl riding his shoulders, the singing man looked like any of the Cherokee or Creek warriors who populated this town. He wore moccasins, leather leggins reaching halfway up his thighs, a breechclout that covered his buttocks and groin but left the sides of his hips exposed. A long linen shirt covered what the breechclout did not, and a woolen, silver-trimmed headband held long dark hair back and away from his clean-shaven face. Only his relatively light skin and the boisterous French drinking song he belted out in an off-key voice identified him as a Frenchman rather than an Indian. This was Michel Freneau, brother of Jean-Yves and a long-time trader among the Indians of the region, and at the moment he was hungry and heading for food, carrying with him the petite Marie Underhill, now about six years old.

His spirits were high—the usual state for Michel Freneau. Unlike his older brother, who had been a serious scholar in younger days and tended to be somber about most of life, Michel had never taken much anything seriously, and was certainly no scholar. His impression of scholars had been shaped by his observances of Jean-Yves and his academic peers in a life long past for both of them: Scholars were a breed of men who didn't laugh as readily as a man should. Michel Freneau would have none of that. He loved laughter far too much. Just as he loved little Marie, who in his mind was his niece.

Michel greeted those he passed in the village, drawing smiles and kind words from the women, who idolized him, and notably less enthusiastic responses from the men. But if the warriors and fighting men of Coldwater didn't consider Michel Freneau a friend, all did trust him. He had been a trader among them for many years and had never cheated anyone, nor betrayed the interests of any Indian to a white man. Michel Freneau, Frenchman, was several cuts above the dishonest English traders many of the Cherokees of Coldwater had been forced to endure back in the Overhill towns farther east.

Finishing his song with a loud crescendo warbling with clumsy vibrato, and giving Marie a shake that made her laugh and dig her fingers into his thick hair, Michel let his nose lead him off the main pathway through Coldwater and ducked into the open door of a particular cabin.

"Ah, Jean!" he said in French, blinking in the darker interior and deftly setting Marie to her feet on the floor. "What is this delicious food I've been smelling all the way across town?" Not awaiting an answer, he made for the fire, where a turkey roasted on a spit, sizzling and sending out a wonderful odor. Michel turned the bird until he found a portion that was substantially cooked, and began picking off strips of hot, roasted meat, cramming them into his mouth at great risk of a burned tongue.

Jean-Yves, seated cross-legged on the dirt floor beside Bushrod, lifted his eyes from the homemade slate he held, and looked at his brother with mild displeasure. "Please," he said in French, with heavy sarcasm, "feel free to help yourself to our supper, Michel."

"Ah, thank you, Jean. You are indeed kind." He put another hunk of turkey into his mouth, wincing at the heat.

Jean-Yves glanced woefully at the boy at his side. "Intemperate," he said in English. "Always intemperate. It will be the death of him someday."

"I don't know what it means, 'intemperate,' " the boy said, also in English, concentrating on every word. He spoke French and Cherokee with ease, but English, though the language of his earliest days, had begun to slip away from him after he came to Coldwater. So Jean-Yves, ever the scholar and teacher, had taken on the task some months ago of bringing Bushrod back to his original language.

"It means, Bushrod, that my brother doesn't know how to

control his own passions. He eats too much, drinks too much, romances too much—''

Michel, who spoke English even more haltingly than little Bushrod, frowned as he tried to interpret what his brother was saying about him. ''No, no, Bushrod,'' he said in French. ''It means that unlike dear Jean, I believe life is not a mystery, not a challenge, not a thing to be taken apart and studied like some pretty toy. No, life is an *adventure*! If there is food, eat it! If there is liquor, drink it deep! If there are women . . . well, someday, when you're not so young, then we'll talk about that, eh?''

''You are interrupting us, Michel,'' Jean-Yves said. ''Why is it that you do that each time we sit down for our lessons?''

''Lessons! Bah! It's foolishness! What need does the boy have of your lessons?'' Michel peeled off more meat and ate it.

Jean-Yves sighed and surrendered. ''Bushrod, you may go. We've done enough for today, I believe . . . and all we'll be allowed to do, in any case, now that Michel has come.''

Bushrod didn't have to be told twice. He bounded to his feet and raced out the door, embracing the gift of freedom with enthusiasm, wondering where Tuckaseh might have gone.

Michel licked his fingers clean, walked over to his brother, and squatted near him. He nodded toward the slate. ''Why do you teach the boy English, Jean? What need does the boy have of it?''

''He comes from English-speaking stock. He should know his native tongue. It is his heritage.''

''Heritage? His heritage is *here*, Jean. And what do you care of heritage, anyway, you, who turned your back on your own years ago?''

''I've turned my back on nothing . . . merely added to what I was born with. A man can choose to embrace new ways of life without forsaking his heritage, can he not? I was born a Frenchman and will die a Frenchman.''

''Nonsense! We are more Indian than French, you and I. And that boy is more Indian than we are. Life among the

Creek and Cherokee is all he has known from the day you brought him here.''

''No. He's known far more than that, thanks to my teaching. He knows about the world around us, the world we came from, which he may never see. And he knows about the world of the white men, the settlers, where he himself came from and to which he will one day return.''

''Why should he return? I for one never will. I enjoy the life I lead here.''

''He'll return because this life will not last. Oh, for you and me, maybe it will, because we have fewer years ahead of us. But it will not last for one so young as Bushrod. He'll remain long after Coldwater and towns like it, and the Indian people, are gone far away and forgotten.''

''So I have heard you say too many times. Why do you think this way? Why are you such a fatalist?''

Jean-Yves quirked one brow. ''Fatalist! I'm surprised you even know so deep a word, brother. I congratulate you! I am a fatalist because *they*—,'' he thumbed northward,''—have superior numbers, an endless supply of themselves ready to spill over the mountains and fill the wilderness and drive the Indians away. I am a fatalist because *they* were exploding gunpowder and fighting wars with rifles while the Indians knew of no greater weapons than blowguns and arrows and spears. Because *they* are more prone than the Indians to make unions and fight together, rather than among each other. Because *they* are not so burdened with superstition that they starve themselves before battle, or turn back from a fight they would have won because some supposed 'sign' presents itself. And most of all, I am a fatalist because I know how badly *they* need this land. It is their hope and chance, the difference between poverty and success. They will fight until it is their own. The Indians may struggle and die with honor and glory . . . but they will be swept away with history, and you and I with them, I do not doubt. But I won't see Bushrod and Marie swept away. I want them prepared to live in the world as it will be.''

Michel shook his head disgustedly. ''I have no intention of being swept away by history or anything else. I believe in survival. If you are so enamored of the *gitlu-ale-tsaqwali*, and see such great victories coming to their people, why don't you go live among them? Add yet another heritage to your list!'' *Gitlu-ale-tsaqwali*. "Hair and horses." It was a common way in Coldwater to refer to the Cumberland settlements to the north, frequent targets for bands raiding out of the hidden town, bands that almost always returned with fresh horses and fresh scalps.

"I am where I want to be," Jean-Yves said. "I have no desire to leave here. But Bushrod, I believe, will someday do so."

Michel stood, looking down his handsome nose at his older brother. "Jean, I do fear for you. You claim to be wise, a man of reason, and yet you believe only foolish things. The whites to the north will not prevail. Don't you realize they don't even know this town exists? The raiders that strike them are like phantoms in their eyes, coming from nowhere, vanishing like fog to the south."

"It won't be that way forever, Michel. It can't be. They will find us one day, and they will come."

"By that time the town will have moved elsewhere."

"How can you be so sure? Do you really believe this life of ours will go on unchanged forever?"

Michel glowered at him and turned, silent. He went to the fire and tore off another strip of turkey meat. He glanced down and smiled at Marie, who had been listening to the conversation but understanding none of it. An infant when her parents died, she knew no English at all but the smattering that Jean-Yves was beginning to teach her.

Chewing on the turkey, Michel left the cabin. A few moments later, Jean-Yves heard Michel's voice ring out again. Another noisy, jolly song, another celebration of his seeming eternal optimism and good spirits. Jean-Yves envied him. It must be grand to be so confident that all the good in life would remain as it was, like a spring that never ran dry.

He looked down at the slate and the word he had been teaching to Bushrod when Michel had come in. He chuckled at the irony.

The word was "destruction."

Bushrod was outside town, setting rabbit snares with Tuckaseh, the day two Chickasaw hunters came into Coldwater. They found the town purely by accident while ranging along the river. When Bushrod and Tuckaseh came back from the woods, they found the predominately Cherokee population of Coldwater welcoming the two roamers, feeding them, telling them with satisfaction of the many raids their warriors had launched against the Cumberland settlements. The Chickasaws listened with remarkable interest, and Tuckaseh, Bush noticed, looked on with obvious displeasure.

"It's unwise to trust a Chickasaw," he said to Bush when the latter inquired about his grim manner. "There will be trouble because of this, Skiuga. The Chickasaw are too closely aligned with the *unakas*. There will destruction to come of this."

"Destruction? Why do you say such a thing as that?" Bush couldn't see anything in the friendly scene with the Chickasaws that suggested anything so extreme.

But Tuckaseh had no more to say at the moment. After watching the Chickasaws leave, bearing gifts, he turned away, a dark expression on his face, and spat on the ground.

Minor as the incident with Tuckaseh seemed, Bush couldn't shake from his mind a sense of deep and impending doom that had settled over him in its wake.

For days, Bush shunned his typical habits of roaming, hunting, and horseplay with the other boys of Coldwater. He shunned even Tuckaseh, and was atypically silent during his daily round of schooling under Freneau. He stayed close to Marie. Protecting her, he thought. Yet her nearness also served to comfort him. She was all that remained of his true family. The only other person in the world, as far as he knew, through whose veins flowed the same blood that flowed in his own.

A few days after the visit of the Chickasaws, Waninahi, who sat beneath the shade of a maple, chewing leather to soften it, watched her adopted son lingering near his sister, and pondered the pair. Though the sun had tanned both of the young ones to a deep nut brown, and both dressed like any Indian children in the town (Marie was young enough yet that she often didn't dress at all when the weather was warm) the *unaka* heritage of both remained as evident as the indelible birthmark on the neck of Marie.

Waninahi was unaccustomed to seeing Bushrod in such an obvious state of worry, and wondered what was wrong with him. Something Tuckaseh said, probably. She knew Tuckaseh to be a wise man, but Bush listened too closely to him sometimes. Waninahi remembered well a time, from the old Overhill Town days, when Tuckaseh, interpreting one of his own dreams, had predicted a storm that would destroy the town with lightning. Several families believed him and took to the woods. When the night of the predicted storm passed with nothing more than a mild, dry wind, the believers came slinking back to town, unwilling to talk, and ready to send Tuckaseh across the mountains for good. For months he was bitterly called ''The Prophet'' behind his back, sometimes to his face. The incident sparked a decline of Tuckaseh's influence among the people. He never fully recovered it.

Waninahi chewed the leather, ignoring the unpleasant taste, evaluating its changing texture with her tongue. It was softening nicely.

Tuckaseh. Yes, she decided, Bush's somber manner was almost certainly the old man's fault. Tuckaseh had always been prone to see the worst of things. Perhaps such an attitude was natural in a man who was slowly losing his vision, and who had long ago lost his prestige, and his wife. Tuckaseh was a declining man living in the house of his unloving daughter. He had reason to be a pessimist, Waninahi decided.

But he didn't have a right to force his dark attitude on a growing young man such as Bushrod. Nor, for that matter, did Jean-Yves, whose attitude lately was as bad as Tuckaseh's, maybe worse. Lately Jean-Yves talked to her by night of coming decline and the end of the life they knew. She was sure he said the same to Bush during their daily tutorials. Thus Bushrod, so deeply under the sway of both Tuckaseh and his adoptive father, was being bombarded with foreboding from two sides. No wonder he was glum!

Waninahi chewed harder on the leather, beginning to feel angry. She would not have Bushrod made unhappy without good cause. He was her son, as much as if he had been born of her own loins. She had not been gifted with children of her own flesh.

Not yet, anyway. She touched her belly, wondering . . . almost sure. There were signs, feelings. She would know soon.

She wondered how Jean-Yves would react when he learned that he was to be a father. Perhaps the news would cure him of some of his pessimism.

She hoped so. No mother desired to bring a child into a world that was unhappy and grim. If there really was a child in her womb, she wanted it to live in a way that was bright as sunshine, happy, and destined to go on for a long, long time.

Bushrod squatted in the middle of his uncle's trade house at the edge of Coldwater, surrounded by the goods by which Michel Freneau made his living: knives, tomahawks, guns, ammunition, blankets, beads, paints, sugar, coffee, clothing, casks of rum. Marie was somewhere amid the clutter, off in a corner, playing. She was here more frequently than was Bush; Marie had won the heart of Michel from the moment he first saw her as an infant, and he spent at least as much time with her, maybe more, as did Jean-Yves.

"So it's fear of destruction that has you so glum, is it?"

Michel was saying to Bush. "You've been listening to Jean-Yves, I take it."

"Mostly to Tuckaseh."

"Tuckaseh! Hah! 'The Prophet.' Don't give him heed, Bush. He's an old, blind fool. I know you admire him, but truth is truth."

"Tuckaseh says a mistake was made when the Chickasaws were welcomed. He says they are friends with the *unakas*, and that they'll bring destruction to us."

"He's like Jean-Yves, full of fear and pessimism. I have no love of the Chickasaws, but there will be no trouble."

Bush played with a round stone he'd found, rolling it about like a marble, and said nothing. Marie was singing quietly to herself, an old children's song taught to her by Waninahi. *"Ua'nu une'guhi' tsana'seha'; E'ti une'guhi' tsana'seha' . . ."* Her voice was high but pleasant.

Bush asked, "Why are you so different than my father, Michel?"

Before he answered, Michel paused to fill a clay pipe and light it from a twig taken from the small fire that burned in the center of the cabin, the smoke pouring out a hole in the roof.

"Jean is an unusual man, Bushrod. He spent his earliest years filling his mind with knowledge, then fell in love with a woman who died the day before they were to be married. Me, I had problems of my own at the time, with the law, and we joined together, fled our troubles and sorrows and found a new life in this wilderness, me as a trader, Jean as . . . well, just what Jean is. A man of the woods. A content man, especially after he found Waninahi. But you know all that already, eh? What I am saying to you here, Bushrod, is that your father is maybe too much a thinker for his own good. He has too much learning, I think. Too much thinking draws lines on a man's brow, and makes him full of darkness and dread. One can study life so deeply that he forgets that life was made to be lived, not picked to pieces. I think maybe that Tuckaseh is much like Jean-Yves, in his own way. What do you think?"

"Well . . . I think that Tuckaseh is very wise. And so is my father."

"Then you, too, will have some deep wrinkles on your brow, my young friend. Don't think too much or too hard, Bush. Better to be like me, eh? Happy, full of joy all the time!" He playfully punched at Bushrod's shoulder, trying to cheer him. "That's what life is for, the pleasure of it."

"Tuckaseh says that life is greater than pleasure. Father says the same."

"And who is happier, those two, or me? Hmm? Forget all this worrying, Bush. It's inappropriate in one so young."

Several days later

The army of frontiersmen moved with remarkable swiftness, considering the winding, twisting route they were obliged to follow. They traveled by the mouth of the Little Harpeth River, along Turnbull's Creek and Lick Creek, on to Swan Creek and to Blue Water Creek, whose course led directly to the Tennessee River at a place nearly opposite to Coldwater.

Boats that were supposed to meet the marchers near the Muscle Shoals, to ferry them and their supplies across, failed to arrive. A leather boat was quickly made, and little by little, as a driving rain set in, the goods and men were shipped across a few at a time. Drenched by the rain, the soldiers took refuge in abandoned Indian cabins south of the river, building fires and drying their clothes and footwear, eating from their supply packs.

Scouts, meanwhile, forged ahead, deeper into the dark land, keeping an eye out for any Indians who might see their advance. When the throng was dried out and fed, the march began again along a six-mile-long path.

The army at length divided, one division heading for the mouth of Coldwater Creek. The rest advanced farther until cornfields appeared. There they paused, checking and rechecking weapons.

Coldwater was just ahead, beyond the corn and across the

creek. Open, unprepared, and utterly unaware of what was about to come.

Bushrod, visiting his uncle again in the trade house, was asleep amid the clutter when the attack came.

Howling frontiersmen charged across the creek and into the very town itself. Sitting up, Bushrod blinked in confusion and looked around for his uncle.

"Michel?" No reply. He stood. "Michel? What is happening?" But Michel was not there.

Shots popped outside; there were yells, the sound of children crying, women screaming, men running.

Hot panic gripped Bushrod. Inside the trade house, he could see nothing but unidentifiable flashes of movement through the doorway. Michel was nowhere around, and no one else was in the trade house.

Bushrod stood still as a tree, scared and confused. Should he hide somewhere among the trade goods? Should he slip out and run? He looked around for an escape route other than the single front door, though he well knew this cabin had no windows. He was terrified by the idea of leaving here, going out into that hellish uproar outside.

Where was Michel? Where was his father? His mother . . . and Marie? *Where was Marie?*

A rifle fired just outside the door; someone screamed in pain. Bushrod dived behind a stack of blankets.

A shadow moved in the room; someone had stuck his head in the door. Bushrod heard words half-shouted in English, something about damned French traders. Bushrod hugged the floor, fearing that the man would come in and find him, then surely kill him. But a moment later he realized that the man hadn't come in at all.

They'll burn this house, he thought. He'd heard about how white men would burn Indian towns, burn every building to the ground and leave the residents homeless. *Maybe he's setting fire to the logs right now! Maybe he's already set them afire!*

Bushrod rose slowly, looking over the heap of blankets. The

door was open. Figures in buckskin and linsey-woolsey moved and fired, and swore, and fired some more in the heart of the town. Bushrod ducked again, huddling, hiding.

I can't hide here forever. They'll come back because of all that's in here. Things they'll want. I must run.

He came to his feet and lunged for the door. He paused a moment in the doorway, then ducked out to the right, heading for his house.

Through the roiling smoke he caught a glimpse of Marie, being carried along beneath someone's arm. Panic hit again. She'd been captured! Then he saw that it was Waninahi who carried Marie. She ran with her around the back of a flaming cabin. Three or four of the raiders circled around after them, the smoke closed in, and Bush could see them no more.

Bushrod saw flames leaping, people running everywhere. The shooting would not stop, and he wondered how there could be so much gunfire from weapons that required painstaking reloading after every shot. He ran in the direction he'd seen Waninahi go with Marie.

He came into view of his own house and halted, gaping.

His house was ablaze. Thoroughly engulfed with fire.

Father!

He ran on, toward the house, having no notion of what he would do when he got there. For all he knew he would run into the very flames themselves.

Something clipped him powerfully on the side of the head and he went to the ground, smacking hard, taking the slam painfully. Suddenly he needed to cry, to sob, but there was no air in his lungs for it and he couldn't manage to pull any in. His ability to breathe had vanished.

He came to his feet again and ran hard toward the house. Ran without breathing, trying with excruciating and futile strain to suck in air. His head began to spin . . .

Suddenly, his breath returned. His lungs, emptied and stunned into paralysis by his fall to the ground, had begun working again, all at once.

He neared the flaming house. The heat seared, feeling as if it might peel the skin off his face.

"Father!" he shouted. "Father! Where are you?"

Someone grabbed him from behind and pulled him into the air. He knew even without looking that it was Michel, come from some hiding place to rescue him and pull him to safety.

He twisted his head to look.

It wasn't Michel. It was a stranger, clad in a fringed rifleman's coat. Red hair. A grinning, freckled, young face.

"Gotcha, injun! Gotcha!"

"No!" Bushrod shouted in Cherokee. "No! Let me go!" Then he realized that this man probably understood none of it. He would speak English, not Cherokee.

Long and dull hours spent at his father's side, crouched over a slate, came back. He sought the right words.

"No . . . let me go . . . please . . . I must find . . . must find my father . . ."

"Hellfire and damnation!" the young frontiersman bellowed, almost dropping him. "You're *white*!"

"I am the son . . . of Jean-Yves Freneau."

The frontiersman reasserted his grip around Bushrod's thin waist, and chortled. "Got me a white one!" he yelled to anyone who could hear. "Got me a white injun boy, son of a Frenchy! *Waaugh*!"

Bushrod struggled but could not break free. The frontiersman, still laughing—Bushrod could only wonder why—ran with him, jolting him along so hard his ribs threatened to break against the frontiersman's bony shoulder. Bushrod's stomach felt like it was trying to crawl out of his mouth.

"Bushrod!"

The boy heard the call as if from a great distance, but when he looked, Jean-Yves was not far away. He was filthy, bleeding, and some of his clothing looked like it had been burned off, and maybe some of his flesh, too.

"Father!"

"Bushrod, I—"

Whatever Jean-Yves would have said, Bushrod never knew. The young frontiersman who carried him threw him hard to the ground. He landed on his face. Rolling over, tasting blood that spewed out his nose and over his mouth, he saw the red-haired man raising his flintlock rifle. Jean-Yves wasn't moving. Just standing, mouth moving with words that Bushrod couldn't make out, one hand extended imploringly.

The shot was louder than anything Bushrod had ever heard. He screamed and spasmed at the sound of it, then screamed again as he saw his father fall, face now a mass of blood, the extended hand falling limply to the side as he collapsed.

''No!'' Bushrod screamed. ''Father!''

''Shut up, damn you!'' the rifleman bellowed. Bushrod saw the butt of the rifle swing down and toward him. He tried to dodge it but couldn't move. It smashed hard against the side of his head, knocking another scream from him, driving him into a darkness, deep as a cavern, where there was only silence and all awareness faded to nothing.

**DON'T MISS *THE GLORY RIVER*
FROM CAMERON JUDD AND
ST. MARTIN'S PAPERBACKS!**

Coming soon...
Don't miss the next two-in-one edition
from bestselling author
CAMERON JUDD

TIMBER CREEK

RENEGADE LAWMEN

ISBN: 0-312-94556-6

Available in September 2008 from
St. Martin's Paperbacks

"The next one I put through your skull," Patterson said. "Give it up. Come up here with me and I'll take you back to Snow Sky."

Lybrand shook his head. "I can't go back. I'll never go back. There's too much against me there."

"You have the same right to a fair trial that any man's got. Come on . . . Don't make me kill you."

"I can't go back . . . can't . . ." Lybrand wobbled on his feet. Even from yards away he looked increasingly weak. He sank to his haunches, then sat on a rock.

Patterson said, "Scoot that rifle away. You're too close to it."

Lybrand slowly reached for the rifle—then suddenly it was in his hands, being levered. Lybrand came up, dodging to the side as Patterson fired. Lybrand fired next . . .

St. Martin's Paperbacks Titles by Cameron Judd

FIREFALL

BRAZOS

DEAD MAN'S GOLD

DEVIL WIRE

THE GLORY RIVER

TEXAS FREEDOM

SNOW SKY

CORRIGAN

TIMBER CREEK

RENEGADE LAWMEN

THE HANGING AT LEADVILLE

SNOW SKY

CAMERON JUDD

St. Martin's Paperbacks

NOTE: If you purchased this book without a cover you should be aware that this book is stolen property. It was reported as "unsold and destroyed" to the publisher, and neither the author nor the publisher has received any payment for this "stripped book."

SNOW SKY / CORRIGAN

Snow Sky copyright © 1990 by Cameron Judd.
Excerpt from *Renegade Lawmen* copyright © 2008 by Cameron Judd.
Excerpt from *Timber Creek* copyright © 1989 by Cameron Judd.
Corrigan copyright © 1980, 1989 by Cameron Judd.
Excerpt from *The Glory River* copyright © 1998 by Cameron Judd.

All rights reserved.

For information address St. Martin's Press, 175 Fifth Avenue, New York, NY 10010.

ISBN: 0-312-94555-8
EAN: 978-0-312-94555-8

Printed in the United States of America

Snow Sky Bantam edition / November 1990
St. Martin's Paperbacks edition / July 1998

Corrigan Bantam edition / August 1989
St. Martin's Paperbacks edition / September 1998

St. Martin's Paperbacks are published by St. Martin's Press, 175 Fifth Avenue, New York, NY 10010.

10 9 8 7 6 5 4 3 2 1

THIS BOOK IS DEDICATED WITH GRATITUDE TO
GREG TOBIN.

A NOTE FROM THE AUTHOR

Some years ago a university professor I much admire expressed the opinion that tales of the frontier are to America what the Arthurian legends are to Britain. I agree. The frontier was not only America's proving ground, but also, in large measure, the forge upon which our national identity was hammered out.

Though the frontier as we once knew it is substantially gone, its memories and images remain in our literature, movies, and television, and are thoroughly American in a way little else is. Go almost anywhere on the globe and display a picture of a fur-hatted frontiersman, a trail-dusted cowboy, or a war-bonneted Sioux warrior, and you will find few who do not immediately recognize those images as distinctly and exclusively American.

Early in my typical small-town, 1960s childhood in Cookeville, Tennessee, I became entranced with tales of the American frontier in all their incarnations: books, comics, television, movies. In those years I never knew I would be privileged to someday personally join the tradition of frontier storytelling. The trail was blazed by James Fenimore Cooper and followed, in various ways, by writers as marvelously diverse as Buntline, Grey, Schaefer, L'Amour, Kelton, and McMurtry. I'm glad to have been given the chance to tread my own route as best I can along that well-worn but ever-fresh pathway.

I could not have chosen a more honorable and meritorious literary tradition. Frontier tales, whether traditional westerns or works of historical fiction, are in the last count the signature stories of the American people, for every person on American soil stands at a place that once was the "untamed frontier," or the "Wild West."

I live today in the northeastern portion of Tennessee, in the home county of both Davy Crockett and President Andrew Johnson. My writing, now a full-time career, is expanding to include not only the 19th-century West of the vast trans-Mississippi regions, but also my home region in its own frontier period the century before.

Sharing and brightening my life is my wife, Rhonda, who became my bride in 1980 in the shadow of the original gateway to the West, Cumberland Gap, and who remains my greatest supporter and best friend. In the meantime, our three children, Matt, Laura, and Katy, keep our homefront frontier appropriately wild and woolly.

Cameron Judd
Greene County, Tennessee

CHAPTER 1

FOR THE THIRD NIGHT IN A ROW, THE MAN forced the boy up the mountain trail. The higher they climbed, the louder pealed the thunder and the harder fell the rain, driving down in bullets and drenching them as they ascended. The man's hat had long ago soaked through and now sluiced water off its downturned brim and onto his wide shoulders.

Rain mixed with tears on the boy's face as the man roughly shoved him forward. "Go on, you," he said. The boy bit his lip and, as always, said nothing.

Narrower grew the trail. Finally the rain slackened, then all but stopped. Clouds drooping heavily from the gray sky formed a drizzling mist about the pair, and fog rose from the emptiness to their right, where the trail gave way to a sheer bluff. The boy's feet slid on the muddy path; twice he fell, and twice the man swore and pulled him up. They went on.

When the land disappeared before them and they finally stopped, they stood atop a high peak, looking down onto dark conifer treetops bending in the wind. Lightning flashed simultaneously with the man's wicked smile. He reached menacingly toward the cringing but still-silent boy. . . .

Florida Cochran woke up with a scream. Man, boy, and mountain melted into the smooth darkness of her bedroom wall.

Tudor Cochran, her husband, bolted up beside her. Florida turned her wide moon face with its watery blue eyes on him; the moonlight was so bright through the window tonight that he could read the silent sorrow in her eyes.

"Same dream?" he inquired softly.

She nodded sadly.

"Flory, what am I going to do about you and your crazy dreams?" he asked, and then wished he hadn't, for he knew already what she wanted him to do. So far he had refused.

Someone approached the closed bedroom door quickly but unevenly; bare feet slapped, scraped against the oiled slab floor on the other side of the door.

"Mr. and Mrs. Cochran! Are you all right in there?"

Cochran called back, "Fine, fine, Reverend Viola. Flory just had that dream again." The inquirer in the hallway was a preacher who had been lodging in the Cochran Inn for two nights now, lingering to let a bruised foot heal before he continued on to Snow Sky. Both nights Flory had dreamed the same dream and screamed herself awake, and the tall, solemn clergyman had limped down to the door on his sore foot to make sure everything was all right.

The preacher padded arrhythmically back to his

room and Flory settled back into her feather pillow. For the next several minutes she sniffed and from time to time dabbed her eyes with the sheet, pretending to hide it so Cochran wouldn't notice while really making sure he did. Cochran listened for a while, then sighed and sat up on the bedside and reached down for his boots.

"It's a curse indeed for a grown man to have a bladder the size of a pea," he muttered. He pulled on his boots, fumbled around on the bedside lampstand for his spectacles, then walked out. An outhouse stood at the edge of the woods behind the inn, over near the stable where the horses and mules shifted about quietly in the moonlight. Cochran crossed the yard. It was a beautiful night blessed with a cool breeze that carried wonderful scents of earth and forest upon its shoulders.

As Cochran walked back toward the inn, he stopped to gaze thoughtfully at the moon. After a few moments he looked at the ground, shook his head, and inwardly surrendered, pondering the sacrifices men have to make to keep their women happy. Over the years he had made several for Flory, and was about to obligate himself to her for one more. But he didn't much mind it, not really. Flory's happiness was worth it.

She was still awake when he returned. He slipped off his boots, tucked his nightshirt down about his knees, and slid back beneath the covers.

"All right, Flory, you needn't bring it up again. I'll go after them," he said.

She sat up, surprised. "You mean it?"

"If you think you and Theon can run things here without me for a while, I do."

3

"Of course we can. Oh, Tudor, you're a wonderful man."

His back was toward her, but he felt her smile beaming on him like sunshine through a window. It was good to know she was happy again, especially after all the worry her dreams had brought her. Cochran wondered why he had fought the inevitable as long as he had, plumped his pillow, and went back to sleep.

Breakfast was salt pork, eggs, and biscuits, the latter so hard that Cochran silently wondered if Flory had saved them from last Christmas. Flory had two main failings: she couldn't sing and she couldn't make biscuits, though she tried hard to do both, sometimes at the same time, which did not improve matters.

The Reverend P. D. Viola sat across the table from Cochran, shoveling big slabs of meat into his downturned mouth and gulping coffee from a china cup. Between bites he was talking about Flory's dream, in which he appeared interested even while also seeming preoccupied and somber. He had said a time or two that he had a dreadful duty awaiting him in Snow Sky, but Cochran was not a busybody and did not pursue the matter, nor had he allowed Flory to do so.

"There is sometimes a symbolism in dreams," the preacher was saying to Cochran. "Of what does this dream consist?"

Cochran described the dream based on Flory's slightly vague descriptions.

Viola said, "An image, perhaps, of Abraham

taking his son up the mountain to sacrifice him.''

''I don't think that's it,'' Cochran responded wearily, not enjoying the subject. ''The boy and man in the dream were in here a few days back. Came late, stayed one night, and left early. The man acted edgy and the boy never said a word. He just looked at Flory a few times in a way that made her worry for him. She's had the dream three nights straight. She feels like the man is going to do bad to the boy. I don't know where she gets her notions.''

The preacher bit off a piece of biscuit so hard it crunched like a bone. ''Despite what you say, I find the imagery remarkably biblical,'' he said. ''But even if not, perhaps her dream is meaningful in some other way. The story of Joseph and his interpretation of dreams gives us verification that sometimes dreams are a vehicle of insight from above and from within.''

Cochran didn't really understand all that and was ready to drop it anyway. He took a swig of coffee and another bite of biscuit. A moment later Flory came in from the kitchen, smiling at Cochran more brightly than she had since their honeymoon nineteen years before.

''Anyone need more eggs?'' she asked. She brushed past Cochran and patted his shoulder lovingly.

''A delicious meal, ma'am, and I'm satisfied,'' Viola said.

Cochran wondered how a preacher could voice such a lie; surely Viola had noticed the biscuits. Then again, maybe a grim fellow such as he enjoyed breaking his teeth. ''A fine tableful to fit a man for a difficult encounter to come, and I'm about to go to one. My foot's in good enough condition, I believe, for me to travel on.''

"My husband is to do some traveling, too,'' Flory said, looking at Cochran and smiling again. "You'll be pleased. He's going off to do a good deed.''

"Oh?'' The clergyman looked inquiringly at Cochran. "Where are you going?''

"Snow Sky,'' Flory answered for her husband. Cochran wished she hadn't, for he knew at once what would follow: a suggestion from either Viola or Flory that the two men travel together. Cochran had nothing against Viola except his overly serious manner. Cochran himself was prone to be serious, but the preacher did not look like he had smiled since childhood.

"You plan to leave innkeeping for mining?'' Viola asked.

"No. I'm just going on an errand for my wife. Nothing, really,'' Cochran responded.

"He's going to help a young boy in trouble,'' Flory said proudly, still beaming at her husband.

The clergyman raised his brows. "The boy in the dream?''

"Tudor told you about that? Yes, the very one. Now, Reverend Viola, I don't claim any gift of secret vision, but I just know in my heart that poor boy is in trouble. Tudor is going to find him and make sure he's safe.''

"I see.'' The preacher turned to Cochran. "How do you know this man and boy are in Snow Sky?''

"Flory heard the man say something to the boy about Snow Sky. Besides, that's where everybody who travels this way is headed anymore.''

"True. Speaking of travel, perhaps we could

conduct ours together. I've been a bit melancholy, I admit, for I have already mentioned the unpleasant matter awaiting me in Snow Sky. A meeting with a person I dread encountering again. I could use a bit of good companionship on the road.''

Cochran was glad he had seen that one coming. ''I appreciate it, Reverend Viola, but I've already got a traveling partner.'' He shot a quick glance at Flory.

''Who?'' Flory asked, surprised. She had thought he was going alone.

''Hiram Frogg,'' Cochran said.

Flory went dark as a snuffed candle. ''If my husband intends to be in the company of Mr. Frogg, Reverend Viola, then you most assuredly do not want to travel with him,'' she said in a much cooler tone than before.

''Who is this Mr. Frogg?'' Viola asked. ''A strange name, Frogg.''

''Just a friend of mine,'' Cochran responded.

''And a no-account of the worst sort,'' Flory added. ''A common criminal. A thief and fighter— and he's been in jail.''

''And got out again when his time was up,'' Cochran reminded his wife. ''He's settled down a lot compared to what he used to be.''

''He's settled, all right. Settled like an old hound too lazy to scratch his own fleas.''

Flory had never liked Hiram Frogg, and had secretly hoped for a long time now that he would be lured away by the silver strikes at Snow Sky. So far, to her chagrin, he had not. Frogg was a most unambitious man, unattracted by anything that required labor. Frogg claimed to be a blacksmith, of all things, though he seldom actually worked. Flory suspected that her husband sometimes slipped Frogg money. He was soft like that, especially where Frogg was concerned.

Flory had never anticipated that Cochran was planning to take Frogg with him; she wondered if he had come up with the idea to get back at her for nagging him to make this trip. The fact was, Cochran actually hadn't considered taking Frogg until he realized a moment ago that he needed an out to avoid traveling with Viola. The more he considered it, though, the notion of taking Frogg along seemed good. Frogg wasn't much for brains or appearance, but he was comfortable to travel with, able to take care of himself. He would be a good companion in a swarming new mining town.

Viola stood, smacked lips smeared with grease and salt, then wiped his mouth on his napkin. "I must be off. I shall pray travel mercies for you and Mr. Frogg," he said to Cochran. "I trust you shall do the same for me. Perhaps we shall see each other in Snow Sky, or you'll catch up with me on the trail."

"Maybe so," Cochran said. "Preacher, that little Bible in your pocket's about to fall out."

"Indeed it is," Viola said, tucking back into his shirt pocket a thin, red-backed New Testament. "Mrs. Cochran, I'll gather my things and return to settle my bill."

When he was gone, Flory said, "I'd much rather you travel with a godly man than with a weasel like Toad Frogg."

Cochran bit off a piece of salt pork. "Don't call him Toad, Flory. You know that makes him mad."

Hiram Frogg leaned over and spat a brown stream of tobacco juice onto the ground. He was sitting on his anvil, which, Cochran had noted, was dusty and strung with cobwebs from lack of use.

Frogg wiped a trace of brown juice from his lower lip and nodded. "I might go with you at that," he said. "Though it all sounds a little difficult. You think you can find a man and boy in that town? Snow Sky had nearly three thousand folks, last I heard, and more coming every day."

"The point isn't so much to find them as just to try, so Flory will be satisfied," Cochran answered. "You're right—it's a lot of trouble for little enough reason, but if you had a woman you loved you'd know why I'm doing it."

"What happens if you do find them?" Frogg asked, resettling his tobacco with his long tongue. That tongue, combined with his wide mouth, slightly bugged eyes, and unfortunate last name, were what had earned Frogg the nickname of Toad. But few dared call him that to his face, for he would fight anyone who did, friend or foe. His reputation as a brawler was one of many things Flory disliked about him.

Cochran shrugged. "I suppose I'll watch them and make sure the boy's all right. Maybe I'll talk to the man to see what his story is, if I think I need to. Mostly I just have to satisfy Flory the boy ain't been thrown off a cliff or something."

"Sounds crazy."

"No crazier than Flory will make me if I don't do it. She's thought of nothing else for days, and she won't let up about it. You see, Flory swears when that boy looked up at her while she was serving the table, she could see he was begging her for help. Begging with his eyes, Flory says, though he never said a word the whole time he was at the inn. Flory says something is wrong, that the man isn't the boy's father. And they didn't look at all alike, that's a fact.''

"Do you know their names?''

"Not the boy's. Man signed in as John Jackson.''

"Sounds made up,'' Frogg said.

"The world's full of John Jacksons. Besides, a man can make up a name if he wants. A lot of them do out here.''

Frogg rose from his anvil and yawned. Some of the anvil's cobwebs clung to his dirty trousers. "Well, Tudor, I'll go with you, crazy and henpecked though you may be.'' He stretched. "I been wanting to get back to Snow Sky anyway, just to see how it's grown since the last time I was there.''

Cochran was glad to see Frogg had at least some interest in Snow Sky. He had always thought that if Frogg could collect even half a basketload of ambition he might head to the mining town to set up a business. He could make a good living if he did. Blacksmiths were much in demand in mining towns, and indeed one of the first acts of Snow Sky's governing body, according to a copy of the Snow Sky *Argus* somebody had recently left at the Cochran Inn, was to put out an offer of a free building and house for any good blacksmith. Lawyers, saloon keepers, gamblers, and soiled doves Snow Sky had aplenty; skilled artisans it sorely lacked. Frogg wasn't a high-quality blacksmith, maybe, but he was honest and could beat out a decent horseshoe when he had to. Cochran had showed the

story in the *Argus* to Frogg, but Frogg had not re-
acted.

Cochran himself had thought briefly of opening
an inn or hotel in Snow Sky, but had decided
against it. He had worked too long and hard estab-
lishing this one, and as long as Snow Sky kept
attracting travelers, he figured he would thrive sufficiently right where he was. His inn's location
about a day and a half from the mining town made
it an almost essential stopover for westbound travelers to Snow Sky.

"When do we leave?" Frogg asked.

"Today. Get your things together, and I'll be
back around in a little while."

"You're too good to that woman, Tudor. Running off on a fool's errand just because she squalls
in the night."

Cochran adjusted his spectacles and said, "You
just ain't been in love with anybody, Frogg. You
don't love nothing but cards and sleeping late."

Frogg snorted. "I been in love plenty. Ain't met
the first dance hall gal yet I didn't fall in love
with."

Back at the inn, Viola was long gone and Flory
was already packing Cochran's bag and bedroll.
Theon, the skinny, slow-witted young man who
helped the Cochrans run the inn, was sweeping out
the main room. "Sure wish you'd take me to Snow
Sky," he said to Cochran.

"You're needed here," Cochran answered.
"You're too important to spare."

Theon smiled at the flattery and swept a little harder.

Seeing his bedroll depressed Cochran, who hated sleeping on the ground. He wondered if that was why he had become an innkeeper—to do his part to keep the human race from having to sleep outdoors any more than necessary.

"Don't you let Toad Frogg get you into trouble," Flory instructed sternly.

"I ain't a little boy, Flory."

"No, but Toad is. I really hate that you're taking him with you. You could have done better. That preacher Viola seemed a nice enough man."

"I'm sure he is. But he had too much starch about him. Frogg you can relax with."

"Oh, I'm sure. His idea of relaxing is gambling and drinking and I don't want to think what else. Don't let him tempt you to go to some cheap crib harlot, you hear?"

"I'm not in the market for crib harlots," Cochran said.

"What's a crib harlot?" Theon asked as he swept.

"Flory'll explain it when I'm gone," Cochran answered, grinning as Flory shot him a harsh look.

But a moment later she came to her husband and put her arms around him. Her gruffness vanished and she spoke tenderly. "Thank you," she said. "That little boy needs help. I know it as well as I know my own name. You'll help him if you find him, won't you?"

Cochran said, "If he needs it . . ."

He started to say more, but she planted a big kiss on his mouth and blocked off the words.

CHAPTER 2

—◄—

THE FIRST NIGHT ON THE GROUND WENT AS
badly as Cochran had feared. He awakened stiff
and aching, thoroughly repentant for his decision
to make this trip and angry at Flory for having
pushed him to it. Frogg, meanwhile, was as cheerful as ever. He had already built a fire and was
frying bacon and corncakes in a spider skillet.

"Morning, Tudor!" he said. "Beautiful day for
riding!"

Cochran rose and stretched, wincing. "I hope
they got a good hotel in Snow Sky."

"Oh, they got plenty of hotels, but nothing as
good as your inn. That's the trouble with a new
mining town. You got to settle for what you can
get, potluck all the way."

They ate breakfast silently. Three big cups of
black coffee slowly brought Cochran back to life
and washed the rust from his joints. By the time
Frogg had rinsed out his skillet and poured off the
dregs of the coffeepot, Cochran was in a much better humor, actually beginning to anticipate with
some pleasure the visit to Snow Sky. After all, a

man had to see different scenes now and again just to keep from becoming stagnant. Cochran wondered if maybe he already was that way; he normally moved around about as much as a farm pond, and saw little more excitement. Maybe the trip would do him good.

As they rode, Frogg talked about Snow Sky, which had been founded beneath an overcast sky the previous year, 1889, on a snowy February day. An idle comment by one of its founders about snowy sky stretching above gave the town an informal name that finally had become permanent.

The silver chlorides at Snow Sky had assayed out at promising levels, and new, even richer lodes of silver and quartz were discovered by the week. Before the summer of '89 had ended, Snow Sky was a full-scale mining camp with twenty-five-cent beer and dollar-a-shot whiskey, flare-lighted streets, and scores of saloons, faro parlors, whorehouses, and lawyers' offices.

"You see if it ain't the next Leadville," Frogg said. "The railroad's already scouting out a route for itself."

"If you think so highly of Snow Sky, how come you don't live there?" Cochran asked.

"Been thinking about that. Maybe I'll stay on this time, open me a smithy."

Now that Frogg was actually talking about becoming a more respectable citizen, Cochran suddenly had his doubts. Frogg wouldn't be able to keep at his work with a lot of recreational diversions close at hand, and Snow Sky had plenty. Minimal law to supervise them all, too, although Cochran had read, in that same copy of the *Argus*, that the town's leaders had banded together to appoint a marshal and a small police force, and had built a jail.

The pair rode slowly but steadily almost half the day, not pushing the horses too hard, stopping twice to spell them. Cochran's mind had drifted away from the man and boy he was supposedly seeking, but when he and Frogg stopped about one o'clock for a meal he thought of them again, and wondered if perhaps Flory was right about the pair. She had good instincts, especially about children. Maybe she really had read a plea for help in the boy's eyes.

Then again, maybe it was just another case of Flory's feelings getting stirred up by the presence of a child. Cochran felt a pang. Flory's inability to give them children was a private wound they nursed together. Life was unfair; Flory would have made the finest of mothers.

They finished their beans and lay back beneath a tree to let them settle while the horses cropped the wild grasses. In a few moments Frogg was snoring with his hat pulled down over his eyes and his hands behind his head. Cochran, though, didn't nap; he got up after a few minutes and walked around, looking at the mountains with their ever-green slopes and barren expanses of stone made brilliant by the sunlight. A while later he went over and gently kicked Frogg awake, and they mounted up and continued.

▬◄

They made better time than they anticipated, for it was not yet dark when they had ridden to within a half hour of Snow Sky.

The sunset was brilliant red and thick as maple syrup when Frogg stopped along the trail and dismounted. He walked over to the trailside and picked up something from the ground. It was a small book of some sort.

"Let me see that," Cochran said, also dismounting. Frogg dusted the book off and handed it to him.

"This is the preacher Viola's little New Testament," Cochran said. "He almost dropped it from his pocket at the table yesterday morning. Must have lost it riding into town."

"Looks like a horse stepped on it," Frogg observed. "Pretty dirtied up."

"Yeah." Cochran wiped more dirt from it and started to put it into his pocket.

"Let me carry that," Frogg said, reaching for it.

"Why?"

"To bring me good luck."

Cochran handed the little volume to Frogg, frowning disapprovingly. "It doesn't seem fitting to use a preacher's lost Bible to bring you good luck in some faro parlor."

"Don't fret—I'll give it back to him, first time we see him. You just point him out."

They were remounting when Cochran suddenly stopped and walked over to the brush at the edge of the forest.

"What is it?" Frogg asked.

Cochran was peering down the wooded slope at the trail's edge. "Thought I saw something move down there on the ground," he said. "But I don't see anything now."

Cochran returned to his horse and mounted. As

soon as he was in the saddle, he sniffed the air and made a face.

"What in blazes is that?"

Frogg grinned. "That, my friend, is the smell of a Colorado mining camp."

"Smells more like an open sewer from here."

"To you, maybe. To most folks hereabouts it smells like money."

Though it was not yet nine o'clock, already Earl Cobb had his hands full and was wondering why he could have been so foolish as to have accepted the job of Snow Sky town marshal. At the moment, as he slammed a hefty drunk against the saloon wall, pulling the man's knife-gripping hand around behind him and twisting it until the wrist almost snapped, he couldn't think of any good reason at all. He supposed he was a peace officer simply because that's all he had ever been, and all he knew.

The drunk roared and cursed as the knife clattered to the ground. Cobb kicked it away.

"Go at it, Marshal!" someone in the crowd hollered. "Whup that old boy real good!"

Keeping his grip on the painfully twisted wrist, Cobb leaned forward and put his face near the drunk's ear.

"You going to come quiet? Or do I break the wrist?"

"I'll kill you, Marshal, I swear it! Break your neck!"

Cobb twisted the wrist a bit more; the drunk screamed.

"I don't think you'll break anybody's neck with

a busted wrist," Cobb said. "What I think you'll do is never threaten me again. You agree?"

With tears beginning to stream down his face, the man quickly nodded.

"Say it!" Cobb demanded with a shake and another scream-evoking twist.

"I won't hurt you, won't threaten you. Promise I won't!"

"Good. Now let's go sleep this thing off and get you human again."

He was grateful this Scofield Saloon and Gaming Parlor was close to the new town jail, which stood on the north side of the street officially named McHenry Avenue, but called Mud Street by everyone in town. Even Paul McHenry, the merchant-mayor for whom the street was named, called it Mud Street. Like most, he had taken a fall or two into the thick muck that made up the avenue after every rain.

Somebody opened the door of the Scofield and let Cobb and his prisoner out. Cobb steered the man rightward and down the crude boardwalk that ran in front of Kerrigan Brothers Hardware and Guns, then immediately right down Irish Alley toward the jail. Irish Alley, a narrow rut between buildings, was so dubbed because of its location between Kerrigan Brothers and O'Brien's Grocery. O'Brien lived in a relatively substantial house northwest of town out among an array of cabins and shacks, but the Kerrigans, two bachelor brothers, had built an apartment on the second level above their store. Right now Clive Kerrigan thrust his head out a window and called, "A good job, Cobb!" and pulled back inside.

"Thanks very much," Cobb muttered sardonically as he cut right out of Irish Alley into Jail Alley, which in turn led to the log-walled jail. Clive Kerrigan was on the town council and had been Cobb's chief promoter for this job.

Deputy Heck Carpenter stood up behind Cobb's desk as the marshal entered, slamming shut the dime novel he had been reading with much effort, limping from word to word like a drunk walking the ties of a railroad. "Why, hello, Earl. Didn't expect to see you so sudden."

"I can tell," Cobb said as he prodded his prisoner toward a cell.

"I won't cause no more trouble if you turn me loose," the drunk said.

Cobb shoved him into a cell. "I'll turn you loose after you sleep it off." He slammed and locked the cell door.

"Watch him, Heck. Don't let him hurt himself or nothing. I'll be back later."

He left the jail and walked back up the street, stretched, and scratched the back of his neck. Another long night ahead. Cobb had learned early on that he was needed mostly at night, and least in the mornings, so he worked the former and slept the latter. Sometimes he got no sleep at all.

He glanced to his right toward the intersection of Mud and Silver streets. In the intersection's center was the town well. At the intersection's southwest corner stood the Rose and Thorn Restaurant, the best eating establishment in town. One of the most substantial buildings, too; in Snow Sky many were more canvas than lumber, and good solid roofs of the sort on the Rose and Thorn were rarities.

The wind had been blowing from the mountains,

northeast to southwest, carrying across town the smell of the Snow Sky livestock pens. A sudden momentary circling of the breeze brought a gust from the west to Cobb's nose, and he savored the aroma of food from the Rose and Thorn's kitchen. His stomach grumbled hungrily. A good slab of pie and a cup of coffee was just what he needed to reward himself for hauling in one more drunk without getting stabbed or shot. Cobb had passed a firm rule against firearms in town, but lots of newcomers either didn't know about it or ignored it, and even those who carried no evident weapons often had hideout guns.

He strode to the restaurant and entered, sweeping off his hat and finger-combing his hair. Rose Tifton, who operated the restaurant with her husband, Kenneth (now, to his chagrin, increasingly being called Thorn because of the restaurant's arbitrarily chosen name), greeted Cobb warmly. Cobb liked coming here; the Tiftons were good people who wanted real law in Snow Sky. That was not a universally shared desire, particularly in the brothels, dance halls, and whiskey mills southeast of town.

"Come in, Earl. You're in luck—your table's clear."

"Why, thank you, Rose. You're a jewel."

"Good job with that drunk," Rose said as she seated him at his preferred spot, near the window. "I saw you taking him in. Ten policemen couldn't have done it better together than you did alone."

"I wish I did have ten policemen," he said. "Couldn't keep peace in a town like this when I had three men, and with Jimmy off with a broke leg I'm down to just two deputies. And Heck only counts for about half an officer. That drunk might be down at the jail hanging himself right now, and Heck would never know it. He keeps his nose stuck in cheap storybooks most of the time.''

''It'd be no loss if that man hanged himself, I figure. I've got little patience for a drunk.''

''Now, Rose. Half the population of Snow Sky are drunks. This one was just a newcomer a little too full of liquor. He might become a fine citizen when he's sober and digs himself into a good lode.''

Cobb ordered vinegar pie, and Rose bustled back to the kitchen. For a moment there was no one else in the restaurant but Cobb. He savored the quiet, knowing it wouldn't last.

And it didn't. The front door opened and Jason Lybrand walked in. He looked straight at Cobb and came toward the table, his ever-present gold cross swinging from its chain around his neck. Cobb felt the same cool distrust for the clergyman that he always felt. Lybrand had been in Snow Sky for some time now, supposedly trying to turn his tent church into a real one, but so far, it seemed to Cobb, the preacher had been more interested in taking up collections than spending them on lumber and nails.

''Hello, Marshal,'' Lybrand said, seating himself uninvited. He seemed rather keyed up—not typical of him.

''Evening, Reverend. Got some coffee on the way if you want a bit.''

''No, no thank you. Actually, I wanted to talk to you a moment. Sorry to do it while you're occupied.''

''Don't worry about it. What's wrong?''

Lybrand looked even more worried. ''Maybe

nothing. It's just that there was a man scheduled to be here, at the latest, a day ago. He's another preacher, named P. D. Viola. He was planning to come here to help me try to stir a little more interest in building a proper church.''

Cobb figured Lybrand had collected enough donations already for three proper churches, but kept the thought private. ''And he hasn't arrived?'' he said.

''He hasn't. And I've known Brother Viola for years. A punctual man. If he were delayed on the road away from a telegraph station, of course, there would be little way for him to contact me, and that's probably what happened . . . but still—''

Cobb's pie and coffee arrived; he smiled as Rose set it before him.

''Still, you're worried, right?''

''Right. I'm afraid some harm has come to him,'' Lybrand said.

Cobb bit into the vinegar pie. ''Well, it isn't uncommon for folks to be delayed on those mountain roads. If he doesn't show up in a day or two we'll see if we can't find out where he is. Good enough?''

The preacher smiled tightly. ''Yes, good enough. Thank you, Marshal. I feel better just knowing you are aware of the situation. I'll tell you if he doesn't show up tomorrow.'' Lybrand stood. ''Good night.''

'' 'Night, preacher.''

The clergyman walked out. A few moments later two more men entered the restaurant. The marshal quietly checked the newcomers over as he sipped his coffee; the action was instinctive and almost unconscious. Neither man struck him as an obviously worrisome sort, though the one with the wide mouth and scraggly whiskers did merit an extra glance. The other man looked particularly benign, like a schoolmaster. Maybe a banker or a preacher.

Preacher. Cobb wondered if this might be the missing P. D. Viola.

He finished his pie and coffee, left payment on the table, and headed for the door. He paused at the table where the two men had seated themselves.

"Evening," he said, extending his hand. His friendly intrusion obviously took the two by surprise. "Earl Cobb, town marshal. Just wanted to welcome you to Snow Sky."

The mild-looking man shook Cobb's hand. "Tudor Cochran," he said. "Pleased to meet you, Marshal."

The wide-mouthed fellow stood, scooting back his chair. He seemed a little nervous.

"Hiram Frogg," he said, also shaking Cobb's hand.

"Beg pardon?"

"Frogg. Hiram Frogg. Proud to meet you, sir."

"Same here." Cobb thought about asking if the pair had run across a preacher named P. D. Viola on the trail, but didn't, for he was having trouble squelching a laugh at the unexpected way Frogg's name fit his looks. Cobb didn't want to embarrass either himself or the other man, so he quickly turned away, saying, "I hope you enjoy your time in Snow Sky."

Thank you, Marshal. I appreciate your friendliness," Cochran said. He sounded weary, and looked like a man ready to find a bed and sink into it.

The marshal waved a goodbye to Rose and left

the restaurant. Outside the wind was blowing in the same direction as before, carrying the stench of manure and livestock. Cobb put on his hat and sauntered down the Silver Street boardwalk, scanning the milling humanity in the flare-lighted street for anyone who looked like a troublemaker, a drunk, or a misplaced preacher.

CHAPTER 3

COCHRAN AND FROGG HAD LEFT THEIR
horses with the old man at the public livery north
of town before going to the restaurant. The livery
was a big barn standing near the bank of Bledsoe
Creek at the base of one of the mountains that over-
looked the town. Scattered in an undesigned jumble
all through and around town were scores of cabins
and tents where the people of Snow Sky lived, most
of them miners, a few with wives and families, the
majority without. The mines themselves were farther northwest, in the rugged hills and mountain
bases covered with evergreens.

True to Frogg's earlier statement, there was no
good hotel or inn in Snow Sky, mostly rental rooms
in various canvas-roofed log buildings around
town. The pair had stopped at the first one they
found. It was a long, narrow structure with a sign
outside reading SCOFIELD RENTED ROOMS. It stood
on Mud Street, next door to the Snow Sky Saloon
and not far from the Blue Belle Dance Hall, which
was little more than a big tent with rough wooden
walls extending part of the way up. Music from an

inept band carried through the thin walls and roof, unimproved by the filtering, and could be easily heard in the room Cochran and Frogg rented.

The music didn't much disturb Cochran, who was bone weary and eager for rest. After returning from the Rose and Thorn, he had immediately stripped to his long underwear and sunk into one of the two sagging bunks in the room. In less than two minutes he was snoring.

Frogg was more restless, and the music did bother him. It made him think of cards, liquor, companionship, women. Frogg had more stamina than Cochran, and was not nearly as weary. After nearly an hour of staring at the underside of the canvas roof, he rose, quietly dressed, left the room, and walked onto the street.

It was only eleven o'clock; the saloons and dance halls would run full steam all night. Frogg grinned as he walked the gaudily lighted street up to the area of the town well. He looked up and down; as in most mining towns, there were abundant options for entertainment. Mining towns were inevitably filled to the bursting point with saloons and dance halls. The only enterprises they typically had more of were lawyers' offices.

Closest by Frogg was the Snow Sky Saloon, but he passed it up in favor of the Silver Striker farther down on Silver Street. This was one of the more substantial saloons and had a reputation for the coldest beer, thanks to the excellent ice house at its rear. Frogg got onto the boardwalk at the front of the Rose and Thorn and thumped down to his chosen place.

He walked into its warm yellow light and looked around, hoping to see someone he knew. He had been to Snow Sky twice before. By his second visit the town had changed dramatically from when he first had come; he had already noted that the same held true this time. Snow Sky was growing, becoming more solid and permanent by the day despite the abundant tent structures and spit-and-wire wooden edifices still dominating the squatty skyline. All around town earlier tonight Frogg had seen the skeletons of new buildings that soon would replace their temporary predecessors. Lumber was stacked all about, ready to be hammered into new offices, businesses, homes, stables.

Frogg was disappointed not to spot a single familiar face in the tavern. But he didn't fret; if he couldn't find old friends he would simply make new ones. Right now a cold beer or two was the main thing he had in mind, anyway.

He went to the bar and got his drink, then followed it up with another. Another man also meandered to the bar. Within five minutes Frogg and he were talking; within ten they were seated at a table with several others, cutting cards for a poker game.

Frogg had little money to put up—he almost always had little money—but tonight fortune smiled. Little by little he gathered winnings, until at last his newfound friends were friends no more, and his broad-mouthed, toady grins were no longer quietly funny to them, but infuriating.

At last the man Frogg had met at the bar stood so quickly his chair tipped over behind him. He was very big and very drunk. "By damn, you look like a frog!" he bellowed. "I think you are a frog—and I'm going to feed you a fly."

Frogg's smile vanished. "I don't cotton to people funning with my name."

"What's the matter, frog? You about to up and hop off your lily pad?"

Frogg stood. "You talk civil or I'll feed you this chair."

The big man leaned across the table, palms flat. His face was six inches from Frogg's. *"Ribbit,"* he said.

By now the other occupants of the saloon had turned their attention to the arguing men, and a general cheer arose when Frogg struck his antagonist in the mouth. This crowd favored a good fight anytime, for any reason.

The big drunk jolted back, and blood spilled from his split lip onto his chin. He dabbed it with his hand, examined it. "Get him!" he directed the others, all of whom were disgruntled with Frogg. "By damn, I will feed me a fly to that frog, I will!"

Frogg backed away, but others were on him at once. They found him hard to restrain, but the big drunk came forward and helped, and before long Frogg was pinned to the floor. The others in the saloon gathered around and looked down on him, grinning.

"He really does look like a frog—a big two-legged frog," a saloon girl said, then laughed.

"Here you go, Bill," somebody said. Frogg saw, to his dismay, a man hold out a wriggling something to the drunk above him. It turned and writhed between his fingers. "It ain't a fly, just a roach. Close as I could come."

"That'll be close enough," Frogg's antagonist said. "Get ready to eat your supper, frog."

Both Frogg and the doomed roach struggled for

freedom, neither successfully. Thick fingers pulled at Frogg's lips and tried to pry apart his clenched teeth. A finger slipped between his teeth and Frogg bit down, bringing forth a yowl as someone pulled back a bleeding digit. But that didn't stop the abuse. The liquored-up crowd was ready to see him devour the bug, and finally, despite all Frogg's efforts, someone managed to pry open his mouth. He closed his eyes as the roach fell onto his tongue. Before he could blow or push it out, his attackers forced his mouth closed. The bug crunched sickeningly between his teeth, and the crowd cheered and laughed.

The saloon owner was saying, "Here now—I don't want such as that in here!" Nobody listened.

Frogg wanted to spit out the crushed bug, but the men holding him would not let him open his mouth. Finally he swallowed it just to get it off his tongue. The crushed, crusty insect slid and scraped down the inside of his gullet.

"Feed him another one!" someone yelled. "Here—this is a big one!"

Frogg opened his eyes again. A much bigger roach wriggled above his face. Once again his mouth was being forced open—

He lunged, kicked, jerked, moved every way he could and found himself suddenly, unexpectedly free. Two of the men atop him had lost their balance and fell back. Frogg bounded up.

The big drunk who had launched the attack was stumbling backward, trying to steady himself. Frogg went straight for him with a loud yell. His fists swung out and connected. The man fell straight back.

Frogg dropped atop him, still pounding as hard

as he could. He felt flesh give beneath his fists, then warm red liquid was on his knuckles. There was now no laughter in the saloon; the people were hushed with panic. It was obvious to everyone that Frogg was mad enough to kill the man who had humiliated him.

For long moments the only noise was Frogg's fists making a dead thud against the face and neck of the supine man. Then the saloon owner yelled, "Get him off him!" and that was enough to break the freeze. Several men came forward at once and dragged Frogg off.

And then Earl Cobb was there, seemingly having appeared like a ghost. In fact, he had heard the noise from outside and walked in unnoticed just as Frogg had begun pounding the drunk. It had taken him until now to push his way through close enough to really see what was happening. Now that he did, he drew his Smith & Wesson Model No. 3 and fired into the floor.

"Hey, now—that's my property you're shooting!" the saloon owner protested futilely. In truth, the damage from the bullet made little difference, for the floor was made of heavy puncheons, and this was not the first bullet those thick split logs had absorbed.

"This ruckus is over," Cobb declared. "I want to know who started it."

Frogg would have spoken up, but his tongue felt like it was wrapped in cotton and his throat burned. He feared that bug he had eaten might make a reappearance.

Others spoke quickly: It was Frogg who started it, they said. Frogg just launched into Old Bill for no reason, just started pounding him in the face like he wanted to kill him, just because Bill had said Frogg looked like his name.

Cobb doubted what he heard, with Frogg being a newcomer. Bill was one of the more popular figures in Snow Sky's lower society. He figured Bill was being protected. But it hardly mattered. He had witnessed Frogg pounding Bill in the face, and that was what he had to respond to.

Cobb took Frogg by the collar. "Come on," he said. "You're going with me."

Frogg found his tongue buried somewhere in that cotton in his mouth. "I didn't do anything but defend myself," he said. "They put a bug down me."

A murmur of chuckles ran through the crowd. Cobb looked sharply around. "That true?"

"He's lying," Bill said, sitting up with his face covered with blood. "He jumped me for no cause."

Cobb suddenly was weary of it all. He pulled Frogg after him out the door, almost dragging him down the street.

"Where you taking me?" Frogg asked.

"The jail. You can spend the night there and think over trying to improve the way you get along with folks in this town."

"I didn't start it. They lit in on me."

"I don't doubt it, but I don't much care, either. Whatever your reason, I saw you just about kill a man, and I can't overlook that."

Frogg thought of Cochran, asleep back there in that rented room. Cochran didn't even know he had left. He started to ask the marshal if he could stop by the room long enough to tell Cochran what had happened, but realized the officer was in no mood to make an extra stop.

"They really did feed me a bug," Frogg said when they reached the jail. The marshal all but shoved him in. He fumbled with the lock on one of the three iron-barred cells.

"Well, Frogg, there's plenty of bugs in there, if that first one gave you a taste for them," Cobb said. "Clean out your pockets."

Frogg did not argue. He felt a mild despair, mostly because he knew Cochran would be angry with him for so quickly finding trouble. Obediently he emptied his pockets and handed his possessions—including a derringer—to the marshal.

Cobb raised the weapon. "It's against town ordinance to carry a firearm in the city," he said. "You just earned yourself a fine."

That reminded Frogg—all that money he had won was still sitting back there on the table in the Silver Striker Saloon. He corrected the thought: used to be on the table. By now it surely was in the pockets of whoever had first noticed it lying there.

Cobb looked at the small New Testament Frogg and Cochran had found on the road into Snow Sky. "Well, you surprise me," Cobb said. "You don't look to be the religious sort."

"It's a good luck charm," Frogg mumbled, turning away.

"Didn't work very well tonight, did it?"

"Nope." Frogg went to the bunk and laid down, his back toward the marshal.

Heck Carpenter walked in from the street, looking tired. With one of Cobb's three deputies laid up at home with a broken leg, Heck and Cap Corley, the remaining lawmen, had been working extra duty.

"Got you another one," Cobb said. "Watch him."

"What did he do?"

"Murdered a bug by ingestion, I hear." Cobb walked out, leaving Heck confused. Sometimes Cobb said mighty strange things.

———

Cochran awakened and rolled over. "Flory?" he said. He remembered then where he was and sat up, rubbing his eyes. A sharp pain stabbed through his back and he groaned. Sleeping on this bunk was hardly better than sleeping on the ground. Worse, really, for it was too soft and made his back sore.

He looked at Frogg's bunk. Empty. Frogg was out early for breakfast, maybe. Yet that seemed peculiar, for the Hiram Frogg he had always known would sleep until noon if given half an excuse.

Cochran got up and dressed. He combed his hair, looking in the little mirror hanging on a nail in the wall, then went out onto Mud Street. He was hungry, though the smell of raw sewage in a narrow ditch beside the little rooming house briefly took away his appetite. This was one of the stinkingest towns he had ever been in.

Also one of the busiest: wagons creaking, people meandering, commerce under way. The rough-cut festival atmosphere of the previous night had faded; replacing it even at this early hour was a sense of rush and enterprise. Cochran walked slowly along, looking over the town, alternating between wondering where Frogg was and wondering if a man could find a good breakfast in Snow Sky without having to draw blood paying for it.

He found breakfast, though not a good one, and paid a price that made his eyes water. He had an extra cup of coffee to make the meal seem more worth the cost and, as he sipped it, considered raising the cost of a night's lodging at his inn to two dollars, maybe more. Based on Snow Sky prices, he wasn't keeping up with the market. The canvas-roofed excuse for a room he had slept in last night cost him a dollar seventy-five. Even sleeping in one of Snow Sky's one-room so-called hotels, which were no more than a dozen bunks scooted together, set a lodger back a dollar fifty a night. Disgusting, the prices of things in mining camps.

Cochran left the restaurant and walked back out onto the street. He felt out of place and rather ridiculous. His agreement to come to Snow Sky to spy on a man and some boy simply to satisfy Flory's whim seemed merely a foolish nighttime condescension here in the morning sunlight. Flory was too pushy. And Frogg, unreliable. Already he had disappeared without even the courtesy to say where he was going.

Cochran walked about the town for lack of anything else to do. All around him rang the sounds of town growth. From several directions he heard the rasp of sawmills that struggled to keep up with the soaring lumber demand. Wagons creaked past, horses clopped along, mules pulled sleds laden with lumber and nail kegs. Quite a town, this place, growing like a miniature version of Leadville at the height of its own boom a decade back.

In the milling crowds it seemed hopeless to spot Frogg or the man and boy Cochran had come to follow. Perhaps the thing to do was to return to the room and hope Frogg showed up soon.

Cochran turned and suddenly stopped. There they were: the man and boy, walking together on the other side of the street. Neither seemed to notice Cochran, who stood stock-still. For some reason his heart began to hammer. The man and boy turned a corner, and Cochran followed across the muddy street.

The pair moved fast, weaving in and out of the crowd. At times Cochran lost sight of them, but always picked them up again. He was glad he had spotted them; now he could truthfully tell Flory he had found them and kept an eye on them. He was pleased to see the boy did not act frightened of the man now; he marched along beside him readily.

They stepped into a boot and shoe shop; Cochran went to the bench outside the door, picked up a copy of the *Argus* that lay on it, and pretended to read. He heard the man inside, inquiring about shoes for the boy. Several minutes passed, then the pair came out again, the boy looking down at his two shining new pieces of footwear. Cochran lifted the paper to hide his profile and let them pass.

Cochran stood and followed them at some distance. All at once the man turned so unexpectedly that Cochran did not have time to react, and for a moment his eyes and the man's met and locked. Cochran broke the gaze and ducked quickly into an alley, wondering if the man had recognized him from the inn. A few moments later he ventured out again. The man and boy were gone.

In an isolated miner's cabin two miles from Snow Sky, a big man with dough-soft hands peered out through the eyeholes of a flour sack mask and pressed a knife to the throat of another man pinned below him. His victim was much smaller than he, though far more muscled and callused, for he was a miner and worked hard. The man with the knife pursued the less strenuous profession of robbery.

"I'll ask you one more time—where's your valuables?" the robber asked in a voice incongruously soft and high-pitched for a man his size.

The man pinned on the floor glared bravely back up at his attacker and said nothing. The blade pressed into the soft flesh beneath his chin.

"For God's sake, Orv—tell him! He'll kill you!" The woman who had shouted the words struggled to free herself from the grasp of a second masked man, who was armed with an old Colt pistol that he alternately waved toward the man on the floor and thrust against the side of the woman.

Wide-eyed and scared in the corner cowered a little girl of about two, watching.

"I'll tell you nothing!" the victimized man said, confirming his wife's frequent observation that he had more stubbornness, and less common sense, than most mules.

Kimmie Brown sent up a despairing wail. The robber with the knife nicked Orv Brown's neck a little, drawing blood.

"Still uncooperative, huh?" he said in his too-soft, too-high voice. "Think I won't really gape your throat, do you?"

"I won't give up what's rightfully mine to the likes of you," Brown said.

"Your life is rightfully yours. You willing to give that up?" The robber punctuated the query by scribing out another thin cut on Brown's neck. The line was pale for half a second, then turned red as it released blood.

"Orv, they'll kill us all!" the woman pleaded through tears.

Attention shifted to her. "Maybe you know where it is, pretty lady!" the man with the gun said, shaking her. "Talk up good unless you and the runt want to see your man smiling with his throat instead of his mouth." He laughed at his own crude attempt at wit.

"Don't say a word, Kimmie!" Brown said, his voice more tremulous now that he had taken a couple of cuts.

Kimmie ignored her husband. "It's under the floor—pull that board there." She pointed.

The robbers smiled beneath the masks. The one pinning Orv Brown moved off him. Brown, whose chest had been pressed under the robber's weight, took a deep, welcome breath and sat up.

"I should have figured that a shack like this wouldn't have a floor without some reason," the high-voiced robber said. "Get up and pull that board," he ordered Brown.

"You shouldn't have told, Kimmie," Brown muttered. He rose and walked across the little cabin to a corner. There he knelt and pressed one end of a floorboard. The other end seesawed up an inch; he got a grip on it and lifted it out.

The bigger robber came up behind Brown, grabbed him by the collar, and pulled him back onto his rump. "Up and over t'other side," he ordered. Brown, looking very sullen, obeyed.

The robber reached into the hole and pulled out a metal box. Popping it open, he nodded as he studied the mix of cash, silver, gold, and jewelry inside.

"The necklace was my mother's," the woman said. "She gave it to me on her deathbed. Won't you let me keep at least that?"

"Why, you're pretty as a picture without it, and your ma surely don't need no necklace no more," he said. "Get over here with your husband."

The woman, trembling, went to her husband's side. The child in the corner began to whimper.

"I'll hunt you down," Brown said to the robbers. "I'll find you and see that you pay dear for this."

"Shut up and turn around."

The woman put her hands over her face and obeyed, but Orv Brown stared defiantly, his chin thrust out, little trails of blood still running down his neck from the slashes the robber had inflicted.

The big robber shrugged. "However you want it," he said. He swung up his pistol and brought it down hard on Brown's skull. Brown shuddered and fell. The woman screamed and the little girl began crying in earnest.

The pistol went up, down again, and Kimmie Brown fell atop her husband.

"That ought to keep them from raising any ruckus for a while."

"What about the kid?"

"Leave her be. She can't do no harm. I ain't without conscience, you know."

The other man looked at the metal box.

"Sweet Mary, that's a pretty sight. But I know a certain partner of ours who'll be fit to be tied if he finds out about this."

"So we won't let him find out. Let's go."

The two robbers rode out onto the road that led into Snow Sky, their masks stashed in saddle pouches. The smaller man, Ivan Dade, halted his horse and pointed.

"Look yonder, Clure," he said.

Clure Daugherty did look, and saw a lone figure walking down the middle of the road toward them.

"He's alone. Let's wait and see what he's got on him," Daugherty said.

They waited, sitting mounted by the road. The figure kept coming, never slowing or speeding. He had one hand to his throat.

"My God," Dade whispered when the man was close enough to see clearly. "Let's get out of here."

Daugherty, who had gone pale, did not argue. The pair spurred and rode toward Snow Sky like they were being chased.

P. D. Viola stopped, lifted an imploring, blood-encrusted hand toward the departing riders, and tried to call out. He did not succeed, and they did not stop.

So he began walking again, staring straight ahead, clutching his throat.

CHAPTER 4

VIOLA WALKED INTO TOWN, STARING straight ahead with his hand still at his throat. The people of Snow Sky greeted him with stunned silence, for he was so bruised and swollen that he looked inhuman. At length a boy of about fourteen approached him as he might have approached a ghost and said, "Sir, do you need help?"

The only response was a faint, gruesome squeak from deep in Viola's throat. He fell to his knees, then collapsed. The boy's face went white. He turned and ran away.

A crowd silently gathered around Viola, who was prostrate and still.

"Is he dead?" someone whispered.

"I think so," another answered.

But Viola squeaked again and moved. "Get the marshal," somebody said.

Earl Cobb had just gotten out of his bed and pulled on his pants when the office door burst open and three excited boys ran inside. "Marshal!" they yelled. "Where are you, Marshal?"

"Here I am, boys," Cobb said, walking out from

his curtained-off bedchamber as he buttoned his shirt. ''What's the excitement?''

Three voices babbled together at top volume. Cobb waved his hands. ''Whoa! One at a time! You—what's going on?''

The indicated boy stepped forward. ''There's a man on the street, beat half to death. His throat's all mashed. He's big and tall, all bruised up. I think he's going to die.''

Cobb nodded quickly. Without a word he returned to his bedchamber and pulled on his boots and hat. He strapped on his pistol as he walked out the door.

The boys ran ahead of him, leading him to the now-enlarged cluster of people gathered around Viola. Cobb pushed through and knelt beside the man, feeling his neck for a pulse. Viola squeaked again as if the mere touch of Cobb's fingers hurt.

''Get Walt Chambers,'' Cobb directed to any and all listening.

''I'm already here.'' A man broke out of the rim of the circle and knelt beside Cobb. Chambers was a self-taught horse doctor, and the closest thing to a real physician Snow Sky yet had to offer. The town fathers had been advertising in eastern newspapers for real doctors, but so far no one had taken the bait, and the town had to be satisfied with Chambers.

''He going to live?'' Cobb asked after Chambers had rolled Viola over, rather too roughly, evoking a pitiful squeak. Chambers examined him cursorily.

''That I can't tell,'' he said. ''Appears to me he's been beat to within an inch of life. Let's get him to a bed somewhere.''

''I've got a little cot off my office,'' said Herbert

Hillyer, one of the town's myriad attorneys, whose office happened to be at hand.

"Thanks, Herbert," Cobb said. "Bring us a good wide board, somebody."

They scrounged a board from a nearby heap of lumber beside the shell of a new store, and on it carried the semiconscious Viola into Hillyer's office. Cobb shooed away the crowd and Chambers examined Viola more closely, breathing loudly through his nostrils in concentration. At last he straightened and shook his head.

"I'm amazed this man was able to walk into town," he said. "Truly astounded. He's about as busted up as old Pellenhymer was when we pulled him from the bottom of that mine shaft." The reference was to a fatality of a month before involving a drunk who wandered through a mining area after dark, looking for a missing dog, and fell to his death in an unmarked shaft.

"I wonder who he is?" Cobb asked.

Viola's eyes opened; the bloodshot orbs rolled about in their sockets, seeming at first unable to focus on anything, then finally picking out the faces of the men with him. The squeak came from his throat again, a terrible sound Cobb didn't like to hear.

"Your throat has been bruised very badly," Chambers said. "I don't think you'll be talking again for a long while." He smiled and touched the injured man's shoulder. "You just rest and let us look after you."

Cobb suddenly remembered the inquiry of Lybrand. He leaned close to the man on the bunk.

"Is your name P. D. Viola?" he asked.

The eyes widened; Viola squeaked again. Cobb understood.

"Who did this to you?" Cobb asked. Then he realized how futile it was to ask such a question of a man who could not talk.

But Viola seemed to want to answer. He moved his hands as if to indicate writing. Hillyer, who had been standing nearby, out of the way, went to his desk and brought back a pencil and paper. He handed it to Viola, but the man's swollen hands could not keep a grip on the pencil. Frustrated, the preacher squeaked some more, closed his eyes, and pressed his lips tightly together. Tears formed in the slits of his eyes.

"You can tell me later," Cobb said. "Right now the important thing is for you to—" He stopped, suddenly remembered the man he had jailed last night, the one who carried, of all things, a New Testament. Frogg—Hiram Frogg. That was his name.

"I got to go for a minute," Cobb said. "I got to check on something. I'll be back."

He went back to the office at a run and all but broke the latch going in through the door. He rushed to the desk and pulled open the drawer.

The red-backed New Testament was there. Cobb flipped it open, gave a mirthless smile, and nodded in fulfilled expectation.

On the inside cover was the inked-in name of P. D. Viola.

Lybrand was in his cabin with the curtain drawn across the window when Deputy Heck Carpenter knocked. The preacher scurried to put away the whiskey bottle and glass on the table, and gestured with finger over lips for the woman with him to be quiet. Straightening his clothing, he went to the door.

The deputy noticed the preacher's disheveled look. "You been sleeping late, Rev?" he asked.

"I haven't felt well," Lybrand answered. "I've been worried about a friend who has not yet arrived in town."

"If you're talking about that Viola, then I got some word for you from Earl Cobb: He walked into town this morning."

Lybrand looked surprised—maybe more than surprised. "What?"

"I said he walked into town this morning. But— sorry to tell you this—he's in a real bad way. Somebody beat him nearly to death on the road outside town, and he may die yet."

Lybrand seemed stunned. He stood silently for a couple of moments, seemingly trying to absorb the news. Suddenly his eyes flashed, and he asked, "Has he said anything . . . about what happened to him?"

"He can't talk. Looks to me like somebody tried to crush his neck. But don't you worry—we already got the one who did it over in the jail. A fellow name of Frogg who got into a ruckus in one of the saloons. Cobb found the preacher's little Bible in Frogg's pocket."

Lybrand stared blankly. "You've got the one . . . oh. Where is Brother Viola now?"

"In a little room off the side of the lawyer Hillyer's office. You know, preacher, this here town needs a hospital. Maybe you ought to lead a campaign to raise money for one, once you get your churchhouse built.''

''Yes. Right. I want to see Viola—is that possible?''

''Course it is. But you'd best hurry, because I think he's going to die.'' Carpenter realized he was talking too frankly under the circumstances. ''I'm sorry to talk so blunt. I shouldn't be guessing about stuff like that. I ain't no doctor—maybe he'll live after all.''

''That is my prayer,'' Lybrand said. ''I'm glad you have his attacker. Interesting that a copy of the very word of God would be the evidence of his guilt.''

''Yeah. Good day to you, Rev. Got to go now.''

''God bless you, my friend.''

Carpenter walked away and Lybrand closed the door and leaned against it, still looking quite stunned.

Polly Coots, for reasons long forgotten called Dutch Polly among the ranks of Snow Sky's army of prostitutes, came to him from the corner.

''You talk awful pretty, you know it?'' she said. ''Almost as pretty as you look. I like that preachery voice. What was that deputy talking about?''

Lybrand was so deep in thought it took him a few seconds to realize she had spoken. ''What did you say?''

''What was that deputy talking about?''

Lybrand shook his head. ''Nothing to concern you. Just a problem I thought I had sufficiently dealt with—though it appears I was wrong. At least he hasn't spoken . . . but never mind that. Get on out of here and go back to your crib. And be sure nobody sees you leave here. I've got a reputation to protect.''

———

When she was with Lybrand she was like a girl again—even thought of herself as one, not as the weary, prematurely aging harlot she really was. Only in his company could she dream. As a child and young woman she had dreamed a lot, building cloud castles in which she played out an idealized future. Now, most of the time, she tried not to think of such things. She was worthless, and worthless women had no right to dream of good things. Their only right was escape—through alcohol, opium, suicide. So Dutch Polly Coots had come to believe.

But with Lybrand she had learned to hope again. Particularly at the beginning, when he had treated her so finely and talked to her like a man talks to a beloved wife. He had told her his secrets, outlined his plans . . . and though it had initially shocked her to find that a man who professed to be a minister was actually preparing to swindle his own church and the local bank as well, she had quickly over-looked it. Let him be what he wants, do what he wants, she thought, as long as he lets me be with him.

Lately, though, it had not always been pleasant to be with him. Lybrand had become cold to Polly—sometimes more than cold. That scared her, but she tried to dismiss his manner as preoccupa-tion with the coming consummation of the scheme he had set up with his two partners, who had come with him from Illinois: the big man named Clure Daugherty and the smaller, weasely one whose name Polly could never remember. She didn't like those men, didn't trust them. Lately, when they had been around, they had acted jumpy and overeager, accusing Lybrand of stringing them along too long. Polly was afraid they might actually hurt Lybrand.

When she thought about that, sometimes she tried to pray for Lybrand's safety, though she didn't know if God heard the prayers of girls of the line. She wasn't the same innocent, gentle woman who had once prayed and sung over a baby's crib and tucked quilts up under a little chin. God had heard her then, and loved her. Now she was sure she was beyond receiving love from anyone who was good, especially God.

At least she had Lybrand. Sometimes Polly could almost believe he was the righteous man he pretended to be. His congregation certainly believed in him. He was faithful in visiting the sick, gentle with children, proper in his public manner and words. He preached a fine sermon, too; Polly had once slipped in the back of his tent church to hear him. His voice had been a ship on a billowing ocean: rising, falling, rolling mesmerizingly onward. She had closed her eyes just to enjoy the music of it. When the sermon was over she had slipped quickly out, and the next time she was with him at his cabin he beat her for having dared show herself in his congregation. That was the first time he had lifted a hand to strike her. Sadly, it had not been the last.

A commotion ahead of her on the road caught her attention and held it. It was a man, woman, and child, riding a wagon toward town. The expression on the man's face was one of either great anger or great fear. The woman seemed only half conscious, and there was blood in her hair. She clung to a child on the seat beside her and seemed addled. Polly wondered if the man driving the wagon, probably the woman's husband, had beaten her.

When the wagon drew nearer, Polly noticed that the man seemed a bit addled himself and had blood drying on the sides and back of his neck. He was doing a poor job of driving, steering the horse team too far one way and then too far the other. The wagon came on more quickly than Polly had anticipated, and suddenly veered toward her. She gasped and stumbled back, barely avoiding being overrun.

"Out of my way, whore!" Orv Brown shouted at her as the wagon grumbled past.

Polly felt her face turn red and warm. She had little pride left, and had long ago faced the fact she had become exactly what the man had called her— but something in the way he had said it stirred a smoldering remnant of pride inside her.

"I was a decent woman once, you know!" she yelled after the man, who now was too far away to hear her over the rumbling wagon. "I was respectable, I was!"

She wheeled and began stalking angrily away. A few feet later she stopped and pivoted, yelling, "And I'll be married soon, married to a preacher! You wait and see if'n he don't marry me!"

She threw back her head and continued on toward the prostitute crib that was her home. "You just wait and see if'n he don't!" she repeated herself, because saying it felt good.

Cochran had continued to wander through the town after losing track of the man and boy. He hoped he would run across Frogg, but so far he had found no sign of him.

He was far across town at the time Viola walked in from the mountains, so he did not learn of the incident at once. But word of Snow Sky's newest arrival, who appeared destined to move soon to more celestial quarters, spread across town like smoke on a wind. Cochran was in a saloon having a sandwich and beer when he overheard talk of it.

"And the deputy said his name is Viola," a man at the bar was saying. "He was somebody the preacher Lybrand was looking for. He was beat near to one solid bruise and the marshal figures he's going to die. But they got the man who did it locked up. Name of Frogg."

Cochran drew a lot of attention as he choked on his sandwich. The men at the bar turned and looked at him. "You all right, mister?"

Cochran managed to slide the last bite down his constricted throat. "Yes, yes. I'm fine, thank you."

The man turned and briefly related to his friends more details of the story of Viola's strange arrival and pitiful state. The event was recent enough that so far it had not been corrupted significantly in passage. Cochran tried not to show further visible reaction to the story, but hearing of Frogg's involvement made his knees tremble beneath the table.

He left the rest of his sandwich, paid for his meal, and rushed out. Outside he walked down the street about a block and went into an alley, where he leaned against a wall to collect himself. At last he straightened his shoulders, adjusted his trousers, took a deep breath, and headed for the marshal's office with as much calm and dignity as he could muster.

Frogg jailed as a suspect in a beating? That would certainly explain his absence—though Cochran could not figure out just why Frogg would have been arrested. Then he remembered the New Testament they had found on the road, and Frogg's insistence he be the one to carry it. A lucky charm, Frogg had hoped it would be. Luck it certainly had brought him, but not the kind he wanted.

Cochran arrived at the marshal's office and three times tried to clear his throat of a lump the size of one of Flory's biscuits. A moment later Cobb opened the door.

"Hello, Marshal," Cochran said, hoping he sounded calm.

The marshal was looking intently at Cochran, trying to place him. Now he remembered: This was the man who had been with Hiram Frogg in the Rose and Thorn Restaurant last night. Interesting he should show up now. He stepped back and let Cochran enter. Cochran took off his hat and felt uncomfortable.

Frogg was seated in a wooden chair beside the marshal's desk, looking like he faced a death sentence. At the moment, with the marshal's attention diverted to Cochran, Frogg gave a flash of his eye and an urgent wiggle of his finger, obviously trying to send a silent message. Cochran wasn't sure what Frogg was trying to convey, but in desperate guesswork he interpreted it as: *Don't link yourself to me. Don't get tied in. Lie like the devil.*

"I met you at a restaurant last night," Cobb said to Cochran. "I'm Earl Cobb. Remember me?"

"Yes. How are you, Mr. Cobb?"

"Just fine. I think you also know my other guest, here."

Cochran looked at Frogg. "Why, yes. We met coming into town," he said. "Decided to share a restaurant meal. Good day to you . . . Mr. Frogg, isn't it? I'm Tudor Cochran, in case my name has slipped your mind."

Frogg said hello.

Cochran looked at the marshal. The innkeeper was not a liar by either nature or practice, and he hoped he would do a good enough job of it now. "I came to report a problem," he said. "I didn't mean to interrupt Mr. Frogg's business with you."

"Mr. Frogg's business is likely to linger for some time," Cobb said. "What's the problem?"

"I saw a drunk strike another with a bottle late last night. I think the man may have been hurt. I should have reported it sooner, I realize."

Cobb blinked. "Is that all?"

"Well, yes."

The marshal chuckled. "Welcome to Snow Sky, Mr. Cochran. You'll see far worse than that before you've been long in this town."

"Oh." Cochran feigned mild confusion. "So you're not interested in the attack I saw?"

"Drunks hitting drunks happens all the time. I can't worry over that. I've got a more significant attack on my mind at the moment."

Good. Cochran had hoped he could steer the conversation around to Frogg's situation. He put on a frown. "Someone attacked Mr. Frogg?"

"The other way around, I suspect. I've got a nearly dead preacher laid up on a cot, and Mr.

Frogg had the preacher's New Testament in his pocket.''

Cochran said, "Oh, my.''

"I'm glad you came in, Mr. Cochran,'' Cobb said. "I've been asking Mr. Frogg some questions about you, given that you two were together in the restaurant when I first saw you. Did I hear you say you only met him on the edge of town?''

The lump in Cochran's throat grew to two-biscuit size. He feared his voice would fail him, so he simply nodded, praying that his lie matched whatever story Frogg had told.

"How far outside town?''

"Not far at all. At the very edge. We both went for the same restaurant and decided to share company.''

"I see.'' There was a long uncomfortable pause. "Well, Mr. Frogg tells me the same story.'' Cochran almost collapsed with relief.

Cobb continued. "A good thing for you, really. I might have had to hold you, too, if I suspected you were with him for much time. Tell me, Mr. Cochran—did you see anything peculiar? Any sign that violence had been done to someone along the road?''

"No, Marshal. Nothing.''

Cochran cast a side glance at Frogg, beginning to feel guilty. Through a mix of lying and luck he apparently had cleared himself of immediate suspicion, but in so doing had left Frogg without any good alibi. Yet Cochran was sure he had read Frogg's silent signals for deception accurately, and the fact that Frogg himself obviously had already lied to the marshal showed he was trying to keep Cochran in the clear. Cochran wished desperately that he and Frogg could talk privately.

The office door opened and Heck Carpenter walked in. "I told Lybrand about his friend," he announced. "I think he's going to go see him."

The marshal had turned when the door opened; Frogg took advantage of the moment to dig a tight little ball of paper from under his cuff and drop it on the floor. It rolled to Cochran's feet. As the marshal turned, Cochran dropped his hat and stooped to pick it up. When he rose he had the paper as well as the hat.

"Mr. Cochran, since you two tell the same tale about meeting up, I don't have any cause to detain you. But I would appreciate it if you would stay in these parts for a time. I may want to talk to you further. Why are you in town, anyway?"

"An errand for my wife." Cochran blushed; the answer sounded inadequate and unconvincing.

"I see," Cobb said. "Stay around for a bit, you hear?"

Cochran's knees were shaking again. "Certainly, Marshal. Well, I'll go now," Cochran said. "And I'll not report any more attacks unless they appear severe."

"A good policy in Snow Sky," Cobb said. "Otherwise you'd be reporting to me all the time."

Cochran left and walked around a corner, where he sank to his haunches. Got to get a new place to stay, he thought. Can't be registered in the same room as Hiram. Can't have that marshal eyeing me all the time.

He remembered the paper, still clutched in his hand. Quickly he unrolled it. It was a note, obviously written earlier by Frogg to be slipped to

Cochran whenever the opportunity arose. It simply said:

Tuder you got to git me cleer of this because if that preecher dies I wil git hungg. Find out who dun it but dont git yourself cawt.

Hiram F.

⁓

Lybrand was at the office door when Hillyer answered. The young preacher's face was pale; he looked terribly worried.

"Is he here?" Lybrand asked.

"Yes." Hillyer's own face was drawn and tight. "You're welcome to come in if you like—I could use the relief. It appears that around here when a man volunteers the use of his office, he's expected to keep it open as a hospital." Hillyer stopped, suddenly looking ashamed. "I'm sorry, Reverend. Pardon that little outburst."

"I understand. Why don't you step out for a walk? I'll sit with Brother Viola. Later I'll arrange to have him brought to my home, where I can tend him until he's well."

Hillyer looked grateful. "You're a good man, Reverend. A walk would do me some good."

When Hillyer was gone, Lybrand took a deep breath, steadied himself, and walked to the back room. He looked down unsmiling upon the pitiful man in the cot.

Viola's eyes opened slowly. When he saw Lybrand standing over him, he blanched, squeaking in an attempt to shout, pulling back on the cot as far as he could.

Lybrand bent over and looked into the gaunt face. "Hello, old man. It appears I didn't do quite as effective a job on you as I thought. I'm impressed with your toughness, I'll admit." He smiled. "Oh, but you've missed one fine performance on my part these last hours. Did you know that after our little encounter outside town, I myself went to the law and told them you hadn't shown up, and that I was worried about you? Clever, you must admit. That would throw the best law-hound off my scent."

Lybrand's expression became darker, more terrible. "You are a fool, old man—you and your flair for drama, your idiot letters saying you were coming here to strike me down. Were you trying to frighten me? Did you think I was trembling at the fear of you? I've never been afraid of you, old man."

Viola raised a weak arm toward Lybrand, as if to grasp his throat, but Lybrand grabbed the arm and twisted it painfully. Viola made more terrible noises in his injured larynx and squeezed his eyes shut in pain.

"Suffering, are you? Well, not to worry. What I didn't complete on the road I'll finish now. You can walk through your blessed pearly gates and tell all the heavenly host about how evil I am and how you went to your death for the sake of your dishonored little girl. You know, old man, you were the closest thing I've had to a father since my real father died. The same endless religious jabber, self-righteous nonsense. . . . I'm going to do to you what I have wished a thousand times I could have done to him."

Lybrand pulled the worn feather pillow from beneath Viola's head and mashed it into his victim's face. He held it tight. Viola, struggling, grasped by chance the crucifix hanging around Lybrand's neck; he squeezed it until his hand went limp and flopped down to the bunk. Even after that, Lybrand kept the pillow over Viola's face for a long time.

When Hillyer returned, he found Lybrand seated in a chair in the corner of his office. Tears streamed down the young man's face. The cross around his neck glinted in sunlight through the window.

"He's gone," Lybrand said shakily.

"Gone? You mean dead?"

"Yes." Lybrand dabbed at a tear. "A hand more powerful than his has taken him to his reward."

CHAPTER 5

EARL COBB WITHDREW HIS HAND FROM P. D.
Viola's pulseless neck and wiped his fingers on his
trousers. "Dead, all right. Sorry about it, Reverend
Lybrand. It's a tragedy, it surely is. Did he have
family?"

Lybrand, his eyes still rimmed with red, shook
his head. He was nervously fingering the crucifix
around his neck. "That is probably the only bless-
ing in this situation," he said. "He had no family
remaining at all. That's why he felt called to join
me here at Snow Sky—he was perfectly fitted to
carry on God's work in a mining camp."

"You say he just expired on you while you were
visiting him?"

"That's right."

"Did he make any sounds you could interpret,
or write any words?"

"No."

Cobb nodded. "Too much to hope for, I suppose. But it would have helped cinch a conviction
if he could have identified our man."

Lybrand looked with interest at Cobb. "Yes. I

understand you've got someone jailed already as a suspect?''

"Man name of Frogg. Typical sort of shiftless type. I had him pegged as harmless. Guess that shows I'm not as good a judge of character as I had thought.'' Lybrand fancied that Cobb cast a deliberate glance at him as he said that, but he wasn't certain. "In any case, that was the dead reverend's Bible in Frogg's pocket. I can't quite figure out why he would have kept that, of all things.''

Lybrand asked, "Was Reverend Viola robbed?'' He knew the answer full well—he had robbed his victim himself to make robbery appear the motive.

"He was,'' Cobb answered. "Though I didn't find any money in Frogg's pockets. Maybe he lost it all at the poker table.''

"Probably so,'' Lybrand said. He sighed and wiped his eyes again. "The criminal mind is a tragedy of the Fall, is it not?''

"It's a source of never-ending trouble, is what it is. Well, Reverend Lybrand, I'm going to leave it to you to notify any who need to be told of his passing. Where did he live?''

"Chicago.''

"That's your old area, too, ain't it?''

"Yes it is. I knew Brother Viola for quite some time there.''

Cobb said, "Now if you'll step out a moment, I want to give the body a last examination.''

Lybrand looked concerned. "Why?''

"Standard practice. I'll need to be able to testify about the state of the body when we put Mr. Frogg on trial.''

"I see.'' Lybrand gave his crucifix another twist; tears rolled again down his cheeks. "Such a tragic thing," he said. "Killed in the course of God's work."

"It's a cruel land God has given us to live in," Cobb said. "I suppose he's got his reasons, but you'd know more about that than I would. Good day, Reverend Lybrand."

Lybrand left, closing the door behind him. Cobb looked after him thoughtfully for a moment, his brows lowered above his pale eyes. Had that been whiskey he had smelled on Lybrand's breath? Surely not; Lybrand was famous for his raging anti-liquor sermons. Still, Cobb had always felt somehow that Lybrand was not all he appeared to be. Well, he thought, maybe I'm just too suspicious about mining town preachers. He turned to the body of Viola.

Kneeling, he began at the top of Viola's head and worked down. He got no farther than the nose when he saw something that interested him. He put his head near Viola's chin and looked closely at the dead man's left nostril. Pulling a pencil from his vest pocket, Cobb extended it slightly into the nostril and pulled out a bit of fluffy white. A tiny feather. He then examined the pillow; indeed, it was torn and leaking feathers. But Viola surely had been on his back the entire time he had been on that pillow; he had certainly been in no shape to roll himself over. How had he managed to inhale a feather?

Cobb examined the man further. The more he looked, the more amazed he became that Viola had been able even to make it into town from the woods. Whoever had beaten him had done so brutally, and surely had believed Viola dead at the end of it.

On impulse, Cobb examined Viola's hands, wondering if there was evidence the preacher had struck or scratched his attacker. The long, supple hands were delicate-looking, and had unbroken fingernails and few calluses. But in the palm of the left hand was a strange red mark, an impression of a shape. Cobb looked closely at it.

He went into Hillyer's empty office and got a paper from the desk. Returning to Viola's side, he carefully sketched the hand and the impression on it. He put the feather on the paper and folded it up inside, and put the paper in his pocket.

Pulling a blanket across the face of the dead man, Cobb left to find the local gravedigger.

Cochran's hand trembled a little as he wrote, and he felt so depressed he worried he might blubber like a woman and wet the paper with tears. He didn't want that, for Flory surely would notice.

My Dear Flory,

There has been trouble here and I know no soft and easy way to tell you. The Preacher Viola who was with us now is dead and Hiram stands suspected of being his killer, though he is innocent. From what I can pick up the preacher was attacked somewhere along the road into Snow Sky and managed to make his way, in terrible condition, into town on foot. I suppose his horse was took or run off into the woods.

I know Hiram to be guiltless, but fear there is nothing I can testify that will convince others. Hiram is suspected because he had in his pocket the New Testament of Preacher Viola, but that we had found on the road and Frogg had kept with the plan to give it to the preacher when ever we saw him. This I could tell the marshal, perhaps, but I am sure he would not believe me, for I am new here and unknown to him, and it would be thought that I only was trying to protect my friend. At the moment Hiram and I are pretending to have no real mutual acquaintance and that we merely met at the edge of Snow Sky, but I do not know whether the marshal believes that because he saw us together in a restaurant the night we reached town. I am hoping he will put that down to the common friendliness of two traveling strangers.

Flory, I must remain here to find a way to help Hiram. I do not know what I will do, but I must do something.

I have seen the man and the boy and both look to be fine. Perhaps it will make you feel better about them to know that when I saw them the man was buying the boy shoes, so perhaps he is a good man after all and cares for the boy.

Flory, I will write you again as soon as I have new word to give. Do not worry for me. I do not think the marshal believes I was involved in the death of the preacher, though it is always possible he could begin to think that way if he perceives Hiram and me as friends. Hiram at the moment wants me to continue saying I do not know him, and so I shall.

I will be well and hope to be home soon.

Perhaps by the time you read this all will be set right.

Your loving husband,
Tudor

He sealed the letter into an envelope, addressed it, and mailed it. After that he walked around aimlessly for a long time, feeling utterly helpless, and wondered what he could do to help Frogg.

Perhaps he should talk to an attorney, who might be able to present his evidence more convincingly. But what evidence? He had nothing but his word—and now, rightly or wrongly, he and Frogg both had lied to the law. He again wished desperately he could talk privately to Frogg.

He continued walking about, thinking. Without real intention to do so, he gravitated toward the jail, approaching from the back. In Jail Alley, he leaned against the wall outside the place where he figured Frogg's windowless cell was. Wishing for some way to communicate with his friend, in frustration he picked at the chinking between the logs.

To his surprise, a big piece of it fell away. He gaped at it a moment, looked around, and then knelt and began digging at the remaining chinking. In only a moment he had made a small hole all the way through. The jail, it appeared, was built no better than most mining town buildings. Cochran peered into it, and saw a familiar eye looking back into his.

"Tudor!" Frogg scolded in a whisper through the hole. "You're going to get yourself hung like me doing such fool truck as this!"

"I had to talk to you, Hiram. This is the only way." Cochran looked fearfully around, hoping no one who passed the alley would look into it. "You know how bad's the trouble we're in?"

"What do you mean, we? It's my tail in the sling!"

"Your problem, my problem. I'm the one who asked you to come to Snow Sky."

"And I'm the one who insisted on carrying that Bible. Tudor, you know I didn't kill that preacher. But there's no way we'll convince the law of that."

"We shouldn't have lied," Cochran whispered back. "I should have come out from the beginning and said I know you and that we were together."

"No! That would just have landed you in here with me. You got to stay free, Tudor. You got to find something to clear my name."

"What, for gosh sake?"

"Find who really killed the preacher."

"How? I'm no detective. I don't know how to dig up information like that!"

"Then find somebody who can." There was a pause. "Shhh! Somebody coming!"

Then Cochran could tell Frogg had moved away from the little hole. Thinking quickly, Cochran scooped up a bit of the broken-out chinking and stuffed it back into the hole so that no flash of sunlight from the outside would betray the opening to the jailers. Then, feeling more despairing than before, Cochran walked away, shoulders slumped. Though the sun beamed down on the active town of Snow Sky, Cochran saw nothing but various shades of dark gray.

Lybrand took a long, deep slug of whiskey, followed by a longer, deeper breath. He looked at his
hand. Trembling. That would not do. A good actor
never loses his nerve. Just keeps playing his scenes
until the show is through.

He rose and walked about his cabin until he had
calmed a bit. This had turned into a nastier business
than he had anticipated. He wished he had done a
more efficient job the first time he had tried to rid
himself of Viola. But how could he have guessed
the old devil could have survived such a vicious
beating as he had given him? By all rights, Viola
should have marched skyward for whatever re-
wards awaited him, rather than coming like an am-
bulant cadaver into Snow Sky to demand even
more lethal attention.

Well, at least he was gone now, and this time
without question. Lybrand took another drink, feeling very tense, though also somewhat relieved. Viola had been a thorn in his side for a long time,
the worst Lybrand had ever been stuck with. Being
the man he was, Lybrand had dealt with a lot of
enemies, but never had he fully understood what
an enemy really was until he had been faced with
a father angered by a daughter's lost honor. He also
had never had to kill before, and though he was
glad to know he had the grit to do it, it had left
him feeling tight, ready to snap.

A knock on his door . . . Lybrand almost dropped
his whiskey bottle trying to hide it. His breath—
surely he reeked of liquor. Quickly he filled and lit
a pipe, hoping the strong tobacco odor would mask
the alcohol. After a few furious puffs, he went to
the door and opened it.

It was Dutch Polly, the crib girl. She grinned

crookedly. "Ain't you going to invite a poor girl in?"

Lybrand swore in a tense whisper and looked furtively around. Seeing no one else around, he grabbed her by the shoulder, pulled her roughly inside, and slammed the door behind her.

"You're hurting me!" she protested.

Lybrand slapped her across the face, hard. She screeched and pulled away.

"Oh! It hurts!" She cowered into a crouch before him. "Don't hit me, Jason, don't!"

"Very well," he said. He drew back his foot and kicked her, sending her sprawling.

Pointing a long finger down at her, he said, "Don't you ever come around to my front door, especially in daylight, you hear? Do you know what it would do to me if I were seen with the likes of you? You're not supposed to come at all except at the arranged times!"

"I just thought—"

His tension boiled into fury; he poured it on her at full temperature. "You're not fit to think. You're fit to do only one thing—and even that's becoming more trouble than pleasure. More trouble than you're worth."

Polly began crying. Her fantasy that Lybrand cared seriously for her was being beaten to death before her eyes. She looked up at him, rubbing her reddened face. "Don't talk to me like that, Jason! I can't bear to hear it!"

"Why did you come here?"

"I . . . wanted to be with you."

"When I want you around, I'll let you know."

"This time it wasn't for what you wanted that I came—I came for myself, just to be near you.

Don't you understand that? I'm a woman, Jason. I have feelings.''

"You're a crib girl, and crib girls can't afford feelings.''

Lybrand looked silently at her as she cried. He had just experienced an unwelcome realization: Dutch Polly was in love with him. He couldn't imagine a more unwanted development. Here he was, thriving in his clerical masquerade, only today rid at last of the long-searching, daughter-avenging P. D. Viola—and now he had a common prostitute in love with him. Sometimes it was terribly inconvenient to be a good-looking man; Dutch Polly wasn't the first of her breed to decide Lybrand was worthy of more than physical affection.

He decided to take a softer approach with her. "You may think you love me, Polly, but you don't. Neither one of us knows a thing about love. That can't be part of your world or mine, and I, for one, am content with that. You need to learn to be the same.'' He dug into his pocket and pulled out a couple of coins. He tossed them to the crouching young woman's feet. "Take it. Learn to get your happiness from that. That's the only thing you could ever really love, and the only god I could ever worship. Neither one of us can afford to take what we offer seriously. Far better to be a seller than a buyer.''

Polly, who felt as if her entire world was being knocked off its course, only cried harder, and pleaded, "No, Jason, please don't do this! I know I shouldn't have come, but I couldn't help it!''

His expression and voice grew cold. "In that case, you're getting out of control, and that makes you dangerous to me. I won't have you behaving in a way that threatens my interests."

Suddenly her grief turned to anger, and she scratched at him. He substantially evaded her, receiving only a scratch on his cheek, then threw out a fist and struck her in the mouth. She fell, lip bleeding.

He swore and grabbed his hand; he had slightly cut his knuckle on one of her yellowed teeth. A little drop of blood trickled down from the scratch on his cheek and dripped to the floor.

"Out!" he ordered. "Out before I snap your pimply neck!"

She was drying her tears on her sleeve; now she wiped her nose along the underside of it. "You can't talk so to me!" she declared. "I'm a lady, not some dog for you to spit on."

"You're a bit less than a dog, my dear, and far less than a lady. Get out—and go the back way. I won't need your services again—don't come around here anymore."

She stumbled toward his back door. As she left she turned. "You haven't heard the last of me," she said. "I wonder what the good people who hear you preach would think to know what you really are? How they'd like to know their preacher's dealings with Dutch Polly? How'd they like somebody to tell them that their preacher and two common thieves are planning to steal their offering plate money right out from under their noses?"

He glowered and stepped forward. "Don't threaten me!" he bellowed. She closed the door and cut him off.

He went to it and threw it open, started to yell after her. He realized suddenly he could not do that.

The Reverend Jason Lybrand could hardly afford to be seen shouting after a crib girl.

Cursing, he slammed the door. Another little drop of blood oozed from his cut knuckle and dripped on the floor.

<hr>

The next time someone knocked at the door, Lybrand opened it and found Earl Cobb. The false preacher uttered a quick and very uncharacteristic prayer of gratitude that he hadn't taken a drink in the last hour. Cobb was the sort who could detect that kind of thing.

"Marshal!" he said. "A pleasant surprise— come in." *What has Polly gone and said?* he wondered desperately. But his concern did not show on his face.

Cobb said, "I don't have long to stay, Preacher, but I wanted to ask you to conduct the burial service for your friend Viola tomorrow morning, ten o'clock. We need to get him under quick, with the weather getting warmer."

Lybrand felt great relief; this was just a routine call by the marshal after all. "Yes. I would have been happy to have conducted the services today, Marshal, if that would have been better."

"I couldn't have obliged you, Parson," Cobb said. "I was busy with the body of the deceased. Examination, you know. And then there was a robbery this morning. Orv Brown and his wife. Members of your congregation, ain't they?"

"Yes. Are they all right?" Lybrand was seriously interested . . . in Kimmie Brown, not Orv.

"A little battered, but nothing serious."

"Thank God. I will have to call on them. Your examination of Brother Viola's body—did you find anything?"

"Just a bit of evidence." Cobb paused, a bit too long. Lybrand felt his heart jump. "I need all that I can get to see that proper justice is dispensed to Mr. Frogg," Cobb continued.

"Yes. Of course. Thanks for coming, Marshal. Ten in the morning, you say?"

"Right, and I thank you," Cobb said. He lifted his chin and looked down his nose at Lybrand's face. "You know, Preacher, you got a scratch there. If you weren't a man of the cloth I'd swear you'd been scrapping with a long-nailed female." Cobb's eyes flickered to look into Lybrand's for a moment, then the marshal laughed.

Lybrand looked unsettled, then also laughed. "Marshal, you're a rather irreverent fellow," he said. "Believe it or not, I like a touch of that in a man. It reminds us men of the cloth not to become too pompous. As for that scratch, I got it from a scrape against a protruding nail this afternoon. Careless construction around here, you know."

"Well, that's a relief. I'd hate to think Snow Sky's only man of the cloth had to be watched to make sure he wasn't violating any commandments," Cobb responded, giving Lybrand another piercing look that did not escape the preacher's notice. Cobb touched his hat. "So long, Parson, and again accept my sorrow for the passing of your friend."

"Thank you."

As Earl Cobb walked away, he could feel Lybrand's stare. He smiled; his little attempt to unsettle the preacher had worked. He had seen

Lybrand's moments of uncertainty, of feverish, quick study of the loaded words he had pitched out. Cobb had played a suspicion and found the results rewarding, if somewhat disturbing.

Back in his office, Cobb sent Heck Carpenter to the Rose and Thorn to fetch a couple of plates of food and, after Heck was gone, unfolded a paper from his pocket and studied by lamplight the tiny feather that had been enclosed, and the sketch of Viola's hand and the peculiar mark upon it. Part of the reason he had gone to Lybrand's just now had been to make a surreptitious comparison of the mark—which looked remarkably like the imprint of a small cross in the dead man's palm—and the crucifix that hung around Lybrand's neck.

Back in his cell, Hiram Frogg snored, sounding like one of Snow Sky's lumber mills. Cobb rose and quietly walked back to the wall of square-crossed flat iron bars and looked at the sleeping man. After a few moments he went back to his desk and sat down again.

Preacher Lybrand, he thought, I think I'll be watching you right close for the next little bit. Right close indeed.

Lybrand really was edgy now. Cobb had stirred him so, with his peculiar and seemingly knowing words, that he felt endangered. He loaded his derringer, slipped it into his frock coat pocket, and left the cabin, intent upon a walk.

Did Cobb suspect him? Surely not. Cobb was nothing but a small-time mountain marshal, nothing like the well-trained police and Pinkerton men

Lybrand had dealt with back in Chicago. Yet Cobb could unsettle him with nothing more than a glance and a change of tone.

Lybrand strode by night toward the northern edge of Snow Sky, keeping in the darkest places all the way. By the flare lights on the street he watched people moving about. At times, when he kept his gaze low and ignored the squatty skyline and the dirt avenues, this place reminded him of some of Chicago's seamier portions, where he had grown up, learning to scrap and fight and hate and devote himself to one cause: improving his own lot at any cost required.

"Howdy, Preacher."

Lybrand was startled; the voice had emerged from the darkness to his right. A glowing red spot, bouncing about six feet above the ground, flared and came toward him. It was the coal of a cigar riding on the lip of a tall, bristle-bearded miner named Corbin Bottoms. Bottoms was built like a small mountain and had features as battered and weathered as the undersides of the federal naval vessels upon which he had served, underage, during the long-past civil hostilities. Rough as he looked, he was as gentle and decent a soul as Snow Sky could boast; even Lybrand had recognized that.

"Hello, Corbin."

"Y'hear 'bout Orv and Kimmie Brown?"

"Yes. Just a few moments ago. Terrible thing."

"Yep. Him and Kimmie both got knocked in the head, but they're not bad hurt. Everybody's talking about it."

"Yes. Good night, Corbin." The preoccupied Lybrand started to walk away. But Bottoms still wanted to talk.

"It was two men what done it. Sacks over their heads to hide them. But one had a real soft way of talking, Orv says. High-pitched. Orv says he'll know that voice when he hears it."

Lybrand frowned. "Soft way of talking?"

"Yep. Well, g'night, Preacher."

"Good night, Corbin."

The big man took the cigar into his hand and walked away; the red glow of the cigar receded and vanished.

Lybrand swore aloud when Bottoms was gone. A big man with a high-pitched, soft voice—that sounded like Clure Daugherty. And if it was, the other robber surely must have been Ivan Dade.

Lybrand knew his partners had been growing restless, and Daugherty even had dropped a hint that he might undertake a venture or two on his own if Lybrand did not give a go-ahead soon on the plan they had worked out together. Lybrand had not taken that seriously; Daugherty was always one for big talk. He had made such threats all the years he and Lybrand had worked together in everything from common theft and burglary to sophisticated confidence schemes. The threats had always proven idle.

But now he might actually have put action into his words and, if so, had endangered Lybrand's plan.

Problems upon problems: Dutch Polly making threats, Daugherty and Dade foolishly acting on their own, a town marshal growing suspicious ...

Lybrand turned on his heel and headed back toward his home. He needed a drink, bad.

CHAPTER 6

———

IT HAD BEEN A VERY FRUSTRATING DAY.
Cochran had roamed the streets of Snow Sky for
hours, trying to think of some way to help Frogg,
and nothing had come to mind. At last he had gone
back to his new rented room and tried to sleep, but
sleep would not come. Almost angrily he had
jumped out of bed and now was out in town again,
walking back and forth up Mud Street, stomping
along the Silver Street boardwalk, cutting from
alley to alley in purposeless frustration under the
light of the street flares.

At the moment he walked in an unlighted area
near the Dixie Lee Dance Hall, which stood off the
main streets behind a row of stores. On the far side
was a thick patch of woods. Raucous music from
a brass band poured from inside the big tent that
housed the dance hall. Cochran thought about going in to attempt to brighten his spirits, but hesitated to do so, for he had heard someone say the
Dixie Lee was the most notorious center for pros-
titution in all of Snow Sky, and Cochran didn't care
for that sort of thing. His father had spent a good

deal of time back during Cochran's Alabama childhood warning his son off strong drink, fighting, and
bad women, and it had stuck. The truth was,
women had always frightened Cochran a little, except for Flory. Flory he was fully at ease with, and
never fully at ease without.

Something moved behind Cochran, startling
him—then suddenly a dark, seemingly huge form
lunged directly at him, and a strong arm crooked
around his neck. He found himself held from the
rear in a stranglehold. A voice, filtered through gritted teeth, spoke directly into his right ear. Cochran's glasses sat pinched at a cocked angle on his
nose.

"Why were you following me?"

Cochran shifted his eyes and tried to turn his
head; the stranglehold tightened. "You know who
I am, innkeeper! Why did you follow me here?"

Now Cochran did know, and his legs went weak,
but only for a moment. He was the sort of man
who occasionally surprised other people, sometimes even himself. So it was now. With an almost
random wrench of his body and gouge of his elbow, he pulled free from the arm that held him,
and at the same time pounded his assailant in the
stomach. The man's breath burst out and he staggered back.

Cochran spun on his heel, straightened his
glasses, and took on a boxing pose that would have
brought forth a roaring laugh from Frogg, had he
been there to see it. His attacker didn't laugh;
Cochran had actually hurt him.

"Didn't expect that from you, innkeeper," the
man admitted. "You don't look the sort."

"Don't attack me again," Cochran said.

"Then tell me why you're in Snow Sky following me around."

Cochran lowered his fists. "I'll tell you if you'll tell me who you are."

The man paused, obviously trying to remember the name he had signed on the inn register. "Joe Jackson," he finally said.

"Really? You signed in as John at the inn."

"Then I'm John Jackson. What does it matter to you?"

"It doesn't matter to me very much at all, sir. But it does matter to my wife. She's worried about the welfare of the boy you had with you—and don't tell me he's your son. Flory knew from looking that he's not kin to you, and she's always been able to tell such things."

The man stepped forward and put out a finger. He was tall, with dark hair, a ruggedly handsome, wind-browned face, and a beard that reminded Cochran of Ulysses Grant's. The only light here was what filtered out through the dance hall tent wall, so Cochran couldn't at the moment see the man's face clearly, but even so the intensity of the black eyes was evident. "What business is this of yours?" the bearded man asked.

"None, I suppose. But I've had a very bad day, and at the moment I'm not all that concerned about what is my business and what isn't. I followed you because my wife worried for the boy. Maybe that's not my affair. Maybe it is."

The man was obviously dissatisfied with the answer. "You're lying. Nobody would follow a stranger just because of some boy."

"It's obvious you don't know Flory Cochran. She happens to care a lot about children—and for some reason, about this child in particular.''

The man was acting more cautious. ''Do you know me?'' he demanded.

Cochran felt he could best keep his advantage by bluffing. ''Maybe I have some suspicions. Where's the boy?''

The man looked silently at Cochran for a time. ''He's fine. Safe. You needn't worry about him.''

''Who is he?''

''Just a boy.'' The man glowered. ''You never mind—I'll see to him.''

''What does that mean?'' Cochran was surprised at his own boldness; he usually did not bear up so well in confrontations.

The man grew angry all at once. He came at Cochran again and grabbed him by the shirt. He pulled Cochran's face close to his. ''Leave it be, innkeeper! Stay away from me! Don't follow me, don't ask about me, and don't worry over the boy! Like I said: I'll see to him.''

He lifted Cochran off the ground and threw him back. Cochran's spine struck hard against a tree, snapping back his head and making it also pound the trunk. Stars burst against the backlighted luminescence of the canvas dance hall, and for a few moments Cochran was stunned. When his head cleared, the man was gone.

Rising slowly, groaning, Cochran rubbed the back of his head and wandered back toward his room. Only now did he begin to realize how much danger he might have been in.

When Cochran was far from the Dixie Lee, the boy who had so captured Flory Cochran's concern emerged from the place at the edge of the woods where he had been hiding, watching, and listening.

He had slipped unseen out of his bed and followed the tall, bearded man, and had taken in all that had just occurred. He looked wistfully in the direction Cochran had gone, but turned and went at a dead run back toward the place where he and his keeper were staying, not wanting it to be known that he had ever left it.

———

Cobb walked into the jail office and took off his hat. Cap Corley was sipping coffee and cleaning his pistol.

"You get that dead preacher planted?" the deputy asked.

Cobb nodded. "Lybrand said a few words and we put him under. Lybrand cried and slung snot like a spanked baby."

"Guess it would put most anybody into a state, having a fellow who was coming to see you get killed like that."

"Maybe so. But at the same time, Lybrand didn't seem all that sincere to me."

"Well, I can't see why he wouldn't be. I thought this Viola was a good friend who was going to help Lybrand start up a proper church."

"That's the story Lybrand tells, at least."

Cobb walked back to the cellblock. Frogg, seated on his cot, was just finishing off a biscuit and the last of a cup of coffee. A tray with the remnants of his lunch sat on the floor at his feet.

"Right good victuals, Marshal," Frogg said.

"Glad you like 'em. Can we have a talk?"

Frogg leaned back against the wall. "I had a few

previous appointments, but I suppose I can cancel them for you.''

Cobb got the key and opened the cell. He sat down on the cot beside Frogg and began rolling a cigarette. ''Want one?''

''Don't mind if I do.'' Frogg borrowed the makings and rolled a smoke for himself as Cobb lit his. Cobb tossed the matches to Frogg, who fired up his own cigarette and tossed them back.

''Mr. Frogg, why don't you tell me exactly what happened the day you came to Snow Sky?''

''I already told you.''

''Tell me again.''

''All right. I rode toward town, and a little ways out from it I saw this book on the road. It was a little Bible, so I decided to keep it for a good luck charm. Thought it might help me win some poker or faro, you know. I put it in my pocket and there it stayed until you took it out.''

''You see anyone?''

''Not until I got to the edge of town and met that Cochran man.''

''Think he might have killed Viola?''

The question chilled Frogg, but he didn't let it show. ''No.''

''Why do you say that?''

''I just don't think he could have done it.''

''You were alone before you met him?''

''Yep.''

''And you never saw Viola at all?''

''Never laid eyes on him. Haven't to this day,'' Frogg said.

Cobb mulled it over. He finished his cigarette, crushed it out, picked up Frogg's tray, and stood.

''Marshal, do you believe me?''

Cobb opened the cell and let himself out. He shut it and shook it to make sure the lock had caught. "I'll be honest: I'm having trouble keeping myself convinced you killed that preacher. Can't shake the notion you didn't do it."

Frogg was obviously surprised. "Then why don't you let me out?" he asked.

"Perhaps it will come to that . . . when I know a little more about a few things. There's one more suspect . . . but I need some more to go on." Cobb leaned on the cell door. "I'm tired, Mr. Frogg. Very tired. Robberies in people's home, dead preachers—it's a wearying thing for a man of the law. And it's worse when what you're trying to piece together doesn't seem to fit. There are some pieces of this situation that are misfits for sure."

"What's that mean?"

"If I knew I'd tell you. Right now I'm just talking hunches and feelings. Good day, Mr. Frogg."

Cobb walked out. Frogg finished his cigarette and wished he had another.

The next morning, a sharp rap on the door pulled Cochran out of deep sleep. He sat up in a stupor. More rapping, sharper than before.

Cochran climbed out of bed and put on his pants. Running his fingers through his hair, he answered the door. From the vigor of the knocking he expected to find someone telling him the building was on fire.

At the door he found a short, slender man with short-cropped brown hair and round wire-rimmed glasses. The fellow struck him first as hardly more than a boy, but at second glance Cochran noted wrinkles around the mouth and the corners of the eyes. In the thick brown hair were a few streaks of gray.

"Oliver Byers, sir," the man said, extending his hand. "I'm sorry to have disturbed you—obviously you were sleeping." Byers had a small mouth and cold blue eyes. His voice was as neatly clipped as his hair. Cochran mumbled out his own name and lamely shook the offered hand. Byers continued. "I hope you'll let me take a moment or two of your time."

Cochran, driven by curiosity, hesitantly stepped back and waved Byers inside. He stretched, yawned, and finger-combed his hair again. "Who are you?" he asked.

"I'm the editor of the Snow Sky *Argus*," Byers said. "I need to talk to you."

Cochran frowned. "What's this about?" With Frogg in jail and himself in a precarious position, he was naturally cautious.

"It's about Abel Patterson."

Abel Patterson? Cochran had never heard of him. "I think you have the wrong man," he said. "I don't know any Patterson."

Byers grinned knowingly. "No? Then why did I see you following him around town yesterday morning? You needn't deny it—I watched you for several minutes."

"So that's his name, huh?" Cochran muttered.

Cochran went to his bed and sat down, wishing for a cup of coffee and wondering if he should toss Byers out. He rested his elbows on his knees and put his face into his hands. "I don't think I should be talking to you," he said. "I don't know what you have in mind. How'd you find me?''

"I saw you come here earlier." Byers paused, then abruptly asked, "What do you think a newspaper should be?'' Cochran looked up at him, bewildered by the question, which carried a menacing hint of a coming lecture on journalism.

"I'll tell you what it should be by telling you first what it shouldn't: It shouldn't be simply a broadsheet for town promoters to boost their developments at the expense of truth. It should be a teller of the hard, bitter truth about a town and the people in it. It should expose secrets, not perpetuate them. I'm from Chicago, Mr. Cochran. I know journalism at its best, not just the throw-away rubbish you see in so many new towns like ours. I came to Snow Sky because I wanted to be part of the excitement of a mining town. I want to show that such a town is best served by a newspaper that doesn't shirk from the facts and doesn't conspire to mask secrets for the sake of some imagined community welfare. And believe me, there are secrets here that merit exposure—Abel Patterson being the newest. Not to mention yourself.''

Cochran asked, "Who is Abel Patterson?"

Byers knitted his brows. "You really don't know?''

"I really don't know. I followed him here from the inn I own, but I don't know who he is, and didn't even know his real name until this moment.''

"Why did you follow him?''

"What makes that your business?''

"Having the sheer gall to ask, I suppose. Look at it this way: I've made it my business, and if you want this story handled as it should be, I suggest you tell the truth.''

"So now I'm a story, huh?''

"Potentially, yes.''

Cochran stared at Byers a few moments. The newspaperman was a problem he didn't need. He played again with the idea of throwing him out, then reconsidered. Angering Byers might just make things worse. Maybe it wouldn't hurt to tell him a little of the truth, just enough to satisfy him . . . Cochran hoped. Maybe Byers could give him some information about this Abel Patterson in return.

"I followed him because of my wife.''

"Oh! He made improper advances to her?''

That really made Cochran mad. His face reddened. "No. Not at all. You'd have to know my wife to understand my reason, Mr. Byers. She worries over folks, especially children.'' He briefly told Byers about Flory's concerns and his agreement to come check on the boy's welfare. "Perhaps you find that foolish. But it's the truth. Not much of a story, is it?''

But Byers' eyes were gleaming. "So the boy really is with Patterson! Fascinating—I can't figure out that one.''

Cochran said, "I've given you what information I have. Now why don't you do the same for me? Just who is Abel Patterson?''

Byers rubbed his chin a moment as if trying to decide how much to tell. He sat down on the room's only chair and crossed his legs. "Abel Patterson is a former Pinkerton agent. He was a good one, too, with an outstanding reputation until a couple of years ago. He was based in Chicago, in Pinkerton's home office. I became familiar with him through my crime reporting. He was aloof, but the best criminal investigator I've ever seen, with the possible exception of his brother, Roland. He was a Pinkerton too.''

''Patterson was a criminal investigator?'' Cochran repeated. The seed of a rather bizarre idea immediately planted itself.

''That's right. When he was on a case it would possess him; he would work without sleep or food, hound the truth until he ran it down. The Chicago police would have loved to have the Patterson brothers on their force, but the two of them liked private work. Let me tell you, they made news in Chicago, right up until the day Roland was killed.''

''Killed? What happened?''

''He was shot down when he walked into a robbery. A senseless death. He and Abel had been investigating a series of such robberies, and the theory is he had detected a pattern or picked up some hint as to where the next would be. He walked in on it, and bang, he's dead. Abel Patterson happened to be elsewhere that night. It was just one of those tragedies that happens, nobody's fault, but Abel Patterson didn't see it that way. He blamed himself. It brought the end of his career with the Pinkertons.

''Patterson left the agency and went to work on his own, doing jobs far below his level of skill— investigating adultery for divorce cases, serving as a bodyguard for rich men with something to fear from one side of the law or the other. He began to drink a lot. Then one day he was gone. Headed west, the talk was. I saw no more of him after that—not until this week. Here I am, walking down Silver Street, and I look and see Abel Patterson, in the flesh, coming out of a rooming house with a boy at his heel. At first I thought my eyes were fooling me, but I followed him a good while, and sure enough, it was Patterson.'' Byers smiled. ''I also detected at one point that someone else had started following him, too. And not too well, I must add.''

''So I'm not a tracker or a detective,'' Cochran said. ''I never claimed to be. Patterson saw me just like you did. Looked right at me.''

''Really? Did he react to you, say anything?''

Seeing no reason to reveal the encounter outside the Dixie Lee Dance Hall, Cochran said, ''No. Just looked and went on.''

''Interesting. Everything about this is interesting—the unexplainable little boy, the money in the bank . . .''

''Money?''

''Yes indeed—big money. I have a contact at the Miner and Merchant Bank. I'm told that Patterson deposited almost fifty thousand dollars there when he arrived in town. And not silver—cash.''

''That's a pile of money.''

''It is. Where did he get it? Where did he get the boy, and who is he? And why did Patterson come to Snow Sky? He's not the sort to become a miner—or to need to, with the kind of money he's got deposited.''

Cochran rolled his shoulders to loosen them. ''Got any answers?''

''Not really. I was hoping you might.''

''Sorry to let you down.''

Byers stood and paced the little room. ''The answers will come, if I keep looking for the connections. I learned in Chicago that even in the big city there usually are links between events and people that don't seem to relate on the surface. Surely that is even more true in a smaller town. For example, you're linked to Patterson, and also to the man over in the jail with a murder charge coming his way.''

Cochran, feeling the newspaperman now was getting around to his real reason for being here, suddenly grew animated, stood, and reaffirmed the lie he and Frogg had created. ''Like I told the marshal, I'm not connected to that man beyond having met him at the edge of town,'' he said. ''I rode in with him and we shared a meal at a restaurant, and that's it.''

Byers laughed. ''Come now! If that's true, why were you talking into his cell through the jail wall yesterday?''

Cochran wasn't a good enough liar to bluff out of that unexpected challenge. He gaped at Byers. ''What right do you have to spy on everyone in town?''

''It's my job. You're a question mark. Another potential story.''

''And that's all that matters?''

''To me, yes.''

''So are you going to print me up in your newspaper?''

The newspaperman shrugged. ''At the moment, no. In the future, maybe. It depends upon what I find.''

Cochran didn't know how to react to this man. Byers had already made him mad; Cochran felt toward him like he would toward an oversized maggot.

But he had to admit the information Byers had given him was valuable. An intriguing idea had already grown out of it. He decided to probe Byers a little further.

"Let's quit talking about me for the moment. Tell me more about Patterson," Cochran said.

"No more to tell just yet. At the moment he's just another question mark, like you. And you two are certainly not the only ones. For example, there's another individual in Snow Sky . . . fascinating character, but not what he seems. I'm expecting an entire package of information from some old newspaper friends back in Chicago—should shine some light on him. See what I mean about connections? He's another former Chicago man. That's the way it is in a boom town. There's not a major city in the country that doesn't have at least a score of its folk here."

Byers abruptly changed his manner. He had become relaxed as he talked, but now he went stiff and formal. "Thank you for your time," he said. "I'll talk to you again, I'm sure."

When Byers was gone, clipping off down the street with his spine as straight as a rifle barrel, Cochran went to the mirror and rubbed the stubble on his face. A shave and wash was what he needed—a good clean appearance to help him do a job of persuading a man who would not be inclined to be persuaded. This Abel Patterson, whomever and whatever he might be, surely would find it quite peculiar that the very man he had attacked outside a dance hall in the night would come to him pleading for help. It was a crazy idea Byers had given Cochran—but even a crazy idea seemed better than none.

Cochran poured water from the pitcher into the basin and began to wash his face.

CHAPTER 7

—

KIMMIE BROWN, FRAMED IN THE DOORWAY OF her home, was as pretty as always despite the bandage tied around her forehead. She looked back at Lybrand in surprise. Her child stood at her side, clutching Kimmie's skirt in tight little fists.

"Reverend Lybrand! I wasn't expecting you to call!"

He flashed white, sparkling teeth. "I hope it is no imposition." He looked over her shoulder into the cabin. "Is Orv here?"

"No. He's . . ." She looked uncomfortable and paused.

"Working?"

"No. Not today." She sighed. "He's probably down in town . . . going through the saloons."

Lybrand lifted his left brow. "Drinking?"

"No, thank God. But it's just as bad. We were robbed, and the robbers struck us." She touched her bandage. "Since then Orv has been dead set to find them. He's convinced that if he roams the saloons enough, he can find the robbers."

"I had heard about the robbery," Lybrand said.

"In fact, I came to see how all of you came through it. Thank God he spared your lives." Lybrand frowned. "What you say about Orv concerns me, though. I hope he knows what he is doing."

"So do I. I wish he would just let it all go, but—oh! Forgive me! I'm rude to have you still standing at the door, Reverend. Please do come in."

"I don't know if I should, with Orv away. A minister must be careful to avoid even the likeness of, well, impropriety, you know."

"Don't be silly." Kimmie stood aside and gestured for him to come in.

Lybrand did, his saintly expression masking most unsaintly thoughts. Kimmie Brown was one of Snow Sky's most beautiful women, certainly the most attractive in his church. Once again he regretted the personal sacrifices that came with masquerading as a clergyman. If not for the economic value of this deception, he would snatch up Kimmie for his own.

"The robbery—tell me about it," Lybrand said.

Kimmie sat on a stool, arms around her child's shoulders. Briefly she described how it all had happened.

"But if they wore masks, how does Orv think he can recognize the robber?" Lybrand asked.

"One had a strange voice. Very high-pitched. Orv says he would recognize it again. I think I would, too. It was a remarkable voice."

Lybrand frowned in concern that Kimmie took to be for Orv but which in fact simply marked an unwanted confirmation. Kimmie's words had cinched his suspicion that Clure Daugherty had in fact been one of the robbers. Surely the other was Ivan Dade. Lybrand mentally swore at his partners.

He didn't need any loose cannons at the moment.

"Will you talk to Orv, Reverend? Try to convince him to forget all this?"

"I'll speak with him, first opportunity." Lybrand stood, feeling the ache that Kimmie always aroused in him. He restlessly fingered the cross hanging on his chest. When his scheme was played out—when he could cast off this pretense and be free of its strictures—then, he vowed to himself, he would come back and take her away with him.

Lybrand said his goodbye and left, trudging down the dirt road into Snow Sky.

Lybrand leaned against a tree near the Dixie Lee Dance Hall, watching people pass, nodding at those he knew from his congregation. "Going to preach you a street sermon?" one asked. Lybrand smiled.

At last he caught the attention of a young boy and called him over. He knelt and whispered to the boy, gave him a coin, showed him another. The boy went to the door of the dance hall and sneaked in. Lybrand waited.

A few minutes later the boy reemerged, Clure Daugherty with him. The boy ran to Lybrand, claimed the other coin, and darted off as Daugherty lumbered over.

"Come on," Lybrand said, not looking directly at Daugherty. "We have to talk."

Together they walked toward a place where a woodshed edged up against a patch of woods. At the front of the shed they were out of potential view from most angles.

"What do you want?" Daugherty said.

"Why the hell did you rob the Orv Brown place?"

Daugherty glared at Lybrand. "Who says I did?"

"I do. A big man with a high voice, they said—you're a fool to not know how easy you are to identify, mask or no mask."

"Don't call me a fool."

"Then don't behave like one. Whose idea was it, anyway? Yours or Dade's?"

Daugherty curled his lip. "Let's just say it was ours together. It's hard to sit in that cabin waiting for you to give word, Jason."

"We've worked together enough years for you to know that patience pays off. You let me get the church's bank account built up high enough, and we'll walk out of that bank with quite a pile. But you try another off-the-cuff robbery or some other damn-fool thing like that, you're liable to wind up dead."

"I can take care of myself."

"Maybe, maybe not. You earned yourself a problem you didn't need when you robbed Orv Brown. Now he's out looking for you. He's got every chance of finding you, too, with that voice of yours. Brown's in my congregation. I know him well enough to tell you he's got more hot temper than religion. He's already looking for you, and he won't quit until he finds you."

That aroused a light of worry in Daugherty's eyes, but he tried to damper it. "He won't find me, and even if he did, I'd take care of him."

"And get yourself jailed for it. You made a big mistake, Daugherty. You endangered our plan."

Daugherty grew angry. "And what about you?

Your dallying around with that crib girl's more dangerous to us than anything I've done. And what about this dead preacher everybody's talking about? Viola—that's your old papa-in-law, and don't deny it. He came looking for you, didn't he?''

''Viola's dead. He can't hurt us. It's living and breathing idiots like you and Dade who'll bring everything down.''

''Did you kill Viola?''

''There's a man over in the jail they say killed him. As long as he's there it doesn't matter who really did it, does it?''

Clure put a finger against Lybrand's chest. ''That's as good as an admission, Jason. Hell, it ain't me and Dade what needs worrying about, it's you! All we done was rob a miner. You kilt a man!''

''Shut up.''

''I won't shut up. It's time you hear me out. Seems to me you're taking too many chances. How much have you told that whore of yours, anyway? She know what we're up to?''

Lybrand didn't want to answer, so instead he lost his temper. His right arm shot out and his fist cracked against Daugherty's jaw.

Daugherty spasmed but did not stagger back. His oak-stout form absorbed the blow easily.

With a snarl and an oath, Daugherty pushed forward against Lybrand, knocking him back with the heels of his hands on Lybrand's chest. The false preacher fell back onto the door of the little woodshed. It fell open behind him and he collapsed inside.

A stack of cordwood fell atop him, and then several slabs of lumber. He was buried.

And at once Daugherty, Snow Sky, Viola, Dutch Polly, and everything else of the present was forgotten. Lybrand was back in Chicago, a boy again. He was no longer inside a woodshed, but in a familiar tiny closet. Outside it was his hated, drunken father, holding shut the door and praying loudly above the sound of his claustrophobic son's screams.

Lybrand had hated small, squeezing places almost from the crib. Even as an infant, his mother had once told him, he had writhed out of his blanket whenever he was swaddled. And as a growing child, the horrors that most dominated his nightmares always centered on closeness, enclosure, entrapment. Lybrand's father, a man consumed by both alcohol and a twisted religious zealotry, knew it and called it the work of demons.

"Let me out! Let me out!" Lybrand screamed. "Please, Papa, let me out!"

The prayers of his father, though muffled by the door, seemed loud to him. "Cast the demon from him, Lord! Purge the evil from his soul!"

Then his mother's weary voice: "Let him out, Jim—for God's sake, please let him out!"

"For God's sake, for his sake, I can't. He's evil, Ruth. Evil from the time he came from your womb. Foul he is, with the devil in him. He must suffer to be made right, just as Jesus suffered."

More feeble pleading from his mother, more screams from his own throat . . . and then he wasn't enclosed anymore. It was not his father or his mother reaching down to him, but Clure Daugherty.

"Jason, what's wrong with you?" Daugherty said, extending his hand. "You were screaming nonsense."

Lybrand grasped Daugherty's hand and scrambled out of the shed. He fell on his knees, gasping like he had been choked.

"You were yelling like I was your daddy," Daugherty said. The big man, the fighting spirit now out of him, thought about that a moment and chuckled. "You called me 'Papa'!"

Lybrand rose to his feet. After a few moments he was more his old self again, though blanched.

"You just forget what happened here," he said. "Concentrate on staying clear of Orv Brown. Get up to the Molly Bee and stay in the cabin."

"I can't spend all my time twiddling my thumbs up there, Jason. A man's got to come to town for a drink or a bite to eat."

"Look, I don't care what you do. Just stay away from Orv Brown, and lay low. You ruin the plan, you'll be held responsible."

"Same goes for you, Jason."

Lybrand wheeled and stalked away.

Abel Patterson watched the boy, as he often did, and wondered if there was a force that brought people together, or if they just met by chance, like leaves falling atop one another in the forest. Patterson had never expected to become guardian of a boy—especially not in the manner he had become unofficial guardian of this one.

The boy was seated in a chair, looking at pictures in a secondhand book Patterson had bought today.

It was a depressing little volume featuring wood-cuts showing the souls of dead children being lifted from coffins by winged angels, and Jesus smiling down from above the clouds at young orphans beside fresh graves marked MOTHER and FATHER, but Patterson hadn't been able to find anything better. Snow Sky opened a new business a day, folks said, but so far few people were selling books.

Patterson walked across the rented room and touched the boy's shoulder. "Spencer, you ready for sleeping now?"

The boy put down the book, stood, and walked to his bed. Silently he undressed and crawled in. He pulled the covers to his chin.

You sure don't have much to say, do you, boy? Patterson wanted to comment. But it would have been pointless, for he had said it a score of times before, and it had never drawn response. In the time he had cared for young Spencer Vestal, he doubted the boy had said enough words to fill one page of that book he had been reading. Given the circumstances in which the two had been thrown together, it didn't seem that should bother Patterson, but it did.

"Good night, Spence," he said. The boy said his own good night—just a faint, quick whisper—and turned his face toward the wall. In a minute or less he began the slow, steady breathing of sleep.

Patterson went to his chair and sank into it, feeling terribly depressed. He was depressed a lot these days, and in a way that made no sense, for he had always figured that if he had money he would be happy, and he had more of it now than he had ever thought he would. He somewhat regretted having put it in the bank, for banked money could be traced much more easily, but he had not felt comfortable with the idea of keeping all that cash in hand. In Snow Sky it would promptly be stolen.

Snow Sky. Here at last in the town that he had hoped would solve his problem, only to find it had not. The sister he had sought was not here, contrary to what he had expected, and no one seemed to know anything about her. Much distance in miles and years stood between his sister and him. Maybe it was just as well he had not found her, for she might have refused to take Spencer off his hands anyway.

Which would have left Patterson in the same predicament: playing guardian to a boy he had not asked for, and whose nearly unbroken silence disturbed Patterson almost as much as the ugly scars on the young white body. What had this boy gone through so far in life? Was it past suffering that kept him silent?

Patterson stretched, shook himself like a wet dog. He had to get out. He couldn't sit here lost in dark thoughts. He rose and picked up his hat. Fingering it, he went to the boy's bed.

"I'm going out for a while," he said, in case the boy was awake enough to hear. "I'll be back soon. You just sleep. I'll leave the lamp burning."

The boy did not respond. He seemed still to be asleep. Patterson put on his hat and walked out the door, wondering why this child could so break his heart.

When Patterson clicked the door shut behind him, Spencer sat up and looked around the empty room. He thought briefly about secretly following his guardian, as he had other times, but tonight he decided not to. He was content to simply stay where he was and think about the man whom Abel Patterson had accosted outside the dance hall. The man from the inn—the man who talked about the woman who worried about the welfare of little boys.

Spencer lay back, his hands behind his head, basking in the knowledge that somewhere, at least, one person cared about him. It was a new feeling for him . . . a good one. He smiled at the ceiling.

———

Cochran had been unable to find Abel Patterson, which did not surprise him, but did worry him. He had already come to think of Patterson's detective skills as Frogg's only hope. Right now Cochran could use a few detective skills himself. But inwardly he wondered if he really would have the courage to approach for help the same man who had roughed him up and threatened him only a day ago.

Still, Frogg had to be cleared, and Cochran had no idea how to do that alone. He was tired now at the end of the day, and ready to give up, but for Frogg's sake he decided to look around a bit longer, poking through a few more saloons and dance halls in hope of spotting the former Pinkerton man.

"Howdy."

Cochran wheeled, drawing in his breath. Lord, but he was tense—jumpy as a cricket in a stove. He was sure that Earl Cobb had noticed that, too; he was standing only six feet away, cleaning his nails with a pocketknife.

"Hello, Marshal," Cochran said, recovering. "You surprised me."

"Thought you looked a bit startled. Sorry. Just trying to be sociable."

Cochran doubted that. This peace officer didn't seem the sort to make idle small talk.

There followed a time of silence that sat uneasily with Cochran but didn't at all seem to affect the marshal, who calmly kept digging dirt from beneath his nails and wiping it on his trousers.

"Still got your friend sitting in the jail," Cobb remarked casually.

"He isn't my friend—I met him riding into town. Remember?"

"Pardon me. I forgot. Anyway, I still got him in jail. But it's a funny thing: I don't really think he killed that Viola fellow. Ain't sure why. You ever get notions like that that you can't quite explain?"

Cochran was so surprised he didn't know what to say.

Cobb continued. "My main problem is, I don't have any good evidence in Frogg's favor—and Frogg did have that Bible on him."

Another long, uncomfortable pause. Cochran wondered if he was about to be arrested. He asked, "Is there anything specific you need of me, Marshal?"

"Need? No. Just passing the time. Things get slow in the law business; you have time to do that. What business are you in, Mr. Cochran?"

"I'm an innkeeper."

"Is that right? Where?"

"About a day and a half's ride up the road yonder. The Cochran Inn."

Cobb nodded. "Heard of it." Then he looked

thoughtful. "So that means that Frogg and maybe even Viola would have come by your inn."

Cochran hesitantly decided to risk giving the marshal one piece of truth. "Frogg I didn't see, but Viola stayed at my inn. It took me some time to realize the man who was killed was him."

Cobb didn't believe that; a name such as Viola is remembered. He didn't challenge Cochran, however.

"Did you talk to Viola while he was there?"

"Some."

"What did he say about his trip to Snow Sky?"

"Not much. Just that he had an unpleasant job ahead and dreaded it."

"What kind of unpleasant job?"

"A meeting with someone, I think. He didn't say more and I didn't ask. Does it matter?"

Cobb folded and pocketed his knife. "Maybe not, maybe so. I was just hoping you'd be able to provide something more to help me. Thanks, and sorry for the bother."

"No bother at all, Marshal."

Cochran walked away, wondering what this encounter had been all about. The marshal's word that he thought Frogg innocent was a profound and pleasing shock—if it had been sincere. Cochran couldn't tell; Earl Cobb seemed a fox-smart peace officer, the kind to pick his way along without revealing exactly where he was going, or how much you had unwittingly helped him along the way. Cochran entered a saloon, mostly to get out of Cobb's sight and think over what had just transpired.

For his part, Cobb had some thinking over to do, too, for Tudor Cochran had just given him an interesting piece of information: P. D. Viola had been fearing a coming meeting in Snow Sky. With whom? Lybrand? But that made no sense if all Viola was coming to do was to help establish a church. Why should a preacher dread that, given that such was his life's business? Once again the pieces didn't fit.

Cobb considered the possibility that the innkeeper himself was lying about it all. Maybe Cochran himself had killed Viola. Perhaps some grudge had developed while Viola stayed at his inn. Maybe he suspected the preacher carried a lot of money.

But Cobb didn't buy that. He could tell by instinct that Cochran was not the killing type. He seemed the sort who would dodge a bug instead of step on it.

Yet Cochran was covering up something, Cobb suspected. Probably about his knowledge of Hiram Frogg; Cobb found it difficult to believe the two men really knew each other as minimally as they claimed. He glanced down the street, wondering where Cochran might have gone. He caught a glimpse of the innkeeper just as Cochran entered the door of the Eagle Wing Saloon.

———

Patterson sat alone at a back table, sipping whiskey. A shadow fell across his table and he looked up. The innkeeper he had attacked outside the dance hall stood there, looking nervously at him.

"Hello," Cochran said. He was holding his hat tightly, rolling and unrolling the edge of the brim. Ironic, Cochran was thinking, that he should chance upon Patterson in the very saloon he had entered to get away from Earl Cobb and his questions.

Patterson shook his head and looked back down at his whiskey. "What do you want? You still trying to poke into my affairs?"

"Please. I'd like to ask you to hear me out about something. My name is Tudor Cochran, in case I never told you." He put out his hand.

Patterson ignored it and looked away.

Cochran lowered his hand and said, "This will just take a moment or two. May I sit down?"

Patterson was not pleased by the request, but waved curtly toward the other chair at his table. Cochran quickly pulled it back and sat down in it, so obviously tense he looked like he would be triggered to the ceiling if anyone around so much as stomped a foot too loudly. Patterson took another sip of his whiskey and glowered coldly at Cochran, thinking of how the man reminded him of a thoroughly unwelcome stray dog who had wandered into his yard and refused to leave.

"Well?" Patterson prompted gruffly.

"I need your help," Cochran said, leaning forward a little, still rolling his hat brim in his lap.

"Help?" That struck Patterson so funny that he laughed aloud. "Why should I help you with anything?"

"Because you're probably the only man in Snow Sky with the ability to clear the name of an innocent man being wrongly suspected of a killing."

Patterson frowned. Those words implied rather uncomfortably that Cochran knew something about his identity and professional background. "What are you getting at?"

"I suppose I'm trying to offer you a job."

Patterson frowned, then laughed again. "A job! What makes you think I need one?"

"I suppose you don't. But an innocent man could be imprisoned, or worse, if you don't agree to help me clear him."

Patterson had to admit that this was becoming interesting. "All right, friend, you've got my ear. This is just loco enough to rouse my curiosity."

"Mr. Patterson, I want you to—"

"Why did you call me that?"

"Well, it's your name, isn't it? Abel Patterson?"

Concern bolted through Patterson, who had thought no one in Snow Sky knew his identity. "My name is Jackson," he asserted strongly. "Where did you hear different?"

Cochran's mouth went dry, and he realized he had made a slip. He should have known Patterson would be concerned when he found out his real name was known. Cochran felt his opportunity slipping away, yet he knew he couldn't reveal where he had gotten his information. If Patterson knew a newspaperman had been talking about him, he would be out of town within the hour. So Cochran blurted, "I used to live in Chicago. I read about you in the papers. You were pointed out to me once. I knew you looked familiar when I saw you at the inn, but I didn't recall who you were until a couple of hours ago." Cochran spilled out the lie, then hoped Patterson would not challenge it, for Cochran had never been to Chicago and knew nothing about the city.

Patterson didn't question Cochran. His mind was occupied with only one thought: He now must leave Snow Sky. Clean his money out of the bank and take off. If someone here knew him, he couldn't afford to linger. But leaving would be troublesome. Could he endure weeks of aimless riding with the responsibility of young Spencer Vestal heavy on his shoulders?

"I'm not trying to cause you worry," Cochran continued. "All I want is your help. You are a fine criminal investigator, or so I was told."

"And you're a man who's followed me for miles and poked his nose in where it doesn't belong."

"I don't deny it. I did that for my wife. But this is a different matter. This is for my friend, and it could be life or death. His."

Patterson drained off his whiskey. "So what are you asking?"

Cochran leaned over a bit more so he could further lower his voice. "You heard of the killing of a preacher named Viola?"

"I did. Why is that your concern?"

"Because the best friend I've got is in the jail, suspected of the murder. He and I have both told the law here that we don't know each other, so I've just now put my safety into your hands."

"Is your friend guilty?"

"No."

"How do you know?"

"Because I was with him all the way into Snow Sky and a little while after that. And even if I hadn't been I would know Hiram didn't do it. He's rough, but no murderer."

"So why not go to the law and tell them what you know?"

"They wouldn't believe me, and likely I'd just become another suspect. And there's some evidence against Hiram." He told about finding the

New Testament and how it had figured into the situation.

Patterson turned his empty shot glass between his fingers, shook his head. "I see no reason for me to get involved in a murder investigation. I don't need money and I don't want the attention, and it isn't my affair. I'm a former detective, not an active one."

Cochran's heart sank. He said, "Surely there is something I can offer you that would make you change your mind."

"Not a thing."

Cochran sank back in his chair. "Then there's not much I can do for Hiram."

"That's your concern, not mine. I got my own concern, and it's more than enough for me."

Interpreting him, Cochran asked, "The boy?"

Patterson said nothing, lifting his glass to let a final drop fall from its rim onto his tongue.

Cochran asked something else that was on his mind. "Mr. Patterson, if you'll do nothing for Hiram Frogg, at least do something for my wife. Give me some word to take back to her about the boy. Who is he? Does she have cause to worry for him?"

Patterson looked at Cochran in silence, not sure he should say anything. Finally he did. "His name is Spencer Vestal. He's a young fellow whose path crossed mine. He's in need of a home. I came here to find him one, but that hasn't worked out."

And at that a new and surprising thought flew like a comet through Cochran's mind—a frightening, probably foolish, but wonderfully possible option. Ideally, it was the sort of thing a man should think about for months and talk over with his wife, but at the moment Cochran had neither months nor wife available. In less than five seconds he made his decision and presented his proposition to Patterson. "Mr. Patterson, if you will help me, then I'll help you in turn. I'll give that boy a home with my wife and me."

Patterson stared at Cochran, then down at the tabletop. Cochran leaned forward again, pressing his offer. "All I ask is that you help me find who really killed that preacher, or at the very least show it wasn't Frogg who did it. Do that, and the boy will become my responsibility."

A home for Spencer was just what Patterson had been looking for, but now that he had found one he was unsure what to do.

"Well? Will you do it?" Cochran prodded.

Patterson stood suddenly, dug money from his pocket, dropped it on the table, and stalked out. Cochran watched him go, then sank back in his seat, more dejected than ever.

CHAPTER 8

JASON LYBRAND AWAKENED WITH A YELL, the dream image of his father's face still clearly before him. Or had it been the face of Viola? Or both—dreams could sometimes twist reality in impossible ways.

Lybrand, who had fallen asleep at his supper table with a copy of the *Argus* before him, put his face into his hands and rubbed his eyes. Got to get in control again, he thought. Can't let myself panic.

He picked up the newspaper and reread Oliver Byers' coverage of the death of Viola, and of the continuing official suspicions that Hiram Frogg was the killer. The story should have made Lybrand feel safe and confident. It didn't. He wadded the paper and threw it into his cold fireplace.

The more time that went by, the more uncertain and threatened Lybrand felt. He had a bitter feeling that bad things were coming; there would be a pay-day, and he would be on the short end.

He stood. Get a grip on yourself, man, he

thought. Things really aren't so bad, no matter how you feel.

He reminded himself of the several matters going in his favor—particularly the suspect already jailed in connection with Viola's murder. And even without such a convenient scapegoat, why should anyone have cause to think the fine young preacher at Snow Sky's House of Prayer would be a killer? He had never given the community reason to distrust him.

Lybrand knew he was a good actor; he had put on many performances under many names through the years, sometimes professionally on stage, sometimes off it. The world of theatrics and make-believe had attracted him as far back as he could remember. In that world an abused city boy could escape the tyranny of an insane father. Lybrand had always felt it ironic that on stage, where every action and word was predetermined and the final climax settled even before the opening line was spoken, he felt more free than anywhere else. The fictional life of the stage was more true and authentic to Lybrand than the cruel real one he lived in.

But being an actor had one drawback: it paid very little. Lybrand thus found himself beginning to use his acting skills in innovative, self-profiting ways. By portraying a down-on-his-luck traveler, he found he could snare a contribution from a church. As a just-discharged, jobless soldier, he could talk his way into a free meal. And as a street-corner preacher, imitating the religious rantings of his obsessed rum-addicted father, he could talk spiritual fervor into the heart of—and money out of the pocket of—the sort of folk who were ready to believe anything that gave them hope and a sense of importance.

Eventually Lybrand had begun calling himself "Reverend" and taking on his preacher persona almost full-time. It had its disadvantages—womanizing, drinking, gambling, and the like had to be done on the sneak—but it was also lucrative.

He involved himself in less sophisticated crimes as well, sometimes participating in robberies, burglaries, and even rapes, with his two old backstreet cronies, Dade and Daugherty. But Lybrand disliked crude crimes; he preferred a smooth swindle to a back-alley pocket-cleaning. As time went by he concentrated most of his attention on his lucrative clergyman persona.

No one except the late P. D. Viola had ever come close to exposing Lybrand—and that had almost happened only because Lybrand let his passions for Viola's daughter make him careless.

P. D. Viola. The man's very name roused Lybrand's disgust. Yet Viola had been useful to him once. Lybrand had successfully deceived Viola and his family for quite some time—so thoroughly that he had gained the secret intimacy of Viola's lovely daughter, Francine. The memory of her stirred Lybrand's blood. Beautiful, passionate she had been. The fifth in a string of wives for Lybrand, who married but never bothered with the legal messiness of divorce, which was troublesome and, in Lybrand's view, unnecessary. In Francine's case it truly had proven unnecessary, for she had died giving birth to the stillborn child Lybrand had planted in her well before their marriage, bitterly shaming her pious father.

Lybrand thought back wistfully on Francine,

then tossed aside her memory like outdated correspondence. She was dead, that was that, and he would have to content himself with the charms of other women. Dutch Polly had hardly been a fit replacement for Francine, but she had served her limited purpose well for a time.

But now Polly was making threats that had him worried. He had been foolish to allow a crib girl to fall in love with him. His own brother years ago had made such a mistake, and had died in his own bed as a result, stabbed by the prostitute who had wanted from him that which he would not give.

Lybrand was only just now realizing that Polly was equally dangerous to him. If she told others of his dallyings with her, that would be the end of the Reverend Jason Lybrand in Snow Sky. Perhaps Daugherty had been right. Perhaps he had been a fool to talk so much to Polly. Yet it had seemed harmless; the woman was so opium-dulled that she had not seemed even to hear half of what he said to her. Now he was sure she had in fact heard him, and understood much more than he had guessed.

He had been fretting over the situation all day, remaining locked away in his cabin. Something would have to be done. Otherwise things might turn sour.

He rose and walked to the window of his cabin. The sky was dull and gray; a change in the weather was coming. Well, let it come. He had to start preparing a sermon for Sunday morning in any case. Perhaps something on the need for the church in civilized society, its role in bringing peace and welfare to the frontier, so on and so on. Something to make his churchmen feel important, righteous—

and to heighten their sense of Christian generosity when the offering plate came around.

Lybrand went to his table and sat down, thumbing through his Bible for appropriate verses. Ironically, the first thing he found was a reference to the Whore of Babylon, which put him in mind again of Dutch Polly and her threats. He slammed the Bible shut and paced around the room, wishing he was free to walk down to a saloon and get thoroughly drunk. Again he despised being tied to a public image of saintliness.

He returned to the window. The wind was up. Lybrand scanned the heavens and then dropped his gaze. To his surprise, it came to rest on Earl Cobb, who was standing leaned against a fence just down the road. He was shaving off a piece of wood with his knife. Lybrand had the peculiar and unsettling feeling the marshal was watching his house. His paranoid sense of doom surged like an ocean breaker.

Lybrand let the curtain fall and turned away.

—◆—

Patterson watched Spencer sleep and mused over the unexpected offer Cochran had made, and the inexplicable reluctance he felt to accept it. At last a chance was at hand to be free of this tag-along boy, but now he didn't want to be. Patterson could make no sense of his own feelings.

Patterson and Spencer had shared a strange companionship; but then, it had begun after a strange meeting.

Spencer had come into Patterson's life—or more precisely, Patterson had come into Spencer's—in a small valley several miles from Denver. His Pinkerton days behind him, Patterson had been making his living doing menial detective and guard jobs, and had become involved in the most menial yet: delivery of extortion money from a wealthy Denver banking baron to some human maggot holed up in the mountains. What sin the extortioner held over the head of the rich man Patterson neither knew nor cared to know—but it must have been significant, for the banker had readily parted with fifty thousand dollars to keep his tormentor quiet. He had hired Patterson to carry the cash because he knew of Patterson's reputation with the Pinkertons, and felt he would be both honest enough and capable enough to safely make the delivery.

Patterson had ridden with the cash in his saddlebags, following the crude map the extortioner had provided, and all the way had fought an inner battle. Why not take the money for himself? Let the rich man's secrets catch up with him—that wasn't Patterson's worry. Likely the man deserved to be extorted and discredited.

But Patterson had not yielded. In the end he found himself riding the final stretch of mountain trail leading to the place where the extortioner was to receive the cash.

At the end of that trail Patterson had found a tiny cabin in a clearing, and outside it, a boy of about eleven very hard at work with a shovel.

He was digging a grave. For the extortioner, it appeared; a fat man's corpse lay stretched out beside the shallow hole. The body matched the description Patterson had been given of the extortioner.

The boy silently watched Patterson's approach.

Leaning on his shovel, he said nothing, but stared as sweat dripped off his brow and soaked through his shirt.

Patterson gestured toward the corpse. "Your father?"

The boy nodded.

"What's your name?"

No answer. It would be days before the boy answered that question. By that time Patterson would have come to understand, through the scars and the eternal, veiled fear in the young eyes, that life had been terribly hard for Spencer Vestal, and that the greatest mercy it had yet shown him was the stopping of the heart of the father who beat his son more than he spoke to him.

From what Patterson could tell, the extortioner had died naturally. Heart, probably. Patterson had seen plenty of death in his time, and knew men of this one's girth had a way of just dropping dead as a run-down clock once their hearts wearied of their task.

"Would you like me to help you bury him?" Patterson had asked the silent boy.

Still unspeaking, Spencer had offered him the shovel. Patterson finished the grave and laid the obese corpse in it, then began shoveling dirt atop him before he realized such a thing might be difficult for the boy to see.

"You want to go somewhere else while I cover him?" Patterson had asked. But Spencer had simply shaken his head and stayed at the graveside, masking any emotion he might have felt. Later, when Patterson would see the boy's scars, he would speculate that the hidden emotion might have been relief.

When the grave was filled, Patterson had leaned on the shovel and considered what to do. Without making a conscious decision, he nonetheless had concluded already that he would not return the extortion payment. His life had made a moral downhill slide for months now, and he simply let himself slide a little farther—and it was surprisingly easy. The old banker surely had plenty more money. Probably much of it ill-gotten, too, judging from the fact he obviously was open to extortion.

Patterson had climbed back into his saddle before he had realized that the boy couldn't simply be abandoned. But what could he, an odd-job drifter with saddlebags full of stolen payoff money, do with a scruffy kid in tow? He couldn't take the boy to the law, or to an orphanage, for someone would ask how Patterson had managed to get him. Even if he lied, they surely would ask the boy, too—and if the lad ever found his tongue, he might just tell about the man who came to bring his father's extortion payment, then decided to keep it.

And that was how Abel Patterson came to be the guardian, against his will and the boy's, of Spencer Vestal.

Patterson had known he would have to find the boy a home—but how? It would have to be with someone who would accept the boy with no questions and no intention of involving the law. In a flash it had come to him: his sister. Living now, last he had heard, with her husband in the mining camp of Snow Sky, Colorado. Even though he had never kept up with his sister as well as he should have, maybe she still would take the boy, give him a home, see to him without getting Patterson himself involved or in trouble. It was the only option he could think of.

Patterson had taken the extortioner's horse for the boy, and man and boy had left immediately for Snow Sky, Patterson as tense as if he had a wasp down his pants, but also excited. He had money now, more than he knew what to do with—and soon he might be rid of the boy. He would have the rest of his days to use that money to buy a new life in which he could forget the old one and its one unforgivable failure—the time he had failed to be there to save his brother from a robber's bullet on a dark Chicago street. Though he had tried at least a hundred times to convince himself his feeling of responsibility for Roland's death was irrational, he had not succeeded. A sense of failure and guilt had continued to haunt Patterson, led him to liquor, ended his career with the Pinkertons, and left him doing jobs as low as delivering—and now stealing—extortion money.

Spencer moved in his bed now and opened his eyes. He saw Patterson looking down at him, and for a moment fear flashed through him. Patterson saw it. It saddened him.

He reached out and touched Spencer's forehead. "You sleeping all right?" he asked.

The boy nodded.

"I've been doing some thinking," Patterson said, hardly able to believe he was about to say what he was. "I was wondering if maybe you might like to stay with me. Let me be your father. I don't know much about boys beyond that I was one myself once—but I can learn. I can give you a good life, better than any you had before. There's enough money for it. Maybe someday there might even be a woman who can be your mother.''

Spencer rolled away, turning his back on Patterson. There already is a woman who could be my mother, he was thinking. She's back at that inn, and I know she cares for me because I heard her husband say so. That's who I want, not you.

He said none of it, but Patterson sensed the rejection. He stood and walked over to his own bed, lay down, and stared at the ceiling.

All right, he thought. Innkeeper Cochran, I'll take your offer. I'll try to help your friend, and you can have the boy.

Even though now I don't want to give him up.

The Next Morning

The marshal's office door burst open with a bang, awakening Cobb from a good sleep that was no more than an hour and a half old. A razor of a voice sliced into his eardrums. Then another voice moaned—or maybe it was a floorboard creaking. Got to find some other place to live besides this blasted office, Cobb thought as he rolled over. Lousy slamming doors, yelling prisoners, creaking floors, belching deputies—won't let a man sleep. . . .

Suddenly he was being shaken. Blearily he opened his eyes. Cap Corley said, ''Earl, I'm sorry to stir you out of there, but we got trouble.''

Cobb sat up, his skull full of cobwebs. ''What is it?''

''Orv Brown just got himself shot.''

Without a word Cobb rose and pulled on his clothing.

Another moan came from the office. Cobb threw back the curtain, walked around the corner, and saw Brown lying on the floor with blood on his side. A couple of men Cobb didn't know were kneeling beside Brown.

"Orv, what the devil have you gone and done?"

"His name was Clure Daugherty," Orv said.

"Who?"

"The one who just shot me, dang it! He shot me and run, and folks leaned over me and said that was Clure Daugherty who done it and it was good that he wasn't drunk because he likely would have killed me then. Oh . . . Lord have mercy, my side's throbbing!"

Cobb knelt and examined the wound. "It don't look all that bad, Orv." To the other men there, he said, "Who are you?"

They told their names, which meant nothing to Cobb. "We seen it happen," the one with the sharp-edged voice said.

"Why didn't you take him to get patched up?"

"We're new in Snow Sky. We don't know how to find no doctor. Besides, he said he wanted to come here first thing, so we brought him."

Orv had pushed himself up onto his rump and was looking at his bloody side. "I think you're right, Earl. Didn't punch too bad a hole." He paused. "The worst of it is that Kimmie's going to kill me. She's been harping on me already for looking for those robbers, saying I'd get myself hurt."

"Smart woman, then," Cobb said. "Smarter than her husband. Dang, Orv, why'd you come here instead of going to get patched?"

"Why do you think? I want you to go after him before the trail gets cold."

"I figured as much." Cobb stood, sighing. He could imagine his snug bed beckoning silently, seductively to him back in his room. But there would be no more sleeping now.

"You do anything to prompt this bullet, Orv?"

One of the other men spoke up. "I can vouch he didn't do nothing but ask the big fellow why he robbed him. The man just up and pulled a pistol, and blam, there was this one on the floor a-bleeding. Then the big one took off on a run. A littler fellow rose up at the faro table and lit out after him. I thought he was chasing him at first, but then they took off together."

"How am I supposed to find this Daugherty?"

"Somebody said in the saloon that Daugherty has been holed up somewhere up at the Molly Bee Pass with somebody. Probably that runt from the faro table."

"Ready to ride, Earl?" Cap Corley asked, spreading his white mustache as he drew his mouth into a thin line.

"Ready as I'll ever be."

They gathered guns, ammunition, jackets, hats. "Orv, get over to Walt Chambers, get yourself patched up, and go home to Kimmie, and next time somebody robs you just leave the responding to the law, you hear?"

Orv's only answer was a groan. Cobb slammed the door as he left. Within ten minutes he and Corley were out of town, riding up the trail toward the Molly Bee Pass. Above them rolled thick clouds, heavy with the promise of rain and lightning.

Cobb reined to a halt beneath an outcrop of rock. He looked around.

"What is it, Earl?"

"I don't know. Just a bad feeling."

"Yeah. I've had the same one for the last ten minutes."

Cobb didn't like to hear that. Cap Corley was an old Texas Ranger who had come through many an ambush by both Indians and Mexican bandits, and his instincts were honed like a keen blade. Cobb trusted his own instincts, Corley's even more. When their intuitions spoke as one, they were worth listening to.

"If this Daugherty hadn't shot Orv I might be tempted to let him go," Cobb admitted.

"But he did shoot him," Corley reminded him.

"So he did." Cobb sighed. "Come on, then— but be careful."

They proceeded. The land tilted up, and rock formations contorted into weird sculptures by centuries of rain and wind thrust up on either side of them. Both men kept their eyes and ears tuned for any hint of ambush.

"Most likely they're on across the mountain by now, Earl," Corley said.

"Maybe. Or maybe they're holed up at Apex McCall's old place. I hear from the mountain prospectors that there's been somebody there lately."

As thunder rumbled overhead, Cobb and Corley made it through the rocks without incident, and when they came out on the other side they were on a wide, smooth level that ended abruptly in a wide gorge. Into the gorge spilled Silver Falls, which was merely a trickle in summer and fall and frozen in winter, but which now was a sizable waterfall, engorged with spring runoff.

The gorge was a big eroded gully about thirty feet deep, filled with rock and fallen timber that had been pulled in by water or gravity. On the other side of it was a mazelike rock tangle, and beyond that the cabin of the late hermit prospector Apex McCall, who had died the previous winter. His cabin had sat empty since—except for lately, as Cobb had been told.

It was a guess at best that Orv Brown's assailant was living at the McCall cabin, but the closer Cobb got, the more he believed that in fact was the case. At several points along the trail he and Corley had seen fresh tracks of two hard-pushed horses.

When they reached the edge of the gorge Cobb and Corley dismounted. Before them stretched a rickety bridge made of logs and puncheons—a crude, very unstable structure built last summer by McCall and several other prospectors who had worked up around the Molly Bee. Their prospecting had not come to much, and by winter all but McCall had abandoned the Molly Bee. The bridge, flimsy though it was, remained in use, though, for the Molly Bee Pass provided one more route into and out of Snow Sky—though a rugged one.

For a long time Cobb and Corley stood quietly, letting their horses rest while they listened for any warning sounds. The crashing waterfall, thunder, and rising winds were all they could hear.

"Suppose we'd better cross," Cobb said.

"Yeah."

Cobb led his horse toward the bridge, but stopped. That same intuitive sense of danger was ringing an alarm in his brain. He looked at Corley and saw something in the weathered face that might have been fear—if the old Texas Ranger was capable of such.

"What do you think, Cap?"

Corley bit his mustache. "That there'll be trouble—but I ain't run from trouble yet."

Cobb nodded, took a breath, and started across the bridge.

The narrow bridge was about fifteen feet long, but seemed twice that long by the time Cobb reached its center. The sagging logs and puncheons creaked and snapped beneath the weight of him and his horse. Cobb's eyes swept the rocks ahead, looking for movement that might indicate ambush.

He had just neared the end of the bridge when Corley led his own mount out onto it. Halfway across, the older man stopped, his eyes narrowing, flashing. Cobb turned in time to see Corley reaching for his saddle rifle, and right then a shot cracked somewhere high in the rocks ahead, and Corley's horse shuddered, spasmed, and fell forward. The old ranger was pinned between the horse and the log rail of the bridge.

"Cap!" Cobb screamed. He dropped his own horse's reins, slid out his rifle, and headed toward his trapped partner.

He was almost to Corley when another shot blasted, Corley's forehead shattered, and the straining bridge rail broke. Corley's body pitched downward, making a full turn in the air before hitting the rocks and the gushing water below. The dead horse fell next, landing directly atop Corley's body, and then both man and horse washed on down and out of sight in the tangle of logs, rock, and muddy runoff below. Cobb's own horse trumpeted in terror and bolted on into the rocks. Cobb saw it no more.

"Cap!" Cobb screamed again, uselessly. Then the unseen gunman in the rocks spat another slug from his rifle, the wind of it fanning Cobb's face. Cobb stepped back, tripped, teetered with his stomach leaping to his throat, then fell off the side of the bridge as a magnificent cannonblast of thunder roared from horizon to horizon.

CHAPTER 9

~

BELOW IN SNOW SKY, OLIVER BYERS LIFTED his head to listen to that same rumble of thunder, and at the same moment heard a knock on his office door. He rubbed his face, which was covered with stiff whiskers, for he had been up both late last night and early this morning, poring over an anxiously awaited packet of information that finally had arrived in the mail. Byers loved his sleep; he did not sacrifice it for much, even for journalism. But what was in this packet had been fascinating enough to make him do so.

He folded his papers together and put them back into the packet, glancing quickly at the last thing to go in: a portrait of Jason Lybrand, actor, dressed as the fur-hatted Col. Nimrod Wildfire in a backstreet Chicago production of *The Lion of the West*.

At Byers' door was a boy with thick blond hair that hung to his shoulders. He was dressed in tatters. Byers recognized him as a son of one of the local prostitutes. The smell of the unwashed young fellow made the newspaperman wrinkle his nose.

''I got something for you,'' the boy said, holding up a note.

"For me?"

"That's what I said."

Smart-tongued little squat, Byers thought, taking the note. "Who's it from?" he asked.

"Dutch Polly from the cribs. You going to pay me for that or not?"

Byers fished out a coin. "Now take your money and get away from here before you stink up the place," Byers said. He closed the door.

Lousy harlot's brood. Byers hated the sort. Snow Sky had more than its share of such cast-off humans, many of them old even before they were grown. Byers often wondered where the beggars, thieves, prostitutes, and gamblers of mining and cattle towns came from, and what made them what they were. It was a question that piqued his journalistic curiosity. At one time it might have also piqued his human sympathy, but years of treating people increasingly as journalistic specimens and subjects for stories and less as human beings had greatly reduced Byers' capacity for caring. When he had first noticed that numbing process beginning he had worried about it, but time finally had taken care of that, too.

He opened the note. In crude, big letters, it said:

Mister news paper, I can tell you abot the precher Jason Librann and the way he lays with harlits and cheets the peple in his church if you will com see me. I am Polly Coots who thay call Dutch Polly.

Byers read and reread the note, hardly believing he had received it at such an ironically appropriate time. He had just spent a full night learning some

damning facts about the supposed Reverend Lybrand—and now a local prostitute was ready to
give him even more information.

Byers smiled, folded Dutch Polly's note, went
back to his desk, and put the note into the packet.
He closed and tied the packet, then looked around
his office for a secure place to hide it. Nothing
seemed to do. Finally he simply stuck it into a filing cabinet. He blew out the lights, put on his
derby, and walked to his little house up the hill
behind the *Argus* office, planning to shave and
clean up before he met Polly Coots—and then he
stopped, realizing how silly that was. Dutch Polly
probably hadn't had a man clean up for her in
years. He turned on his heel.

Entering the street, he headed for the southeast
portion of Snow Sky, where the cribs stood. It was
not an area much frequented by him, except when
he was there to gather facts about one more shooting or stabbing. Byers loved vice in others because
it generated good news copy, but personally he
shunned it—not out of moral fortitude, but because
a man could hardly keep up a schedule of sin and
mining town journalism at the same time.

Byers reached the cribs, which stood in a row along
Scofield Street's south side. Their purpose was
made blatant by the sign above the crib row—
SALLY'S PARADISE ROW—and the smaller signs
naming the individual crib occupants. The latter
were tacked onto the small, windowed gablelike
protrusions beside each crib. Byers walked down
the row, reading—JESSICA, KATHLEEN, SALLY

RUTH, JEZEBEL . . . and at last, DUTCH POLLY.

Byers took off his derby and knocked on the door. He heard an answering shuffle inside, then fumbling at the latch, and the crib door swung open.

Byers fought off an impulse to recoil. Dutch Polly, in the diffused light inside the doorway, was a disconcerting mix of youth and age. She surely was no more than thirty and just as surely no less than fifty. She reeked of gin.

"You that newspaper man?" she asked after she had looked him over.

"I am. Oliver Byers."

She hiked up the shoulder of her dress, which had been pulled low. "Come on in," she said.

He stepped inside. He was hard-pressed to breathe in the cramped, unventilated little room. The crib reeked of spilled liquor, crushed-out cigars, sweat, unclean flesh. On a shelf sat a new bottle of gin and a half-empty quart bottle of laudanum. Dutch Polly, obviously, was addicted to the only type of escape available to most crib girls. In many cases it was the final escape they turned to when living wasn't worth it anymore. Looking at Dutch Polly, Byers could only wonder how long it would be until she made that ultimate decision.

"Sit down," Polly said, waving at a chair. She picked up the bottle of gin and poured some into a greasy glass on her bedside table. "Want some?" she asked.

"No, no," Byers said. "Too early for me."

Polly took a long swallow. "The earlier the better, I always say." When the glass was empty, she poured it full again. "I didn't know if you would come."

"I was intrigued by your note," Byers said. "I happen to be quite interested in Lybrand."

"You ain't in his church, are you?"

"No. I'm not a churchgoing man. And I don't trust Lybrand."

Her breath was strong with alcohol. "You're smart, then. He's bad. I know how bad he is. Stands in that pulpit and tells people to be good and takes their money and then does every bad thing he tells them not to. Even with the likes of me."

"Why are you telling me about this?" he asked.

"So you could put him in the paper for what he is."

"You hate him that much?"

To his surprise, she began to cry. He understood: her hatred was the bitter kind spurred by love. Now there was a twist to enliven a story—a crib girl in love with a preacher.

"What do you want me to do about Lybrand?"

"I want you to ruin him, make him so he's no better in folks' eyes than me," she responded, wiping her eyes. "Then people will hate him. Nobody will give money to him anymore or come to his church." She took another drink; some of the liquor ran down her chin and dripped onto her dirty dress.

"You really want to see that happen to him?"

"Yes," she spat, wiping her tears. Her sadness was becoming anger. "He deserves it. I ain't going to let him do to me what was done before."

"What do you mean?"

"I had a man once. And a baby. They're gone now. My man took my baby and run away. Left me on my own . . . left me nothing but this way to live." She waved her hand, indicating the crib. "I couldn't bear to be left again. I won't let him do that to me.''

Byers cleared his throat and decided to open up more to her. Maybe he could shake loose some information more substantial than the mere fact that Lybrand used the services of a prostitute. With what Byers had learned of Lybrand from the packet, and what he further suspected, fornication was probably the man's most minor sin. ''Polly—may I call you Polly?—let me tell you a few things. I have received some information in the mail about our good reverend . . . the results of investigation by an old friend of mine back in Chicago. Lybrand is, as you well know, no holy man. Far from it, farther even than you may suspect.

''Back in Chicago, he did just about every common crime you can name—robbery, extortion, swindling, rape. The closest thing to a legitimate profession the man has ever pursued is acting. He received some excellent reviews early in his career. But his best acting has always been done outside the theater. And he's still doing it, pretending to be a clergyman.

''Lybrand is married—several times over, in fact—and he's not had one marriage legally broken except his last one, and that only because his wife died in childbirth. Her maiden name was Viola.'' He waited to see if that name drew a reaction, but it did not. Obviously Polly Coots didn't keep up with the news, or was too mentally slow to make the connection to the murdered preacher.

So he continued. ''At any rate, the child had been conceived before their marriage, and was still-born well after Lybrand had deserted his wife and gone on to new pursuits. The scandal caused a minor flurry in Illinois, since Lybrand's wife's father was a preacher of some note, named P. D. Viola. Viola was all but destroyed by his daughter's death. He blamed Jason Lybrand for the whole thing.

"And matters only became worse. Reverend Viola's wife died a little while after the daughter did. Grieved herself to death, I suppose. Viola about lost his mind then. He resigned his church and announced to his congregation that he was going to punish the man who had shamed him. He had found out somehow that Lybrand had turned up in Snow Sky, still posing as a preacher. Viola supposedly stood before his congregation and waved a handful of letters, copies of ones he had been mailing to Lybrand, telling him that P. D. Viola was coming like the righteous wrath of God to strike down Lybrand and expose him for what he was. It was a crazy thing to do, because it forewarned Lybrand. But you know how folks can get when they're torn up about something.

"Viola's congregation must have figured he had gone insane . . . which maybe he had. At any rate, it stirred up attention in the Illinois newspapers. NOTED MINISTER OF THE GOSPEL VOWS REVENGE ON YOUNG FAKIR. Quite a story, huh? But listen to this: When P. D. Viola finally showed up in Snow Sky, he was murdered. Beaten to death. Maybe you heard about it. They say they have the man who did it locked up in the jail, but now I've got suspicions that someone else waited by the roadside to kill Viola. Someone who knew he was coming, and who had cause to stop him."

He stopped to let her draw the obvious conclusion herself, but she simply stared at him, almost stupidly. He saw the tragedy in this woman, with her abused body and laudanum-dulled mind. Her future was as gray as the clouds were thick on the horizon outside. For a moment Byers felt an almost forgotten emotion: pity.

"You say he had wives?" she asked.

"Yes."

She silently looked away. Now she seemed sad again rather than angry.

"What was that your note said about cheating his church?" Byers asked.

In a listless voice, she answered, "He's building up a big bunch of money in the bank from the church folks. Going to build a church building, maybe a school, he tells them. But he ain't going to. He's got him two partners who are going to take him into the bank and pretend to make him draw out the money, with him looking scared and all. Then they'll ride off and take him with them like he's their prisoner. They're going to split up the money, and turn him loose. He's going go back and say his life was threatened and the church money stole. The church folk will feel so sorry they'll give even more money to make up for all that was took. Then he'll take it out of the bank again, and this time run off with his partners . . . and me, he told me. Then there would be another town and they'd do it all again. They've done it several other places already, before they came to Snow Sky. They always go to the little towns, the new places where folks won't know them."

"So that's what Lybrand has been doing since he left Chicago!" Byers smiled. Now he was getting some worthwhile information. "Who are his partners?"

She tried to find the names in her dulled mind and could not.

"Ivan Dade and Clure Daugherty, probably," Byers said. "Those names were in the packet—a couple of long-time partners of Lybrand's. Substantially of his ilk but not as sophisticated, according to what the Chicago police told my old newspaper associate." Hesitating, he put out his hand for her to shake.

She did so, limply. Her eyes began to cloud over. "Maybe I shouldn't have said none of this," she said. Suddenly fear came over her. "You won't put in your story that it was me who told on him, will you? If you do, he'll kill me, he will!"

Byers said, "Don't worry—he'll be jailed because of this. He won't be able to hurt you."

"He *will* hurt me! He'll find a way. . . . Oh, why didn't I think of that before? Please don't put my name in your paper!" She began to sob.

"I have no choice," Byers muttered. "Good day." He quickly left the crib. A block away he stopped and looked back. She was standing in the doorway, watching him, wiping tears on her sleeve. For a moment he wanted to go back and reassure her he would do nothing to endanger her, but the moment passed. He went on.

The air smelled wet. Two men walking down the street were talking of the coming storm.

Frogg knelt and whispered to Cochran through the hole in the jail wall. "You'd best be careful about this, Tudor. If the marshal comes back around and catches you here, you'll be sharing this cell with me.''

''That marshal's an interesting case,'' Cochran returned. ''He's talking now about how he doesn't think you did it. I really believe he means it.''

''I've been getting a similar notion from his way about me—but if he thinks I'm innocent, why don't he let me go?''

Cochran glanced around, feeling exposed there in the alley as he whispered through the gap between the logs. ''No evidence in your favor,'' he said.

''Then why does he think I didn't do it?''

''I don't know. Maybe he thinks I did it. Listen, Hiram—I'm trying to get you some help. Believe it or not, that man Flory sent me after is an old Pinkerton detective. I found him and told him if he'd help clear your name, Flory and me would take that boy off his hands. He's been trying to find a home for him—that's why he's got him.''

Frogg whistled softly in surprise. ''You're a wilder fool than I took you for, then. What will Flory say?''

''I hope she'll welcome him. But nothing will happen if that detective doesn't agree to my bargain.''

''He said no?''

''Not exactly, but he hasn't said yes either. I won't give up, though. He's the best hope we've got.''

Frogg said, ''The time's fast coming, Tudor, for you to get out of here and leave me to work this out on my own. No point in you getting dragged in. Think of what that would do to Flory. What if that marshal really is starting to suspect you?''

"I'm not leaving you. Don't even suggest it. I wouldn't in any case, and besides, the marshal told me flat out to stay in town."

"Deputy's coming!" Frogg whispered suddenly. Cochran quickly slipped the loose chinking back into place, turned on his heel, and walked rapidly toward the street. At the end of the alley he made a sharp left and ran straight into Polly Coots, knocking her down.

"Sorry, ma'am, I didn't see you there." He reached down and helped her up. Then he saw she had been crying.

"Ma'am, are you all right?"

"I got to go tell him what I did," she said, her voice slurred. "If I tell him then he'll forgive me. I know he will."

Cochran didn't understand the incoherent talk. He smelled gin on her breath. He realized suddenly that this was one of Snow Sky's soiled doves.

Polly walked on, brushing him aside, her head down, butting into the rising wind that swept dust into billows and whirling devils along the street. Cochran watched her go, feeling pity for her.

In the distance a serrated bolt of lightning flashed from cloud to cloud, followed by another that cut a swath to the ground.

A follow-up blast of thunder shook the town, and trailed off. Storm coming in the mountains, Cochran thought. I'd hate to be up there when it hits.

Earl Cobb had managed, when he fell from the bridge, to catch hold of the end of a small evergreen growing almost horizontally out of the side of the gorge. The trunk bent under his weight, swinging him down and against the wet rock wall. His hands slipped on the dampened needles and let him fall. Cobb closed his eyes, expecting to crash into the roiling water below, but he did not. Instead he fell onto a little ledge beneath him. His rifle clattered on down and was lost in the foam that already had swallowed Cap Corley and his horse.

For a few moments there was no noise but that of the waterfall. Cobb lay dazed on the ledge. Groaning, he rolled—the wrong direction. He fell over the edge, barely managing to grab the ledge and stop himself from sliding down the nearly sheer slope into the water.

He looked up. A man appeared above, looking down from the top of the gorge. There was a still-smoking rifle in his hand. A big fellow he was, one Cobb had seen before in town. Clure Daugherty, no doubt.

Daugherty laughed; his voice was remarkably high, almost falsetto. "Got you a good grip there, Marshal?" Then he lifted the rifle and took aim.

Cobb let out a yell and pulled himself up. To his amazement, he made it, and rolled back onto the ledge as the first shot sang down and smacked the rock below him. He rolled into a shallow depression in the wall. It was enough to keep him safely concealed from the rifleman directly above, but left him still dangerously exposed should the man come out onto the bridge.

Cobb reached for his pistol and was relieved to find it still there. His holster thong had a way of slipping off, and he easily could have lost the pistol when he fell. He thumbed off the thong and drew the pistol. The grip was cold and wet in his hand.

"Where is he, Clure?" This was a new voice, coming from somewhere around the near end of the bridge. Daugherty's partner, probably. Cobb scrambled to a squatting position, backed up against the stone wall, and readied himself to shoot should anyone show himself on the bridge.

"He's back up under me," Daugherty said. "I took a shot at him and missed."

"Daugherty!" Cobb yelled. "You're making a bad mistake! You'll get yourself a death sentence if you kill a peace officer!"

"Then it's too late to worry—I already killed your deputy."

Good point for him, bad one for me, Cobb thought.

Dade appeared on the bridge and fired off a quick shot that *spang*ed into the rock directly above Cobb's head. Cobb leveled his pistol and fired quickly in response. Dade ducked back, then returned, firing again. A slug nicked the side of Cobb's leg and another ripped a hole through his sleeve, missing him by a sixteenth of an inch. Cobb fired again, again—and thought he saw Dade spasm once before he withdrew this time.

A silence followed. Smoke from Cobb's pistol floated up from the gorge, mixing with the mist of the churning water. Another gunsmoke cloud dissipated above the bridge where Dade had been.

"I'm hit, Daugherty!" Dade said in a pain-tightened voice. "Plugged me through the arm!"

Daugherty responded in a lower tone; Cobb could not hear him clearly over the roaring of the water and a new peal of thunder that here in the mountains was twice as loud as it would have been below. He knew, though, that they were making a plan to get to him.

He couldn't stay here, yet he had no way off the ledge. Taking a chance that neither of his assailants would show themselves on the bridge for the next few moments, Cobb emptied the three spent shells from his pistol and replaced them with live ones, then slipped a final one into the cylinder he usually kept empty beneath the hammer. He could not afford an empty cylinder right now.

He groped for a plan. To stay here meant nothing more than draining off his limited ammunition until finally his foes would be able to walk safely out onto the bridge and shoot him at their leisure. But the ledge was a mere lip of rock sticking out at this one place, and even if it had extended farther in either direction, Cobb could not leave the protection of the depression that hid him. He had no desire to take a slug in the crown of his head.

No way out to either side or straight up—leaving only one option: down.

He craned his neck and looked over into the boiling torrent below. The waterfall was close and to his left; its mist was soaking him right now. It crashed onto rocks that were largely obscured by the water. To throw himself down there might mean to impale himself on some upthrusting stone spear or to burst his skull against an unseen, water-covered boulder. He hesitated, unsure.

Two things happened right then. The first was that a tiny avalanche of dirt and gravel fell before Cobb, letting him know that his two enemies were still directly above. The second was that it began to rain—not a mild sprinkle, but a gushing storm, as if the water-gorged belly of some cloud had exploded.

If it was to be done, now was the time. Cobb stood, took a breath, and lunged forward out of the rock depression, twisting and firing blindly upward at the same time. The shot was simply to drive the men above back away from the edge; there seemed no chance it would actually strike either one.

Cobb quickly reholstered and restrapped his pistol, took another deep breath, and leapt off the ledge toward the left, aiming for a small gap between the edge of the waterfall and the gorge wall, hoping he could land behind the descending wall of water and be hidden.

"Yonder he goes, Ivan!" Daugherty yelled. "The damn fool jumped!"

Dade did not respond and Daugherty looked at him. Dade had a look of surprise on his face, and his chest was flooding with bright red blood, washing all the way to his legs in the rain. Dade wobbled and turned bedsheet white.

Cobb's unaimed bullet had taken him in the side of the throat, cutting a path upward to come out below his right ear. Dade's eyes glazed and he fell limply to his knees, leaned forward, and silently fell over the edge of the gorge into the crashing turbulence below.

CHAPTER 10

——————

ABEL PATTERSON PAUSED, HIDDEN BEHIND A parked wagon, and let Cochran pass on the other side of the street. Cochran strode on to a hotel and entered. Patterson stepped out and began his search again. He noticed the mountains. Raining there— he could see the gray, slanted mist of it in the distance. It would roll into town soon—and it looked like a big storm. Knowing it was coming only increased the sense of pressure he felt to find Spencer.

He reached into his pocket and looked at his watch: almost four o'clock. Spencer had been gone for hours, and still he had not found even a hint of where the boy might have gone. Patterson had dozed off late in a restless night, and when he had awakened in the morning, Spencer's bed was empty. The boy had slipped out and run off.

Patterson knew he probably should have flagged down the innkeeper and recruited him to help with the search, but he didn't really want to talk to Cochran. Not yet. If he failed to find Spencer on his own, he might have to approach Cochran. At least now he knew where Cochran was staying. He wondered if perhaps Spencer knew too—maybe even was there. If he didn't find Spencer elsewhere, Patterson decided, he would come back and check.

Outside the door of the Pardue Boot Shop Patterson stopped a man with a waxed mustache. "Excuse me—you seen a towheaded boy, about eleven, wandering around, maybe looking lost? New pair of shoes on him."

The man frowned thoughtfully, twitched the mustache as if it moved with the gears of his brain, and finally shook his head. " 'Fraid not. Yours?"

"Sort of."

"Could be he's in O'Brien's Grocery sneaking licorice out of the jar. O'Brien, he lets the young-uns get away with that."

It was a possibility. Patterson got directions to the store, thanked the man, and went on.

He was more worried than he would have thought. In one way that made little sense, for Spencer surely had faced much bigger challenges, growing up with an abusive criminal father, than getting by on his own in a mining town. Likely the boy was in his element on the streets—unless his late father had simply kept him penned up in their mountain cabin all his years.

O'Brien's Grocery had four children inside, gathered at the glass-topped candy counter, but none was Spencer. Patterson turned and walked back onto the street, then sat down on the bench on the store porch. He leaned back against the wall and crossed his arms over his broad chest. His longish hair fanned back over his collar.

What really hurts about all this, he thought, is that Spencer ran off only after I suggested that he stay with me for good. I don't know what possessed me to make such a suggestion anyway. I don't have what it takes to raise a boy right. I'm just a worn-out old Pinkerton who can't even locate a lost runt in a mining camp anymore. Can't seem to keep anybody safe in my care—just like I couldn't keep my own brother safe on the streets of Chicago that night.

He stood, listening to the thunder, then walked off the porch and up the center of the street, looking for Spencer in the crowd around him.

He saw the tent church and it gave him a thought. Spencer might have sought out somebody he thought might protect him, like a law officer, or maybe a preacher. The former Pinkerton wasn't inclined to approach the law, given that he didn't know if his absconding with a bag of extortion money had managed to land his name on police dodgers. But the preacher might be worth asking. At the least a clergyman might be willing to keep his eyes and ears open to help out. He might even organize a search if he was a particularly helpful fellow.

Patterson walked to the frame and canvas church and pushed open the door. Gray light from the clouded sky came through the canvas like thin-strained coffee, barely lighting the bench-filled structure, at the front of which stood a crudely made pulpit on a little rostrum, and a small altar table. There was no one and nothing else here.

Patterson stood in the silence a few moments, trying to remember how long it had been since he had set foot in a church, even one as makeshift as this one. A lot of years. Tomorrow was Sunday, he realized. Lord, he prayed, if you keep Spencer safe and let me find him, maybe I'll come to the service in the morning. Put a few dollars in the plate.

He walked back out onto the street and glanced at the name painted onto the door frame: HOUSE OF PRAYER. Then the name of the minister—JASON LYBRAND.

Lybrand . . . vaguely familiar. Something from the past, from Chicago. Perhaps someone of the same name was in a Pinkerton file. It was not unlikely, given that the Pinkertons never closed a case until the parties involved were either dead, jailed, or cleared.

Patterson buttonholed a passing man. "Where's this preacher Lybrand live?" he asked.

The man singled out the cabin that was Lybrand's. Patterson thanked him and headed for it, glancing again toward the mountains. The wall of rain was moving closer to town. A mist hung in the air. Patterson hurried toward the preacher's cabin.

Lybrand drew back his fist and drove it into Dutch Polly's jaw. The impact made her thin body shudder like a leaf, and knocked her back, where she tottered against a table before sliding to the floor. She cried out and grasped her injured face, tears streaming down her cheeks.

"Oh, Jason, please don't . . . I told you I was sorry!"

"Sorry! Do you know what you've done to me? Flapping your mouth to a newspaperman! You've ruined me! How could you have been such a damned fool?"

"I was mad at you—but I'm sorry now! I came back and said I was sorry, didn't I?"

"You don't know what sorry means yet, my dear! When I'm through with you, you'll have real cause to regret what you've done to me."

She looked at him with honest fear. "Please . . . I wish I hadn't done it. I've thought of nothing but that since I did it!"

Lybrand's lip curled back; he advanced on her. Her tears streamed faster, and she put the back of her hand over her eyes and cowered down on the floor as he bent toward her. His fist went up simultaneously with the knock on his door.

Lybrand froze, lowered his fist, and pointed his thin finger into the prostitute's face. "See? Already he's here! All your crying and sorrow can't fix what's been done. Now you keep quiet—hear me?"

Lybrand straightened his clothing and hair and walked to the door. Rolling his shoulders, twisting his tension-stiffened neck, he opened the door a crack.

Lybrand had seen Oliver Byers in town before and knew the visitor outside was not the newspaperman. This was a tall, broad man with a salt-and-pepper beard.

"Are you the Reverend Lybrand?" Patterson asked.

"I am. What can I do for you?"

"I'd like to speak to you if I could."

"I'm terribly busy at the moment," Lybrand said in an artificially pleasant voice. "I'm in the midst of preparing a difficult sermon, and my home is too strewn about with books and papers to be fit to accept company."

Funny attitude for a preacher, Patterson thought. He said, "I don't want to come in—just to ask you something. My boy is missing. I'm sure he's somewhere in town, but I can't find him. I thought maybe you might have seen him, or be able to help me out some way or another."

Lybrand seemed irritated by the request. Patterson was fast developing the feeling something was amiss here. He had learned in his Chicago years that intuition often ran in advance of reason, like a scout, and flashed warning signals best not ignored.

"I don't know how I can help you," Lybrand said. "Why don't you go to the town marshal?"

"I saw your church tent down there and came up here on impulse." Patterson smiled coolly. "I guess that was a mistake."

"Like I said, I can't help you. I'm sure the boy is fine. Good day. God bless you."

Lybrand abruptly closed the door, leaving Patterson blinking in surprise—and wondering if that in fact had been a flash of skirt and female leg he had seen for half a second in the background as the door swished shut.

Halfway down the hill, he met a man emerging from another cabin. He nodded hello, then asked, "Does the preacher up in that cabin have a wife?"

The man looked up, grinned, and shook his head. "Nope. Surely doesn't." He leaned close. "But the fact is, I've seen one of the town crib harlots sneak up there. What do you think of that out of a preacher, huh?" The man cackled gleefully; obviously he thought the situation was hilarious.

"Not what you expect from a preacher," Patterson said.

"Amen to that! I had him pegged a fake from day one."

Patterson headed back into town through the drizzle to continue his search.

Back in his cabin, Lybrand let his curtain fall back straight. He had been looking covertly around the edge of it, watching Patterson descend. Lybrand had witnessed the brief meeting and conversation of Patterson and the man below, and could tell from their gestures that he was their subject. Maybe talk was out already about him. Maybe that newspaperman had a loose tongue and was mouthing his story even before putting it into print. Lybrand raged inwardly; Polly had ruined him.

She had gotten up and moved to his bed, holding her injured jaw. She sobbed quietly. Dutch Polly had been humiliated often in life, but never so much as now.

She wasn't sure why she had felt so compelled to inform the newspaperman about Lybrand's secret life. Last night and this morning she had been driven by a sense of vengeance. Now that seemed alien; she wanted only Lybrand's affection and forgiveness, and the assurance he would harm her no more.

"That jaw hurt?" he asked her. She thought she detected some tenderness in his voice. Looking up through her tears, she nodded. Without a word, he struck her again.

The pain was more than pain; it spasmed through her in a convulsion like that of a beheaded snake. For a few moments she blacked out. When she came to, she was on the floor, on her back, with Lybrand kneeling beside her.

"You should have never betrayed me," he said.

"That's all womenfolk know how to do—to betray. I grew up with a mother who stood by and watched her husband try to destroy her own son, giving no more help than a feeble plea or two. My father might have killed me for all the help she gave. But he couldn't overcome me, Polly. I overcame him in the end . . . just like I'll overcome this Oliver Byers and his little rag newspaper. Nobody has ever been able to destroy me, Polly—not my father, not my mother, not Viola, not Byers, and not you." Then he hit her again.

It all became hellish after that. In the midst of it she stood and tried to run from him on legs wobbly as chicken fat. Repeated blows jolted her, knocking her down again and again, but always she arose. She was keenly aware, for some reason, of the wind moaning around the house. Listening to it, suffering blow after blow, she fell and passed out again.

Daugherty crept along the bank of the gushing stream, cautiously watching the waterfall that was growing bigger and more violent in the rain. Lightning flared and crackled in the sky, and clouds drooped like sodden sponges between the mountains.

The big outlaw still could not believe the marshal had managed to put a bullet through Dade's neck with a randomly fired shot. It was enough to make a man start believing in providence . . . though Daugherty surely didn't want to, especially if providence was on the side of Earl Cobb.

He stopped, standing there in the drenching rain.

Maybe the best thing to do was get out of here. Take off across the mountain and let the storm wash away the trail. Most likely the marshal had died when he threw himself toward the waterfall anyway. Daugherty couldn't tell for certain, but it seemed to him that Cobb had made a poor jump and had gone straight into the falls. But maybe he had managed to come up behind—and if so, Daugherty wanted to know it. He didn't want any law close on his tail if he could help it.

Too bad all this had to happen before he, Dade, and Lybrand got around to cleaning out the church bank account down in Snow Sky. Now Dade was gone, Daugherty could not return to town, and the plan was finished. It was Lybrand's fault. Lybrand was just too slow—wait, wait, wait was all he ever would do.

Daugherty mentally voiced his complaint and then put the subject behind him. All that was over now; there was nothing left for him but running. On his own this time.

But not until he knew for sure that the marshal was dead. Daugherty readjusted his hat to make the water sluice off it to the side, and advanced toward the waterfall.

He stopped with a gasp when something rose in the turbulence and vanished. It was Dade, eyes open, white face upturned. No blood on him—all that had washed off. A moment later the corpse reappeared, still facing up, staring at the sky for three or four seconds before washing down again. The body was caught like a leaf in a circular up-and-down movement of water created by the nearby falls and the shape of the rocks below. Daugherty shuddered.

He advanced again. The waterfall roared like an angry devil.

No movement that looked human, no voice, nothing. For all Daugherty could tell, he was alone here. By himself with nothing but dead men around. He wondered if the marshal might have washed down the stream like the deputy who had plunged off the bridge.

The outlaw backed up against the side of the gorge as he neared the waterfall. Only a narrow gap between the wall of water and the rock around it was there to allow access to the area behind the falls. If Cobb was hidden anywhere, it had to be there.

Daugherty stopped suddenly, and grinned. If Cobb was back there, waiting to surprise him, then Daugherty had his own surprise to hand out first. He swung the rifle around at hip level and swept the falls with bullets. With any luck, if Cobb was back there he took one or two of them, mortally.

Daugherty hugged the wall and reloaded, then advanced with more confidence. At the least Cobb would now be spooked. The outlaw reached the edge of the falls, held his breath, and rushed on through the gap.

Now he was behind the plunging water, on a sandy, gravelly patch shielded by an arch of rock. The falls were to Daugherty's right, a curtain of water blocking all view of the world on the other side.

No Earl Cobb. The moist little enclave, dark as late twilight, was empty. Daugherty breathed in relief. Obviously Cobb had been washed under the falls when he jumped. That meant he was dead.

The outlaw nodded in satisfaction and lowered

his rifle. At that moment his eye fell on the wet sand and gravel beneath him.

Tracks. Fresh. Cobb's tracks.

Movement beside him—and Cobb came out of a shadowed crevice in the rock. Cobb's pistol swung around in an arc and laid open Daugherty's jaw. Blood and a scream came out of the big man's mouth. He lifted his rifle. Cobb grasped its barrel and pushed it aside before Daugherty could fire. When the outlaw did get off a shot it ricocheted off the stone behind them and out through the waterfall. As it did, Cobb shoved backward on the rifle. Daugherty danced clumsily and then stumbled into the falls. The water grabbed him like a clutching hand and pulled him in.

Cobb let go of the rifle so Daugherty would fall in without taking him with him, but Cobb's sleeve was torn and Daugherty's rifle caught in the tear. Cobb, already unsettled because of the fight, found himself dragged into the water with Daugherty.

They came up together on the other side. Both had lost their weapons. Daugherty's face was bleeding, turning the foam around him pink. The outlaw saw the marshal bob to the surface and let out a lionlike roar. Daugherty's stone of a fist shot up from the water and caught Cobb on the side of the head.

Cobb absorbed the blow well, but it did daze him. He pulled away, trying to get a grip on a rock to avoid being swept away. But what he took for a good handhold actually was a badly fractured and eroded stone, and as he grabbed it a big fragment snapped off in his hand. Cobb was pulled downstream, then sucked under.

Beneath the water he found himself struggling

with Daugherty—struggling, but Daugherty wasn't struggling back. He opened his eyes, and in the foaming water saw that it was not Daugherty at all, but Daugherty's partner. The man was dead, a bullethole in his neck. He couldn't believe it—that wild shot he had fired off when he jumped must have actually hit this fellow. There was one for the books.

Suddenly Cobb's head broke water and he sucked in a lungful of air. The corpse came up, headed back down, and Cobb was pulled after it. He groped out blindly and managed to get a grip on a firm rock this time. Pulling upward, straining his arm terribly, he drew himself out of the circling current that was moving the corpse in an endless cycle.

Cobb wrapped his arms around the stone that held him and drew in more air. The storm was going full fury, pelting the water all around him. Lightning flashed and Cobb saw Daugherty's face appear before him, rising from the water.

Dead? Maybe so. Daugherty was pale as a bedsheet, and his eyes were closed. But a moment later a big arm rose from the water and grabbed the same rock to which Cobb held. Daugherty's eyes opened; his lips drew back to expose his teeth like those of a snarling animal. The gash Cobb had inflicted on his face looked hideous.

Daugherty swore at Cobb and with his free arm went for the marshal's throat. Cobb lunged out almost blindly and connected with Daugherty's forehead. New blood gushed down Daugherty's face as Cobb heard the crunch of rock against bone. He had forgotten that the broken-off shard of rock from his first failed handhold was still gripped in his hand. It had done the job well. Cobb knew even as Daugherty let go of the rock and slipped beneath the water that the man was dead.

Suddenly Cobb's head began to spin. Pain rippled a dull electric path through his frame. It felt like he might have bruised some ribs somewhere along the way. He dropped the piece of rock that had killed Daugherty and held to his perch with both arms, but he was growing weaker. In the lightning glare he watched Daugherty's body wash down the stream, and then his own eyes closed and he slid beneath the water.

When Dutch Polly awoke it was dark in the room except for a circle of light cast by a lamp on Lybrand's table. He was seated there, drinking, looking at her hatefully.

"Back around for some more, huh?" he said. His voice was slightly slurred, either by liquor or the distortion of her own ringing ears.

"No . . ." she said as he rose and walked to her. She tried to stand but fell back onto the floor. He hit her and she began crying again.

He cursed her and kicked her. This time she managed to get up. She stumbled toward the door but, staggering to one side, reached the window instead. Grabbing out for something to balance her, she pulled down the curtain and rod. It was dark outside. She had been unconscious a long time. The rain pounding the windows was fierce. A lightning flash lit the terrain outside, and in its glare the heavens gave Dutch Polly the last gift she would ever receive: a final glimpse of the world she was about to depart.

Cursing at her now for having pulled down the curtain, Lybrand grasped her shoulders and pulled her back, then pushed hard. She screeched and spun against the table; the impact made a horrible smashing sound.

Lybrand fumbled with the curtain, feeling exposed, and finally got it back in place. Still swearing, he turned to renew his abuse of Polly.

Something in the way she lay stopped him in his tracks. He looked closely at her—no breath. No movement. Panic rising, he dropped to his knees and crawled to her. Rolling her over, he saw her eyes stare up at his, but there was no light, no life in them. He had killed her.

He pulled back up from her and clasped his hands together, then drew his shoulders up tight around his neck, taking the tense posture of a child at bedside prayers. Polly's head rolled to the side and she seemed to look at him again, blood dripping from the corner of her slightly open mouth. Lybrand stared at her, trying to figure out if he had killed her intentionally or by accident. He wasn't sure it really mattered. Dead was dead.

He returned to the window and peeped through the curtain. Lightning showed him an empty town below. The handful of cabins near his were shut tight; lights burned in only a couple. Thank heaven for the storm. Many people, apparently, had turned in early because of it. The street flares were out, and even the saloons, dance halls, and restaurants had apparently closed, their proprietors probably huddling now in the safer confines of their squatty log cabins.

No need to worry, he told himself. No one is out there tonight. No one saw what happened. I'm safe. In fact, maybe I can use this storm to my advantage.

Got to get rid of her body, make it look like she died somewhere else, some other way. . . .

His mind clicking off a new plan, Lybrand let the curtain fall, and thus did not see Spencer Vestal dart from beneath the overhanging evergreen branches of a tree not thirty feet from the cabin. The tree had kept the runaway boy somewhat dry, but no longer was he willing to stay there, for he knew something bad had happened in that cabin. He himself had lived with abuse long enough to know the sound of it when he heard it—and that familiar sound, though muffled, had been audible. He had seen the woman at the window, the man dragging her back. After that there had been no sound at all, and that made Spencer even more afraid, for he feared the woman was dead. He could feel death in his marrow, smell it in the wet air.

He ran back down toward the town in the rain.

CHAPTER 11

EARL COBB HAD COME BACK TO THE LIVING about sunset.

Rain on his face was the first thing he was aware of. The second was that he hurt quite a lot. He was crumpled awkwardly on the bank of the stream, where he had washed up—with his nose turned toward the sky rather than buried in the water, to his good fortune. It took him a long time to gather the courage to move, and when he did he was both sorry and gratified: the former because the movement brought him pain, the latter because he could move at all.

Cobb got up carefully, slowly, and examined himself. At the same time he pulled together his memories of what had happened here. He remembered the death of Cap Corley and felt a stab of sorrow that hurt as much as his battered frame. At least Cap had not left behind a family to grieve for him.

When Cobb tried to walk he found it brought wracking pain. His left ankle throbbed. After only a few steps he sank to the earth again, coming down in a gathering pool of rain. Falling down made his damaged ribs hurt that much worse. Lightning sizzled through the atmosphere and tinged the air with a clean electric smell.

New wet-weather waterfalls gushed here and there around him as the mountain shed the falling rain. Silver Falls was massive now, hammering water against rock with terrible force. Down in town, Cobb figured, Bledsoe Creek surely was gushing to its limits. Possibly some of the streets would flood.

Cobb was still down in the gorge, the storm was still raging, and the stream was rising. Good thing he had come to when he had. Even now he had best get out or his feet might be knocked from under him, and in the shape he was, it was even money whether he would be able to get out of the water if he fell into it.

He remembered the Apex McCall cabin, where Daugherty and Dade apparently had been holing up. There he could wait out the storm, and in the morning make it back down to Snow Sky—if he wasn't too sore to move by then.

The cabin was, at the moment, to Cobb's right, on the far side of the gorge from Snow Sky. The slope on that side was far too steep for him to climb. The other side was much less so, though it was across the stream. Now this was a fine fix: either climb a nearly sheer rock wall in the rain, with a busted ankle and banged-up ribs, or try to wade a gushing stream that obviously was trying to fill its year's quota for dead men.

"Ain't been your day, Cobb," he said to himself. With that he put out a foot and stepped, with much pain and wincing, onto one of the rocks thrusting out of the rising stream, his idea being to cross to the more shallow bank, climb it, and double back to the bridge, where he could cross to the side where the cabin stood.

"So far so good," he said. He stepped again, reaching another rock, and from there half stepped, half fell onto another, this one a long slab buried sideways in the water. On it he made it three quarters of the way to the other side, pain shooting up his leg with every careful step.

But from there on there were no rocks on which to step. Cobb stood, feeling both ludicrous and frightened there on the rock in the stream, rising water lapping at his toes as the storm sizzled through the mountains around him.

"Here goes," he said.

Sitting on the rock, he slid on his rump into the water, praying it was not as deep as it looked.

It was. Cobb was pulled under at once and washed fifteen feet downstream before he could find the surface again. When he pulled his face out of the water he was clinging to a big log, part of a tangle of other logs wedged among the rocks.

"What the—" Suddenly he realized it: This was the bridge, or the remnants of it. Sometime while he was unconscious, the rickety structure had yielded to the pounding water and washed away. He twisted his head and looked at the far side of the gorge. Too high. No way to reach the top and the cabin.

"Well, Cobb, looks like you're going to make a nighttime trip to Snow Sky after all," he said to himself.

Painfully he worked his way along the timber rubble to the bank, where he pulled himself out. After another ten minutes of slow, agonizing climbing, he made it up the shallow bank and back onto the trail that led down the mountain to Snow Sky.

"I'd best find myself some sort of crutch," he said aloud.

He had to limp a long way before he finally found a crotched sapling that might make a decent crutch. Propping up in the driving rain, he dug his folding knife from his pocket. Night was falling now, and he had to strain to see what he was doing. It took a long time to cut, twist, and break away a makeshift crutch, and when finally he had, he found the crutch wobbly and prone to slide on the wet rocks. Still, it was better than having no extra support at all.

The storm was terrific, and lightning danced around him. Cobb had never been much afraid of lightning, but from the way bolts were firing out of the sky, he could almost suspect the heavenly host was holding a turkey shoot, with him as the prize bird.

Oh Lord above, Cobb prayed inwardly, I surely hope I make it. Please let me make it.

He began walking. Water bounded past his feet toward the base of the mountain. His improvised crutch slid and almost failed him. Cobb prayed for the storm to slacken, but it did not. Town seemed a long way off.

Cochran cautiously answered his door. The caller was Abel Patterson, standing there drenched from rain, staring back at Cochran without expression.

"Hello," Cochran said. "This is a surprise."

"Is he here?" Patterson asked, walking in without waiting for an invitation. He swept off his hat, in the process flinging about a pint of water off it onto the floor. Another quart drained off his slicker, leaving a watery trail across the room. It hardly mattered; the roof was leaking at three places anyway.

"Well, is he here?" Patterson asked again.

"I don't know what you mean."

"Don't you? Are you saying Spencer hasn't been here?"

"No, he hasn't. Is he gone?"

"Since this morning. I've looked for him all day. Not a sign. I thought maybe he had found you. You're the only other man in Snow Sky he knows at all."

"Well, I wouldn't say he knows me, just from staying at my inn. In any case, he didn't come here. Did you tell him the bargain I offered you?"

Patterson wouldn't meet Cochran's eye. "No. Instead I asked him if he would let me keep him, raise him. I never thought I'd reach the point of wanting anything like that, but that boy has a way of growing on you."

Patterson now looked at Cochran. "He's got scars on him, you know. He's lucky he survived his childhood. He had no mother when I ran across him, and he had just lost his father, poor excuse for one though he was." Patterson stopped, then fought out the rest of what he had decided to say. "That boy needs a good raising. I'm accepting your offer."

Cochran drew a deep breath. "He'll get a good raising, Mr. Patterson. That I pledge to you. But first we'll have to find him. Do you have any idea where he might go?"

"I don't. I suppose he's just hiding out some-where. I'm worried. A stormy night's no time for a boy to be roaming loose in a mining camp."

Cochran said, "I'll get my hat and coat. We'll find him together."

Bledsoe Creek was more like a river now, raging through Snow Sky like a mad beast. Brush, leaves, trash, scraps of lumber, and occasional drowned animals came sweeping along its angry current.

Less than a yard above the rising surface of the rushing water, Spencer Vestal perched. He was in-side an outhouse—one of several built at the end of the platforms that extended out from the creek bank and over the water. It wasn't the most sanitary way to dispose of human wastes, but it was effi-cient, legal, common to mining camps, and pref-erable to another system many people used: dumping their raw sewage out the back door.

Spencer was glad to at least be dry. He had never been afraid of storms; he even liked them, partly because his despised father had not. But this storm was the worst Spencer had seen. Several sheds now were flat, several porch roofs completely blown off, and a few house roofs on the verge of going the same way—but this outhouse above the creek was shrugging off the weather rather well. It shook a bit in the wind and had one small leak in its roof, but Spencer felt safe here.

Before finding this little refuge, he had consid-ered returning to Abel Patterson. Now he was glad he had not; he did not want to go back to Patterson for fear he would never be free of him again if he did. He knew Patterson cared for him more deeply all the time, and wanted the best for him, but he also knew what he really needed: a mother. He did not want to spend another day being raised by a man alone. He had experienced enough of that.

He could barely remember his own mother, but he clearly recalled that her touch was soft and loving, and that she did not beat and curse him as his father did. A new father Spencer could take—if he was kind and caring—or leave, as long as a loving mother came with the bargain. And that woman at the Cochran Inn, the one he had heard worried for him, would do just fine. When the storm was over, Spencer decided, he would try to find the man who apparently was her husband, and if he could not find him, he would walk all the way back to that inn on his own, and ask that woman to become his mother. If he had the courage.

Spencer tried to think about how nice it would be to have a mother again, but that pleasant thought kept giving way to memory of the horrible encounter he had witnessed a little earlier through that cabin window. He wondered if the poor woman being so beaten was someone's mother—and if she somehow might have survived. He felt reasonably sure she had not.

He looked down through the hole of the outhouse and watched the rising water below. If it kept getting higher he would have to leave here; the outhouse might be swept away. Turning, he stepped to the door and cracked it. Looking out, he saw that the rain was continuing, a little slackened from before, but not much.

Something moved out in the rain. Pulling the door almost completely closed, Spencer squinted.

A lightning flash revealed what it was: a man, walking through the storm, carrying something on his shoulder. The thing apparently was heavy and wrapped in a blanket. The next lightning flash brought Spencer a shudder, for he realized that the man was the one he had seen pulling the woman away from the cabin window, and the thing on his shoulder was a body. Her body.

Eyes wide, Spencer watched the man descend to the creek. Spencer now noticed a coil of rope over the man's other shoulder. When the man passed out of Spencer's view, the boy closed the outhouse door and went to a knothole on the side wall. Pressing his face to the hole, blinking against the rain that battered in against his eye, he watched the man proceed on to a similarly constructed outhouse a few yards up the creek.

The man looked around furtively, then went inside the outhouse with his burden. When he came out again about a minute later, he had only the blanket and rope in hand. He tossed the blanket into the creek, where it twisted and swirled away downstream on the current.

The man then stepped down into the edge of the roiling stream himself, gripping the outjutting beams that supported the outhouse. He worked his way slightly beneath the structure, the water swirling to his waist and threatening to pull him out into the stream. As Spencer watched, the man looped the rope firmly around one of the two tree-trunk poles that provided the main support of the outhouse.

The man struggled back up onto the bank again. Holding both ends of the rope firmly, he began to pull in the same direction the pole already was being pushed by the current. Spencer heard the creak of the moving timber. He realized how fortunate he was that he had hidden in this privy and not that one; he could not guess what the man would have done had he found a little boy looking back at him when he opened the door.

Lightning danced through the sky, turning darkness to day and then returning it to darkness. Bit by bit the pole support leaned, and then with a wrench pulled free. The man fell back onto his rump, still holding the rope. The horizontal outhouse supports sagged downward, pulling up on one side from the muddy, weakened bank. The outhouse descended partially into the water. The man rose and went to the other side, where he apparently loosened the remaining support pole, for although Spencer could not see him there, suddenly the tilting outhouse fell completely into the creek, broke loose from its platform, and was caught in the rush of the stream. It began to sink even before it swept out of Spencer's view.

Spencer crept around to the other side of the outhouse, but could find no opening through which to watch the damaged little building wash down the creek. He returned to the knothole on the other side and looked back out.

The man was gone. He had taken his rope with him.

—◆—

Cobb made it almost to Snow Sky before he collapsed. He had reached the place almost at the base of the mountain where the way leveled off across a narrow plateau, and from there descended toward two hills and the footbridge across Bledsoe Creek.

The marshal lay still for a minute, then got up again. The rain had nearly stopped, but the creek was higher than ever as water hammered down from the mountain. He continued, slowly, until at last he passed between the twin hills and saw Snow Sky.

The town, illuminated by the now more sporadic bursts of lightning, looked much abused by the weather. Canvas flapped, brush and limbs lay strewn everywhere, and fallen trees lay across woodsheds and telegraph wires. Cobb saw all that in the momentary flashes of light. To him the battered town was beautiful, for the mere fact he was seeing it reminded him he had cheated death.

But he was terribly weak and his ankle hurt worse than ever. Cobb feared he might collapse in exhaustion.

He began his walk toward the creek. The trail was slick and wet, and his crutch slipped. With a yell he fell onto his back.

He dragged himself the rest of the way to the footbridge. He blacked out a few moments, then awakened suddenly and realized his face had been all but submerged in a puddle. He considered how ironic it would have been to survive a gun battle and a long, lightning-lit descent down a mountainside in the worst storm he had seen in a decade— only to then drown in two inches of puddle water.

His crutch lay beside him, and he used it to push himself up. Grasping the handrail of the bridge, he began working his way across, his vision unfocused and dim.

That was why he did not see that one section of the footbridge was no longer there. The gorged creek had swept a loose section away. Cobb put his crutch out for one more step, and it pierced the surface of the still-rising creek. He fell straight forward into the water.

The experience was something like being buried in a grave, but not a normal, hole-in-the-earth one. This grave was out of a nightmare. Instead of dank earth around you, there was liquid darkness that turned you like a roasting duck on a spit. Cobb groped out beneath the water, finding nothing, feeling himself carried along in a silent rush. He had no idea which way was up, which was down.

Got to relax, he thought. Got to let myself rise.

But relaxing wasn't easy, for he hadn't been prepared for his tumble into the water and thus hadn't drawn in a deep breath. He longed for air. Got to relax. Got to relax if I ever want another breath.

Suddenly he broke the surface. He threw back his head and took in a big gulp of air before being pulled back down again. Only a moment later he slammed into something hard. For a few seconds he was pinned to a flat surface by the current, like a butterfly smashed flat against a window in a windstorm. His hands found a corner; he got a grip and pulled up.

He was on the edge of a smashed little shed of some sort, jammed firmly up against rocks on the edge of the stream. He managed to drag himself, by some amazing gift of strength, atop the little building, which appeared to be lying on its back in the water. There had been a door on the front of it, but it had been ripped away by the current. Cobb, panting, laid himself on the now-horizontal front beside the dark, rectangular opening where the door had been. He could tell from the solid feel of the wood surface beneath him that the building was firmly lodged and would go nowhere.

Lord, I'm tired, Cobb thought. If it's all right with you and my guardian angel, I'll rest here for a moment. Not for long, I promise . . . just for a moment. . . .

His eyes closed and he passed out, lying flat atop the tight-wedged little building, his body in the space between the door and the edge of the wall. His left hand slipped over and dangled into the water inside the outhouse, where Dutch Polly's hair floated out from her upstaring corpse to brush his unfeeling fingers in the current.

~~~

Oliver Byers rolled over in his bed and resettled himself. He dreamed of being at the office, working with his noisy old hand press. It thumped and knocked, irritating him as always. When it made a particularly loud bump, Byers opened his eyes, and knew that the noise was not a product of his dream, and that he was not alone in his house. He sat up, looking into the darkness.

A match flared, moved, touched the wick of a lamp. Byers drew in his breath as the light revealed Jason Lybrand, soaked in rain, his hair matted on his forehead.

"You're Oliver Byers, I believe," Lybrand said. "Oliver Byers the newspaperman."

Byers wished he had kept his own pistol within reach of his bed. Instead it was in a drawer all the way across the room.

"What are you doing in my house? Get out of here!" Byers stormed.

Lybrand laughed in an ugly way. "Get out? Why? I hear you might want to talk to me, newspaperman. I hear you've already done some talking about me, behind my back. Well, here I am. You want your interview? Take your chance! Or maybe you don't want to talk to me. Maybe you planned to print up stories about me without even asking me about them."

Byers said, "You get out of my house."

Lybrand did not move.

Byers, becoming more frightened by the second, decided that the truth he normally valued so highly perhaps wasn't the best option at the moment. "I haven't been speaking to anybody about you. Why should I? I don't know what you're talking about." He hoped to the heavens Lybrand would believe this.

But the intruder simply shook his head. "You needn't lie. Dutch Polly Coots came to me and told me what she had done," Lybrand said. "She told me you said you already had something on me you were ready to put into your newspaper." Lybrand paused. His eyes flashed. "She said you told her you think I killed P. D. Viola."

Byers knew he could not lie his way out now. "Look," he said, "I'm sorry. Just forget all this and I'll do the same."

"She said you told her you had something on me that had come in the mail." Lybrand reached behind him. When he brought his hand around again it held a knife that flashed in the lamplight. "Where is it?"

Dutch Polly obviously had picked up more of what he had told her than Byers would have thought. "There's nothing, I swear!" he said.

"Where?" Lybrand smiled and leaned forward, turning the blade for Byers to see. "You might as well tell me, Byers, because I'll find that information even if you don't, even if I have to burn down this house and your newspaper office." He paused. His face became ugly with contempt. "Ah, hell with it, hell with you. You're right about me. When this week started I had never killed another man. Then I had to kill Viola. A little while ago I rid the world of Dutch Polly. . . . That's right, I killed her, too. Two killings in one week. A third won't clutter up things much worse."

Byers moaned, drew back. "The packet—it's in my file, in the office."

"Thank you. You've saved me some time." Lybrand lifted the knife.

"Please . . . please . . ."

"Don't beg. It doesn't become a grown man to beg."

Byers scrambled backward and slid off the bed. He dived for the drawer that held his pistol.

Lybrand was on him before he could even reach it. The knife stabbed down; Byers cried out and fell. He rolled onto his back, clutching his shoulder, looking fearfully into Lybrand's unsmiling face.

"Too bad you won't be around to write up your own obituary," Lybrand said.

The knife descended and Byers screamed.

CHAPTER 12

———

LYBRAND'S HEAD WAS REELING AND HE FELT
he might faint. Hidden in darkness, he clung to a
tree behind the *Argus* office and tried to calm himself. He had found Byers' slaying distressing, much
more so than the murder of Viola. Maybe it was
because he was still edgy from killing Dutch Polly,
though that had been as much accident as outright
murder.

Byers had died too noisy a death; that was the
problem. His screams had been upsetting, but also
dangerous. Lybrand hoped the newspaperman's
cries had not roused any neighbors. Fear of that
had forced Lybrand to flee after only three stabs;
he would have liked to have stayed longer to be
fully sure Byers was dead.

Only a soft drizzle remained from the storm, and
even that was diminishing. No more lightning
flashed, and the thunder was just a distant grumbling, gone on to other parts.

After a few minutes Lybrand began to feel better. The fainting feeling passed, to be replaced by
weariness. But there could be no rest yet. He went

to the back door of the newspaper office; as he expected, it was locked. Looking around to make sure no one was about, he picked up a stone, wrapped it in a handkerchief, and as quietly as possible broke out a pane of the door's window. He reached in and opened the latch, then let out a faint yelp and pulled back his hand. He had cut it on the broken glass. Swearing softly, he wrapped the handkerchief around the cut to stanch the blood. He opened the door and entered the office.

—◆—

Patterson shook his head. "It's no good, Cochran. It's taking too long, and Spencer could be anywhere."

"Then let's divide and look separately," Cochran suggested. "Either of us finds him, we take him back to my room and wait for the other."

The rain-soaked pair split up, Cochran heading back toward Bledsoe Creek, Patterson continuing to explore the main part of town.

After several more minutes of fruitless searching, Patterson turned down Silver Street and passed the Silver Striker Saloon and the San Juan Sign Company, and there stopped. He was at the office of the Snow Sky *Argus*, and he had seen movement inside it. He noticed through the front window that the door apparently was slightly open.

He circled the building and approached the back door carefully. It creaked open at his touch. "Spencer?" he asked as he stepped inside.

Patterson dug out a match and struck it. Simultaneously with the flare he saw a man near him, the face covered partially by a hand. A hard fist struck Patterson on his bearded jaw and he fell, stunned. His attacker ran; Patterson saw that he had a packet beneath his arm.

"Hey!" Patterson shouted. "Come back here!" He dived after the fleeing man and caught his ankle. The man fell, hitting hard, driving the breath from him.

Patterson jumped atop him, pinning him. The man struggled, still clinging to his packet. He had a handkerchief wrapped around one hand.

"Figure a storm's a good cover to rob somebody—that it?" Patterson said. He didn't bother to wonder why he even cared; years of Pinkerton work had ingrained a get-involved attitude into him when it came to crime.

Suddenly the pinned man rolled and swung up a fist, hitting Patterson in the jaw. The ex-Pinkerton was knocked back, and the man beneath him writhed and pulled free. Patterson grabbed for him again and missed, but he did manage to grab the packet. It tore, and something fell out. The man put his hand over the tear and ran as hard as he could out of the office and down the street.

Patterson stood slowly, rubbing his jaw and working his mouth from side to side. He thought about chasing the man down, but decided he had best concentrate on finding Spencer.

He had caught only a glimpse of the man's face, but it seemed familiar. Where had he seen him before? He rubbed his jaw again and glanced down.

At his feet lay a bloodied handkerchief. Must have come off his hand, Patterson thought. That fellow had a wound.

He stepped over and picked up what had fallen from the torn packet. It was a photograph—the same man he had just fought, dressed in some sort of frontier costume, a fur hat on his head. He was on a stage. Now Patterson recognized him: the preacher Jason Lybrand, the one who had acted so cold toward him when he came asking about Spencer.

Now, there was a mystery. What would a preacher be doing breaking into a newspaper office in the night? Patterson put the photograph in his pocket. He stepped out the back door and started around toward the street, and as he did so he happened to look up the hill toward the nearest cabin. Something moved in its doorway. Patterson squinted but could not make out what it was.

"Spence?" He headed toward the cabin at a lope, then heeled to a stop when he saw the moving thing was not Spencer, but another man, dragging himself out of the door.

Patterson approached him. "You drunk or hurt?"

The man groaned and lifted a hand. Patterson pulled his box of matches from his pockets and struck another light. The wind snuffed the match after only a moment, but in that moment Patterson saw enough.

The man's hand was drenched in blood. Patterson couldn't help but marvel at what a mind-boggling night this was turning out to be.

He knelt at the man's side. "You shot?"

"Cut . . . stabbed . . ."

"Who?"

"Lybrand . . . Jason Lybrand."

Patterson glanced down at the newspaper office. "That your office down there?"

"Yes . . ."

"I'm getting you back inside."

"No . . . got to get the packet . . . before Lybrand does. . . ." Byers could barely speak.

"He's already got a packet, so the odds are you're too late. I'm taking you inside, like it or not. You'll die otherwise."

Carefully he lifted Byers, who promptly passed out, and carried him inside. He laid him on the bed. A lamp already burned in the room.

Byers opened his eyes. "Abel Patterson—it's you!"

Patterson frowned. "How do you—"

"Listen to me, Patterson. It was Lybrand who killed the preacher Viola . . . said he killed Polly Coots, too."

"Killed Viola—"

"Yes . . ."

"Who's Polly Coots?"

"Town prostitute—in love with Lybrand. . . . He said he killed her. Now he's killed me, too."

"Not yet he hasn't. You're still with us, friend. I'm going to get you some help."

"Too late. You go after him, Patterson . . . get Lybrand for me . . ."

"But how do you know who I am?"

Byers did not answer. He closed his eyes and let out a slow breath. He did not take another.

Patterson pulled a blanket across Byers' face.

Cochran, standing near Bledsoe Creek, could just make out the overturned outhouse in the water, and a man atop it. Moving now, he was. The front of the outhouse was barely above the surface of the creek, making the man appear to be lying on the water itself. Cochran heard him groan, saw him stir again.

"Are you all right?" Cochran called, drawing near to the bank. The outhouse was lodged on the far side of the creek from him.

The man groaned once more and slid off into the water.

Without hesitation, Cochran splashed out after him. He miscalculated the creek's depth and went under as soon as he reached its middle. Floundering, he found the base of the outhouse underwater. Something touched his face. He reached for it. A foot.

He grabbed it, thinking at first it was that of the man who had fallen in the water, but then he realized this foot was far too small. And it was bare and cold—cold as the foot of a corpse. With that thought Cochran let go of it quickly. He pushed up on the base of the submerged shack and came to the surface. Pulling up on top of the shack, he caught his breath and looked for the man who had fallen.

He saw the man dragging himself up on the bank, and was surprised to see it was Earl Cobb. Remembering his underwater discovery, Cochran looked down into the vacant, upturned door of the outhouse and saw a murky shape inside, below the surface of the water. Summoning his courage, he reached down. His hand closed on sodden cloth; he pulled up.

A woman's pale face, eyes open, emerged for a moment from the water. Cochran shouted and let her go, then fell backward into the creek. He splashed quickly to the bank and pulled up beside the marshal.

"There's a dead woman in there!" he exclaimed.

Cobb groaned, then said, "Mr. Cochran, I've had quite a long and difficult day." He obviously had not grasped what Cochran had said.

"But Marshal, there's a—"

Cochran stopped, for on the other side of the creek he saw the shadowy little figure of Spencer Vestal, looking at him. Cochran whipped off his spectacles, shook the water from them, and put them on again. It really was Spencer.

"Mister?" the boy said. His voice was so soft Cochran could barely hear it. Cochran stood. "Wait there, Spencer. I've been looking for you."

Cochran splashed out into the water, its temperature and his awareness of the corpse making him shudder.

Halfway across he saw Abel Patterson running toward Spencer from behind, waving his hand. Obviously Patterson had just now spotted him. Spencer whirled, saw Patterson, and ran away into the darkness.

"Wait!" Patterson shouted. "Come back, Spencer!"

By now Cochran had reached the bank and Spencer was fully out of view. Cochran and Patterson ran after him, looking all about, but the night was too dense; they could not see him.

"Hiding from us!" Patterson said. "I don't understand it."

"Neither do I," Cochran said. "He actually called to me a moment ago, like he wanted me to come."

Patterson said nothing for a while. He looked at Cochran. "It's obvious, then. It isn't both of us he's running from. Just me."

Cochran said, "Do you know there's blood all over your shirt, Mr. Patterson?"

Cobb, despite his injuries, was in surprisingly good condition. Cochran and Patterson together helped him down the street toward the jail. Patterson was edgy around the lawman, but felt obliged to help.

"Cap Corley is dead," Cobb said. "Shot down. Them who did it are dead, too."

"It's been quite a night for dying," Patterson muttered so low the others did not notice.

"How'd you wind up on top of that outhouse, Marshal?" Cochran asked.

"That I can't rightly remember."

"There's a dead woman inside it," Cochran said.

"Good Lord!" Cobb said. Patterson could have provided another grisly surprise, but decided to wait. Oliver Byers was beyond human help, in any case.

They reached the jail; Patterson pounded the door. In a moment it opened, and Heck Carpenter looked out. The deputy obviously had not slept at all, nor changed clothing for many hours. When he saw Cobb, his eyes went big and bright.

"Marshal! Thank heaven! I thought you were surely dead and gone!"

"I ain't dead. But Cap is."

"Dead! What happened?"

"Get me to bed and maybe in a bit I can tell you," Cobb said. "In the meantime, Heck, there's a privy in the creek that needs cleaning out." Then

Cobb almost collapsed; Patterson caught him.

Heck looked at the others. "Privy? Is he delirious or something?"

They helped Cobb to his bed, and Heck freed a sobered-up drunk and sent him after Walt Chambers. Patterson and Cochran stepped outside. The eastern mountains were backlit by the coming dawn. "Sun will be up in a couple of minutes. I'll go looking for Spencer again," Cochran said.

"I'm coming too," Patterson said.

"No. I think I should go alone. Remember how he ran when he saw you? I know it's hard to take, but it's obvious he's just going to keep running as long as you're after him."

Patterson knew Cochran was right.

"All right. You go alone. I know when I don't belong." At that moment he would have been willing to give away every cent of that fifty thousand in the bank across town just to feel like Spencer wanted him instead of someone else.

Patterson stepped off the porch. "By the way, Cochran—there's still another dead body to be dealt with. Don't know his name, but he runs the paper here. He was murdered. He's lying on a bed in a house behind the paper office. I found him and put him there."

Patterson walked away, leaving Cochran wondering if it was some gruesome joke. Finally he shrugged. "I guess that explains the bloody shirt," Cochran wryly said to himself. He turned and went back into the jail office to report what Patterson had just told him. Behind him the sun spilled fresh light onto the weather-battered town.

Patterson walked back toward the creek, bitter at Spencer's latest rejection. Never should have let that boy come to mean anything to me, he thought. Care about somebody, and you're bound to hurt when you lose them. Just like when Roland died.

Patterson drew close to Bledsoe Creek. Several men were fishing Dutch Polly's body out of the water. The people gathered around were silent as pallbearers. The prostitute's body was a ghastly sight when it came out of the water, even from the distance Patterson saw her from. Someone had quickly covered her with a sheet.

Patterson started to walk on, but something made him stop. After a pause, he went to the crowd, pushed through, and knelt beside the body. He pulled back the sheet and looked at Polly's face.

"Hey—there's no call for that," someone said.

Patterson did not seem to hear. He put the sheet back in place and rose. "She was a whore?" he asked.

Someone protested the frank question, but another answered. Yes, she was a whore, name of Dutch Polly Coots. Must have gone into the outhouse to get away from the storm, and it washed away and drowned her.

"She didn't drown," Patterson said. He had seen enough bodies in his time to know. "She was hit in the head."

"No loss either way," one of the cruder members of the crowd said. "She was just a whore."

Patterson did not respond. He turned and walked away. The crowd parted to let him through.

———

Lybrand also had watched from a distance as Dutch Polly's body was fished out of the waterlogged outhouse.

He was in turmoil. Should he stay in Snow Sky or run? He had eliminated the threats posed by both Polly and Oliver Byers, but he had been caught at the newspaper office. Had the man seen his face? He wasn't sure. Lybrand had caught a glimpse of the other fellow, and he looked familiar—but many faces in this town were familiar to him.

He wondered how long it would be until Byers' body was found, and if there would be any way his death could be traced back to him. Probably not, now that he had the packet. But something had fallen out of it when the man at the *Argus* office grabbed at him. Lybrand had seen it happen but had been unable to recover the item. What if it was incriminating? The other contents of the packet scared Lybrand to death; he had no idea so much damning information about his past could be dug up by a mere Chicago newspaper reporter. He also had found Dutch Polly Coots' note to Byers in the packet; seeing it had taken away any hint of regret he had felt about killing her.

Suddenly he realized what day this was: Sunday. In a little while he would be expected to deliver a sermon. He had nothing prepared—not that he couldn't pull something from the air. He was a good improvisor.

But what if the law was looking for him? If somehow they had the goods on him? After having seen Byers' packet, he no longer could be sure that what he thought was secret really was. What if Byers had already talked to someone? What if Polly had?

That settled it. He would leave. Couldn't chance staying around to be arrested right in his pulpit. He went to his closet, flung open the door so roughly he jostled and hurt his injured hand, and got down a pair of canvas trousers and a rough cotton shirt. He would need stouter clothing than his preachery town garb when he traveled. He changed clothes, then went to his bureau and began unloading the drawers.

As he did so, the loose curtain rod Polly had pulled down in her final struggles fell again of its own accord. The rod clattered against the floor, startling Lybrand so much he yelled. He took a breath in relief when he realized what it was, and walked across the room to replace it, for he did not want to be observed from outside.

As he lifted the wooden rod back into place, he looked out. Down the slope a lone man loped past, stopping to stare up at the cabin. Lybrand's tumultuous mind for half a moment overruled his eyes and he actually saw the figure as P. D. Viola. But Lybrand did not believe in ghosts any more than he believed in the religion he pretended to teach. It was not Viola below, but the man who had come to the door shortly before Polly had died.

Lybrand could not remember if the man had told him his name. Why was he out there, and why was he looking up here?

Suddenly his memory completed itself—not only was this the same man who had come to the door yesterday, it also was the man whom he had fought with in the *Argus* office in the night, the one he had only just now been struggling to identify.

Lybrand's hands trembled. He went to his bedside table and got his derringer, which he placed in his pocket. He had a larger pistol, a Remington, but it had been damaged and he had not bothered yet to have it fixed. Now he wished he had.

He went back to the window and looked around the curtain. There was no one below. The man had gone.

Lybrand spent the next ten minutes hurriedly finishing his preparations, then put on his hat and went out his back door. Suddenly he remembered the packet he had taken from the *Argus* office. He had not had time to destroy it. Not wanting to leave it around, Lybrand went back inside, picked up the packet from the bureau top, and went out again.

"Hello, Preacher," a breathless Abel Patterson said, stepping around the back corner. "Would have been up to see you quicker, but I had to run back to my room to get my pistol. They won't let you keep them on you in town, you know."

For a moment, Lybrand knew what sheer panic was. He backed up against his door, eyes big as dollars.

"What's the matter, Preacher? I scare you?"

Lybrand forced himself back into control. His eyes flicked down; this man indeed did have a pistol, but it was holstered—though the thong was loosened so the weapon could be quickly drawn.

"Is there something I can do for you?" Lybrand asked. "I'm in a rush at the moment."

"I'll bet you are. I'll bet you're hurrying to get out of town before they find that newspaperman's body yonder in his house. I'll bet you're hoping he didn't tell anybody else about you putting a knife into him—and about you confessing to him that you killed that poor dead woman they pulled out of the creek."

Lybrand forced a laugh. "You're insane!" he said. "I don't know what you're talking about. Who are you?"

"Don't you remember? We've met twice, once at your front door, once in the *Argus* office. You dropped this, by the way." He pulled the photograph from his pocket and tossed it at Lybrand's feet.

"Look, I don't know what you're trying to do here—"

"I'm here to bring your judgment day, Lybrand. I'm here to call you killer and deal with you for it."

"You're mad!"

"You bet I am. As mad as hell is hot. I looked at a dead woman just a little while ago and saw the face of a woman I came to this town to find. That little boy I came looking for at your door, he needs a home, and I came to give him one with my sister. I hadn't kept up with her like I should—you know how that goes. But I did write her a little and she wrote to me, telling all about her happy little family, her good life. Last I heard from her she was moving to Snow Sky. Husband was going to run a big store and they were going to live in a big house and be happier than ever. I was glad for her, Preacher. She had the good things I missed out on. At least, that's what I thought. It appears she lied to me about all that, because when I saw her lying dead beside that creek this morning they told me she was just a whore. No loss, somebody said. No loss. A woman's murdered and they say it's no loss."

Lybrand was so amazed he almost forgot his

own desperate situation. "You're Polly Coots' brother?"

"She was always Polly Patterson to me. Still signed her letters that way, even after she got married—or claimed she had. Did she ever really have a husband, Preacher?"

"Look, this is crazy. I—"

"Answer me!"

"She had a man at one time, I'm told. His name was Coots. She bore his child, and later he ran out on her. Took the child." Lybrand backed away half a step. "But that's just what I hear. I've never met Polly Coots. And I'm told she died from accidental drowning, not murder."

"You're a liar. You confessed to the newspaperman that you killed her."

Lybrand felt new panic. "But Oliver Byers is . . ."

"Dead? Yes, he is now. But he wasn't when I found him crawling out of his house last night, bleeding like the devil. He lived long enough to tell me you're the one who cut him up—not to mention that you're also the one who beat that Viola fellow to death and killed Polly. God above, you killed my sister! Scum like you killed my brother in Chicago. I know all about you and your ilk, Lybrand, and I intend to see you go to your death for what you did. I don't know if they'll be able to convict you for Polly's death, but it doesn't matter to me what name's at the top of the case sheet. You can die for killing the preacher, the newspaperman, any of them—to me it will be Polly you're dying for. I'm ready to testify to what Byers told me."

Lybrand backed off again. "No," he said. Secretly he sneaked one hand into a pocket.

Patterson touched the butt of his pistol. "Give it up, Lybrand."

"No!" Lybrand pulled his hand from his pocket. In it was the derringer. He fired, point-blank, at Patterson's head.

"Spencer? Wait! Spencer!"

Cochran had seen a flash of color through the gaps in the wall of a nearby shed. He was far from the main part of town now, among the mines, having left the marshal's office to continue searching for Spencer. Before he had left, Cochran had conveyed Patterson's message about the dead newspaperman to Cobb, and Heck Carpenter had been sent to investigate. Cochran had not hung around to wait for the results.

"Mister?" It was a boy's voice. "Is that you?"

"I'm Tudor Cochran. You stayed at my inn on the way to Snow Sky. Do you remember?"

Spencer stepped out. He looked small, damp, frail in the sunlight. "I remember. I remember the lady there with the nice face."

Cochran knelt to bring himself more down to the boy's level. "She does have a nice face, doesn't she? That's my wife, Spencer. She cares a lot about boys like you. She worried for you and sent me after you."

"I know."

"Did your friend Mr. Patterson tell you?"

"No. I heard you say it that night outside that big tent with the music. And he's not my friend, not really."

Cochran had to think back to understand. He remembered the Dixie Lee Dance Hall, where Patterson had jumped him, and where he had described Flory's concern about the boy.

"You heard that? Where were you?"

"In the woods. I followed Mr. Patterson out."

To Spencer, Cochran's eyes looked small and glittery beneath his spectacle lenses. "We've been worried about you, Spencer. Mr. Patterson and I."

"He wants to be my father. I don't want him to be. I had to run away from him."

Cochran said, "I understand. But he cares about you, you know. He's told me that."

"But I don't want him." He paused. "I want the lady with the nice face. I want her to be my mother, because she cared enough about me to send you."

Something in that made Cochran swallow hard. He thought of the times early in marriage when he and Flory had talked about the children they would have—and how as the years passed such talk had faded along with hope.

Cochran wanted to tell Spencer that he was going to see his wish fulfilled, but he feared that if he did, the boy would just think it was a ruse to lure him back to town and Patterson. So he merely said, "Spencer, I think you are going to find yourself a very happy boy soon. I can't tell you all about it here, but I want you to trust me, and come back with me. It's all going to be all right. I promise."

Spencer seemed to relent, but then pulled back again. "I'm scared to go back to Snow Sky," he said. "There is a really bad man there."

"I don't understand."

"A bad man. He killed a woman and put her

into an outhouse over the creek, and made it fall in. I know, because I saw him do it—last night.''

Cochran was stunned by this information, delivered in such a matter-of-fact way. He reached out his hand.

''Spencer, now I know you've got to come back with me. There is a man you must meet; his name is Earl Cobb. He's a good man, and he needs to hear what you just told me.''

Spencer hesitated only a moment, then came forward and took Cochran's hand. Together they walked back toward the town.

CHAPTER 13

—◆—

LYBRAND ROUNDED THE REAR OF THE ROSE
and Thorn and stopped to catch his breath. He had
run a winding, hidden route from behind his cabin,
where the man named Patterson now lay crumpled
on the muddy ground. The fugitive preacher was
in a panic, desperate to get out of Snow Sky but
unsure of the best way to do so.

He needed a horse. On foot he could easily be
followed and run down. Even though Patterson had
been dealt with, Lybrand feared he ultimately
would be pursued by someone else.

A jumble of voices . . . Lybrand edged up to the
front of the alley to see where the noise was coming from. He saw a group of men, all very excited,
slogging rapidly up the muddy street. At their lead
was Heck Carpenter, the deputy. The group passed,
agitated voices still mingling. Lybrand caught the
eye of a little boy on the fringe of the group and
called him over.

"What's happened?"

"Dead man found!" the boy said. "Oliver
Byers, from the newspaper. Somebody stabbed him

to death.'' The boy, unashamedly thrilled by all the excitement, rejoined the group of men on a run. They were heading for the marshal's office, Lybrand figured.

Got to find a horse, and quick, Lybrand thought. He walked back around to the rear of the Rose and Thorn and looked up the hill toward the cluster of miners' cabins standing there. Orv and Kimmie Brown's place was on the far side of that hill—and Orv had several good riding horses. One of those would do nicely. Lybrand took off at a trot.

———

Cobb, seated in a chair in front of his desk, made a face as Walt Chambers bound up his ankle. ''What are you trying to do—squeeze it off?'' he complained.

''You nearly broke your dang ankle bone, and this won't do you no good unless it's tight,'' Chambers said irritably. Cobb had griped about everything Chambers had done to him in the last several minutes, and the horse doctor was tired of it.

''Won't do me no good when my foot rots off from lack of circulation, neither,'' Cobb said. At that moment the door opened and Tudor Cochran walked in with Spencer Vestal beside him.

''Well, hello there, gentlemen!'' Cobb said. ''Come here and meet our local medicine man, Walt Chambers—'cept I'm giving him a new first name: Torture. Torture Chambers.'' He laughed, but not for long; his bruised ribs, now bound up tight as his foot, throbbed too badly.

Cochran was serious; he did not laugh. ''Marshal, this is Spencer Vestal. He's a . . . Well, it's a long story. Just say he's a young friend of mine. He told me something a few minutes ago that was quite disturbing. It seems he may have witnessed a murder last night—the woman in the creek.''

''Witnessed it?'' Cobb sat up straighter, too quickly, bringing another jab of pain. ''That right, son?''

Spencer, nervous and shy, nodded. He stood close to Cochran.

''Who did you see committing this murder, son?''

''I don't know his name,'' the boy said. ''But he lives in a cabin up the hill behind that church tent. He was beating a woman.''

''Exactly which cabin was it, Spencer?''

''That one sort of off by itself, almost to the top of the hill. There's a big tree down from it and I hid under it when the storm started.''

''Merciful heaven, that would be the preacher's place!'' Chambers exclaimed.

''So it would,'' Cobb said. ''Spencer, did you see clear the man who did it? Was he young, old, fat, thin . . . ?''

''Young,'' answered Spencer, who judged age relative to his late father, older than most fathers of boys Spencer's age. ''Thin . . . He carried the woman out and put her in that outhouse. Then he made it fall in the creek.''

''That's for sure Jason Lybrand,'' Cobb said. ''Wouldn't you know it! I've had a bad feeling about that fellow from the first day he showed up here.''

''Well, I for one don't believe it,'' Chambers said. ''He's a preacher, for landsake.''

At that point they were distracted by the rising noise of a small mob approaching the office. Chambers went to the door and opened it; Heck Carpenter came bursting in, several other men following.

"Earl, it's true! We found Oliver Byers dead on his bed."

"Sweet Jehoshaphat! What's happening to this town?" Cobb exclaimed. "Dead preachers, dead crib girls, dead newspaper editors, even a dead deputy."

"What do you want us to do?" Carpenter asked.

Cobb lifted his hand for silence and turned to Cochran. "Mr. Cochran, I believe I need a few answers from you. That man who helped you get me back here, the one who told you Byers was dead—who is he?"

Cochran knew the time for covering up was over. Enough lies had been told, and he was weary of them. "His name is Abel Patterson. He's a former Pinkerton agent from Chicago, and I came to Snow Sky following him."

"Following him? He's a friend of yours?"

"I rather feel like he is now, or might be . . . but when I followed him it was because of Spencer here. Spencer has been in the care of Patterson. The pair of them spent the night at my inn, and Flory— that's my wife—got one of her feelings about them. She thought the boy was in danger or something, so I followed them to Snow Sky to make sure he wasn't. Hiram and I—" He stopped, reddening, realizing the slip he had just made.

But Cobb didn't seem surprised. "Hiram? Hiram Frogg, I presume—the man you keep telling me is not your friend?"

Cochran stammered, then confessed. "I lied to

you, Marshal. Yes, Hiram is a friend of mine, and
we rode in together. I lied because I knew he did
not kill P. D. Viola, and I had to be free of suspicion myself in order to prove it.''

Carpenter was becoming edgy. ''Earl, shouldn't
we be—''

''Hush up, Heck. I have a feeling I need to know
this before we do anything. In fact, why don't you
take your gaggle of gooseneckers there and wait
out on the porch? You too, Walt. I'll pay you when
I can.''

''I've heard that before,'' Chambers muttered.

Carpenter gave a sour look but complied with
Cobb's order. When the door was closed, Cobb
said, ''Let's get back on track. How did Patterson
know Byers was dead?''

''He told me he found him. You see, we were
out searching together for Spencer last night—
Spencer had run away—and he must have run
across him.''

''Did you notice there was blood on Patterson's
shirt?''

''Yes.''

''Think he might have killed Byers?''

Cochran hadn't had time to think about it, but
now that he did, it seemed possible. ''Well . . . I'd
hate to think of it. The truth is, though, that Byers
is the one who told me most of what I know about
Mr. Patterson. Byers had recognized him, knew of
him back in Chicago, he said, and also saw me
following Patterson around. He came asking what
my interest in him was. And he said—'' Cochran
stopped, not really wanting to say much more.

''Go on.''

"He said that Patterson came to Snow Sky with fifty thousand dollars in cash."

"That's a heck of a lot of money to be carting into a mining town. Where did he get it?"

"I don't know. Byers didn't know. I never asked Patterson about it. Our contact has been very limited—most of the time I've spent around him was last night, looking for Spencer."

"I know where the money came from," Spencer said. He had been so quiet the men had almost forgotten he was there.

"Then by all means, son, tell us," Cobb said. The man leaned over in his chair—slowly, given his hurt ribs—and smiled at Spencer to make the boy feel more at ease.

"That was money Mr. Patterson had with him when he found me," Spencer said. "He was bringing it to my father."

"Why?"

"My pap knew something bad about a rich man, and the money was from the rich man to pay Pap to keep it a secret."

"And Mr. Patterson was the delivery man, then."

"Yes."

"So why does he still have the money?"

"Because Pap died. Died right before Mr. Patterson came with the money."

"I'm sorry, son. I lost my own father, and I know it hurts."

"Not me. Pap was bad. He beat me."

A moment of silence. Hiram Frogg, oblivious to all that was going on, coughed back in his cell. Cobb said, "Are you telling me that Mr. Patterson

decided to keep the money that was supposed to
go to your pap?''

''Yes.''

''And he kept you, too?''

''Yes.''

''Why did he bring you and the money to Snow
Sky?''

Spencer said, ''He was bringing me to give me
to his sister. Said she would give me a home. But
when we got here we couldn't find her.''

Cobb turned to Cochran. ''Mull this over, Cochran—Oliver Byers goes to Patterson and starts talking about writing him up in the *Argus*, him and his
fifty thousand dollars. If Patterson wanted to keep
that quiet, which he would under the circumstances, what might he do to Byers?''

''I suppose he might kill him to keep him
quiet,'' Cochran said. ''But if he did, why did he
tell me about the body? Why didn't he just keep
quiet and not link himself to the situation?''

''I can't answer that. Perhaps Mr. Patterson has
something the average criminal doesn't. The fact
he didn't just abandon young Spencer here is evidence of it.''

''What?''

''A conscience. Maybe Patterson killed Byers in
a rage and after he had cooled down felt compelled
to tell about the death. I've seen that sort of thing
before.''

''Or simpler than that,'' Cochran said, ''maybe
he didn't kill Byers at all. Sometimes people are
innocent when they look guilty—like Hiram
Frogg.''

''Or guilty when they look innocent, like Jason
Lybrand. Speaking of whom . . .'' Cobb twisted his

neck and yelled toward the door. "Heck! Get in here!"

The deputy, still looking irritated at having been run out by his own boss, came inside.

"I want you to deputize some men and go bring in the preacher Lybrand. We got a young fellow here who says he witnessed Lybrand committing a murder."

Carpenter, stunned to hear the preacher connected with murder, bugged out his eyes so he looked somewhat like Hiram Frogg, said his yes sir, and started to turn away. He was still too irritated at being sent out onto the porch to lower himself to ask for an explanation from Cobb.

"Wait, one more thing," Cobb said. "Did I see Fred Apple out there?"

"Yep."

"Call him in."

Apple was the town postmaster. If he hadn't held that job Cobb would have liked to have had him as a deputy, for Apple had once been a policeman in Missouri. Experienced help was hard to come by in a Colorado mining town.

"What do you need, Earl?"

"I want to make you temporary deputy and head of a posse, Fred," Cobb answered. "Got a man you need to search for."

"Wait a minute," Carpenter said. "I thought you wanted me to head the search."

"You're looking for Lybrand, Heck. He might have killed Polly Coots. I want Fred to look for a man named Abel Patterson. He might have been the one who killed Oliver Byers. Of course, if the wrong posse brings in the right man, or however you'd say it, I won't fuss.

"We all know Lybrand. Patterson is a tall fellow, trimmed beard, blood on his shirt last time I saw him. Consider that he's likely dangerous. I want both of you to deputize as big a posse as you need, and I'd make it a fairly big one, if I was you. And Cochran, I want you to be part of Fred's posse. You know Patterson and Fred doesn't."

Cochran had never been asked to be on a posse before. "I don't have a pistol on me," he said.

"Good for you, in that you'd be in violation of the town ordinance if you did. You can borrow something from me. Fred, go out and start gathering men, quick as you can. I suggest you group up right outside here. Blast this busted-up body of mine—I wish I could go myself."

"What about Spencer?" Cochran asked.

Cobb smiled at the boy. "You pretty good at checkers, son?"

"Don't know how."

"Then you're about to be taught by a wore-out, out-of-practice master. The set's in that desk drawer there. Move it back in my bedroom—I got a bad need to lie down."

Lybrand crept around the corner of Orv Brown's horse shed, his eye on a shave-tailed beauty that looked like it could run. Lybrand had never been much of a horseman, but had enough of an eye to know a decent mount from a poor one.

"Easy, girl," he cooed, slipping toward the horse with one eye on the Brown cabin. "Easy now . . . easy . . ."

He stepped in fresh mud and slid. Instinctively

he reached for the shed door, which was standing ajar, to keep from falling, and as he did made a loud thumping sound against it. The horses moved and whickered.

"Who's there?" It was Orv Brown's voice, coming from the cabin. Lybrand ran around the other side of the shed and hugged the wall. His glass-cut hand throbbed and still leaked a little blood. "Somebody up there?"

Lybrand figured that as long as he stayed quiet, Brown would take a look around and head back inside. But a moment later the cabin door thumped shut. Lybrand heard Kimmie's voice. "Orv, you're not in shape to be up—"

"Got to see what's spooking the horses, Kimmie. I'll not be robbed again."

Lybrand heard the door open and shut, and Brown's approach. Stubborn fool, that Orv Brown, Lybrand thought. He's his own worst enemy. Lybrand placed Brown's location by sound, crept around toward the front of the shed, heard the creak of the pen gate . . .

Twenty seconds passed; Lybrand heard Brown slog through the mud, step by step, closer, closer . . . Lybrand wheeled around, cleared the corner, and drove his good fist right into Brown's nose. Brown grunted, flung out his arms, and fell. Lybrand deftly caught the rifle before Brown hit the ground.

Brown, his face red with gushing blood, looked up. "Preacher?" Lybrand hit the bandaged man with the rifle butt, knocking him cold as Kimmie's scream came piercing out of the house. She had seen it all from a window.

Kimmie . . . now, there was an idea! Lybrand

headed down, opened the gate, and ran onto the porch. Kimmie slammed the door shut just as he got there, but he pounded the latch open before she could lock it and threw his weight against the door, bursting it open and knocking Kimmie to the floor. Lybrand aimed the rifle at her. Kimmie's toddler daughter came around from the kitchen, saw her mother on the floor, and began to cry, not under-standing what was happening but sensing some-thing was wrong.

"Hello, Kimmie. Get up from there—you and I are going for a ride."

"My God, Reverend Lybrand—why are you do-ing this? Why did you hurt Orv?"

"Shut up. Get up from there and out of here—we got horses to saddle. You got two saddles?"

"Yes—"

"Good. Get moving."

"The baby . . ."

"Forget the baby. She'll be found soon enough, safe and sound, I'm sure. I need you. Protection, you know, if things get sticky. And later, other things." He smiled.

Kimmie did not know why this was happening, but it was clear that Lybrand was in some desperate situation—and also clear that he was not what she had thought he was.

Lybrand scouted around the house and found Brown's pistol and belt. He had been too discon-certed to think of taking Patterson's after he shot him. He loaded the pistol and strapped it on, and dumped extra shells into his pocket. "Come on," he ordered.

A few minutes later, Kimmie was mounted on one horse, her hands bound to the saddle horn, and

Lybrand was on another. He walked his horse out of the pen, and led Kimmie's.

"We're going into the mountains," he said. "They'll check the main roads first, figuring I'll go that way for speed. But we'll be up around the Molly Bee Pass, hooking up with a couple of partners of mine."

Keeping away from town and the outlying populated areas, they circled back toward the base of the trail that led to the Molly Bee Pass. As they rode, Kimmie bowed her head and refused to let tears come, even though the fading cries of her abandoned daughter tore at her heart.

The old man at the livery stable crammed a near-handful of tobacco into his cheek; his jaw bulged out as the wad settled naturally into his fist-sized pocket that had formed over years of chewing. He leaned back against a stall door and watched the bearded man who was rather hurriedly saddling his horse.

"Pardon me," the old man said as the other tightened the cinch, "but did you know you have a right smart furrow plowed along the side of your head?"

"I was aware of it," Patterson answered.

"Looks like a bullet done it." He leaned over and launched a coffee-colored stream from his mouth. "You been in a fight of some kind?"

"Now you've gone to meddling," Patterson said in a friendly tone.

"Got blood down your shirt, too. I'd say you was running from the law, if I had to guess."

"You don't have to."

"Don't you worry none about me—I run from the law plenty myself in my younger days. Did you know I holed up with Jesse James one night? Down in Tennessee he was at that time. And I rid for a week with Simon Caine during the hostilities. Hard as nails, Caine was. Yes sir, I was a wild buck in my young days. Man running from the law's got nothing to fear from me. My lip's sewed tight when law comes looking."

"I'm not running from the law, if it makes any difference," Patterson said. "Not that I know of, at least. But I'm looking for a fellow who is, or will be."

"He give you that gully in your head?"

"Sure did. He assumed he had killed me, I think. Knocked me clean out for a few minutes, but I'm still kicking."

Patterson dug money from his pocket. "Keep the change—if you'll tell me the way a man on the run would most likely leave Snow Sky."

"Well sir, there's any number of ways out. You could take the main road if you wanted to go fast, or any of these mountain trails if you wanted to hide in the hills."

"Any of those mountain trails connect with main roads farther on?"

"None but the trail through the Molly Bee."

"Where's that?"

"Yonder way." The man pointed. "Go out back, cross the creek, and take the road between them two hills you'll see." The old man put on a devilish grin. "My compadres and me calls them hills Molly Bee's breasts." He cackled. "Yes sir, that's what we call 'em, no fooling!"

"Clever bunch, you and your compadres," Patterson said. He wiped away the last of the blood exuding from his head wound; the rest had scabbed to a crust. He then led his horse out the big double back door of the livery, just as another man came running in the front. He was a boyish version of the older fellow.

"Papaw, they's two posses forming down at the marshal's office!" the young man said. "They's looking for the preacher Lybrand and for another fellow too. The preacher Lybrand, they say he kilt Dutch Polly Coots, and the other fellow kilt the man running the newspaper. I going to get me my rifle and go down and—" The flood of words stopped as the speaker noticed Patterson. "Papaw—that there looks like he might be the fellow one of them posses is after."

The old man pivoted his hoary head toward Patterson. "You told me there wasn't no law after you!"

"Didn't know there was," Patterson said as he drew his pistol. "I suppose I ought to ask you to open that stall door."

The old man spat. "Reckon you orta." He opened the stall and stepped inside. "Come on, Dwayne." He pronounced it Dee-wayne. "He'll want you in here too."

"If'n I had my pistol I'd take him to the law," the younger man said as he stepped inside.

"Good thing for me and you that you didn't," Patterson responded. He closed the door, wedged it shut with a long board jammed up against another stall on the far side, and then tied a rope across the door to keep it from opening even if the board was knocked free. "That ought to hold you awhile," Patterson said.

"It orta."

Patterson mounted and headed for the trail up to the Molly Bee. When he reached the twin hills the old man had chortled about, he saw fresh horse prints in the muddy trail. Two horses, traveling fast. He hoped one of them carried Lybrand. Perhaps the second was a spare mount.

No way to be sure if Lybrand had come this way, but his intuitions felt right, and at the moment that was all he had to go on. He passed between the hills and continued up the trail.

CHAPTER 14

—◆—

THE AIR BECAME COOLER AND THINNER THE
higher they went. Kimmie Brown shivered uncontrollably, but it wasn't from the cold. She felt
doomed, and every lurching, upward step of her
horse made her husband and deserted child seem
more distant. For all she knew, Orv was dead; she
had not even been given the chance to check before
Lybrand stole her away.

She could hardly believe the roughly dressed,
profane man who held her hostage was the same
polite gentleman she had seen behind the pulpit so
many Sundays past. She wondered if he had gone
insane . . . or if she had.

Her horse stumbled and she almost fell from the
saddle. The ropes binding her hands to the saddle
horn tore at her wrists. Lybrand twisted in the saddle, glared at her, and swore. He stopped, dismounted, and pushed her back into the saddle. She
kicked at him.

Lybrand drew his stolen pistol and stuck it under
her chin. Slowly he clicked back the hammer.

"It would be ironic for you to die from a bullet

fired by your own husband's pistol, wouldn't it? Come now, Kimmie—it needn't be this way. You can enjoy your life with me, I assure you . . . or you can throw your life away if you refuse to cooperate. You decide.''

She glared at him, still refusing to give in to tears.

''Don't think I'd hesitate to get rid of you, Kimmie, no matter how I feel about you. I've killed three people already this week, and I don't have much to lose by adding a fourth. But I don't want to kill you. I care about you, Kimmie. I always have. I used to look at you from the pulpit, think about you. Could you feel it? You could, I know you could.''

She shuddered. His talk made her feel sick.

Lybrand tried to read her expression. ''Worrying over your family? Don't. I didn't kill your husband. He'll live to take care of your child. Forget them. You're with me now.''

''Orv will come after you. He won't stop until you're dead.''

''No fool worse than a stubborn fool. If he follows, I'll deal with him later.''

Lybrand thumbed down the hammer and holstered the pistol. He remounted.

Cochran wasn't sure how to feel about riding in a posse, particularly one searching for Abel Patterson. While looking for Spencer last night along with Patterson, Cochran had come to like the ex-Pinkerton. It was hard now to picture Patterson as a potential murderer, despite the convincing case

Cobb had outlined. And Cochran knew firsthand that Byers had been the aggravating sort who easily could drive someone to kill him in anger.

Posses, Cochran had assumed, were fast-moving, powerful bands that swept the land like righteous angels bringing in wrongdoers. But Apple's posse just sort of plodded along. No one had any idea where to look for Patterson, or even if he was in town. Only Cochran knew first-hand what Patterson looked like.

Apple rode beside Cochran at the head of the ten-man party. The riders wound through town, looking about, asking questions of people on the street, all in all seeming to Cochran like a rather ineffective force.

At length they wound up outside town, riding up the road that led toward the Cochran Inn, a day and a half away. "Maybe we'll meet somebody coming in who might have seen Patterson going out—if he went this way," Apple said.

It seemed to Cochran that finding Patterson like this was about as likely as shooting a crow through the head by firing blindfolded at the sky. But he kept his peace; Apple was the one with law experience, not he.

Two miles out of town, Apple raised his hand and stopped the posse. "Take a look." He nodded forward.

Two riders were coming toward them. Both wore dusters, big-brimmed hats, and broad mustaches. From the looks of them they had been on the trail quite a long time.

Apple waited for them to approach. When they were twenty feet away they stopped. Both touched their hats as one.

"Gentlemen," Apple said.

"Good day, sir," one of the pair returned. He cast a glance across the group. "This has the look of an official party."

"A posse. Looking for a man name of Abel Patterson. You see anybody come out this way?"

The men glanced at each other. "No sir," the first man said.

"You're sure?"

"Had we seen Abel Patterson, I assure you we would know it. We're looking for him too." The man reached beneath his duster and pulled out a folding wallet. He opened it, rode up a few feet, and handed it to Abel. "My credentials. I'm J. B. Fulton, Pinkerton agent. My partner here is Ken Lambertson. Also affiliated with Pinkerton."

"Pinkertons! Why are you looking for Patterson?"

"We'll be glad to answer that—if you will do the same."

Apple glanced at Cochran and shrugged. "No harm in that, I guess." Then to Fulton: "He's suspected in the murder of a local newspaperman. Somebody stabbed the fellow to death."

Fulton shook his head. "It wasn't Patterson. I know him too well. Under no circumstances would he murder a man. If he's killed anyone, it's in self-defense."

"How do you know him so well?"

"Used to work with him. And as I said, we've been sent after him. He took a bad turn. A very wealthy fellow is alleging that Patterson took a large sum of money that belonged to him. Some sort of payment—extortion, I figure—that Patterson was to deliver. Our man got wind the fellow who was to receive the money died before it ever came—but Patterson never brought back the money. We were hired to find him, and a hard trail it's been, I'll tell you. Patterson knows how to cover his tracks. He was good when I worked with him, and he's good now.''

Apple asked, ''You gentlemen interested in joining our search party here?''

''No thanks. And I suggest you look elsewhere—Patterson has not come this way.''

Apple sighed, turned to his posse, and said, ''Gentlemen, let's turn it around. We're going back to Snow Sky.''

—

Lybrand stopped when he saw the bridge over the gorge was gone. Disbelieving, he dismounted and walked, rifle in hand, to the edge of the gorge. He had all but forgotten the storm, and the possibility it could have wiped out his only way across this obstacle had never crossed his mind.

He scanned the fallen bridge, now a crumpled mass of logs and puncheons, then raised his eyes to the maze of rocks on the far, steep side. Beyond them, out of his view from here, stood the cabin in which Dade and Daugherty were holed up. If they were there, perhaps they could tell him some other way across. He cupped his hands and started to shout, then realized there could be someone trailing him. If so, he didn't want to advertise his exact location. He would have to find an alternate way across on his own—though that could only mean cutting along the length of the gorge and going back through the forest itself. That would slow him down considerably, especially with Kimmie along.

But there was one other option. They could abandon their horses, climb down in the gorge, and scale the other side. That would put them on foot, but also would have them across the gorge much more quickly. They could connect with Daugherty and Dade in the cabin and leave together. Daugherty and Dade had only one horse each, meaning Lybrand and Kimmie would have to double with them until they could steal other mounts, but that was a minor problem. The worst thing Lybrand would have to face would be the anger of his partners at having to abandon their scheme to clean out the House of Prayer bank account.

Lybrand, turning, happened to glance to his right and downward into the churning water at the base of the gorge, near the waterfall.

A body was there, half out of the water, half in, caught between two rocks sticking out from the bank. It was Ivan Dade. Breathing faster now, Lybrand scanned the rest of the area. Farther up from the waterfall he saw Daugherty's corpse, caught by the shirt collar on a protruding limb, his feet pointing downstream with the current.

Dead. Both of them dead. How? Had the bridge fallen with them on it?

He heard her behind him a second before he saw her, and when he wheeled she was already upon him, pushing him back and over the edge of the gorge. He fell, hit the slope, and rolled down it toward the water, losing his rifle along the way.

Kimmie, her wrists bleeding from having slipped the tight ropes, let out a spontaneous scream, then wheeled and ran back down the way they had come, too distraught even to think of taking one of the horses.

———

Patterson heard the scream echoing back down the trail. A woman? He pieced it together: The extra set of hoofprints on the trail were not left by a spare horse, but by a second rider—apparently female.

A girlfriend? A hostage? Patterson could not know, not yet. But a few moments later he saw a pretty woman coming back down the trail. When she saw him she stopped so quickly she fell.

He dismounted and went to her. "It's all right, lady—relax. I won't hurt you." He pointed up the hill. "Lybrand?"

Kimmie was too breathless to answer, but she nodded rapidly.

"You were his hostage, maybe?"

Another fast nod.

"Where is he?"

"Knocked him . . . into a gorge . . . just up the hill."

"Here . . ." Patterson led Kimmie to his horse. "You ride on down to Snow Sky. Don't stop for anything. I'm going after Lybrand." He helped her mount, turned the horse, slapped its rump. As Kimmie rode away, he drew his pistol and headed up the slope.

Kimmie rode like she had never ridden before. Patterson's horse was swift despite weariness, particularly on this downslope. The farther she got from Lybrand, the safer she felt. Happiness began to rise. Ahead was her home, her husband, her baby.

When she came out from between the hills at the base of the trail, she careened toward town, crossed the Bledsoe Creek bridge, the horse gracefully leaping the missing portion, and sped past the livery, not noticing the crowd of men there. She was bound for home, and nothing would distract her.

"Hey—that looks to be the same horse!" the old man said, pointing after her. "That woman's riding the horse that belongs to the fellow what shut us up in the stall!"

Heck Carpenter asked, "Are you sure?"

"No doubt. Saddle's the same, too, ain't it, Dee-wayne?"

Carpenter singled out two of his men. "Go after her. See what's going on. I think that was Kimmie Brown." He turned back to the two men he had just freed from the stall. "Good thing you gents know how to holler loud. That man, was his name Patterson?"

"Don't rightly know. When he put his horse in here t'other day he used the name Johnson."

"Yeah, but when I come in talking about joining the posse, that's when he locked us up," Dwayne said. "Must have been Patterson."

"Which way did he take off?"

"Right up toward the Molly Bee."

"Let's go after him, then," Carpenter said. "If he lost his horse to Kimmie Brown somehow—and don't ask me to figure that one out—then likely he's on foot. That ought to make him easier to catch."

"Don't count on that," the old man said. "That fellow, he struck me as a slick one. And I can tell things like that. I was wild in my younger days, you know. I was with Jesse James once't."

"Tell me about it one of these days, then," Carpenter said, trying not to act impressed but in fact being very much so, for he had read a score of Jesse James dime novels. "Right now I got work to do. Forget about Lybrand, men—we're going after Patterson. At least we know where he went." Carpenter was determined to outdo Apple, whom he knew Cobb held in higher regard.

The posse galloped off toward the Molly Bee trail. The old man and his son walked to the back of the livery and watched them head for the twin hills. "Been a sweet sort of day, ain't it, Deewayne?" the old man said. "Ain't had this much excitement since I rid with Simon Caine. No sir."

Patterson saw the horses first, standing where they had been left. From the horn of one of the saddles hung a curl of cord, wet with blood from Kimmie Brown's wrists. He noted that beside the other horse lay a packet that apparently had been half stuck into a saddlebag, but had fallen out. It was the packet Lybrand had taken from the *Argus*, he figured.

No Jason Lybrand in sight. Patterson saw the gorge ahead. He crept forward, pistol out, trying to be as silent as he could, hoping that any noise he might make would be masked by the sound of the waterfall. The distance to the gorge seemed infinite, every step an effort. His pulse pounded inside his temples, making the bullet furrow on his head throb.

He came to the edge of the gorge and saw Lybrand too late to duck, so he was fully exposed when Lybrand fired. Lybrand had only then regained his rifle, for he had been stunned by the roll into the gorge, and his rifle had fallen into a crevice and had been hard to find. In fact, he had literally plucked it out of the crevice, whipped it up, and fired it just as Patterson appeared. Haste made for bad aim, and he missed. Patterson backed off.

"Show yourself again and you're a dead man!" Lybrand yelled.

Patterson figured surprise was his best hope. "All right, all right . . . I'm not foolish. I'm backing away—I'll leave . . ."

With that he plunged forward, landing on his stomach at the edge of the gulch. He fired a quick shot at Lybrand. The false preacher screamed and grabbed at his shoulder. The rifle hit the ground. Blood streamed between Lybrand's fingers.

"Next one I put through your skull," Patterson said. "Give it up. Come up here with me and I'll take you back to Snow Sky."

Lybrand shook his head. "I can't go back. I'll never go back. There's too much against me there."

"You have the same right to a fair trial that any man's got. Come on—live. Don't make me kill you."

"I can't go back . . . can't." Lybrand wobbled on his feet. Even from yards away he looked increasingly weak. "Can't go back." He sank to his haunches, then sat on a rock.

Patterson said, "Scoot that rifle away. You're too close to it."

Lybrand slowly reached for the rifle—then suddenly it was in his hands, being levered. Lybrand came up, dodging to the side as Patterson fired.

Lybrand fired next, and it was Patterson's turn to scream. A slug pounded through the flesh of his upper arm. He dropped his pistol and it fell into the gorge. Patterson rolled back away from the edge.

Lybrand was a good actor; he had certainly fooled Patterson. Obviously the bullet Lybrand had taken had not harmed him as much as he had pretended. Patterson quickly examined his own wound, which was bleeding freely, but was relatively superficial. That made twice today that Lybrand had tried to kill him but had managed only to wound. Patterson doubted he would be so lucky a third time—especially without a gun to answer with.

Realizing that if Lybrand came back up the slope on this side, there would be nothing to anticipate but a quick slaughter, Patterson headed back down the trail toward Snow Sky and then on a rocky stretch cut into the forest to his left. He hoped Lybrand would not attempt to follow him, but if he did, at least he would lose all sign once he reached the rocks. In the forest Patterson edged back up toward the gorge, staying far from the trail so he wouldn't be seen should Lybrand be on it.

He saw a knoll ahead and went to it. He scrambled up it and from the top found, as he had hoped he would, that through the evergreens he could see into the gorge a little. He waited there, wondering what Lybrand would do. A few minutes later he saw him—on this side of the gorge—heading back toward the edge, carrying the packet that had been on the ground beside the horses. Lybrand must have gone back to the horses and picked it up. The young man, seemingly ignoring the wound Patterson had given him, descended into the gulch on the shallow side. After three minutes had passed, Patterson saw Lybrand climbing up the other side, moving relatively fast up the steep rock face, his rifle thrust through his belt, the packet in his teeth. Patterson had to grudgingly admire Lybrand's determination and ability to ignore pain.

A minute later, Lybrand cleared the far side of the gorge and vanished among the rocks there. Patterson stood, slid down the rounded front of the knoll, and headed for the gorge himself, cutting straight through the forest.

He waited a few moments before coming out into the clear, for he feared Lybrand might be hidden in the rocks on the other side, waiting for him to appear. When finally Patterson did come out in the open, no gunfire greeted him. He ran forward, paused at the gorge to assess the smoothest way down, then made another slide.

He looked for his dropped pistol at the bottom but did not find it. It must have been lost in the water. He splashed through the water, which was not as high now that some of the storm runoff had drained away, and made it to the other side. He stumbled across something and was stunned to see it was a dead body . . . and not far away was another. Two mysteries—two he would have to ignore. Catching Lybrand was the important thing.

He scaled the wall on the other side, which was not easy, given his arm wound. Using the muscles hurt him terribly, but he would not give up. He kept seeing the face of his dead sister, kept thinking about the fact that the man who killed her was even now escaping. With a final heave, Patterson pulled himself up and immediately ran into the rocks.

There was more trail here, and it led to a cabin. The little log hut was tucked back against a low bluff. Beside it was a crude corral, the gate open. Patterson eyed the cabin until he felt reasonably confident it was empty, then went to the edge of the corral. Fresh tracks of two horses pockmarked the dirt; Lybrand had probably just now taken a horse from this corral, and either turned the other loose or trailed it along.

Patterson edged over to the cabin; the door was open. He peered in. As he had thought, no one was inside, but it was obvious someone was staying here—or had been. He remembered the bodies. Perhaps those men had lived in this place.

A glint of light on something in the corner caught his eye. A rifle! Lybrand must have overlooked it; he would not have left it behind willingly, Patterson figured. Beside the rifle, on the floor, were a box of shells and a Colt pistol.

Patterson checked the rifle—loaded. The pistol as well. He tucked the pistol behind his back, in his belt, pocketed the extra rifle shells, and walked out. Scanning the ground, he picked up hoofprints, and followed them on a run.

Once again the land began to rise, the air to become even thinner. Patterson panted as he ascended. It was easy to follow the tracks of the horses; here there was only one trail they could follow in any case. It wound up between rocks, heading toward the timberline.

Patterson stopped, leaning over with his hands on his knees, gasping. His injured arm hurt badly; so did his head. He began to lose the hope he had gained when he found the firearms. Patterson could not outperform a stout horse used to the mountains.

Lybrand was going to get away after all.

The thought brought despair. Patterson remembered Polly as a young girl, a baby he had held in his arms when he was just a child himself. Too bad he had lost touch with her as much as he had. Perhaps he could have steered her off whatever course finally had made her a mining town prostitute. A sad thing Polly's life must have been.

"I'll try, Polly. Try to get him for you," Patterson said aloud. He stood and began trotting up the slope again.

As he rounded a turn, a horse stood before him, bridled but barebacked. Patterson scanned the high rocks, looking for evidence of ambush, and found none. Slowly he advanced to the horse.

The reins were bloodied. Apparently Lybrand was bleeding worse; perhaps the blood itself had made the reins slip from his hands. Probably this was the second horse, which he had led away to keep any pursuer from using it against him.

Patterson hefted himself up onto the horse and headed up the trail again. He rounded a bend, came around a monolith of stone, and knew even before he heard the shot that he had brought himself squarely into a trap.

Lybrand fired from somewhere above; the slug tore through Patterson's side, to the left of his stomach. He fell from the horse, landing on his right side. He tried to raise the rifle with his left arm, but Lybrand fired again and put a bullet through his forearm, breaking it. The rifle fell. Patterson struggled not to pass out.

Lybrand stood up behind the boulder that had hidden him. Smiling broadly, he approached. There was little blood on him; the wound he had received was obviously superficial. He must have smeared blood on the reins of the horse deliberately, to make Patterson think he was worse off than he was. Patterson had to hand it to Lybrand: the ruse had worked.

Patterson twisted, moving his right arm from beneath him, putting his hand behind him . . . and Lybrand approached, laughing now, bearing down on him as he levered his rifle again.

"Viola, Polly, Byers—and now you," Lybrand said.

Still walking, he raised the rifle to hip level, aimed it at Patterson's upper chest—and Patterson heaved up, clearing enough room between himself and the ground for his right arm to come forward, the Colt pistol in his grip.

Lybrand never got a chance to squeeze off a shot. Patterson's bullet took him in the gut, doubling him over. The next shot caught his right shoulder, kicking him back, making him stumble, screaming, toward a steep slope behind him. His arms flailed and then he was gone.

Patterson closed his eyes for a few moments. Then he opened them, made himself get up. He staggered to the edge of the slope, looked down.

Nothing. Just a barren, rocky slope, nothing on it big enough to hide a man, no vegetation into which a body might disappear—but no Jason Lybrand, either. It seemed impossible. Even if Lybrand had been able to run away, he still would be well within view.

But he wasn't. Patterson was mystified, but the feeling gave way quickly to one of sickness. He sank to his knees, then fell forward, almost rolling down the slope himself.

Near the base of that slope, fifteen feet deep in a narrow crack in the rock that Patterson had not even been able to see from the top, Jason Lybrand lay wedged sideways, his throat crushed against a bulge of stone so tightly that he could barely get breath into his constricted lungs, yet could make no sound other than the same sort of squeaks P. D. Viola had made in his last hours. Lybrand wanted to scream for help, but could not, and even if he had, the only man who could have helped him would have been unable to do so, downed as he was by bullets Lybrand himself had fired.

The worst of it was, the pinching rock was hampering Lybrand's loss of blood from his gut wound. Eventually, he knew, he would bleed to death . . . eventually. But before that would be hours in this living hell of constriction, enclosure—the things that Lybrand had feared and hated more than anything else for as long as he could remember.

Life had seemed short so far to Jason Lybrand. But he knew that would be made up to him, for what time remained would seem long indeed.

Time passed; he heard Heck Carpenter's posse arrive, heard them exclaiming over Patterson, heard them search the area, saw their shadows pass above, heard them find the horses and the packet. He tried again and again to scream but could not. Then they were gone.

Time dragged on and torment drove Lybrand's sanity from him. He shifted his eyes upward and saw a man crouching above the crevice, looking down at him, smiling. Lybrand squeaked again and the man laughed and waved. It was P. D. Viola. Lybrand closed his eyes, and when he looked again Viola was not there.

For the rest of his life, Jason Lybrand was alone.

CHAPTER 15

———

Two Days Later

COCHRAN WALKED UP TO THE DOOR OF THE marshal's office, knocked, then went on in. Heck Carpenter, sliding his dime novel into a drawer, nodded a hello.

"The marshal wanted to see me?" Cochran asked.

"That's right." Then, over his shoulder, "Earl! He's here!"

Cobb came out of his side room, hobbling stiffly on his crutch, making a face with each step. But he looked more rested than the last time Cochran had seen him. "How you coming along?" Cochran asked.

"Tolerably well. And what about Patterson? You seen him today?"

"Yes. Just came from there. Walt Chambers was with him, and he's optimistic. Says he'll make it, though it may be a long time before he's fit to travel."

"Them Pinkertons hanging around still?"

"Yes, just waiting on Patterson to heal up so they can take him back. And Spencer stays by Patterson's side every waking hour. Funny thing how the boy has grown so close to him all at once. When he found out how hard Patterson looked for him, and how he went after Lybrand all alone, he started seeing him as a hero."

Cobb sat down slowly, then eased his crutch to the floor beside his chair. "I plan to talk to Patterson soon as he's more fit. When he gets clear of this stolen money problem he's facing, I want him to know he's got a job here if he wants it. Probably he won't—being a Snow Sky deputy don't pay a heck of a lot, and it ain't got the prestige of being a Pinkerton."

"Amen," Carpenter muttered from over at the window, where he was looking out onto the street.

"He may take you up on it in any case," Cochran said. "There's not much prestige in being an ex-Pinkerton ex-convict, either."

"Let me get to the thing I called you here for," Cobb said. He laid his hand atop a big pile of papers on top of the desk. "Judge Worth was in town this morning and we conducted us a quiet little hearing. The judge looked over these papers and such, the stuff that came out of the packet they found on Lybrand's horse. The packet was addressed to Oliver Byers, and came from somebody on the Chicago *Tribune*—an old friend of Byers', we gather from the letter in it. It's all about Jason Lybrand, and sheds a lot of light on that bird. Seems he had a past relationship with P. D. Viola that wasn't what he presented to us." He briefly outlined the story of Lybrand and the Viola family. "Viola wasn't coming to Snow Sky to help Lybrand build his church at all. He was coming for revenge.''

''Which supports what Patterson and Kimmie Brown say about Lybrand being Viola's killer.''

''It does, and the judge sees it the same way I do. We've decided there is no case to be made against Hiram Frogg. I called you over thinking you might want to be here when we let him go. I would have freed him sooner, but I wanted to see how the judge saw it.''

Cochran let fly a wide grin.

''Heck, you do the honors, huh?'' Cobb said.

A minute later, Frogg was standing in the office beside Cochran, beaming in the joy of freedom as he shook hands with Cobb and Heck Carpenter.

''I thought there for a bit that my time had come,'' Frogg said. ''I figured the law would see me dead.''

''You didn't kill Viola,'' Cobb said. ''There's no doubt in my mind Lybrand is our man. Another hearing or two, and I think we can officially lay three murder charges on Lybrand's back.''

''But he's not here to bear them,'' Cochran said.

''No. That's a puzzle, too. Don't know if Lybrand's alive or dead. Never heard of a man vanishing like that before. Maybe someday we'll know what happened. It's as if the earth itself swallowed him up.

''We'll put out notice Lybrand is wanted, but I have a feeling we'll see no results from it. I only hope there's enough justice in this world that he somehow got what was coming to him, and that Snow Sky never sees the like of him again.''

Cochran and Frogg headed back to Patterson's bedside and found the man much improved. Cochran introduced Frogg; hands were shaken. Spencer was at Patterson's bedside, as before.

"Well, I told Cochran I'd investigate to see you cleared, and it didn't really work out for me to do it," Patterson said to Frogg.

"The end result came out right for me, and you had your part in it," Frogg said. "That's what matters."

"And what's ahead for you now, Mr. Patterson?" Cochran asked.

"Fulton and Lambertson are hovering around like two buzzards waiting to haul me off," Patterson answered. "Suppose I'll do some jail time for keeping that blackmail money." Patterson reached down and fondly ruffled Spencer's hair; the boy grinned. "I don't look forward to what I'll have to face, but still I'm ready for it. I'm tired of running and worrying. I'll do my time, then after that, who knows?"

"The marshal just informed me he'll make you Snow Sky deputy anytime you want to be," Cochran said.

Patterson lifted his brows. "You don't say! Well, I could give it some thought. Lord knows being locked up will give me plenty of time to think."

"Whenever you're free, and if you come back through here, I hope you'll stop at the inn," Cochran said. "Free room and board for you anytime. Me and Flory and Hiram will be glad to see you."

"I'll take you up on that. And you can bet I'll be there. I'll want to see how this boy here is shaping up.'' He scruffed his hand through Spencer's hair again.

''Well, you won't see me about the inn if you come through,'' Frogg said.

Cochran turned, surprised. ''What?''

''I'm staying in Snow Sky. Opening up a smithy. Like Mr. Patterson said, being locked up gives you time to think. I thought about it, and decided that a man has to settle down sometime or another.''

Cochran smiled and stuck out his hand. ''Glad for it, then,'' he said. ''I'll miss having you about, though, Hiram.''

''Yeah, but think how happy Flory will be that old Toad ain't around no more. But don't worry— I'll be in to visit, and you can let me stay in that free room you offered Mr. Patterson.''

Cochran gave Frogg a friendly frown and then turned to Spencer. ''Son, are your feelings still the same about coming to live with Flory and me?''

''Yes,'' Spencer said. ''If yours are.''

Warm relief spread through Cochran. He had feared Spencer's newfound affection for Patterson would change his notions about whom he wanted to spend his life with—not that Patterson would have been able to take care of the boy for a long time to come, in any case.

''I still feel exactly the same way,'' Cochran said. ''Come on. Let's let Mr. Patterson rest a bit. We'll go to the Rose and Thorn and have us a good piece of pie.''

''With cream on it?'' Spencer asked.

''A gallon, if you want it. You come too, Hiram.''

''Sorry. I'm more in the humor for a beer.''

Outside on the boardwalk, Spencer slipped his

hand into Cochran's. "You called me 'son' in there," he said.

"I did. And from now on, that's what you are."

"But what if your wife doesn't want me?"

"She will. I know Flory mighty well, Spencer. You're the answer to her prayers."

Spencer looked down; Cochran could feel him shyly hiding his smile. "First thing when we get there, I'm going to shine up these shoes," Spencer said. "They're the ones Mr. Patterson got for me, and that makes them special."

"That it does, son."

The next day about noon, Cochran saddled his horse, listening to the talkative old liveryman drone on about his much-prized wild past, and then he bought a cheap mount and battered old saddle for Spencer. That was the best Cochran could afford at the moment.

All the way back, Spencer talked—endless chatter, a young lifetime's worth of observations, questions, feelings, too long pent up inside but now flowing like a dam had been broken.

They slept on the roadside and the next morning rode on, taking it slow, until the sunset brought them to the Cochran Inn.

Flory stood at the door, having seen them coming down the road. The ruddy glow from the west shone on her face, and Cochran watched her expression. He could tell from here that when she saw the boy she began to wonder if maybe, just maybe . . .

Cochran spurred his horse and galloped in the

rest of the way. Spencer, nervous now that the moment of arrival had come, hung back and watched Cochran talking with excited expression and sweeping gestures to his wife. Her look of confusion gave way to a smile, and she turned toward Spencer and opened her arms.

The boy, alone no longer, rode into the yard of the Cochran Inn and the beginning of happiness that was not to fade.

KEEP READING FOR AN EXCERPT FROM *RENEGADE LAWMEN*, COMING SOON IN A TWO-IN-ONE EDITION FROM ST. MARTIN'S PAPERBACKS:

CHAPTER 1

IT WAS HARD TO KNOW WHO TO SIDE WITH: the skinny fiddle player with the missing ear or the hefty trail bum with the harelip. The former was taking some fierce punishment from the latter, but then, he had brought it on himself by his heartless teasing. I am a man with little sympathy for anyone who taunts another because of his looks, for there's not a one of us who can control what nature gives us, or fails to.

Of course, I couldn't stand by and see a small man beaten to death by a big one, either, no matter what the circumstances. That made my decision for me. I hefted up a big cuspidor, advanced, and brought it down as hard as I could on the back of the bigger man's head. It made for quite a messy explosion.

I had hoped it would drop him. It didn't. He turned and glared at me in disbelief, stinking cuspidor muck running all down both sides of his wide head. He had eyes that drilled like augers. His nose was wide and flat, like his face; his whiskers were as coarse as wool and thirstily soaking up the foul stuff I had just baptized him with.

The whiskers hid his mouth deformity fairly well, but his speech betrayed it. I couldn't make out all he said—mostly just catch cusswords that came out with their edges rounded off. His general point came through even if his words didn't, that being that I had been mighty foolish to cut into his business in so rude a manner.

His partner had been holding the fiddler from behind during the beating. He gave me the ugliest, most threatening grin I had ever received. He was a shrimpy man with a beard worthy of Elijah; his eyes were bright with the prophecy of my impending doomsday.

The fiddler was the only one who welcomed my intrusion. He took advantage of the distraction to wriggle free and dance off, very spritely, to the corner. From there he poked fun at his interrupted tormentors, obviously having gained no wisdom from suffering.

I felt surges of both anger and fear. I had butted into this situation only because I had thought that the fiddle player was about to be killed, for he had howled pitifully at every blow he took. Yet now it seemed he hadn't been hurt at all—in other words, I had endangered myself for darn little reason. That accounted for my anger. The fact that the harelipped man was big enough to single-handedly separate me from my limbs accounted for my fear.

"Have yourself some tobacco, rabbit-mouth, have yourself a chew!" the fiddle player chortled from his safe distance. His fiddle and bow lay at his feet, kicked into the corner earlier by the two hardcases. The fiddler stooped and snatched them up. The rosiny bow dragged across the strings and made a high, scratchy drone that melted into music. The fiddler's voice rang out, shouting more than singing in raucous jubilee—"Well, I went down in Helltown, to see that devil chain down . . ."

Now I knew how the Romans felt as Nero fiddled while their world crumbled to ash around them.

The hardcases advanced and I backed up, promising myself that if I lived to get out of this place I'd never lend a hand to any more one-eared fiddlers for the rest of my days.

"Here now, let's have no more trouble!" pleaded the wiry barkeep from behind his protecting counter. He had been yelping and begging for peace throughout the whole thing.

The harelipped man said something to me that I couldn't understand. Elijah the Prophet interpreted: "Peahead says he's going to pluck out them curls of yours like the feathers of a roasting hen."

Meanwhile, the exuberant fiddler was scratching and shouting away, ". . . Johnny, won't you ramble? Hoe, hoe, hoe . . ."

I wanted to ramble myself, not that there was any way with these two between me and the door. If the side window had been open I would have made a dive out of it, but it wasn't open, for outside the February cold still crawled over the western Nebraska landscape.

"Listen, friend, you've got my apology," I said placatingly. "I thought you were getting a little rough on the fiddler, that's all."

Another muffled statement, another interpretation: "Peahead says the fiddler made fun of his mouth. Peahead don't stand for nobody making fun of his mouth."

"I don't blame you, Peahead, I don't blame you at all," I replied. "He had no right to tease you. Listen, I'm mighty sorry about the cuspidor. I'll pay right out of my own pocket for a bath for you, I promise."

The white-bearded one shook his head. "You shouldn't have called him Peahead. Peahead don't like nobody but his friends calling him that."

"Peahead!" yelled the fiddler at once, having heard the last statement. His fiddle droned up high like an excited bee. "Well, I went down in Helltown, to see old Peahead chain down! Peahead, won't you ramble, hoe, hoe, harelip!"

"Here now, don't do that," the barkeep said feebly.

The fiddler's mockery proved helpful to me this time, for it snatched the attention of Peahead and his partner away from me for a moment. In that moment I balled up my fists and lunged forward, striking two blows in tandem, the first pounding into Peahead, the second into his companion.

The effort jolted me worse than my victims. These fellows were solid, even the little one. My attack did no more than draw their attention back my way.

"Fiddle man!" I yelled, backing up again, wishing my gunbelt was hanging around me, not that wall peg behind the bar. "Fiddle man, this is your fight, not mine! Get over here and help me!"

". . . Peahead, won't you ramble? Hoe, hoe, hoe!" He was so caught up in his mocking music that I'm not sure he even heard me.

They fell upon me then and the world became a confusing whirl of grit, muscle, motion, and the stink of the tobacco spittle that dripped from Peahead. Then came pain, the dull pain of repeated blows that pounded me like spikehammers and made me sink toward a floor that was beginning to spin beneath me. I tried to fight, but there can be no fighting when your main foe weighs twice what you do and doesn't mind using it to full advantage. How long this went on I did not know; time had come to a halt.

I heard my voice yelling for help, calling out to

the fiddle player, the barkeep, anyone at all, to give me aid, but aid did not come. A fist struck my jaw and I called out no more. I felt tremendous weight atop me, felt the floor hard as an undertaker's slab beneath my back. My eyes, already swelling, opened enough to let me see the fearsome faces above, the massive fists that went up and down like shafts on a locomotive—and then a bare blade, glittering and sharp, that sliced open my shirt and exposed my chest. For some reason I noticed right then that the fiddle music had stopped.

I didn't hear Peahead speak, but he must have, because his partner said, "He says he's going to carve his initials on your chest for you to recollect him by."

I was near passing out when the knife pricked my chest. Writhing, I tried to pull free, but couldn't. The blade was cold and stinging. My eyes began to flutter shut and the images above me were almost gone when a third figure appeared behind the two that leaned over me. A heavy chair hovered, descended, crashed against the rocklike skull of Peahead. My last light dwindled and everything turned black. All I could hear as I sank away was the voice of the barkeep saying here now, don't do that, here now, don't do that, over and over.

The face that slowly put itself together before my blurry eyes was slender and brown and wore a mean expression. I groaned and swiped a hand across my eyes. When I looked again, the face was in sharper focus, and glittering somewhere below it was a badge on a blue shirt.

"What's your name?" the man with the badge demanded.

"McCan . . . Luke McCan," I answered in a whisper.

"Luke McCan, you think I need your ilk drifting through our town and stirring fights with the locals?"

"I . . . didn't stir any fight . . . just tried to help out . . ."

"You've helped yourself into a cell, that's what you've done. The barkeep says you lit into Peahead Jones with a spittoon, then fisticuffed with him and his brother before they raised a hand against you. Is that true?"

"The fiddler . . . they were slapping that fiddler . . ."

I pushed up a little and groaned. Somebody had put me on a bed in a small room. It might have been a spare bedroom in somebody's house, or maybe the sickroom of a doctor's office.

"It was to help out the fiddler that I got into it," I reaffirmed. I found a window to my right and looked out it. The sun was edging down.

"Well, this fiddler was gone when I got there, and the barkeep seems to hold you most at fault," the man with the badge said.

"He's a coward, then. Blaming it on me because he's afraid the other two will come back on him if he tells the truth."

"You can argue about it with the judge, Mr. McCan. You're under arrest on a charge of brawling, city ordinance number fifteen. However, if you'll make restitution for the saloon damages, I'll drop the charges and let you go. Fair enough?"

"Restitution? I'll pay no restitution for a fight I didn't start."

"Have it your way, then. If you won't do the

responsible thing on your own, we'll let the city judge make the decision for you." The lawman reached over to a chest of drawers and fiddled with a pile of bills and change lying atop it. I recognized the prior contents of my pockets. "Let's see—three dollars and seven cents, a folding knife, and a handkerchief. Not a lot, but the cash I'll take to be applied toward your fine and the knife I'll take as a potential weapon. The handkerchief you can keep."

"Thanks very much. You're too kind." My attention was somewhat diverted from the lawman at the moment because I was examining my chest to see if there were any initials carved onto it. There weren't. The fiddler had brought that chair down on my attackers in time to save me a slicing.

"Old Doc says he wants you to stay here a few more hours so he can keep an eye on those bumps and bruises. I'm going to chain one of your ankles to the bed, in case you think you might like to run away. Tomorrow morning I'll move you to a cell, unless you've had more cooperative thoughts about paying that damage bill. Do you own a horse and saddle?"

"No." It wasn't really a lie, because the horse and saddle I possessed technically were property of my brother-in-law. In a way, you might say, I had stolen them from him, but not really, for he was dead when I took them. And he would have gladly given the horse and saddle to me, anyway, had he been alive. We got along well, my brother-in-law and I.

Without more talk the lawman produced a chain and linked me up firmly to the metal footboard. "That will do, and that's all for now. Good evening, Mr. McCan."

I gave an ill-tempered grunt in response, and closed my eyes. Every inch of me hurt, and from the feel of my face I knew I was probably no beautiful sight. But at least I was alive and uncut.

A little later a boy brought me supper on a tray. It must have been provided by the doctor, whom I had yet to talk to, rather than the jail, because this was better food than any jail would put up for a small-time prisoner like me. It was hard to chew the chicken because the left side of my jaw hurt every time I moved it. As I ate I wondered what had become of my pistol and gunbelt, which I had left hanging on the peg in the saloon. The lawman had not listed them among my personal effects, which must mean he was unaware of them. After supper I dozed off.

A pecking on the window beside the bed awakened me. I sat up. There was a face looking back in at me. It was lean, battered, familiar . . . the fiddler. He pecked lightly on the window again and made motions to indicate I should be careful and quiet.

The window was stuck, my muscles sore, and my ankle chained to the footboard; sliding up the lower window section proved difficult. With help of the fiddler outside I finally got the job done.

"Come on—I got your horse out here—we can ride out of this sorry town!"

"Not with me chained to a bed, I don't reckon."

He looked in over the sill, saw my situation, and swore beneath his breath. He clambered in through the window, making too much noise even though his thin, Lincolnesque form moved with the lightness of a wind-blown feather.

There proved to be strength as well as suppleness in those long limbs. He squatted at the end of the bed, wrapped a hand around the picketlike metal post I was chained to, and with a few grunts and twists worked it out of the footboard top-piece. My ankle chain slid off. The fiddle player stood and grinned.

"The name's J. W. Smith, but call me Fiddler," he said in a low voice. "You're . . ."

"McCan. Luke McCan."

"Pleased to know you, McCan, and thanks for your help today. This here's my way of repaying the favor."

"What's going on in there?" came a gruff voice from the other side of the door. The knob began to turn.

Fiddler Smith turned and dived headlong out the open window. Without a moment's hesitation I followed, hitting the ground with a grunt as the wind was knocked from me. I rose and ran, ankle chain jingling, struggling for breath that would not come, as behind me I heard the exclamation at discovery of empty room and open window. It gave me a joyful feeling, and as soon as breath returned, I laughed.

CHAPTER 2

WE RODE LIKE WIND BLOWING THROUGH A narrow mountain gap. For an hour we did not speak to each other, and we looked behind us often to see if there was sign of pursuit. There was none, and at last we slowed our pace to a lope, then a walk. Fiddler Smith's violin bounced on the side of his horse, hanging from the saddle horn in a large flour sack.

"Reckon I'm not enough of a criminal to merit a chase," I commented.

Fiddler Smith grinned. "Reckon not." He dug into his pocket and pulled out a twist of hot tobacco. Carving off a chew with his knife, he shoved the twist at me. I declined.

"Thanks for helping me out," I said.

"No, sir, it's me who owes thanks to you. Them two in that saloon might have done me in if you hadn't stepped in."

"You didn't look much scared, not with the way you kept on teasing that Peahead gent."

"I never had much sense, I admit. Once somebody pushes me, I push the other way. He gave me a hard time about my fiddling, so I gigged him about the lip." He grinned again. "Right mean of me. A man can improve his fiddling, but he can't change a harelip."

I reached down and touched the butt of my pistol, finding it reassuring to have it there again. "You must have took my gunbelt off the peg," I said. "I didn't figure I'd have it again."

"A man needs his weapons. Hey, that is your own horse I gave you, ain't it? It was the only one tied out front of the saloon. I figured it for yours."

"It's mine. Thanks for fetching it."

We rode a while longer, me sizing up Fiddler. He was an interesting-looking man and as ragged a one as I had ever seen. He wore nankeen trousers that had gone out of fashion a decade and a half back, a shirt that once had been yellow and now had faded to a sickly tan and white, and a dark broadcloth coat that hadn't been sponged down for a year or more. His hat was a battered derby greased from much handling. It fit his head as perfectly as a cartridge case around a slug.

We made camp in a grove beside a little stream. Fiddler gathered wood and built a roaring fire. I commented that maybe the fire was a bad idea, in that followers were still a possibility. Fiddler just shook his head.

"Never could abide to camp without a big fire," he said. "A man needs the comfort of light and heat out in the wilderness."

Fiddler had several cans of beans in his saddlebags and broke out two of them. I was glad to see them, being down to dried-up biscuits and a bag of jerky. My plan had been to resupply myself in town, a plan ruined by the row in the saloon.

After we had food under our belts, we fell to talking. Fiddler Smith spoke cheerfully—he seemed one of those types who are always cheerful—and told of a most unillustrious past.

"The mountains of West Virginia's where I come from—that'll always be home to me, though I doubt I'll ever again live in them. Never had a thing as a boy except two good parents. But they died young and left me alone, and that's how it's been for me ever since. My daddy left me nothing but that old fiddle yonder. My two sisters are dead these six and seven years, and the only brother I've got lives up in Powderville, Montana. I ain't seen him in twelve years.

"I took to roaming when I was sixteen. Even though I'm a slender fellow, I was a lot stouter in my younger days, and I've always been strong. The only two things I've ever known how to do is fight and fiddle, and that's how I've made my living. I'd fiddle in saloons, and toss out drunks who got too rowdy and such. Every now and again I'd serve as deputy or policeman in this or that town back east. Mostly I roamed through the cities, doing whatever I had to do to keep body and soul together. I was in Colorado awhile, too, at a little mining camp called Craig City. You might have heard of it."

"I think I have."

"McCan, I'll tell you, I ain't seen a bright prospect in a long time, not until now. Back when I was living in Chicago, I got myself fired from a saloon over a bit of trouble. Well, right after that into town comes this fellow named Walden, Ike Walden, a big white-haired man who called himself a 'freethinker for temperance and health.' He lived in a big house and had some sort of bee in his bonnet about closing down this saloon that had fired me—he claimed it was destroying the community or something like that.

"He held a big rally to close the place down and

drew the biggest bunch of old women and teeto-
talers you ever saw. I was at the rally because of the
food they were handing out. Things got hotter and
wilder and before you know it, here goes Ike Walden
and an army of these ax-carrying liquor-haters
down to bust up the saloon. I went along, hoping to
see the fellow who fired me get his come-uppance.
Things got still hotter and before you know it, Ike
Walden was staring down the barrel of a pistol. He
decided to fight and was just about to get his brains
blown out when I jumped up and wrestled my old
boss to the ground and took the gun. To this day I
ain't sure why I did it.

"Ike Walden declared me the finest fellow he had
run across. He gave me a job doing general work
around his place for almost a year. I got restless then
and left for the West, but he told me to keep in touch
with him and I did.

"Well, about two weeks ago I got a message from
him, offering me new work. He's in Colorado now,
and built himself a town about forty miles west of
Fort Collins."

"What's the new work?"

Fiddler beamed with pride. "Town marshal. Town
marshal of Walden City, Colorado mining town.
Bound to be the best durn job I've run across."

"Can you handle it by yourself?"

Fiddler cocked his head and looked closely at me.
"Don't know. That's a good question. I'll tell you
this—Walden's not allowing saloons or gambling in
the town. He says that draws 'undesirable' folks. It
seems to me that marshaling in a town without
saloons and gambling halls ought to be a right easy
job."

"Sounds like it."

Fiddler loaded and fired a corncob pipe. "Well, that's my story. Let's hear yours. You got family, McCan?"

There's no way Fiddler Smith could know the stab of pain that question brought to me. I doubt it showed on my face, for pain had been a constant companion of mine for months now, and I had grown accustomed to hiding it. I didn't want to answer his question, but given his openness with me, I felt obliged.

"I had family," I replied. "No wife, just a sister and her husband. And there would have been a wife by now, except . . ." My will failed me.

He gave a perceptive look. "She's dead?"

I nodded. "Not only her. My sister, too, and her husband. They were together on a train in Chatsworth, Illinois. It was last August when it happened. A railroad bridge caught fire and collapsed beneath the train. More than a hundred people died." I paused, my voice growing tight as it always did when I talked of this. "I was going to go with them at first, but at the last minute I had to stay behind. I was running a hardware store in Independence with my brother-in-law, you see, and our clerk quit on us just in time to knock me out of the trip. It saved my life, but when I think of what that accident took from me, I swear that sometimes I wish I had been on that train, too. Life without Cynthia hasn't been much of a life."

"I'm sorry," Fiddler said.

"Me, too. Me, too."

"So what brought you out here in the midst of this godforsaken territory?"

I rolled a smoke as I talked. "I wasn't brought out here. I was driven. Loneliness, mostly, and bad memories. After Cynthia, I didn't want to stay in Independence. The business didn't matter to me anymore, even though it passed to me after the . . . tragedy. I sold out, tucked some of the money into the bank to draw on as I needed, then took out roaming. Just like I did during my younger years. Roaming, working here and there. Mostly gambling. I gamble a lot. Too much. I had given it up for Cynthia, but after she was gone, it kind of reached out and took hold of me again."

"You tell a sad story, McCan. Too sad to have happened to a fellow young as you. You can't be out of your twenties."

"I'm well into the thirties now, Fiddler. I've always looked boyish, everybody tells me."

"Losing a woman is hard for a man of any age. Look at it this way, McCan, there'll be other women. Odds are the next one you won't lose."

"I've already lost two in my time."

"Two?"

"Yes. Before Cynthia, there was a girl in Montana. Maggie Carrington was her name."

"She died, too?"

"No, but as far as cutting herself off from me, she might as well have died. She married another man, name of Rodney Upchurch. Your talk about this Ike Walden and town-founding put me in mind of Upchurch. He set up the Upchurch community near Timber Creek."

"You talked about roaming in your younger days. Was that in Montana?"

"Mostly. I started out in Dakota. I freighted into Deadwood from Pierre during the big boom and stayed on to mine for a time with a man named Caleb Black."

"Caleb Black . . . sounds familiar." Fiddler drew on his pipe and his eyes suddenly lit up. "Wasn't it a Caleb Black who trailed the outlaw Evan Bridger for so many years?"

"One and the same."

"No! You mined with him? Well, I'll be, I'll be!"

"More than mined with him. We rode together up in Montana. I worked for the Timber Creek Cattle Enterprise, then finally just drifted out of the business and went back to Independence. That's tended to be my way, just drifting in and out of things, never settling down. Kind of funny, in a way. I thought when I met Cynthia that my wandering days were over. Now here I am, drifting again, shiftless as ever. I've already gambled away half of what I got from selling off the store."

"Montana," Fiddler said thoughtfully. "Sure got to get up to Montana myself one of these days, and see that brother of mine. Lord knows he might even be dead by now."

Fiddler sat quiet with his thoughts and eyed me through his pipesmoke for a while, then got up, stretched, and pulled his fiddle from its flour sack. He sat by the fire and played a couple of slow tunes, real strange and pretty, then laid down his bow and put the fiddle across his lap. I had gone to work on the ankle chain with a file from Fiddler's saddlebag. When at last the chain fell free, we both grinned. I rubbed my ankle in relief.

"Think you might want to cut out the drifting for a while and settle into some steady work?"

I shrugged. Fiddler must have found more yes than no in it, for he spread his easy grin again.

"In that case, why don't you stick with me and go

to Walden City? Town marshaling might be too hard a job for one man, after all. I could use a deputy."

He surprised me with that one, I admit. "I don't know, Fiddler . . . this Ike Walden might not have in mind to hire more than you."

"Why, he feels he owes me. I can talk him into it or I ain't Fiddler Smith. What do you say, McCan? I like your company. You're good folks—I can spot it right off."

"Well . . . I got no other offers pending."

"That a yes?"

"Just a maybe. I can ride in with you and see how the place feels, and what this Ike Walden has to say."

Fiddler grinned all the broader. Picking up his fiddle again, he sawed out a new tune, this one lively and bright. I lit up my cigarette and lay back, smoking and watching the sky and wondering what kind of place Walden City would be, and whether I would stay there for any length of time.

A little later Fiddler brought out a bottle and took a long swallow. He waved the bottle at me but I turned it down.

"What's a champion of temperance like Ike Walden going to think of a town marshal who pulls on a flask on the side?" I asked him.

"Why, Ike Walden don't have to know everything," he replied. "And I don't have to be no angel of teetotalism to safeguard a town—at least as long as everybody else stays sober."

I chuckled, but the incident gave me my first pause as to the likelihood of Fiddler's success as a town marshal. Surely Ike Walden wouldn't put up with an enforcer who broke his own rules, not if he really was the authoritative type that Fiddler painted him.

We slept a little while and rode out with the dawn, crossing into Colorado just south of the South Platte. It would take some long traveling to reach Fort Collins, especially in that Fiddler planned to get there by way of Denver. Clearly he was in no real hurry to claim his new job, even though he seemed to be looking forward to it.

The longer we rode together, the better I got to know Fiddler Smith, and the greater my doubts about his ability to perform his awaited job became. He drank too much, usually not to the point of full drunkenness, but enough to become tipsy by sundown. "Don't worry," he reassured me. "I can hide it. Anyway, maybe a town without saloons will give me the nudge to throw the bottle away once and for all."

"Maybe so," I said. "And maybe a town without gambling halls will break me of my card habit."

Hours rolled into days and miles stretched behind us. We reached Denver and remained there three days, then rode north to Fort Collins and west into the rugged mountains, following the narrow trails that led to the new mining town of Walden City.

CHAPTER 3

PICTURE A TRAINLOAD OF NEW LUMBER hammered together into two rows of nondescript buildings, spread a wide street of mud between them, throw in abundant swinging shingles and windows with painted-on business signs, almost all incorporating the name "Walden," and you have a good image of what Walden City, Colorado, looked like the midmorning that Fiddler Smith and I finally rode in. There had been rain since dawn, and it had only just stopped, so the Walden City we saw was a wet one.

It was a typical new mountain town in most ways, built along the contours of the narrow valley in which it sat. The main street had a slight curve that was mandated by the rocky bluffs bumping up almost against the backsides of the row of buildings facing north. The opposite row wasn't so pressured and therefore in most mining camps would have been built straight, but here it curved right along with the other row, keeping the street a uniform width. I didn't understand the reason for that until I got to know Ike Walden. Then I knew: Walden wasn't the kind of man who would put up with irregular streets in any town bearing his name. Everything in Ike Walden's world was orderly, rigid, militarily precise. He permeated his town like the smell of fresh-cut pine lumber.

"She's a beaut, ain't she?" Fiddler Smith said as we slogged down the muddy street. He bent to the side and shot an amber dollop of tobacco juice into the mud. "This here town's going to be dancing to Fiddler and McCan's tune before long. We've come into our own, son, into our own."

Truth be told, though I was glad to be here, I wasn't nearly as excited as Fiddler. Maybe it was because I wasn't being awaited here, like he was, and so didn't feel the town was quite so much mine. Or maybe there was more to it. Maybe it was that beneath the town's facade of commonality with every other mining community, there was something remarkably different.

It took me a few minutes to realize what that was, and I chided myself for having been surprised by what I should have been expecting, considering Fiddler's earlier talk. The difference about Walden City was that among its plethora of buildings and businesses, there was not a single saloon. In most towns like this, a saloon was the first place built, before people got around to throwing up the less-important enterprises, such as hardware stores, restaurants, and livery stables. Niceties such as schools, churches, and doctors' offices usually came much later.

I scanned the buildings and picked out what looked like a brand-new schoolhouse still in the works. There was even a four-roomed hospital already open for business; a young medical-looking fellow stood leaning in its doorway, watching the bustle outside. I wondered if he would make much of a living in Walden City, given its lack of saloons and, presumably, knife- and gun-happy drunks.

"This Walden must be quite a powerful man, if he can dominate a whole town," I said to Fiddler.

"Dominate? Durn, he owns it!" Fiddler replied. "Most every one of these businesses here, he owns. Them he don't he leases out the buildings for. Even that there hospital belongs to him."

"How the devil did he manage to set up such a place?"

"Friends in high places, as the phrase goes. He worked out some special grant of land up here, some deal there ain't nobody else got. He even controls all the mineral rights—gold, silver, everything. I don't understand it all that much, but suffice it to say, this here town is Ike Walden's all the way, and anything you get you get only because he deals it out to you. There may not be kings and such in this country of ours, but there sure as Sally is a king in Walden City."

We turned down what would eventually become a side street but which was now only a short, rutted thoroughfare with a handful of small houses and huts along it. Our horses splashed through a deep puddle of brown water, beyond which the fledgling street became a lane, then a mere trail that threaded into the trees.

"Where we going?" I asked.

"Open your eyes, McCan! Were you so smit with that muddy town that you didn't look up on the hill-side?"

I looked now; through a gap in the trees I saw a house, painted a neat white, perched on a plateau above the western end of the town. From its front window you could look right down the center of the street. It wasn't all that big a house—just a typical two-story that would have looked modest in an Eastern city neighborhood—but it had a pretentious round tower and was set high up enough that it seemed bigger than it was. As I studied it, a shaft of sunlight cut through the clouds and gleamed off the white clapboards, making the house stand out against the mountains like a diamond among pebbles.

"That's got to be Walden's house," I said.

"Reckon so. His letter described the place right well. 'The Walden Palace,' he calls it."

"Palace, huh? Well, it's got a tower, but it falls pretty far short of a palace."

"Don't get picky about Ike Walden or his things. He's not a man who likes pickiness in other folk. He figures that being picky is his job."

We circled up the trail and onto the big flat on which the house stood. We approached it from the side. Glancing up the tower, I saw a figure standing in the big window row that curved all the way around the top. I couldn't make out much about him other than that he was portly but tall and had a gray topknot and long hair that stuck out wide on both sides of his head. It made him look from here like some wild-eyed Puritan expositor from long ago.

Fiddler threw up his arm and waved eagerly at the figure, smiling brightly. The man in the tower stood up straight and waved back, very dignified and haughty. So far my impressions of Ike Walden were falling out just as I expected they would.

We dismounted beside the house and were about to tether our horses to a tree when out of the house came two black servants, both wearing uniforms that made them look like railroad-station baggage carriers. "We'll be happy to take your horses, gentlemen sirs," one of them said. "If one of you gentlemen sirs is Mr. J. W. Smith, Mr. Walden is waiting to see you."

"I'm Smith," Fiddler said. "This here's my partner, Luke McCan. You want we should just walk in?"

"I'll show you in, Mr. Smith, sir," the servant said. He had a beaten-down look in his eye, and you could tell at once that being handservant to the king of Walden City was a draining job. I felt sorry for him.

He led us into the house, which was as spanking new as the rest of the town but more finished. I figured Walden had seen to the completion of his "palace" before anything else. The interior was fancy, though again only in comparison to the rest of the town. In any other setting it would have been nice but nothing to gape at. There was carpet and wainscoting and a shiny ceiling, but a close look revealed seams and gaps that showed the place was rather hastily built.

The servant took us over to a big oak door that was still awaiting a sanding down and a coat of paint. It creaked open to reveal a circular staircase, made of rough lumber, leading to the tower.

"You sirs will need to take care 'cause there ain't yet no banister," the servant said. He began plodding up the stairs. We followed, making one full circle around the tower before we reached the landing at the top and faced another oak door.

The servant knocked, then opened a little metal slide three quarters of the way up the door and through it said, "Mr. Walden, sir, Mr. J. W. Smith and his partner Mr. McCan are come to see you."

"Bring them in, then, Bob," came a booming voice. I was thinking how peculiarly formalized this process was, given that Walden had already seen us through his window and we had seen him. I suppose a "king" has to maintain some sort of protocol when he gives audience to his subjects.

As the door swung open, I was already thinking to myself that I wasn't going to like Ike Walden

much, not if such airs as this were common to him.
Ever since I had had trouble with a pompous little
Iowa-born snoot named Henry Sandy back at the
Timber Creek ranch in Montana, arrogance had set
poorly with me.

Walden was a broadcloth expanse of belly, vest,
and watch fob, peaked off with a wide and somewhat pasty face. What I had from a distance taken
for long hair hanging down either side of his head
actually were big stiff sideburns that ran down
almost to his deeply dimpled chin. He had no mustache, but needed one: the space between his mouth
and the bottom of his little nose seemed overly wide
and could have used some filling in.

"J. W., it's good to see you," he said to Fiddler,
thrusting out his delicate hand. "I can't tell you how
thrilled I am that you've accepted the job."

"I've been slow to get here, Mr. Walden," Fiddler
said. "I hope that ain't given you no problems."

"None at all, sir. We have peaceful folk in this
town." He glanced at me. "Mr. McCan—isn't that
the name you gave?"

"Luke McCan. Pleased to meet you, Mr. Walden."
His handshake was soft and moist, the kind that
leaves you conscious of your own palm and makes
you want to wipe it on your pants leg, which of
course you can't do.

"I'm glad to know you, sir, but I admit to being at
a loss. I had expected only Mr. Smith."

Fiddler stepped forward. "Mr. Walden, McCan
here is a longtime partner of mine. We've known
each other for years, and he's a fine man with peace-
officer experience. He and me served together under
Masterson back in my early days at Dodge City."

I fired a shocked glance at Fiddler, who was lying

through his tobacco-coated teeth. He had laid out his life fairly thoroughly to me by now, and had never mentioned being a deputy in Dodge—and I sure as heck knew I had never been. Obviously Fiddler had greatly inflated his credentials to Walden even before now, for the Dodge City reference had been given in the easy manner of a mutually familiar subject.

"Well, I'm impressed, then," Walden said. "Am I to presume you wish Mr. McCan to assist you in the job?"

"Well, sir, I had hoped you'd consider it."

Walden scratched the deep cleft in his chin and looked at me in a way to make me feel like I was on an auction block. His brows came down in an evaluative frown, then he shook his head.

"I have nothing in the budget for an assistant, even one who looks as fit and promising as this young man," he said, making me feel flattered even in rejection.

"Oh, he'll work for free," Fiddler promptly replied. "All he requires is room and board."

I didn't even try to hide my glare of shock, but Walden had gone into a coughing fit and was looking down, hacking into his fist, and didn't see it.

When he had cleared his throat, he begged our pardon and picked up where Fiddler had left off, "Labor in return for only room and board? Are you really willing to do that, Mr. McCan?"

"Well, actually I—"

"McCan is a former hardware-store man out of Independence, Missouri," Fiddler chirpily interrupted. "He sold out his business and is fairly well off, and might set up in trade right here, if he likes the place." I could only listen in amazement as Fiddler revealed to Walden plans and dreams even I didn't know I had. "Free room and board in return for some part-time marshaling would set him ahead just enough to make this town a mighty appealing place for him—and I could surely use his help from time to time."

Walden seemed impressed. I started to speak up to burst the bubble of illusion Fiddler was blowing—then I decided abruptly not to. Making Fiddler out for the liar he was might cost him the job he had come for, and I didn't want that to happen. Besides, it would be fun to see what Walden would say.

"Well . . . well . . . all right, then. There's a small house set aside for you behind the jail, Mr. Smith. With only a little effort and expense I can quickly add another room . . . if Mr. McCan is serious in this offer."

I opened my mouth, honestly not knowing what I was going to say. What came out was, "I'm serious." What the devil, I was thinking. I've got nowhere else to go, I've got to stay somewhere, and a free room is better than one with a price tag.

"Fine, then, fine," Walden said. Suddenly he faced me and spoke in a surprisingly forceful tone. "You understand, I hope, that in Walden City I tolerate no drunkards or opium fiends, no gamblers, sluggards, harlots, or any such ilk?"

"I understand. Fiddler . . . Mr. Smith, I mean, has told me all about it."

"Good. And no preachers, either. Purveyors of unscientific superstition have no place in Walden City. We are overshadowed not by steeples but by reason, by intelligence and rationality. If anyone waves a Bible on a street corner in this town, you may summarily escort them past our borders, gentlemen."

"Seems to me a good preacher or two might help you keep out the gamblers and drunkards you despise so."

Walden's eyes seemed to pop in their sockets. He stepped forward, suddenly a foot taller than before. "I am a freethinker, Mr. McCan, unfettered by belief in some bearded overseer on a heavenly throne. This is my town. It will operate in accordance with my lights, not yours. If you work for me, you must understand that."

I said nothing. He stared at me a moment or two, then his harshness faded and he smiled. "You understand me, I can see. I like you, McCan. You have a healthful look about you—the kind of man who can serve as a good example for the people of this town." He looked at Fiddler. "And I must confess, Mr. Smith, that I detect in your eyes the tracks left by the beast alcohol. I do hope you'll not fail to live up to the standards I require."

"No fear of that, Mr. Walden. I know what you expect."

"Good. Very good. Now, if you gentlemen will return downstairs, I'll join you in a moment and show you your new office and quarters."

While we were waiting below, I commented, "Strange character."

"No doubt of that. But once you get used to him he ain't bad."

"I'm talking about you, not him. What was all that Dodge City nonsense, and when did I tell you I was willing to work just for lodging?"

"Well, you took the bargain, didn't you? Shows I was right."

A door across the room opened and in walked a woman who was obviously barely into her twenties.

She was rather plump but very pretty, even though her eyes were red as if she had been recently crying. She stopped short when she saw us, stared at me for a couple of moments, then withdrew quickly back into the door from which she had come.

"Who was that?" I asked.

"Vera Ann Walden, Ike's daughter. He's a widower, you see. Pretty thing, ain't she!"

"Easy enough on the eyes, I suppose." I felt prideful over the way she had looked at me. "Did you notice how she—"

"How she looked at me?" Fiddler cut in. "You bet I did. Reckon I must be a handsomer gent than I had thought."

I stood with my mouth half-open, on the verge of correcting his obvious misperception. No—it wasn't worth it. "You are a fine-looking specimen of a man, now that I notice it," I said.

"Wish I could say the same for you."

"You can. All you got to do is lie about it like I did. Ought to be no difficulty for you. I've had occasion to notice today that you're adept with the falsehoods."

He just grinned. That was a good thing about Fiddler Smith: You could gig him and he'd take it without a flinch . . . most of the time.

Coming soon...
Don't miss the next two-in-one edition
from bestselling author
CAMERON JUDD

TIMBER CREEK

RENEGADE LAWMEN

ISBN: 0-312-94556-6

Available in September 2008 from
St. Martin's Paperbacks

AND LOOK FOR CAMERON JUDD'S EPIC *TIMBER CREEK*, ALSO COMING SOON FROM ST. MARTIN'S PAPERBACKS. AN EXCERPT FOLLOWS.

CHAPTER 1

AS LUKE MCCAN STRODE THROUGH THE gate of the Tolliver & McClelland freight yard, a black man scrubbing mud from a wagon turned to watch him. McCan nodded a greeting, but the big fellow gave not even a grunt in return.

At the doorway of the unpainted building of rough lumber, McCan took off his hat. Shifting it in his hands, he tried to swallow his tension; he couldn't. He straightened his shoulders and walked inside.

It was dark there, and musty. McCan stood blind a couple of moments as his eyes adjusted. He found himself facing three somber men on a bench against the opposite wall. They slumped more than sat, expressionless as tomcats. McCan nodded, and got no more reaction than he had from the man outside. Like wooden Indians in a cigar store, he thought.

"Could you tell me where I'd find Ira Tolliver?" he asked.

Wooden Indian number three raised a hand-rolled smoke to his lips and took a slow drag as he tilted his head toward a door at the far corner of the room. It was ajar, and beyond it McCan saw the corner of a big pigeonholed desk, as cluttered as a postmaster's, and an equally paper-laden oaken filing cabinet. He nodded his thanks and headed for the door.

Inside the office sat a fat man with an unlit cigar stub jutting over an impressive collection of chins. He looked up; the chins danced gelatinously beneath broad jowls.

"What is it?" he gruffly asked.

"Are you Ira Tolliver?"

"I am."

"I'd like to speak to you a moment."

The man shrugged, and McCan entered. The office was cramped, and looked as if it had never been cleaned. It was a refuge for stray odors. Tolliver shuffled papers as McCan looked for a seat. The businessman's rubbery mouth wrapped itself around the well-chewed cigar, a duplicate of any one of a score of others that lay about on the floor.

McCan evicted an ancient gray tabby from a chair and took its place, then waited until Tolliver turned his somnolent gaze to him.

"You got business?"

"My name is Luke McCan. I'm looking for work."

"Uh-huh. Somebody say I'm hiring?"

"No, sir. I just figured to ask."

Tolliver dug out a match and lit his cigar. Through the smoke, his face was that of a bulldog, fat and lazy. "What work you after?"

"I'd like to be a teamster." He anticipated the follow-up question. "I've got experience—I hauled freight in Missouri almost a year."

"Oxen?"

"Mules."

"We use oxen." Tolliver looked to his papers again, conversation concluded. The cigar made a four-inch roll to the other side of his mouth.

"I can drive oxen, Mr. Tolliver. I've done it a time or two, and I can pick up what I don't already know."

"How long you been in Pierre, son?"

"About a week."

"Where are you from?"

"St. Louis."

"You're young."

"Twenty-five. I'm told I look younger."

"You got folks?"

"No parents. They died just over a year ago, a wagon accident. I've got one sister living in Independence."

"What brought you to Dakota?"

"I just wanted to come, and saw no reason not to."

"You know where my freight line runs, son?"

"Deadwood, I hear."

"That's right. Black Hills. Gold country. A lot of young bucks looking for a way to get there." He leaned back in his chair; it creaked and moaned as if in pain. McCan caught his implication and shook his head.

"I'm not looking for a ticket to Deadwood," he said. "If I wanted to go there, I'd get on my horse and ride." He didn't mention he had lost his horse in a poker bet a week ago.

Tolliver flipped an ash. "This line cuts through Sioux country. There's highwaymen too. We got a one-mile-wide right-of-way through to Deadwood, but that don't mean a lot to the lower types. And Deadwood, once you get there, is about as dangerous as the trail."

"I'll try to take care of myself."

"Bill Hickok tried too. He's moldering in his grave on Mount Moriah."

McCan saw Tolliver was trying hard to sell him on *not* deserting the freight line in Deadwood. It was not something he had thought of doing, but all this talk was making him wonder if he *should*.

"I'm just looking for a job," McCan said. "Can you use me?"

Tolliver pondered. "A teamster quit me last week, and we got a shipment going out Monday. You come back in a couple of days, and we'll start breaking you in."

They talked pay, shook hands, and McCan left. He headed to a café and, in celebration, ordered a steak, biscuits, and coffee. As he ate, he looked out the café window at the busy street.

Pierre stood at the bend of the Missouri in the southern Dakota Territory. Since the discovery of gold in the Black Hills, the freight business out of Pierre had flourished, for the Black Hills had only two links to the world beyond: freight lines and stagecoaches. By those conduits people and goods were funneled into the Black Hills, and carried out again were stories of gold-mining towns such as Deadwood. Talk had it that Deadwood was a place of intense living and easily found death. The murder of Wild Bill Hickok there a few years back had only bolstered the gritty mystique of the town.

McCan sipped coffee and tilted his chair back against the wall. He was a slender man and rather tall, his features smooth and appealing if not outright handsome. He dressed well for one who had been without a job for a year; his inheritance from his parents had been modest, but enough to finance a few months of wandering. He should invest what

was left in something practical, he knew, but such
was not his way. He had dreamed of roaming like
this from the first time he'd toddled across his nurs-
ery. Had he not gambled away his horse, he might
have been content to remain jobless a bit longer;
applying for work with Tolliver had been a momentary inspiration, a way to get in a little more
travel with no investment of his own money.

Now McCan was thinking of Deadwood, and
wondering why he had not thought of it before.
Tolliver, in his eagerness to steer his thoughts from
it, had instead turned them to it.

McCan left the café and walked without aim
along the street. In front of a store whose window
sign read MINING TOOLS—HIGH QUALITY
AND LOW PRICE, he paused to roll a cigarette.
The door opened and a man emerged, arms filled
with supplies. Blinded by his load, he walked directly into McCan, and tools and other goods fell
all around.

The man cursed, but it was directed at the situation rather than McCan, so McCan took no of-
fense.

"If I had seen you coming, I would have
moved," McCan said.

"Not your fault."

"Let me help you," McCan said. He and the
man picked up the items and loaded them into a
small covered wagon parked by the curb of the
boardwalk.

McCan thrust out his hand and said his name.
The other man took the hand and said, "I'm Caleb
Black. I'm obliged for your help."

McCan gestured toward the wagon. "You're
bound for Deadwood?"

"Like everybody else."

"I'm heading that way myself. I'm a teamster for the Tolliver company yonder. Just hired on."

"Maybe I'll see you in the Black Hills then."

"Maybe so."

Caleb Black climbed to his seat and rode away. Luke McCan watched him depart, then looked westward toward the horizon that hid the Black Hills.

McCan wrote a letter that night by candlelight.

Mrs. Martha Hyatt
Independence, Missouri

My Dear Martha,

As I write you now, I'm a teamster. When you hear from me next, I likely will be a gold miner in the town of Deadwood. That is where the freight line that has given me a job runs, and likely I will stay on once we get there, for it is the talk of everyone I see. There is money to be made there at honest labor, and I will be glad to make my part.

Our father would have been proud of me, would he not? "Make a living with the sweat of your brow" always was his theme—with me at least—though as a female you probably were spared some of that, it being more your duty to marry well, in his eyes, than to work hard. You've done both.

It is late and I will not write you long, but you will hear again from me when I am settled at the Black Hills mines. To answer the question of your last letter: no, I have not gambled away all my inheritance, though I have kept to my poker-playing ways. I see no harm in it, though I know in your eyes it is the fatal vice that will ruin my life, if not damn my soul, for you were well-taught by Mother about the wicked ways of men. But do not worry about me, and be sure you will hear from me soon.

Your affectionate brother,
Luke

CHAPTER 2

MCCAN LABORED THROUGH SATURDAY
night, filling canvas sacks, heaving crates, stacking
goods, covering the loaded wagons with tarpaulins.
It was grueling work, with more to come on Sunday, for the loading was behind schedule.

McCan worked with Bob Webster, the black
man he had seen washing wagons in the freight
yard. Webster was talkative now, warmed to
McCan through the brotherhood of labor. McCan
asked questions, and Webster answered them in de-
tail.

Tolliver, he said, would not come along on the
journey. He was a businessman—at home behind
a desk, but a stranger to a freight wagon seat. Ira
Tolliver had founded the company three years before with a man named Zeke McClelland, and the
latter had actually led the freight runs. McClelland
had died after the first year, and Tolliver had kept
the company running alone, amid rumors that he
had swindled McClelland's window. Now the
freight runs were led by an employee named Benjamin Weaver.

Webster pointed Weaver out to McCan; he was thin-featured, with a mustache that drooped around fleshless lips. The left side of his face was ballooned incessantly with hot-twist tobacco. But he never spat; Webster claimed he swallowed the juice as if it were sugar water.

"Weaver is a good man to have leading," Webster said. "Better than Zeke McClelland was on his best day. Listen to him and you'll learn a lot about this business."

On Sunday the crew headed to the plains north of town to round up and herd in the oxen grazing there. It was easy; the oxen were accustomed to the process and all but fell into line. They plodded willingly back to the freight yard, where they were penned in a makeshift corral. Webster and McCan watered them and gave them hay, and the big beasts consumed both in placid contentment, watching the crew finish preparations for the Monday run.

Webster began McCan's education in the freight business. He gave a rapid-fire description of the train: ten teams of twenty oxen, each team pulling three wagons hitched together, each wagon carefully weighted. Lead wagons would carry seven thousand pounds, middle or swing wagons about five thousand each, and trail wagons about three thousand.

Before dawn Monday the train began its roll toward the Missouri. Ben Weaver led, followed by McCan. McCan sat astride his lead wagon, traces in his hands and the whoops and curses of the teamsters behind him ringing in his ears. The earth made a sodden, crushing noise beneath the big wheels of the wagons. As the sky turned from black to lavender to pale gold, a sense of adventure filled McCan.

The wagons reached the Missouri, and Weaver halted his team near the ferry that would convey the entire train across. Morning rays splintered over the river's chopped surface, brightening as the sun rose. Weaver's figure etched itself against the silver background as he talked to the long-bearded ferryman. McCan threw the brake and leaned back, knowing the crossing would be slow.

Indeed, it was almost noon before the chuck wagon at the end of the train was parked across the water, with a huge kettle of stew bubbling beside it. None of the teamsters had eaten that morning, because of the early departure from Pierre, so they accepted the food with the eagerness of dying souls grasping a sacrament.

Webster sat beside McCan, who was propped against a wheel of his swing wagon. Webster pulled away his hat and wiped the sweat off with his sleeve. "Mighty hot," he said.

"It is. How long will we stay here?"

"Most all day. The oxen can't take a lot of heat. We'll travel from the later part of the afternoon until we can't see no more. Then we'll camp, get up before dawn, and roll until it gets hot tomorrow. Good thing about this business is, you don't work much the hot part of the day. The bad part is, you don't get breakfast until about noon."

"How many miles will we cover a day?"

"It depends on the ground and the weather. On a good day, maybe almost twenty miles. On a bad one, maybe five or six."

McCan swatted a fly on his knee. "Slow way to get to Deadwood."

Webster looked at him sidewise. "You in a particular hurry?"

"I don't suppose. But I hear it's quite a place."

Webster smiled vaguely. "Oh, it is. You thinking of becoming a miner, maybe?"

"Would I tell you if I was?"

"There's nothing wrong with mining," Webster said. "A man sure can't get rich driving a team of oxen."

McCan had a sudden insight. "You're not coming back, are you, Webster?"

Webster's dark eyes flickered around. "Don't say that so loud. Old Weaver listens for such, and there's the devil to pay if he hears. I've thought of leaving, sure, but it can be hard for a colored man to get work if the mining goes bust. I can't let go of what I've got without a lot of thinking."

They passed the hot hours around the wagons. Men napped, smoked, talked among themselves. Except Ben Weaver; he stayed alone, staring at nothing, whittling a stick of pine.

"He's always like that," Webster said. "Either he's had some hard times in his life, or one of these oxen kicked him in the head. He's a smart man and a good leader, but he's always alone."

When the afternoon waned, the teamsters yoked up and rolled out. The oxen were full and rested and made good time. Weaver's wagon left deep ruts behind, so McCan pulled off his trail. Others behind him did the same, and soon the train stretched a quarter of a mile long and a sixth of a mile wide.

Dark came, but the sky was clear and moonlit. Weaver called back to McCan, and he in turn passed the message back: "Clear night! Roll on!"

Roll they did, a good two hours past dark. Such a thing was rare, McCan would learn. Usually darkness marked the end of the working day.

The wagons finally halted, and the oxen were freed to graze. Leftover stew was served, bedrolls came out, and Harvey Lane, the night guard, emerged from his sleeper wagon, which trailed along after Webster's wagons. He went to work as the others lay down, and sleep swept in with the song of crickets and the whisper of grass.

Lane's jarring call awakened McCan just before dawn. He crawled out, longing for coffee, knowing there would be none until they were far down the trail.

It was while the teamsters yoked their oxen under the paling sky that the first hint of trouble came.

CHAPTER 3

IT WAS A FREAKISH EVENT, BUT IT SET OFF hard feelings that had stewed, mostly unnoticed, for months.

Webster was yoking two oxen when Roy Sturley, a teamster from Arkansas, passed him. One of Webster's oxen moved suddenly and threw him off balance. Webster staggered back against Sturley who dropped a yoke he had been carrying. It hit his foot.

Sturley spat, "Watch yourself, nigger!" and threw a hard right against Webster's jaw.

Webster squarely faced the man who had uttered and done what he would tolerate from no one. Sturley stared back, brushed dirt from his sleeve, and breathed loudly through his teeth.

"Nobody calls me that, Sturley," Webster said.

The teamsters gathered. Some grinned, others looked worried. McCan edged in and touched Webster's shoulder; Webster pulled away as if it burned him.

From the other side of the circle emerged Jimmy Wyatt, one of the youngest teamsters. He was a short, slight fellow with flame-orange hair and a ruddy face dotted with pancake freckles. He looked at McCan and said, "Stay out of it. It ain't right for a nigger to push a man."

"It was the ox moving that done it," somebody said.

"No. He pushed me a-purpose," Sturley interjected. "You seen it, didn't you, Jimmy?"

"Sure did."

McCan turned to Bob Webster, "Bob, just walk away from it."

Webster glared at him. "Shut up, Luke. I fight my own fights."

"Listen at that!" Wyatt chortled. "You gonna let a nigger talk that way to you?"

McCan was going to respond, but suddenly Sturley lunged forward, swinging wildly. Several blows connected against Webster's neck, chest, and jaw. A gout of blood squirted as a final swing hammered his nose. He fell back, and Wyatt whooped in tent-revival ecstasy.

Webster recovered quickly. He threw himself on his opponent, slammed a hard fist against his eye, and pounded a left into his gut. Sturley grunted, cursed, and groped for Webster's neck. He gripped it and squeezed until his fingernails were white, but Webster seemed unaware of the hands at his throat.

The black man pounded two more bruising punches into Sturley's stomach, then brought up his fists and spread them between Sturley's forearms, knocking the hands from his neck. He heaved forward, head lowered, and butted a granite forehead against Sturley's skull. The crack was like mountain goats colliding.

Sturley fell, but rose with a knife in his hand.

"Yeah!" Wyatt exulted. "Cut him!"

The men nearest Sturley parted suddenly, like a stand of wheat divided by a twister. Weaver came through the gap, walked up to Sturley, and punched his jaw with one hand while deftly taking the knife with the other. Sturley fell back two steps, then looked into the train leader's cold eyes. His face flared livid, then drained to funeral-parlor white.

"But the darky pushed me," he said feebly.

"Bob's my best teamster," Weaver said. "I won't have you cutting him up. And as for you, Bob, I won't tolerate troublemaking or folks with chips on their shoulders. The rest of you, clear out. We're losing time."

Sturley straightened and turned to Webster. The two stared like wary cats as Weaver walked away, confident from experience that his warning was enough to end the fight.

The atmosphere crackled with back-and-forth tension until at last Sturley turned away, muttering. Webster watched him go, then dug out his handkerchief and wiped away the blood. The other teamsters scattered, knowing Weaver meant what he said.

Webster returned to his oxen. McCan thought of going to him, but didn't. He hitched his own team and awaited the order to roll.

The journey continued until the sun raged hot. They stopped the wagons, and the cook provided beans seasoned with big hunks of bacon. The men lined up with pewter bowls in hand; McCan fell in behind Webster.

The cook, Sterling Slater, dished out huge portions and fat biscuits. When Webster received his, he stared first at his bowl, then at Slater.

"Where's the rest?" he demanded.

"What are you talking about?" Slater's confusion was justified, for he had given Webster the same amount as the others.

"You heard me."

Slater twitched thick brows and emphatically spit a dollop of tobacco juice earthward, but he dished out an extra heap for Webster, who then stepped down the line. He was a volcano seething toward explosion.

Jimmy Wyatt thrust his bowl under Slater's nose. "Fill it up. As much as the nigger got."

McCan's eyes darted to Webster. The big teamster sat with his back toward him, shoveling beans into his mouth. He hadn't heard, or at least didn't let on.

For two days there was no further trouble. Webster calmed down, but remained brooding and distant. McCan spoke to him only a little, for most of the time it was obvious Webster wanted to be left alone.

Rain came, and the going was slow. The daily mileage dropped to six, and often the wagons had to be pushed through mud. Streams swelled to twice normal size, and Weaver worried aloud about the Cheyenne River farther on.

On the fourth day out from Pierre, the train encountered an emigrant wagon beside a stream. McCan recognized it as Caleb Black's.

"Stuck trying to cross?" he asked Weaver.

"Could be. Or maybe redskins, or bandits. If you know this fellow, come with me."

As they drew near, McCan pointed out two dead

mules lying nearby in blackened blood, covered with flies.

"He was jumped for sure," Weaver said. "Keep a sharp eye."

McCan could see now that the wagon had bullet holes in the sides and rips in the canvas. From inside it a voice rang out: "Hold it there—come around where I can see your faces."

It was Caleb Black's voice, coming over the long barrel of a Henry that jutted out of the wagon. McCan and Weaver raised their hands.

"Easy, friend," Weaver said. "We're teamsters, here to help you if you need it."

The flaps moved and Black peered over the tailgate. He lowered the Henry. "Come on, then."

He stepped from the wagon as they approached. He recognized McCan, even remembered his name.

"Redskins?" Weaver asked.

"No, white men. Dressed like redskins to try to fool me, but I seen their faces. I'll know them when I see them again."

Weaver said, "You won't see them. Most of the highwaymen keep hid out. A few turn up in Deadwood from time to time—Tom Branton and Evan Bridger, mostly. Nobody bothers them. The law has no proof on them, and most folks are scared of them."

Black snorted contemptuously. "I'll teach 'em scared!"

"You can ride into Deadwood with us," Weaver said. "We'll hitch your wagon behind McCan's team. You can pay your way as an assistant night guard, or by helping the cook, or whatever."

"I'm obliged."

They tied on Black's wagon and moved on; Black rode in the seat beside McCan. The sun grew hot, and the oxen slowed after a few miles. At last Weaver signaled the halt.

CHAPTER 4

WHEN THEY STOPPED, CALEB BLACK crawled inside his wagon and went to sleep. By then, McCan had received a nutshell history of Black and kin.

Black's brother, Walter, was already mining in the Black Hills, and had invited Caleb to join him. The brothers had one younger sister, who lived in Minnesota with her husband, a farmer. Caleb hoped to persuade them to join him in Deadwood after he became settled with Walter.

He answered McCan's questions. No, he had not mined before. Yes, he had read all about it. No, Walter was not rich—not yet. But yes, he would be, and Caleb too. He was sure of it.

The rains stopped, but the mucky land—called gumbo by the veteran teamsters—continued to hamper their progress. The Cheyenne, however, had receded by the time they reached it, and fording was easy. From there on the journey went speedily.

The first sight of the Black Hills reconfirmed to McCan his plan to stay. From a distance they truly were black, because of the pine and spruce on their summits. They crumpled the land like a scuffed-up carpet for a hundred miles on the western border of the territory, down to the Badlands farther south. At places, the hills humped like knuckles or pointed like fingers at the sky.

They approached Deadwood through the Centennial Prairie, where the oxen would graze after the wagons were unloaded. There would be only one day of rest and one night of carousing in Deadwood before the trip back to Pierre—a trip McCan would not make.

McCan had picked up some of Deadwood's history along the way. The town had been founded in 1875, after the discovery of gold there, and at first had been called Deadwood Gulch. The latter title was appropriate; the town was bordered by hills, and thus had grown in a long strand. Along its rutted course sprouted businesses—some legitimate, others not. There were those who called Deadwood the Gomorrah of the West.

Deadwood prospered. The Black Hills swarmed with prospectors; the town was populated with those who made a living, in a variety of ways, off the earnings brought in by the miners.

Deadwood had a decidedly lawless streak, and every kind of human castoff infested its alleyways and dark corners. Prostitutes, gamblers, thieves, murderers—they were plentiful in this hell-pit of a town, and many were those who predicted that one day the Almighty would swallow Deadwood into the bowels of the land and be done with it. The straight and narrow did not pass within a hundred miles of the Black Hills. Deadwood was a rough and cruel town, a place men did not go if they valued their mortal lives and immortal souls. Naturally enough, it was crowded.

The freight wagons rolled into Deadwood late in the afternoon. Unloading them proved difficult and slow. McCan had time only to glance over the town before the return to camp. The narrow street was little more than a wide gully with squatty buildings along it, all of them drab and crude, some consisting more of canvas than lumber.

McCan noted Carl Mann's Saloon, supposedly one of the wildest in town, where Jack McCall had blown out Bill Hickok's brains. They had buried Wild Bill behind the saloon at first, but later moved him to Mount Moriah, overlooking the town. He had plenty of company there; violent death happened frequently in Deadwood. ''When the gold pans out,'' Webster observed, ''they can start mining lead out of the corpses on the hill.''

Weaver didn't hand out pay until the teamsters were back on the Centennial Prairie; it was his way of making sure they returned. A few slipped back to town immediately, but McCan was exhausted from the day's work. He crawled into his bedroll and fell asleep.

Caleb Black had remained in town. McCan thought about him just before he went to sleep. Probably he was looking for his brother right now. A stake waiting for him—a lucky man.

In the morning, McCan and Webster took two horses from the train remuda and rode into town. Weaver stayed behind with the wagons, ostensibly to guard them, but McCan figured that for an excuse. Weaver seemingly had no need for recreation or release, even company. He was a mystery McCan never would solve, for he knew when he waved his good-bye to him he would see him no more.

McCan and Webster sought out Hardin Crowley, a fellow teamster Webster said was honest, and gave him payment for the horses. "Take it back to Weaver when you leave," McCan said. "We'll not be thought horse thieves by any man."

Crowley pocketed the money. "Good luck to both of you," he said. "Next run, I'll be staying on myself. Wish I could now."

They left their horses at a livery and took to the street. Webster said there were days Deadwood was lifeless as its name, others when it teemed even at noon. This was one of the latter.

Men walked the boardwalks and muddy street, horses milled about, wagons creaked by, merchants sat in the doorways of their shops or tended customers inside. It was an incredible jumble, alternately thrilling and exhausting to observe. As the sun rose, the drab town took on a surreal light that made it almost beautiful, in a primitive way.

McCan stopped; approaching from the other end of the street were Sturley and Wyatt. He felt Webster bristle.

The pair approached and stopped, keeping out of reach of Webster's long arms. Wyatt grinned cockily. "You're keeping some bad company, McCan."

McCan said nothing. Wyatt and Sturley smelled like whiskey, even at this early hour. Wyatt weaved where he stood.

"Can't you talk?" Wyatt said. "It ain't polite to stand and stare at a man like a bug-eyed jackass."

"Just move aside and don't cause trouble," McCan said.

Wyatt presented a look of offended innocence.

"Trouble? Did I talk about trouble, Roy? We're just trying to be nice. We're nice to everybody. Even to niggers like you, boy. I'm talking to you, Webster."

Webster moved almost imperceptibly, but managed to squelch whatever he was about to do or say. Wyatt saw he had touched a nerve. He grinned broadly.

"What's the matter, black boy? I make you mad?"

Webster nodded. "You did." His hand flashed out with amazing celerity, and his whole body lunged like a rattler's to within striking distance. Bone crunched horribly as Wyatt's nose went flat under Webster's fist. He grasped his injured face; tears poured out to mix with blood. Shirley gaped, open-mouthed and silent, at his injured partner, who now sat on his rump in the street with blood gushing down his shirt.

Wyatt struggled to his feet again, gripping his nose. He pointed at Webster and said, "You're dead, nigger."

His hand fell to the ivory-handled Colt he always wore. He drew and leveled it, clicked the hammer, and aimed the pistol between Webster's eyes.

McCan pushed the barrel aside as Wyatt squeezed the trigger. There was an empty click. Wyatt raised the pistol and stared crazily at it.

Webster laughed. "They don't work unloaded," he said. He kicked upward and caught Wyatt full force in the groin. Wyatt's body rose a foot off the street and fell backward. His eyes bleared; he tried

to scream, but couldn't. As for Sturley, he backed off, then ran.

Webster knelt beside Wyatt and gently took the pistol from his hand. "I unloaded this while you slept the night after you decided mine and Sturley's business was yours. I never take a chance with a fool. And I figured you to be fool enough not to bother to check your own pistol before you came to town. You won't make it here, Wyatt. There's men what can eat you alive."

Webster tossed the pistol into an alley. A drunk scurried to it, stooped, then he and the pistol were gone.

Webster stood and he and McCan walked away. Sturley was gone. Wyatt still writhed in the dirt.

"It isn't over, Bob," McCan said.

"I know it," Webster paused. "Maybe I ought to get me a pistol."

"Both of us," McCan said.

They heard laughter, and McCan turned. A tall man with graying hair and a leathery face stood in the doorway of a tent saloon, a painted girl under his arm and a beer in his hand. He laughed at McCan and Webster, and when McCan looked at him, raised his beer in salute. The man turned back into the dark saloon interior.

"Who was that?" McCan asked. But Webster didn't know.

TIMBER CREEK—ANOTHER UNFORGETTABLE CAMERON JUDD SAGA—AVAILABLE IN NO-VEMBER FROM ST. MARTIN'S PAPERBACKS!